ANNIE OF ALBERT MEWS

had gone to the races at Epsom. She bent down and took a feather duster from under the counter.

"'Allo there, Annie. Gonner flick the dead flies off the bacon fer yer dad gits back?' An elderly woman waddled into the shop and sat on the bentwood chair that stood beside the counter. 'Sorry, love, did I make yer jump? You were miles away then.'

Annie smiled. She knew there was no malice in the old woman's comments. 'Hello, Mrs Turner. Don't often see you in here on a Wednesday afternoon. What can I get you?'

'Yer, well. I need a pen'orf o' broken biscuits.' She looked about her. 'Yer see me son's just walked in wiv 'is new wife and yer got ter make a bit of a show, ain't yer?'

'That's nice,' said Annie, walking round to the front of the counter. She pushed her shiny scoop with a wooden handle into one of the brown sacks that contained the factory rejects. 'How they getting on?' she asked.

'Not bad. Got a couple o' nice rooms round in Clover Street.'

Annie put a brass weight on the large scales at the far end of the long counter, and gently let the biscuits slide into the pan. She watched the arms level out, then went back behind the counter and tipped the biscuits into a blue paper bag, turning the top over with the expertise her two and a half years in the shop had given her.

'Put it on me slate, love,' said Mrs Turner, picking up the bag.

'Dad told me to tell you your bill's getting a bit high,' Annie answered quietly.

Mrs Turner stopped, her large bulk filling the doorway. The sunlight filtering past her gave her a kind of aura, and once again the dust from outside flitted and danced in the sunbeams. ''Ow much is it?'

Annie took a black book from the shelf behind her. She quickly thumbed down the index and turned to a page. 'You owe one and ninepence three-farthings now.'

'Can't be.' She came back into the shop. 'Let's 'ave a look.'

Annie handed her the book, knowing Mrs Turner couldn't read.

'I'll 'ave ter send young Tommy James round wiv a bit when 'e gits in from school. Bye.' Mrs Turner pulled her black shawl round her shoulders and hurried from the shop.

Chapter 1

Annie Rodgers sighed, and looked up at the large white-faced clock that hung high on the wall of her father's grocer's shop. It was half-past three. It would be another three hours before Lil poked her head round the door to give her all the latest gossip about the girls at the tea factory. They would laugh and giggle when Lil told her what some of the women wore, and what they got up to. Annie, like Lil, was sixteen. They both looked very young for their age: Lil with her wistful hazel eyes, and short, light brown hair, scragged to one side and held flat against her head with a clip, was skinny against Annie's nicely rounded figure, but neither knew much about the world beyond Rotherhithe.

Annie sometimes felt she knew nothing about the world beyond Albert Mews, even. Many times she wished that when she'd left school at fourteen, she, like Lil, could have worked with lots of other girls instead of being here on her own. Although her mum and dad gave her plenty of freedom, it wasn't the same, and she would dearly love someone to talk to, and laugh with, other than the customers. Annie sighed again, her elbows resting on the counter, and let her gaze travel on out through the open door and on to the cobbled mews. The light shower had made the stones glisten, dampening down the dust that seemed to be forever hovering and settling on the display in the neat bay window. The steady drip of the leaking gutter and the ticking of the clock were the only sounds that afternoon. In the distance the muffled noise of the traffic drifted in.

It was 5 June 1935. Derby day, and because they knew trade would be quiet, her parents had left her in charge of the shop and

1

This one is for Nannie's darlings,
Emma and Samantha

This edition published 1993
by BCA
by arrangement with Headline Books Ltd.

Copyright © 1993 Dee Williams

CN 1275

Printed and bound in Germany
by Graphischer Großbetrieb Pößneck GmbH
A member of the Mohndruck printing group

ANNIE OF
ALBERT MEWS

Dee Williams

LONDON NEW YORK SYDNEY TORONTO

Annie grinned, and picked up the feather duster once more. 'That's if she can get it off her old man first,' she said to herself.

Standing on the first step of the ladder, she busied herself flicking the duster over the tin boxes. They held mustard, cocoa and other loose groceries, and a few of them were beginning to rust: they had been sitting on the shelf for a long time. Annie then rearranged the jars before stepping down and putting the steps to one side. She walked round the counter. The sacks that lined the wall were full of dried goods, and they squatted on the worn wooden parquet floor like little fat men. Annie rolled down some of the tops a bit more to show off their contents. She then stepped back to admire her handiwork before quickly plunging her hands into the bright yellow lentils, letting them slowly trickle through her fingers. She smiled to herself – she loved doing that. Annie moved back to the counter and ran her fingers up the side of one of the three large stone jars displayed at the far end. Two were filled with jam, while the other held thick chunky marmalade. She licked the strawberry jam off her finger and mumbled out loud, 'I'll get a damp cloth and given them a wipe.'

It was dead on six-thirty when Lil came bursting in. As usual she was smiling. ''Allo there, me old mate, can't stop. Been busy?'

'No,' said Annie. 'We going out tonight?'

'Should fink so. 'Ere,' she moved closer to Annie. 'Guess what? I fink me mum's 'aving another baby.'

'No. Why do you think that?'

Lil's hazel eyes twinkled, lighting up her pale face; her mouth widened as she laughed. 'She was sick this morning, so I can't stop. Must go and see how she is. See yer later.'

Annie's gaze followed Lil as she left and the shop fell back into silence. On the surface it appeared nothing seemed to bother Lil; she was always happy-go-lucky. Even though Lil had very little to make her laugh, Annie envied her having two younger brothers and two younger sisters, whom she had helped bring up. Annie thought about her own brother John: he would have been nineteen by now. He died when she was seven. She still missed him, even after all these years. Her thoughts went back to Lil and her family. Lil's father made Annie shudder. He was fat and always looked unshaven and scruffy. He was dirty and smelt of stale beer and tobacco, and he never seemed to be in work. Lil said it was because he had a bad back. Her mother was a short, thin, mousy sort of woman with sad, watery blue eyes. She was quiet and never grumbled, was always very kind and nice to talk to, and Annie liked her. Very often Annie would tell her mother a frock or coat was too tight just so she could give it to Lil, who was a lot thinner, and a few inches shorter than herself. Lil always seemed glad of anything Annie could come up with.

Suddenly she was brought out of her daydreams as a horde of grubby dishevelled kids came laughing and pushing their way through the door.

''Allo, Annie,' one yelled out. 'We want some sweets.'

'Oh yes, Jimmy Bently, and where have you got money from to buy sweets?' she demanded.

As he shoved and elbowed his way up to the counter, the little boy grinned, showing the gap his two missing front teeth made. He flicked his straight brown hair out of his eyes. 'Been chasing the charra's, ain't we. It was Fisher's outing terday, they've been to the races. They must a 'ad a good day, they've just got 'ome.' He plonked two halfpennies and two farthings on the counter. 'I'll 'ave two rolls of liquorice, and two farthing Golly bars.'

'That was quick.'

'Been finking about it all day, ain' I?' He stood back proudly after Annie had handed him his wares, and let the others through.

'What do you want, Rene?' asked Annie.

A little blonde girl with startling blue eyes looked at the display of sweets in the glass case. 'I don't know,' she lisped, tucking a strand of tangled hair behind her ear. 'I ain't got much. 'Arry Martin pushed me over and trod on me 'ands, so I didn't git much.'

Annie smiled. 'Well, take your time while I see to the others.'

Billy Kent wanted some gobstoppers.

Annie liked it when she was busy weighing out a ha'penny worth of aniseed balls, or acid drops, dolly mixtures and jelly babies, passing the goodies to eager hands, who in turn passed over money, warm through being clutched in hot sticky hands for so long.

She remembered the fun she and Lil used to have when they

4

chased the charabancs yelling, 'Throw out your mouldies,' and how they clambered for the money that was tossed out of the windows. Derby day was always the best, especially if the men had had a good day, had plenty of booze and won a few bob.

Billy Kent was standing in the corner, and every time Annie looked at him he was taking the gobstopper out of his mouth to admire the different colour. He was still there after most of the children had left. Rene, the little blonde girl, was patiently waiting to be served.

'Please, Annie,' she whispered. 'Can I 'ave a 'aporf of broken biscuits?'

'Of course.' Annie didn't bother weighing them out, just put a couple of good handfuls into a bag.

As they left the shop Billy Kent took hold of her hand. 'I'll let you 'ave a suck of me gobstopper if yer give me a biscuit.'

''Ere are then, but let me finish me biscuit first.'

He took his sweet out of his mouth and put it into his pocket for later, and Annie shuddered, wondering what other things were hidden in the depths of that bulging pocket.

It was a warm and pleasant June evening, and before Annie and Lil went for a walk in the park, where they knew plenty of boys would be playing cricket, they stopped in a shop doorway to put on some lipstick and rouge.

Annie pouted her lips and pressed them together before passing her lipstick to her friend. 'D'you know, one of these days I'm going to forget to wipe it off 'fore I go home, then I'll be in trouble.'

'Your old man won't give yer a good 'iding though, will 'e?' said Lil sadly.

'Course not, but I'll get a good telling off. Don't know why they can't let me wear a bit of lipstick.'

'They think you'll turn out ter be a hussy, that's why. I don't wear it 'cos I can't afford it.'

Annie laughed. 'Come on, let's have a look at you.'

Lil too pursed her now scarlet lips.

'That looks all right, now come on.'

Arm in arm, they laughed and giggled as they wandered into the park. They watched the boys chalk the stump marks on a tree, calling out to them, encouraging them when they got a run. Life was very simple and easy.

'We going to the pictures Friday?' asked Annie as they sat on the grass.

'I can't,' said Lil lying back.

'Why not?'

Lil rolled over on to her stomach, and pulled at a buttercup.

'We must go,' Annie persisted. 'Elsie Coombs was telling me that they've got a film of the King and Queen's Jubilee. It's better than what we saw on the news. Look, don't worry about paying, it'll be my treat.'

'Fanks, Annie. I'd like to see that,' said Lil softly. 'I wish we could 'ave gone to a street party like some of the other streets 'ad.'

'We couldn't have got many tables down Albert Mews. 'Sides, there's not many kids in the flats now, only the ironmongers. And what about where you live: you couldn't get a chair in that yard, let alone a table.'

A smile lifted Lil's face. 'Could yer see us all sitting in that yard? Old man Reeves keeps 'is smelly 'orses in there. Yer'd be up ter yer knees in 'orse dung.'

Annie laughed. 'That's better. Come on, cheer up. What's made you so miserable?'

She turned over and sat up. 'It's me dad. 'E's been 'aving a go at me mum again. 'E reckons it's 'er fault she's 'aving another baby. D'yer know, sometimes I wish I could get away from 'em altogether – leave 'ome.'

'No you don't. Besides, where would you live? Who would have you? And what about your poor old mum? You wouldn't want to leave her, now would you?'

Lil shook her head, and a smile spread across her face as she patted the back of her hair. 'You tell me what's what. But honestly, Annie, I wish I could keep more of me money, and not 'ave ter give it all ter me mum.'

'One of these days you'll meet a nice rich young man, and then you'll have everything you've ever dreamed of.'

Lil laughed. 'I don't mind if 'e's a rich old one, but I'll 'ave ter wait till pigs learn to fly. Come on, let's be going 'ome, or else I'll 'ave me old man 'aving a go at me an' all.'

Once again they linked arms, and left the park, happy with each other's company.

'Come on, love, move yourself, take this tea down to your father.' Mrs Rodgers was wiping the kitchen table when Annie walked in, still sleepy-eyed. Her mother, slim and energetic, always seemed to be busy. 'I think he's got a few orders to deliver this afternoon, and I might go with him and get some veg from the market – you'll be able to manage the shop for a while, won't you?'

Annie nodded as she wistfully combed her short dark bobbed hair into place. She resembled her mother, with her dark brown eyes and hair, and Annie knew from her photographs that she used to have a nice figure. Her father had worked in the shop since the day he left school at fourteen. After the previous tenant had died, and he had taken it over, he'd met and married her mother. He'd told Annie many times of the way, at first, they'd had to struggle to keep the business going, and how they worried about paying for the meagre amount of stock they had in the beginning. Annie often wondered if that was one of the reasons for her mother's gaunt look. But her father had built up the business despite all the problems, with many local people being out of work, and he said he was always grateful for Fisher's factory being at the end of the Mews. They were fortunate, and lucky too to have a home above the shop. Her father worked hard, and was determined to give them a good life, and Annie didn't want for anything – not like some of them round here.

Her mother tutted loudly. 'I've told you before, do that in your bedroom. I don't want hairs all over the kitchen.'

'Sorry.'

Mrs Rodgers continued bustling around and moved the rickety wooden clothes-horse away from in front of the gas oven, where the clothes had been airing. She began folding the ironing, ready to put away. She took a dry towel, shook it out with a loud crack, folded it, then added it to the neat pile on the table. 'He's very proud of the way you've taken to the shop you know,' she said, calmed by her tidying. 'It's given him a bit more time to himself.'

Annie smiled and, picking up the cup of tea, made her way down the stairs and through the door at the back of the shop. 'Here's your tea, Dad . . .' Her voice trailed off when she saw Mr Barrett, the landlord, deep in conversation with her father. 'Sorry, I didn't know.'

'That's all right, Annie love,' said Mr Barrett. 'I was just telling your father here that my son's just finished college and got a good job in the City.'

'You remember little Peter?' said her father.

Annie nodded. She remembered the little devil all right. He was about four years older than her, and his father used to bring him with him when he came round to collect the rent; and when no one was looking, he used to get her in a corner and pull her hair.

'He's not so little now,' said Mr Barrett, sticking out his chest and fiddling with the gold chain that was stretched across the front of his royal blue silk waistcoat. He tucked his fingers into the small slit pockets either side of his large paunch and rocked back on his heels. 'Proper City gent he is now, in shipping.'

'That's nice,' said Annie.

'Well, I had better be going. Got a few more to call on. Only wish they were all like you, Mr Rodgers, and paid up on time.' He picked up his black Gladstone bag. 'Might bring young Peter with me next time. He's got to take an interest in the business. After all, being the only one, this'll all be his one of these days.' He waved his arm nonchalantly behind him. 'Bye.'

The small bell suspended on a spring on top of the door tinkled excitedly as he left.

'Don't often see him round here collecting the rent,' said Annie.

'No. It seems the old boy that does it for him has got a bad back.'

'Dad, your tea's got cold,' Annie noticed. 'Shall I go and get you another?'

'No, that's all right, love, get used to drinking cold tea. D'you know old Barrett must be worth a bob or two,' her father said thoughtfully. 'He owns all of Albert Mews, and the flats in Victoria Gardens where young Lil lives.'

'They're slums,' said Annie aggressively. 'He don't do anything to them. D'you know the water drips through the ceiling when it rains, and Lil says there's rats there as well.'

'That could be because of old man Reeves. I'm surprised Mr Barrett lets him get away with it. That place looks like a right old junk yard with that pile of rags, and rubbish all over the place.'

'Still, Mr Barrett could do something.'

'You do have to look after your own place a bit. You've got to keep it up to scratch. After all, you can't expect him to be at everybody's beck and call.'

'He could put a few slates on the roof. I don't know how Lil's mum puts up with it.'

'Well, her old man don't do a lot, now does he?'

'I know,' Annie admitted.

'Right, enough of this idle chatter, let's get some work done before the factory turns out for lunch and they all want their fags and baccy.'

Annie smiled, making her dark eyes sparkle. She liked it when the apprentices from Fisher's tool factory came in for their sweets and cigarettes. Some of them were a bit cheeky, and once young Georgie Bates had asked her for a date. But she didn't fancy going out with him as he was noisy and had lots of spots. Will Hobbs was a nice quiet boy, though, but he was in the Salvation Army.

Her father was still talking. 'I bet Barrett's son's turned out to be a nice young feller. You could do yourself a bit of good if he comes round here.'

'Dad. You trying to get me married off or something?'

He laughed. 'Well, I'm not keeping you for ever.' He playfully pinched her cheek.

'I don't like him,' said Annie, her thoughts still on the boys from Fisher's factory.

'He's going to be worth a few bob later on.'

'I don't care. I still don't like him.'

Chapter 2

It was the end of November, and a month after Annie's seventeenth birthday. It was dark and miserable outside, and had been drizzling rain all day. Annie, alone in the shop as her mother and father had gone to their normal Monday afternoon pictures, was busy getting a list ready for her father to take to the wholesaler's, for goods they would need to stock for Christmas. She thoughtfully chewed on the end of her pencil. This wasn't a rich area, and for some Christmas would be like any other day if they couldn't find something to pawn, or had been fortunate enough to put a bit by in a Christmas club all year. Many were jobless in Rotherhithe, and the Means Test man, together with the Tally man, were a familiar sight cutting through the Mews on their push bikes. Lil's mother hated the Means Test man: she always made sure her youngest were around when he came knocking, and the kids knew how to cry when ordered.

Annie looked at the black book on the shelf at the back of the counter. It told of the money that was owed and, though her father was a kind man, if people didn't pay him, he too could find himself in difficulties. The sudden tinkle of the bell over the door made Annie look up. A tall, well-dressed man in a dark suit, complete with bowler hat, was standing in the doorway vigorously shaking the rain off his black umbrella. This wasn't the sort of person that frequented their shop. He turned, and Annie found herself staring at a good-looking young man.

He touched his hat. 'Sorry, did I startle you?'

'That's all right.' She looked more closely. In the flickering gas light, something about him seemed familiar. 'What can I get you?'

11

'Actually, I've come on behalf of my father.'

'Peter Barrett.' Annie stood back. 'After all this time! Well, you've certainly changed.'

He smiled. 'For the better I hope.'

Annie was flustered, his smile was disarming. With both hands she smoothed down her neat bobbed hair. 'Well, yes.'

'And you have certainly changed.' He looked her up and down. 'And I may say very much for the better. Gosh, I remember when I used to come here with my father.' He glanced round the shop. 'I pulled your hair.'

Annie blushed and felt embarrassed. 'Yes, you did . . . you said you were here because of your father – he's not ill, is he?'

'No, he asked me to call to invite you and your parents to a little get-together he's having at our house.' He fished in his pocket and brought out an envelope. 'He was going to post this but I said it wasn't that far out of my way. You see, on the last Monday of the month, I go to a club near here, so I said I'd deliver it.'

Annie took the invitation. 'But why? Why us? We're only his tenants, why should he invite us to his house?' She quickly looked up. 'He's not selling up, is he?'

'No of course not. He thinks a lot of you and your parents. You seem to be a cut above the rest of them round here. Besides, he thought . . .'

The door flew open and Lil came rushing in. 'Oops, sorry. I'll wait till yer finished serving this gent.'

'Lil, this is Mr Barrett's son.'

'The landlord's?' she inquired quizzically.

Annie nodded.

'Pleased ter meet yer, I'm sure.' Lil almost did a little curtsy.

'I must go. Hope to see you Saturday week.' Peter Barrett touched his hat and left.

As soon as the door closed, Annie and Lil collapsed with laughter. Lil sat on the bentwood chair while Annie held on to the counter. Neither could speak for a moment, and tears ran down their faces.

'What a ponce!' shrieked Lil. ''Ere, what did 'e look like in that bloody 'at.' She wiped her eyes. 'What did 'e mean, 'ope ter see yer Saturday week?'

Annie too wiped her eyes. 'You'll never guess, we've been invited to the Barretts' house.' She waved the envelope under Lil's nose. 'So, what d'you think of that?'

'No? Who's we?'

'Me, and me mum and dad.'

'What for?'

'I don't know. I can't open it, it's addressed to me dad, so I'll have to wait till he gets home.'

''Ere, d'yer reckon they'll invite all 'is tenants?'

'Shouldn't think so. Could you see old Mrs Turner going there wearing her greasy old flat cap.' Annie laughed.

'And what about my old man.' Lil held her nose. 'Phew, yer wonner smell 'im when it gits warm.'

'Well, it's not easy having a bath in your house with your lot.'

'No. It's all right for you, only three 'as to share the water. When it gits ter me dad after all the kids, the water's black.'

'I'd love a house with a bathroom,' sighed Annie.

'I reckon the Barretts 'ave got one. I wish I was going with yer.' Lil laughed. ''Ere, p'raps I could marry Peter Barrett, then I'd let yer come and use me bathroom.'

'Thanks. I wish you was coming with us. That's if there's no strings attached, and we do go.'

'D'yer reckon 'e's after something?'

'Don't know,' said Annie wistfully.

'Cheer up.' Lil gave Annie a nudge and whispered out of the corner of her mouth. 'D'yer know, I reckon they're gonner whisk you off to the white slave market like Amy Day.' She laughed again.

'What – with me mum and dad there. 'Sides, Amy Day ran off with her sailor when her mum wouldn't let her marry him.'

'Yer I know. Some say she was up the spout an' all.' Lil picked the letter off the counter and turned it over. 'Couldn't we steam it open?'

'No.' Annie snatched the letter back.

Lil looked up at the clock. 'Cripes, is that the time? Me old man will skin me alive.' She rushed out of the door yelling, 'Don't fergit, you've got ter tell me what it's all about as soon as yer knows.'

As Mr and Mrs Rodgers walked into the shop, Annie rushed up to them waving the letter. 'We've been invited to the Barretts' house. Quick, Dad, open it, I'm dying to find out why.'

'I'll go up and put the kettle on,' said her mother.

'Don't you want to find out what it's about?' asked Annie eagerly.

'I can wait. I need a cup of tea first, and, Dad, get those wet things off.'

'I'll just lock up. Turn the gas lights off, Annie, we can read this upstairs.'

Annie reached up and pulled at the chain that hung low from the high ceiling. The shop gradually became darker as, one by one, she moved round the shop and the gas lamps under the white enamel shades that looked like Chinese coolies' hats flickered and then popped out. She followed her father through the door behind the counter and up the stairs. In the warm, cosy kitchen, the kettle was sitting on the gas stove with blue flames leaping up and licking the sides. Her mother was busy laying the table, and the delicious smell of the casserole that had been simmering all afternoon filled the air, making Annie's stomach churn with hunger.

'That smells good, Mother,' said her father.

'What was the film like?' asked Annie.

'Not bad, your mother had a little weep.' With Annie looking over his shoulder, he tore open the envelope. 'Here look, Mr Barrett says he's having a few people round for a pre-Christmas drink on Saturday 7 December, and he requests our company.'

'All of us?' she asked.

Mr Rodgers, with his head still bent reading, nodded.

'What does he want with us?' asked his wife.

'How should I know? It's very kind of him, don't you think?'

'Don't know,' she replied.

'Well, I think it's nice,' said Annie, sitting at the table. 'It was his son Peter who brought it in. He's very grown-up now, bowler hat an' all.'

'No?' laughed her father. 'That young whipper-snapper in a bowler; I would have liked to have seen that.'

'You might if he comes in the shop again.'

'Well, I don't like the sound of it,' said her mother. 'I think there's something fishy about it.'

'Don't be daft, Mother,' said Mr Rodgers.

'Come on, Mum, let's enjoy it. 'Sides, you could do with a nice evening out.'

'Got nothing to wear.'

Mr Rodgers put the letter on the table. 'I tell you what, you and Annie go out and get yourselves a new frock each. Could be me Christmas present to you both.'

Annie leapt out of her chair and threw her arms round her father's neck. 'Ooo, thanks, Dad.' She kissed his cheek. 'When can we go?'

'When I get back from the wholesaler's tomorrow.'

'We can go over to Peckham, Mum, or would you rather go to Brick Lane?'

'I don't mind.' Mrs Rodgers lent over and patted her husband's hand. 'Thanks, love.'

Ben Rodgers turned the family's grocer's van into the gravel drive of Forest Hill, Dulwich, and they all sat quietly looking at the large, impressive, red-brick house. It looked warm and inviting as white smoke puffed straight up from the chimneys high into the dark, crisp, starlit sky. It was a cold, still night, and the house seemed to have lights blazing from every window.

'It looks very posh,' whispered his wife. 'I don't want to feel out of place.'

'Don't be daft, Mother,' said Mr Rodgers. 'You're just as good as them.'

'Not as rich, though,' said Annie, leaning forward to get a better view.

'Well, that's just the luck of the draw when you're born,' said her father. 'Now come along. You both look very nice. In fact I bet you'll outshine everyone.' He clambered out of the van and helped his wife and daughter down the high step.

The front door was opened by Mr Barrett. He took a large cigar from his mouth. 'Welcome, my dears. Welcome to my house.' One by one he shook their hands vigorously. 'Hang your coats there.' He pointed to a tall dark hat-stand with a number of hooks, many of which already carried some very smart coats. 'This way.' As he led them across the square hall their feet echoed on the highly polished wooden floor, the noise only deadened when they stepped on to one of the richly coloured ornamental rugs. They passed a dark long-legged stand which held an aspidistra that hung like a gigantic green spider over the pot and went through an open door at the far end of the hall. Annie's feet sank in to the rich red carpet as she stepped into the noisy, smoke-filled room. The gramophone at the far end was adding to the general hubbub with one of the latest hits, 'Anything Goes'. She stared around her and moved tentatively into the room. There were about a dozen people in there, and they were evenly divided into two groups. Most of them were standing around with glasses in their hands, while some of the women, who were draped over the arms of the long red plush sofa, were waving long cigarette-holders about as they talked. The evening dresses of the younger ones were very fashionable, tight fitting and cut very low at the back and front, revealing their pale, delicate-looking skin. Annie's wasn't full-length, and she felt young and overdressed in her pretty pink petal-sleeved silk dress. Those lounging near the gramophone were listening intently to a tall, fair-haired young man standing with one hand in the pocket of his navy blue blazer. Annie noticed he had a yellow cravat at his throat. Suddenly, all those in his party laughed very loud.

'Hello there.' Annie turned to face Peter Barrett. 'Glad you came. Would you like a drink?'

Annie quickly looked towards her father who was already deeply engrossed in conversation with a man she knew vaguely who owned another shop. 'Yes please. Lemonade.'

'Nothing else?'

She shook her head. Annie noted her mother had also found a soul-mate.

Peter was back at her side in no time. 'Thank you.' She took the drink. 'Why did your father invite us here?' she asked instantly.

Peter laughed. 'I'll let you into a little secret. It was me really.'

'You? But why?'

'Cigarette?'

'No, thank you, I don't smoke.'

'You don't smoke, and you don't drink. Don't you have any vices, or will I find out more about those in time?'

Annie blushed. 'I'm sorry, I don't know what you mean.'

He laughed. 'I must say you look stunning tonight. That's a lovely dress.'

'Thank you,' she murmured, looking down at her hands and away from his intense gaze.

He bent his head closer and whispered, 'It's much better than your old brown wrap-over overall.'

She quickly brought her head up. She didn't have that on when he came into the shop to deliver the invitation. She only wore that when she was cleaning. 'How . . . ? When . . . ?'

'Ahhh-ha. That's got you interested. I told you the other day that I pass your shop on my way to my club, and over the months I've seen you change from a gawky schoolgirl into quite a nice bit of stuff.'

She turned to go. He grabbed her wrist. 'What's your hurry? You can't go anywhere without your father, now can you?'

'What do you want with me?' As Annie twisted her arm free she knew she was making herself look silly.

'I'd like to take you out sometime. I could show you how the other half live.'

'I don't think I want to know – thank you.'

'Oh come on, now. Wouldn't you like to go up West to the theatre, and see some of the great shows that are on at the moment? And then perhaps on to a really good restaurant for a meal afterwards?' He hesitated.

'No thank you,' she said, trying to sound grown-up. Although deep down she really wanted to say, yes please, she was afraid of appearing too eager.

'I bet your friend Lil would.'

'What do you know about Lil?'

'Nothing, but she looks as if she wouldn't need asking twice.

17

Come on, how about next Saturday?' He gently took her elbow.

'I don't know.' Annie felt awkward and out of place and, shaking off his hand, stepped to one side. She looked across at her father for support – he smiled, and nodded approvingly.

Annie stood toying with her glass. She knew Lil would jump at the chance to go out with someone like Peter Barrett, and was wondering if she had been too quick to refuse him.

'I'm sorry,' said Peter sincerely. 'Look, perhaps I started on the wrong foot, shall we try again?'

She nodded.

The gramophone was playing 'Cheek to Cheek'.

'How about a dance?'

'I don't know. I'm not very good.'

Peter pulled her close. 'I'll let you into a secret, neither am I.'

They danced all evening, and Annie, much to her surprise, found him easy to talk to. He told her that his mother was dead, and that his father had inherited a lot of buildings as well as houses. She knew he had had a good education. But she was still intrigued as to why they had invited her and her family to their house. She was introduced to some of Peter's friends, but they seemed affected and stuck up, and she was sure a couple of the girls, with their long tortoiseshell cigarette-holders, painted nails and faces, were laughing at her behind her back. They made her feel young, plain and insignificant.

As the evening wore on, one or two began to leave. Annie glanced across at her father who pointed to his watch.

When she left the room she met her mother at the bottom of the stairs. 'Have you been up to the bathroom?' she asked.

Annie shook her head. 'Is it nice?'

'It's lovely, and don't you just love walking into a room and switching on the light.' She giggled. 'I wish we had electric.' Her mother's face had a rosy glow and her eyes sparkled. 'Get your coat when you come down, as we've got to be off now.'

Annie laughed and whispered, 'I think you've had just a drop too much.'

Her mother pulled her fur stole round her shoulders and smiled. 'I don't care.'

'You ready, Mother?' asked Mr Rodgers when Annie joined them in the hall.

His wife, who was sitting in an armchair, nodded, and gently rose to her feet.

'Have you said your goodbyes, and thanked everybody, Annie?'

'Yes, Dad.'

Peter Barrett, who was standing next to her, pulled her to one side and whispered, 'I'll pick you up at seven on Saturday.'

Annie quickly glanced at her father, who was ushering his wife through the door. 'All right,' she whispered.

When she was settled in the van she asked, 'Did you two have a good time tonight?'

'Yes we did,' said her father over his shoulders. 'What about you? You seemed to be with young Peter most of the evening. You see, I told you he's turned out to be a nice boy.'

'He's asked me out on Saturday.'

'That's good.'

'Did you find out why they invited us?' asked Annie, thinking about what Peter had said about him having been the one who wanted them to come tonight.

'No, didn't see any point, we were all enjoying ourselves.'

'Did you see the bathroom?' sighed Annie.

'Yes, it was very nice.'

'I wish we had a bathroom.' She paused. 'Mum's very quiet.'

'She's nodded off, that's why.'

Peter drew hard on his cigarette.

'Well, old boy, did she come across?' asked Julian, tossing back his fair hair.

'I'm taking her out on Saturday,' said Peter, stubbing out his cigarette in the ashtray.

'Right everybody,' called Julian. 'All those that took on the first bets, gather round while I pay out.' He looked at Peter. 'You will tell us if you get intimate, won't you? Don't go keeping it to yourself, and don't go getting all silly and sentimental over this girl. After all, a bet's a bet.'

'Do I look like a welcher?'

'It has been known, old boy.' Julian pulled at his yellow cravat. 'It has been known.'

'Yes, well, keep your voice down – I don't want my father to know about this.'

Chapter 3

A week later when Peter tenderly kissed Annie's lips she felt grown-up and happy. She liked him, he was polite and attentive, not like most of the rowdy Fisher's boys. As he left her at the door she was still bubbling over with excitement, and though it was late, she wasn't tired. Peter had been the perfect host, and now, she knew what he meant when he referred to 'the other half'. All evening she'd felt like pinching herself when she took in her surroundings. Although she felt a little intimidated at being taken out by someone like Peter, and worried as to why he'd chosen her when he had the pick of all those girls at his house, nevertheless it had been the most wonderful evening of her life, and as she slipped out of her clothes and into bed, she knew her parents were still awake and probably dying to ask her where she had been.

As promised, Peter had called for her dead on seven. Annie had spent a long time preparing for her first real date, and when she walked into the shop wearing make-up, her parents looked shocked but said nothing.

To begin with Peter had taken her to the Palladium to see a variety show, and for the first time in her life she had sat in the stalls. Before, when she had been with her parents, they always sat high up in the gods, and Annie would cling to the arms of the seats, terrified that one day she would slip, and roll down the steep steps and tumble on to the people below. Now Annie was below, and she had excitedly laughed and sung along with the artistes, clapping till her hands stung. Once or twice Peter had tried to hold her hand, but she had quickly pulled it away.

After the show he had taken her to a small restaurant off Argyll

Street. Inside it was warm, and the Christmas decorations gave it a heady festive atmosphere, so different to Lyon's, the only other eating place she had been to. Peter had insisted they had a bottle of wine with their meal and, much to Annie's surprise, she found she liked it. In the taxi home when he had put his arm around her shoulders, she had relaxed and enjoyed the feeling of comfort, and the pleasure his kiss had given her.

She snuggled down in her bed and smiled to herself. I'll have Lil round in the morning asking me all about tonight, she mused. She turned over and cuddled the stone hot-water bottle her mother had thoughtfully put into the bed earlier. Gradually Annie drifted off into a contented sleep, and the smile remained.

'Well, where did you go?' Lil was at the door at ten o'clock. Annie knew she wouldn't be round any earlier, as she had to help her mother.

'I'll just get me hat and coat, then we can walk up the road and I'll tell you all about it.'

'It's perishing out 'ere,' said Lil as they strolled along arm in arm.

Lil listened eagerly as Annie told her all about her night out. 'Cor, yer come 'ome in a taxi then? What did yer mum and dad 'ave ter say about that?' Lil pulled her long multi-coloured knitted scarf tighter round her throat. Over the years it had grown, and had so many runs from where Lil had dropped stitches when she'd made it, that it almost looked lacy.

'Mum didn't say much – I think she was more upset over me wearing make-up. But I told her I can't go out with him looking like a silly schoolgirl.'

'Yer seeing 'im again?' screamed Lil.

'Not till after Christmas.'

'What about yer dad?'

'He likes him.'

'What about you?'

Annie giggled and tried to appear nonchalant. 'He's all right, I suppose. But I don't know. He's very . . . I don't know, I suppose it's because he's worldly, but he is very nice.'

Lil laughed and nudged her friend. ''Ere, fancy you drinking wine. What's it like?'

'Not bad. I only had a small drop. I was worried in case me dad found out.'

''Ere, 'e wasn't trying ter get yer drunk, was 'e?'

'No.'

''E didn't try anyfink on, did 'e?'

'No, course not. I wouldn't let him.'

'Did 'e kiss yer goodnight?' inquired Lil eagerly.

'Yes.' Annie blushed and, looking away, pulled her blue woollen beret down over her ears. 'This wind's cold.'

'I reckon you'll end up marrying 'im.'

'What? I'm not getting married for years. I want to see a bit of life first.'

'Yer, but just fink. 'E's got a nice big 'ouse, and from what yer told me it sounds smashing.' Lil sighed. 'I wish it was me.'

On the next corner, the Salvation Army were grouped outside the Eagle pub, singing their hearts out. Lil joined in with a few choruses of 'Good King Wenceslas'.

'I love singing carols,' said Lil, her face beaming as Annie pulled at her arm.

'Come on, it's too cold to hang about.'

Will Hobbs was banging the big drum with fury, his face red with the effort. Although he worked at Fisher's and was a few years older than them he was always shy with the two girls. But today as they walked passed, he winked.

'Did you see that?' Lil said in a loud whisper. 'I fink 'e fancies you.'

'Go on. Did you see his sister peering out from under her bonnet, she didn't half give him a look. And the way she waggled her tambourine at us.'

'Never did like school teachers,' muttered Lil.

'She only teaches infants, and at the Sunday school. You can't have been in her class.'

'No, I know. Good job she wasn't at our Sunday school.'

'You would have made her life a misery.'

'Never did like it, I only went ter git away from 'ome. I didn't

23

like any of 'em.' Lil laughed. 'She looks frozen. I wonder if she wears woolly drawers.'

'She's so high and mighty, when she comes into the shop for her cough drops, you'd think she owns the street.'

'She was always like that when Will was at school. I wonder if she'll ever git married. I'd like to be behind 'er when she goes in the pub selling 'er *War Cry*. I bet she gits some right old remarks.'

'I feel sorry for Will. Ever since his mum died he's had to cower down to his dad and sister. He was telling me the other day, when he came in the shop, that his dad's going to be made up to sergeant.'

''Is old man frightens me. I bet 'e can be a right whatsit at 'ome, don't you?'

'Could be.'

'Good job 'is old man didn't see 'im winking at yer – 'e would 'ave cast 'is eyes up ter heaven and yelled out Alla Yulla.' Lil bent over laughing.

'Will once told me if it wasn't for his father and sister he wouldn't be in the Sally Army. Oh, I've just remembered, I've got to get some shrimps and winkles for tea.'

'You can get 'em on yer way 'ome.'

'All right.'

Gradually the girls, laughing and giggling, arrived at Reeves yard below where Lil lived. 'Yer coming in?'

'No, I best go back. We going out this afternoon?'

'No, it's a bit too cold.'

'Come round to my house, we can have a game of draughts or something, and you can help me wrap up me Christmas presents.'

'OK.'

Christmas was the usual quiet affair in the Rodgers household. Auntie Ivy and Uncle Fred had sent Annie the customary two-and-sixpenny postal order with their Christmas card. Annie liked her mother's sister, her husband, and her cousin Roy, all of whom lived in Sussex. Once she and her mother had gone to stay with them for a holiday. She had had so much fun playing in the fields and helping Roy and his friend Matthew collect the hay and stack it on the cart. She liked Roy, who was five years older than her but never treated her like a little girl. During that week she'd even got a tan. She sighed and put the card back on the mantelpiece. That week had been her only holiday and she had been so happy there. Among the cards was one from Peter Barrett, addressed to all the family.

On Christmas morning, after exchanging presents, they went to church. For dinner they always had a capon with all the trimmings; afterwards they listened to the King's speech. While her father settled down with a newspaper, Annie and her mother did the washing-up, then Lil came round to tea. It was always so predictable.

The Friday after Christmas Annie was upstairs when her father called up from the shop. 'Annie, come down here, there's someone to see you.'

At first she was puzzled. It was too early for Lil, and besides, she would come on up – Lil didn't wait to be invited. As she passed the mirror hanging over the fireplace in the kitchen, Annie automatically patted her hair, and bit on her lips to make them red.

She pushed open the door behind the counter and wasn't really surprised at her visitor. 'Hello, Peter.' Her father was busy serving a customer, but gave her a knowing smile as she walked through and moved away from him and the customer.

'I've come to ask you if you would like to come to a dance with me on New Year's Eve.' Annie cast her eyes down to his hands which were twirling his bowler hat round and round.

'I don't know. Where is it?'

'At my club.'

'What do they wear?'

'Evening dress?'

'I don't have an evening dress.'

'Can't you buy one?'

'I don't know. I can't expect me dad to fork out again.'

'Oh, dear. Well, I'll call in on Monday and you can let me know then if you'll be able to come.' He took her arm and whispered, 'I sincerely hope so.' As he moved nearer the door he called out, 'Goodbye, Mr Rodgers.'

'Goodbye, son.'

Annie knew her father was dying to ask her what he wanted, but he resisted till the shop was closed and they were sitting down to tea.

'Are you going out with young Peter again?'

'He's asked me to go to a dance with him.'

'Oh,' said her mother, cutting up the last of the Christmas cake. 'Where?'

'It's a New Year's Eve dance at his club.'

'So I suppose that will mean you'll be putting that muck on your face again?'

'Come on now, Mother, Annie looked very nice when she went out with him before.' Her father broke off a piece of icing and popped it into his mouth.

'I still don't hold with plastering your face with that stuff.'

'Mum, I'm seventeen. Besides, look at all the girls at the Barretts' party, they all wore make-up. I felt a right little girl when we were there, I can tell you.'

'They looked like a lot of hussies, with those low necklines showing off half their bodies, smoking and drinking. I hope you don't drink when you're out with him. I don't like the idea of you going out with that crowd. You could end up looking like one of those floosies.'

'Thanks,' said Annie disdainfully.

'Now come on, Mother. Our Annie's not like that – she knows how to behave herself.'

'Anyway, I don't think I'll be going,' said Annie, smoothing out the wrinkles in the white damask table-cloth.

'Why not?' asked her father.

'Well, I haven't got a long frock for one thing.'

'Is that all that's stopping you?'

Annie continued running her hands over the cloth. 'Yes.'

'Well, I'm sure we can overcome that little problem. I'll give you the money, and you can go and treat yourself.'

Mrs Rodgers' head shot up.

'But, Dad . . .' said Annie.

Her father held up his hand to silence her. 'If I'm going to help

26

you get up the ladder, I've got to be prepared to support you.'

'But, Dad,' repeated Annie. 'You bought me a new frock for Christmas.'

'Well, we'll call this a New Year present.'

'Well, I still don't like the idea of Annie hobnobbing with that lot. Some of them looked shifty. That fellow wearing the blazer and yellow cravat for one. Did you see his crafty-looking eyes? I ask you, a yellow cravat.'

'Mother, our little girl is growing up, and if we want her to go to the right places, and meet the right people, we've got to be prepared to let her spread her wings.'

Annie leant over and kissed her father's cheek. 'Thank you,' she said solemnly, and then got up and went. She knew this issue was going to be a bone of contention between her parents all evening.

At eight o'clock on New Year's Eve, Annie, holding her pale blue satin dress above her ankles, rushed down the stairs to answer Peter Barrett's knock on the door at the side of the shop.

He looked handsome standing there in his black overcoat, with his white silk scarf draped loosely round his neck. His dark eyes appeared to be taking in every detail of her dress, its discreet neckline and small lacy puff sleeves. Annie could just see his black bow tie, and the contrast against his brilliant white shirt was dramatic. He held out a corsage in a cellophane box.

'For me?' asked Annie, her large brown eyes shining.

'If you let me come in you can pin it on your very lovely dress before we go.'

'I'm sorry. Of course, come in.'

Peter removed his black Homburg hat, his dark hair smoothed flat against his head with Brylcreem, and climbed the stairs behind Annie.

In the warmth of the kitchen Annie's face felt flushed, and she wondered if she had perhaps put a little too much rouge on her cheeks. 'Look, Mum. Look at my lovely flowers.'

Mrs Rodgers looked up from her sewing. 'Very nice.'

'Hello there, son.' Mr Rodgers stood up and shook Peter's enthusiastically.

Annie stood in front of the mirror and pinned the spray of white flowers on to her dress. 'How does that look?'

'Very nice, my dear,' said her father, beaming with pride.

'I'll be bringing Annie home about two, if that's all right with you?'

'Two?' inquired her mother.

'Yes, I'm afraid it doesn't finish till after one, and I wouldn't want Annie to miss anything.'

'Well. Yes,' said her father. 'If that's the time it finishes.'

'We'll come home in a taxi, of course.'

Mr Rodgers coughed. 'Look after our little girl, won't you?' He moved towards the fire and placed his foot on the wide brass fender that his wife spent hours polishing on her knees. 'She's all we've got, now,' he said solemnly. Unconsciously he ran his fingers along the bobbles of the green cloth that covered the mantelpiece.

'Yes, sir. Ready, Annie?'

She nodded. Her smile disappeared when she looked at her father's sad face. He was looking at the photograph of John. She was instantly reminded of her dead brother, and the pain that day had brought. John, three years her senior, had been struck down with pneumonia just after his tenth birthday. Her mother and father's tears, and the way they had held her close when they heard the news that sad day, would stay in her memory for ever.

Annie picked up her mother's fur wrap and Peter placed it round her shoulders. 'Thank you,' she whispered.

'Have a good time,' shouted her father after them as they left the room.

When Annie stepped inside the ballroom it took her breath away. The walls were lined with mirrors. A glittering crystal ball hanging from the high ceiling was slowly rotating, sending arrows of coloured lights darting off in all directions. Annie stood wide-eyed, taking in her surroundings.

'This way,' said Peter. 'Our table's over there.'

They pushed and edged their way through the milling crowd of dancers, and made their way across the room.

All evening Annie was so happy. The music, and the carefree

atmosphere as they danced and laughed, was everything Annie had ever dreamed about, and she didn't want it to end. Peter was wonderful and he introduced her to many of his friends, some of whom she recognized from the party at his house before Christmas – including the one her mother had said had got shifty eyes. His name, she discovered, was Julian.

It was nearing twelve o'clock and Julian had insisted on dancing with her. She was nervous – she didn't like the sneering way he looked at her. He was holding her very close, and his lips were caressing her neck. At the stroke of twelve he kissed her lips hard, forcing her mouth open. She pushed him away and looked anxiously around for Peter. He too was kissing a girl – everyone seemed to be kissing and laughing and shouting 'Happy New Year' to all and sundry. Nineteen thirty-six was being heralded in with streamers, paper hats and balloons cascading from the ceiling, and the noise from those blowing trumpets and hooters, popping the balloons, laughing and shouting, mingled with the band who had just struck up with 'Auld Lang Syne'.

'What's up, you silly little thing? Never been kissed before?' Julian had to raise his voice to be heard above the noisy revellers; his steely blue eyes seemed to be mocking her. 'Or is it that you're afraid you're going to turn into a pumpkin or something?' He grabbed her again and as she struggled to free herself from his grip, his lips came down on hers, hard and demanding.

When she broke away he laughed and, pushing back his blond quiff of hair, turned his back on her. Shouldering his way through the crowd, he kissed the first girl that was available – leaving Annie standing alone on the dance floor.

Suddenly someone linked her arm and she was swept along with the line singing 'Auld Lang Syne'. Peter was nowhere to be seen. The crowd then went on to do 'The Lambeth Walk', and Annie was once more thrown into the fray.

The noise was pounding in her head as she pushed and staggered her way back to the table. The smoke was smarting her eyes, and she was beginning to feel dizzy from the drink. She looked at the table. Empty and half-full glasses were strewn all over it. Some of the glasses had been knocked over, and the red stain from the wine had spread across the cloth. The ashtrays were filled to overflowing. It was a shambles, and looked a very sorry sight. She felt alone and dejected. Where was Peter? How was it possible she could be so happy one moment and so miserable the next? She picked up her evening bag and made her way to the ladies' room.

As she pushed open the door the sound of high-pitched laughter greeted her.

'Hello, it's little Annie,' said one of the girls through the mirror of the dressing-table she was sitting at. She put the long tortoiseshell cigarette-holder she had been waving about back in her mouth. Annie knew her name was Belinda.

'Hello,' said the girl sitting next to her. She turned on her red velvet stool to face Annie. 'Enjoying yourself then?' She wet her fingers and twirled a curl in front of her ear. 'You want to hang on to that Peter, he's a good catch.' Iris's voice was squeaky, like a little girl's.

'Darling, I've been throwing myself at him for years,' said Belinda. 'And I've given him everything,' she threw her head back and laughed. 'You know what I mean, darling – everything.'

Annie felt embarrassed as the two girls laughed loudly. 'Excuse me,' she said, moving towards the lavatory. They must have thought she was out of earshot as they continued their conversation.

'I wonder if she and Peter have . . . you know?' said Iris giggling. 'Had it?'

Annie was shocked, and gently pushed the door ajar.

They both shrieked again.

'Look's like we'll have to wait for Peter to come clean and tell us. Can't see little Miss prim and proper letting on.'

'Doesn't look as if old Julian's got to pay out just yet.'

Annie was furious. How dare they talk about her like that? She moved slowly to where she could see them. She was still out of their sight – she wanted to confront them, but what could she say? Iris, the girl with the curl, giggled and put her finger with a long scarlet nail to her scarlet lips. 'Shh,' she whispered loudly. 'Perhaps tonight's the night Peter will have his wicked way.' They both threw their heads back and screamed with laughter.

'Not to worry, darling, Peter will let us know as soon as he does it. He's never been known to welch on a bet yet.'

Annie was shocked. What did they mean? She locked herself in the lavatory. What did they mean, a bet? Had he just her asked out for a bet . . . Just to see if he . . . And he'd done it before.

'Bye, Annie, see you outside,' Belinda yelled, and slammed the door.

For a few moments the powder room was deadly quiet, then the door was pushed open and another noisy crowd came in.

She didn't know for how long she had been sitting on the closet. Her head was swimming with drink and anger. Tears filled her eyes. She liked Peter, and felt happy with him, but now . . . Did he really only take her out for a bet? Was that why he'd asked her parents to his father's party? Annie looked in her compact mirror, and saw her make-up was all smudged. She felt miserable and so unhappy. She tried to work out how she could get home. She had no money, and if she took a taxi, her parents would be in bed by the time she got home, and she didn't want to wake them to pay for it. Besides, what would her father say about Peter? He must never know what he was really like, and why he'd taken her out. Although he wasn't a violent man, if he lost his temper, well, anything could happen. She shuddered. Peter's father was the landlord – they could even lose the shop.

Finally, after repairing her make-up, she gathered up enough courage to leave the quiet of the ladies' room, to find, to her surprise, a completely different scene back in the ballroom. They were playing a waltz and, apart from the mess on the floor, the room and the music were serene and beautiful.

'Where on earth have you been?' Peter, who was wearing a silly pink pointed hat with streamers hanging down the back, came up and took hold of her arm. Even though she was angry and upset, she wanted to laugh at the contrast between this party hat and his bowler. 'I haven't even wished you a Happy New Year yet.' He put his arms round her waist and kissed her long and hard. Her lack of response made him step back. 'Oh dear. Am I in the dog house? I'm very sorry, but I got caught up with this crowd.'

'Would you please take me home?'

'What? Why? I thought you were enjoying yourself.'

'I was till . . . It doesn't matter. I'll get my wrap.'

'It's not one o'clock yet. What's your hurry?'

'I just want to go home.'

'Please yourself. I'll just go and tell the others. We had planned to go on to a party after this.'

In the taxi Annie sat in the corner and stared out of the window. They passed plenty of rowdy crowds, all eager to greet the New Year with lots of noise and laughter. If only Annie could feel as happy.

'What's wrong? I thought you were enjoying yourself. Do you feel all right?' Peter sounded genuinely concerned.

She nodded. How could she bring herself to tell him she knew why he had taken her out.

He moved closer, and went to put his arm round her shoulder. Annie pushed it away and squeezed herself as far away from him as she possibly could.

'Please yourself,' he said, sliding back along the seat. 'It's just that I'd like to know what I'm supposed to have done.'

She looked down at the flowers pinned to her dress. They were crumpled and dying, and that's how she felt. She had tears in her eyes – her feelings were all mixed up. What should she tell him? She was angry, but she wanted Peter to hold her and touch her, and to tell her they were wrong, and that he'd taken her out because he liked her. Was she being silly and naïve? She felt frightened, knowing she could never show her feelings even if he did really like her; she would be afraid of the consequences – afraid that if he did have his way it would be just her luck to end up with a baby. Then what would her parents say? Bewildered by everything that was happening to her, Annie furiously blinked back her tears.

Chapter 4

'Good morning, love. You were quiet coming in last night. A bit early, wasn't it? Didn't expect you in till after two. Did you have a good time?'

'Yes thank you, Dad.' Annie kept her head down as she buttered her toast.

'Well, you'll have to tell us all about it tonight, won't she, Mother?'

'If she wants to.'

'Best get back into the shop. Come down later after you've finished helping your mother.'

'OK, Dad.'

'You all right, love?' asked her mother after her father had left the room. 'You're very quiet this morning – thought you'd be full of it.'

'It was very nice.' Annie sat with her elbows resting on the table. She clutched her cup with both hands. How could she tell them Peter Barrett had only taken her out for a bet. Just to see if he could add another virgin to his list. She knew her parents would be shocked at that – she would have to make up some sort of story for them, but what?

At six-thirty Lil came into the shop. ''Allo, Mr Rodgers.'

'Hello, Lil. All right then?'

She nodded. 'Well?' she asked Annie. 'Did yer 'ave a nice time? Did yer frock look nice?'

Annie moved away from the counter. 'All right if I walk home with Lil, Dad?'

'Yes, but wrap up mind, it's bitter out there.'

Annie waited till they were well away from the shop before she went into details.

'No,' uttered Lil, her mouth falling open with surprise. 'That's all 'e took yer out for? The dirty little toe-rag. Some of the tarts at work tells us about blokes like that. Sounds like these toffs are just as bad.'

'Worse, I reckon,' said Annie.

'Yer dad'll go mad when 'e finds out.'

'Yes, well, I'm not going to tell him.'

'But what yer gonner say when 'e asks if yer going out with 'im again?'

'I'll just tell him we don't really hit it off.'

''E'll be ever so disappointed. I finks 'e 'ad 'igh 'opes for you.'

'Yes, well, that's as maybe, but I'm not going to be another one of Peter Barrett's conquests. I best be going back.'

'I can't come out tonight, I've got ter 'elp me mum with the washing, so I'll see you termorrer.'

'All right.' Annie turned and headed for home. She knew she would have to tell her parents something, but didn't want to disillusion her father's idea of Peter Barrett.

The snow that had been threatening all day began falling, and when Annie pushed open the door the sound of the bell tinkling over her head and the warmth of the shop was comforting.

Mr Rodgers pushed his plate away. 'That was lovely, Mother. Now, Annie, sit down and tell us all about last night.'

'Well, it's a smashing place. It has this large crystal ball hanging from the ceiling, and you should have seen all the balloons, and paper hats, and at midnight we all sang "Auld Lang Syne".' She began genuinely to enthuse as she recalled the evening. Suddenly she realised she'd made it sound very exciting.

Her father leaned back in his chair. 'I'm glad you had a nice time. Are you seeing Peter again?'

'I don't think so.'

Her father sat forward. 'Why not?'

'Well, I did feel a bit out of place. His friends are a bit la-de-da.'

34

'Nonsense. You're just as good as them, don't you think so, Mother?'

'Well, I don't like them, and I don't like her going out with all that muck on her face,' said her mother as she cleared the table.

'A lot of young women wear that stuff now. I was only looking at Bill Armstrong's oldest the other day when she trotted past – done up to the nines she was, and I don't think she's as old as our Annie.'

'She's not,' said Annie.

'Well, what do you expect,' sniffed her mother, 'they were totters before they took over the ironmonger's.'

'Yes, but that was his father, and it was years ago. You must admit they've got a good business there.'

Mrs Rodgers tutted. 'I don't know how they all manage in these poky little holes.' She swept the white cloth off the table, folded it and, placing it in the drawer of the dresser, banged the drawer shut.

'There're not poky,' said Annie, sticking up for her father as usual when there was a family disagreement. 'Our flat's very nice.'

'Yes, when there's only three of you, but not with their brood. What she got, five kids? I don't know where they all sleep.'

Annie giggled. 'P'raps they sleep on the counter.'

Mrs Rodgers gave Annie one of her looks, and she knew her mother was going to have the last word. 'I'm going to get a book,' Annie said, quickly leaving her parents to it.

It was two weeks later and Annie, busy serving Mrs Turner, was only half listening to her going on about Mrs James's boys.

'D'yer know, those little perishers let all the tyres down on me boy's bike, made 'im late fer work they did. I started ter give 'em a clip round the ear-'ole, then she came out.' Mrs Turner adjusted her position on the chair. 'Yer should 'ave 'eard 'er leading orf at me.'

'That all?' asked Annie as she added up the bill.

'I'd better 'ave a couple of rashers as well. Well, I told 'er, if she give 'em both a bloody good 'iding now and again, they wouldn't be such little buggers. They ain't got no discipline in that 'ouse. Fanks, Annie,' she said as Annie put the bacon on the counter. 'And what about 'er old man? 'E's just as bad.'

Annie looked up when the door bell tinkled and was taken aback when Peter Barrett walked in. He stood in the far corner of the shop.

Mrs Turner adjusted her flat cap and pulled her shawl round her shoulders. 'I fink that's all fer now, love.' She cast her eyes over Peter and leaned forward on the chair. She put her hand to cover her mouth and asked, 'Is this the landlord's son?' She inclined her head towards him.

Annie nodded.

Mrs Turner continued. 'The young man yer dad was telling me about?' she said in a loud whisper.

Again Annie only nodded – she didn't want to make any comments. 'Are you paying for this, or is it to go on your bill?' Annie knew her voice was high and unnatural.

'Shove it on me slate fer now, love.' She stood up. 'See yer later,' and gave Annie a knowing wink. ''Allo there, young man. Bit cold, ain't it?' she said, going towards the door.

Peter Barrett touched his hat, and held the door open for Mrs Turner.

'Ta very much,' she grinned.

As the door closed Annie hurried from behind the counter. 'Well. What do you want?' she asked angrily.

He held up his hands in surrender, then quickly took off his hat. 'It seems I'm not the most popular person at the moment. I was telling Belinda, I didn't know why you were so off-hand the . . .'

'Oh, so you discuss our affairs with your friends?'

'No. It's just that . . .'

'I know now why you took me out.'

He looked down as he twirled his bowler round and round in his hands. 'I'm sorry about that,' he said softly. 'Belinda told me what was said in the ladies' room. And she thinks you may have overheard. She told me to tell you she's very sorry, it was the drink talking, not her. So here I am, cap in hand, to apologize. Am I forgiven?'

36

The door behind the counter opened and Mr Rodgers walked in carrying some boxes. 'Hello there, Peter. How are you?'

'I'm fine thank you, sir. I was just trying to persuade your charming daughter to come out with me.'

'Is she playing hard to get?'

Peter laughed.

'Well,' said Mr Rodgers. 'You know what these young women are like, they want you to throw yourself at their feet.'

'Dad,' said Annie blushing.

'I'll just put this new display in the window.'

He moved away, and Annie and Peter wandered to the far corner of the shop. When she knew they were safely out of earshot she said forcefully, 'I'm not going out with you. I know you had a bet, and I'm not going to help you collect your money, so I think you'd better leave.' Her face was burning with anger.

He took her arm. 'That's not the reason I want to take you out. I've called off the bet.'

The shop bell went again, and Annie quickly pulled her arm away.

It was one of the men from the factory. 'Give us 'alf ounce o' shag, Annie love.'

Annie went behind the counter.

'Shove it on me slate.' He picked up the tobacco and meandered out of the shop.

Peter looked amazed. 'Doesn't anybody ever pay?'

'At the end of the week, when they get paid. Most of them clear their bill then. Remember, this is a very poor area.' Her reply was curt.

'As I was saying,' continued Peter. 'Come out for a drink.'

'No thank you.'

'Why not? I've said the bet's off, what more do you want?'

Annie looked anxiously at the window. She could see her father busy moving objects around. 'I don't want to go out with you.'

'Look, Annie,' he whispered. 'I promise I'll behave myself.'

She turned her back on him. 'Go away.'

'You could make it a foursome if you'd feel safer.'

'No thank you.'

'I'm sure your friend would like to go out somewhere nice?'

She slowly turned and looked at him suspiciously. 'Who would come with us?'

'Would you bring your friend?'

Annie nodded. 'Lil would like that,' she said thinking out loud.

'I'll bring a fellow from the office. Is that a date then?'

'I'll think about it.'

'Right, I'll call in on Friday and you can let me know if Saturday would be all right for both you and Lil. Must dash, see you Friday. Goodbye, Mr Rodgers,' he called out.

Mr Rodgers poked his head out of the window. 'Bye, son.'

Lil was round early on Saturday night to get ready for her first date. Standing in her washed-out pink Celanese petticoat, she wrapped her pale thin arms around herself. 'I'm ever so excited. Fanks ever so much for letting me come out with yer. What d'yer fink 'e'll look like?'

'I don't know.' Annie wanted to laugh at Lil's skinny matchstick legs. She had never seen her undressed before, and never realized her friend was so thin. 'You must try to sound your aitches, and act a bit more refined.'

''Ere, 'ark at you. What, yer mean like this?' She picked up a bottle top from Annie's dressing-table and, putting it to her lips, she stuck her little finger high in the air. 'This better?' asked Lil, emphasizing her t's. Throwing her head back, she giggled excitedly.

Annie laughed. 'What frock you going to wear?'

'I don't know. It's ever so kind of you to let me choose one of yours. Which one d'yer fink I should 'ave?'

'This blue one should suit you. Try it on.'

Lil slipped the light wool dress over her head and preened in front of the long mirror on the wardrobe door, turning this way and that.

'Put this belt on, it'll show off your waist.'

'It's smashing,' purred Lil. 'Oh look, it shows off me bosoms.' She pushed her small breasts together, then slowly smoothed the dress down over her hips. 'Fanks, it's really lovely. You're ever so kind.'

'Go on with you,' laughed Annie. 'Remember you're going to be my bodyguard tonight. So don't have too many drinks and get squiffy.'

'Will we 'ave wine?'

'Shouldn't think so. Keep your voice down, I don't want Mum to know.'

'I've only ever 'ad a drop of me dad's stout, and that's when 'e wasn't looking.'

Annie sat at the dressing-table and began to put her make-up on.

'You'll 'ave to do me face,' Lil laughed. 'Look, me 'ands are all of a quiver.'

'I'll have to do something with your hair. You wait till you see the way some of the girls dress.'

'Yer, I still look like a kid.' She looked sad as she leaned forward and peered in the mirror. 'I wish I 'ad a bit o' money ter spend on meself. Annie, d'yer fink I might let yer down?'

'Don't be daft. Come on, cheer up. I'm glad to see you've not still got your socks on.'

They laughed and giggled as they did their hair and made up their faces. At last they were ready for their big night out.

At seven-thirty Peter knocked on the door and, after quickly poking her head into the kitchen to tell her parents they were off, Annie and Lil raced down the stairs, shouting their goodbyes on the way down. At the bottom Annie ground to a halt. 'Right, remember to try and act like a lady,' she said. 'Let me look at you. You look smashing. Ready?'

Lil nodded nervously.

'OK. Now I'll open the door.'

Annie was taken back when she saw Peter standing there with Julian.

'Well, aren't you going to introduce us to your friend?'

'This is Lillian,' whispered Annie.

Lil giggled. Nobody called her Lillian. 'Please ter meet yer, I'm sure.' She held out her hand.

'I'm Peter, and this is your date for tonight. Julian.'

Julian took her hand and kissed it, making Lil giggle again.

'I'm looking forward to a very interesting, and hopefully, pleasant evening.'

Annie wanted to run in and slam the door, but from the sparkle in Lil's eyes she could see it would be wrong to deny her friend a nice night out. And Lil was trying so hard.

They walked through Albert Mews, and on past the Eagle pub on the corner where Will Hobbs was banging on his drum – his sister Rose shook her tambourine with gusto, and added extra verve to it as they passed. Mr Hobbs gave them a slight nod.

When they reached Jamaica Road, Julian put his fingers in his mouth and whistled loudly for a taxi. Lil's face was a picture as she climbed in. 'Where're we going?' she asked eagerly, sitting forward.

'Thought we'd take you to a little place we know in the West End.' Julian sat back and placed his arm along the back of the seat. 'It's good fun – the kind of place we think you would like.'

Annie shot him a glance of disapproval which he chose to ignore as he continued. 'They have a small stage, and people get up and do turns.'

'Yer mean like amateur night at the pictures?' inquired Lil enthusiastically.

'Sort of – most of them get a small remuneration which helps bring the punters in.'

'Oh,' said Lil with a blank expression on her face.

Peter added, 'They get paid.'

'Oh, that's nice.'

Although Annie wasn't happy with the situation she had to smile at her friend. Lil was sitting on the edge of the seat, excitedly looking this way and that, almost as though she was seeing this area for the first time. Annie too was sitting on the edge of her seat in the taxi, but through apprehension and suspicion. Why had Peter brought Julian along for Lil? She would be totally out of her depth with him. Had he done it to make her angry? Were they just using them, was it something they would boast about at the office, going out with a common shop girl and a factory girl? Her mind was turning over and over; only Lil's happy and excited laughter brought her out of her grey mood.

'Right, this is it,' said Julian, helping them from the taxi.

It was a lively bar, and on the corner of the small stage was a piano player, a fellow playing a banjo, and another older man on the drums. Many different artistes took it in turn to sing, tap-dance, or play their speciality instruments, and there was even a juggler, who when he dropped his clubs got booed and whistled. Despite being nervous and uneasy, after a while Annie felt herself relax amidst all the jokes and singing, and noted with pleasure the smile of delight on Lil's face as she clapped, laughed and sung her heart out.

In the ladies' room Lil was still giggling at her new surroundings. 'Annie, this is the best night of me life.' She peered into the mirror. 'I never knew people could 'ave such a good time. I could get used ter this sort a life. And I tell yer what, I rather like that port and lemon, it's much better than me dad's stout. Lend us yer lipstick.'

Annie smiled. 'Don't you go having too much to drink. I don't want to end up putting you to bed.'

'I'm keeping me eye on what *you* 'ave. Come on, the boys will be wondering where we've got to.'

All evening Peter was attentive and chatty. Julian also seemed to climb down off his high horse, and the way he laughed and talked with Lil, encouraging her to sing, made Annie wonder if she had misjudged him.

It was finally time to go, and once more they climbed into a taxi. 'I could get used to this,' laughed Lil once again, throwing herself back on the seat.

Eventually they reached the spot where they had to get out and walk. It was cold and their breath formed small clouds in front of them as they hurried along. Annie pulled her scarf tighter at her throat. When they came to Paradise Street, the road before Victoria Gardens, Julian said, 'You two go on, while I take Lil to her door.'

Annie panicked. 'It's all right. Me and Lil can go the rest of the way on our own.'

'Don't be silly, I wouldn't dream of letting you walk home on your own,' said Peter. He turned to Julian. 'I'll be back in a jiff.'

'Please, we'd rather,' said Annie.

41

Julian laughed. 'Why's that, Annie, don't you trust him?'

'It's cold standing around here,' said Lil, stamping her feet. 'Come on, let's git a move on.'

Julian took Lil's arm and tucked it through his. 'See you later, Peter. Goodnight, Annie.'

'I'll be round in the morning,' called Lil over her shoulder as she tripped along beside Julian.

'But Lil, Lil,' cried Annie as she walked away. At the corner Lil turned and gave her a wave.

'What's the matter with you?' asked Peter as they slowly moved on. 'Didn't you enjoy yourself?'

'Yes, thank you. Why did you bring Julian along?'

'I told you I was bringing a fellow from the office to come out with us.'

'Yes, I know, but you didn't say it would be Julian.'

'Don't you like him?'

'No.'

'Lil seems to. I like her, she's good company, and I love the way she sings all the latest songs – you know, she's got a good voice.' He laughed.

'Yes, I suppose she has. Never took a lot of notice of it before. Lil's been my friend for years, we went to school together.' She looked behind her. 'And if Julian tries anything I'll . . .'

'You'll what? Besides, surely she's old enough, and capable of looking after herself.'

They turned into Albert Mews, their feet echoing on the cobbles. 'Thank you for a nice evening,' said Annie quickly.

'Can I see you again?'

'I don't know.'

'Annie, I told you, all that business with the bet's off. So why can't I see you again?'

She turned on him. 'What is it you want from me? You've got the pick of girls – your type of girls. Girls who come from your background. I'm only one of your father's tenants' daughters.'

Peter pushed her against the wall. 'I like you, Annie. All those other girls are false, loud and demanding. You . . . You, are differ-

ent. I must admit at first it was only a game, but now . . . Well, I
enjoy your company.'

In the Mews' gaslight she looked at him. Was he telling her the
truth? 'I'd better go in,' she said quickly.

'Can I see you again next week?'

'I don't know,' she whispered. With her back to him she slipped
her key in the door and stepped into the passage.

He didn't attempt to kiss her, just turned on his heel and walked
away.

On Sunday morning Lil was round well before ten.

'You're early,' said Annie, ushering Lil into her bedroom.

'I've brought yer frock back. Fanks.' Lil's eyes were sparkling,
and she was on edge. 'I 'ad ter come round as soon as I could. I'm
sorry about last night – not coming all the way 'ome with yer.'

'That's all right.'

'Did 'e try anyfink?'

'No.' Annie looked at Lil. 'Did Julian?'

Lil grinned and shook her head. 'No, but 'e kissed me "long and
passionately", as they say in them books you read. She giggled. 'It
was smashing. 'Ere Annie, what d'yer fink?' She sat on the bed.
''E want's ter take me to that pub again next week.'

'What? Why?'

She clasped her hands in front of her, hardly able to contain
herself. ''E's gonner ask the governor if I can sing on the stage,
you know, like those other women and blokes did.'

Annie laughed. 'You on the stage?'

Lil looked downcast. ''E finks I've got a nice voice, and 'e reckons
I could make meself a few extra bob singing. Those people gits
paid yer know.'

'I'm sorry Lil,' Annie apologized, 'but I never thought of you
singing for your supper.'

'Are you going out with Peter next Saturday?'

Annie shrugged her shoulders. 'I hadn't planned to.'

'Well, d'yer fink yer could? Ter keep *me* company this
time.'

They laughed, long and heartily. Annie wiped the tears from her eyes.

'This is a right turn up fer the books, ain't it,' said Lil. 'You being my chappa . . . what ever they call it.'

'Chaperon.'

'I told me mum and she's tickled pink. I told 'er I've got ter buy meself a lipstick. Well, I can't keep borrowing yours, now can I? And, Annie – ' Lil sat back on the bed – 'd'yer fink I could borrow one of yer frocks?'

'I don't see why not. Then when you're a big star I'll be able to say I helped you get started.'

They laughed again.

'Well, they can't stop us from dreaming, can they?' said Lil wistfully.

Chapter 5

The following Saturday Annie was waiting for Lil to come round to get ready for her big night.

'Well, I don't like the sound of it,' said Mrs Rodgers. 'Those sort of people could lead that young girl into anything. And I don't like the idea of you going out drinking.'

'Oh, Mum, we don't have that much to drink, only a shandy. I'm not a child you know.'

'Annie, don't speak to your mother like that.'

'Dad, Lil's only going to get up on the stage and sing. We'll all be watching her.'

'Yes, this time maybe,' said her mother. 'But what if they entice her with promises of greater things?'

Annie laughed. 'Oh, Mum. You sound like Mrs Day, she's always going on about her Amy being whisked away into the white slave market.'

'Don't be so silly. Her Amy ran off with a sailor, we all know that. What about Lil's mother, what does she have to say about all these goings on?'

'I don't suppose the poor woman would have much to say, especially if Lil's bringing in a few extra bob.' Mr Rodgers picked up the newspaper. 'Has anyone seen my glasses?'

'On the mantelpiece.'

'Where?'

'Under that letter, look.' Mrs Rodgers jumped to her feet and handed her husband his glasses, tutting loudly.

'Thank you, Mother.'

She settled back in the armchair at the side of the fireplace and

45

carried on with her knitting. 'I was talking to that nice Mr Hobbs today. Did you know he's going to be made up to sergeant soon?'

'Yes I know,' said Annie in a disgruntled tone. 'Will told me.'

'Annie, don't talk to your mother like that.'

'Sorry. It's just that I get a bit fed up with Mum always on about Will Hobbs and the damn Salvation Army.'

Her father looked up from his evening paper. 'Watch your language, my girl,' he said irritably.

'He said you should go along to one of their meetings one evening, just to see if you like it.'

Annie laughed. 'What, me join the Sally Army?'

Mrs Rodgers' knitting needles were going at a great speed, and she continued. 'You could do a lot worse, young lady. I don't hold with you going out to pubs and that, with that crowd.'

'Dad likes me going out with Peter Barrett.'

'Well, yes. Don't let's start on all that again,' said Mr Rodgers. 'There's the knocker.'

'It's Lil.' Annie rushed from the room thankful at the excuse to get away from what was going to be another long drawn-out disagreement about her going out with Peter.

In Annie's bedroom they laughed and giggled while Annie made Lil's face up with extra care, and fixed a bow she'd bought from Miss Page in the haberdashery next door in Lil's hair. The two Page sisters had been very interested when Annie told them about Lil singing, and she'd promised to tell them all about it on Monday.

The dress they had decided Lil would wear was dark blue, and Annie carefully draped a pale blue chiffon scarf round her throat, and fastened it high on her left shoulder with a pretty brooch. Annie stood back.

'There, look in the mirror.'

'Is that me?' Lil leaned forward and peered at her reflection. 'Fanks, Annie.' She rubbed her hands together. 'Me 'ands are all sweaty.' She laughed nervously. 'I 'ope I don't make a fool of meself.'

'Don't be daft, course you won't. Come on, before you put your coat on, let's go and show me mum and dad what you look like.'

'I wish me mum was coming,' she said sadly.

'I told you before, when you're a star you can send a taxi round for all of us.'

'Daft a'porth,' laughed Lil, giving her friend a playful push as they made their way to the kitchen.

'Well, Mum and Dad, what do you think?'

Mr Rodgers stood up. 'You look very nice, my dear. Don't she, Mother?'

His wife looked up from her knitting. 'Yes, very nice.'

Lil was nervously moving the black handbag Annie had given her for Christmas from one hand to the other. She pushed up the tortoiseshell clasp and quickly clicked it shut again. A knock on the door eased the tension.

'They're here. Grab your coat, Lil. Bye, Dad, bye, Mum.' Annie hurriedly kissed their cheeks, picked up her handbag and raced down the stairs.

'Good luck,' Mr Rodgers shouted after them.

Inside the pub Julian ushered them to a corner table, and went off to have a word with the manager.

'I'll get the drinks,' said Peter, and headed towards the bar.

Lil looked anxiously around her. 'I ain't 'alf nervous.'

Annie too looked about her. 'There's a lot of people here.'

'Oh my Gawd,' Lil fretted. 'What 'ave I let meself in for?'

Annie patted her hand reassuringly. 'Don't worry, you'll be all right.'

Peter arrived with the drinks. 'Looks like a good crowd in here tonight.' He waved to someone across the smoke-filled room then sat down at the table. 'One of the chaps from the office,' he explained. 'I told them a friend of mine was singing here tonight.'

Lil giggled and gently pushed his arm. 'Fanks. So I'm a friend then.'

'Right,' said Julian, joining them and sitting next to Lil. 'It's all settled. You're on after Poppy, the tap-dancer.'

Lil laughed nervously. 'Poppy? What a name.' She pulled at Julian's sleeve. 'Does 'e know what I'm gonner to sing?'

'Yes, I told him. He wanted to know what key. I said you'd sort that out with the pianist.'

'What key?' She threw her head back and laughed again. 'Christ, 'ow the 'ell do I know?'

'Don't worry, you can sort that out with him.' Julian picked up his glass. 'Cheers everybody, and here's to my little cockney sparrow.'

'Cheers,' they all said.

Lil quickly downed her port and lemon and, smiling, moved closer to Annie. 'Do I look all right?'

'For the umpteenth time, yes. And watch the drink.'

'Don't get uppity. It's just that I need a bit o' Dutch courage.'

'Sorry, Lil, only I'm nervous for you.'

'Blimey. How do you fink I feel? I'm sorry I started this.'

'Don't be daft, you've got a nice voice.' Annie glanced across at Julian who was deep in conversation with Peter. She couldn't hear what they were saying above the noise and clatter all around them. The three-piece band had warmed up and they were now playing some of Marie Lloyd's old music hall songs, and when Lil joined in with the rest of the audience, it seemed to relax her.

The announcer got up and introduced the acts. First came the good-looking tenor they had seen last week. He was popular and did a medley of the latest songs, and they all joined in with the chorus. Then there were some performing dogs who barked and did all the wrong things, and it was only when one of them cocked his leg up against the piano stool that everybody laughed and applauded. They were quickly followed by a fat lady in a low-cut evening gown who sat herself at the piano. She closed her eyes, and, giving some sort of recital, pounded the keys with gusto. Her large fat arms wobbled and she looked to be in ecstasy, but when the audience began stamping and banging on the tables she quickly changed to a pot-pourri of popular tunes.

Then it was Poppy's turn, who, when she danced on to the stage with her short curly blonde, Shirley Temple hairdo, and her very short dress, received plenty of whistles.

'She looks about forty,' whispered Lil.

Annie smiled at her and nodded in agreement. She clapped eagerly when Poppy finished and the announcer strolled back on to the stage.

'Tonight we have a new little lady who's going to sing "Who" for you. Ladies and Gentlemen, please give Miss Lillian Grant a big hand.'

Lil stood up and walked on to the stage. The audience gave her a polite clap as they did most of the other new performers. Annie's mouth went dry as she watched her friend talk to the pianist. Then Lil moved to the centre. Annie could see her shaking with fear, and she closed her eyes and prayed for her friend.

Suddenly a faltering little voice, accompanied by the band, began to sing, but the words were lost in the hubbub around them. Gradually, as she gained confidence, it got louder. The noise in the bar quietened considerably, and Lil suddenly became herself. She strutted on the stage, belting out the song like a polished performer. Annie's mouth fell open. She couldn't believe this was her friend, whose voice she had always taken for granted.

At the end of her song, Julian and Peter jumped to their feet, shouting and clapping. Annie too was on her feet, tears of joy running down her face as she laughed and clapped. Lil ran off the stage with her arms open. Annie turned to embrace her, but she ran to Julian who swept her off her feet, twirling her round and round.

'Was I any good?'

'Good, my little darling – you were sensational.' Julian took her in his arms and kissed her long and hard.

Annie was speechless as she stood watching the scene.

Peter too kissed her, but only on the cheek, and Lil was glowing when it was Annie's turn to embrace her friend.

'Did yer like it?' Lil's eyes were sparkling.

Annie had never seen her look so happy. 'You were great. I can't believe it. You were so confident. I'm so happy for you.' She hugged her warmly then they all sat back down at the table.

'I was ever ser nervous when I stood up there on me own, but once I got started, I loved it,' Lil said, breathless. She laughed, and for the rest of the evening Lil continued to laugh, sing loudly, and cuddle up to Julian with adoration in her eyes.

At the end of the evening the manager came up to them and gave Lil two shillings and sixpence.

'That fer me? All fer me?'

'Yes, my dear, and I'd like you to come back next Saturday – that's if you can, of course.'

'Course I can. Yer really want me to sing again next week?'

'Well, you went down very well this evening.'

'Don't worry. We'll be here,' said Julian.

Lil sat back and looked at the money in her hand. ''Alf-a-crown, just fer standing there singing. D'yer know I only get a pound fer a whole week's work.'

'Well, my little cockney sparrow, looks like you could be making yourself quite a few bob one way and another,' said Julian.

Annie quickly shot him a glance – his condescending tone worried her.

Lil was still smiling. 'Wait till me mum 'ears about this.'

Julian was on his feet. 'More drinks everyone?'

'Not for me, thank you,' said Annie.

'Why not?' inquired Peter. 'We've got to toast Lil's success.'

Lil quickly looked across the table at Annie, and Annie could feel the hurt in her expression.

'Sorry, yes, of course we must,' said Annie.

All the way home Lil was the centre of attention, and she was wallowing in it. When Lil and Julian left Annie and Peter at the corner of Paradise Street, Annie didn't make a fuss.

'You seemed a little surprised at Lil's talent?' said Peter taking hold of her elbow.

'I was. I can't believe it was her up there on that stage.'

'So, what about next Saturday? Are we going with them?'

'If you want.'

When they reached her door Peter took her in his arms and gently kissed her.

Annie's feelings were mixed as she bade him goodnight and went indoors. She did like him, but she was afraid of him too. She still didn't know if she trusted him – and certainly she didn't trust Julian. They were both out of her class, and what if Peter still wanted to . . . ? She quickly dismissed that thought – her mother and father would never forgive him if they knew why he'd first asked her out. And she did want to carry on going out with him.

In the comfort of her bed she lay reflecting on the evening's events. She was happy for Lil. But she also knew she was a little jealous of the attention she was getting, and was annoyed with herself over it. Little mousy Lil was happy for once in her life and doing something she liked, and getting paid as well. An extra half-a-crown was going to make a great deal of difference to Lil's life. But, Annie thought, where was her own life going?

Chapter 6

As usual on a Sunday morning, Lil raced round to Annie.

'I didn't 'alf enjoy meself last night. Did you?'

'Of course. You were very good.'

'And I got paid fer it.' Lil sat on the bed and swung her skinny legs back and forth. ''Alf-a-crown, just fer standing there singing. Ter fink I only gits a pound fer standing in that dirty old tea factory all week. When I told me mum she didn't believe me, and me old man finks I've been out on the game.'

Annie looked shocked. 'He didn't say that, did he?'

Lil nodded. 'Yer.'

'D'you want me to come round and tell them?'

'Na. 'E shut up when I gave 'em the money.'

'What, all of it?'

'They let me keep tuppence fer a lipstick. I'm going ter Woolies and get meself one termorrer.'

Annie felt guilty at her jealousy of her friend, ashamed of her thoughts last night. 'You'll have to tell me what frock you want to borrow next week,' she said, trying to sound cheerful.

'D'yer mind? D'yer know Julian,' she laughed, 'what a poncy name. Julian' – she said it in a cocky manner – ''e reckons I could earn meself pounds a week.'

'What doing?' As soon as she said it Annie felt cross with herself for being a bit off-hand.

'Singing, of course. 'E's gonner try and see if 'e can get me in another pub.' She lay back on the bed. 'Just fink, if I got pounds and pounds . . . I'll be able ter buy meself a nice frock, and shoes.' She sighed. 'Cor, it'll be like a dream come true.'

Annie smiled at Lil. 'What you going to sing next week?'

'Dunno. Ju said 'e'll bring me round some music so I can learn the words.'

'You're going to see him before Saturday?' asked Annie. Her tone was one of shock.

'Yer. I forgot ter tell yer, 'e's taking me to this other place Wednesday night ter see the boss, and ter see if I can do a turn there.'

Annie began tidying her bedroom. 'I expect Peter will call in the shop tomorrow and ask me to go with you.'

'Yer, I 'ope so, that'll be nice.'

'How's your mother?'

Lil sat up. 'She's all right. Look, I'll 'ave ter go. I'll call in termorrer from work, then you can tell me if you're coming on Wednesday.'

'OK.'

It was after six on Monday, and Annie eagerly waited for Peter to come into the shop. But at six-thirty it was Lil who pushed open the door.

'Well, yer coming with us?'

'I don't know.'

'Ain't 'e asked yer?'

'No. He hasn't been in yet.' Annie began wiping down the counter. 'He may have been held up somewhere.'

'Yer, could be. I won't be round ternight, me and me mum are going ter 'ave a go at tarting up one of 'er old dance frocks.' Lil laughed. 'I didn't know it, but it seems she was quite a girl before she got married, and she's kept a couple of 'er old frocks. They ain't all that bad.'

'You can always borrow one of mine, you know,' said Annie eagerly.

'Yer, well fanks. We'll see 'ow this turns out first. See yer termorror.'

'OK.'

As Lil closed the door Annie felt very down. Why hadn't Peter been in to ask her out with Lil and Julian? Had she been too off-hand towards him? The bell tinkled and she looked up. 'Oh, it's you, Will.'

'Hello, Annie.' He politely snatched his cap from off his head. 'How are you?' he asked amiably. 'You look a bit down.'

'I'm all right. What can I get you?'

'Just a tin of Zubes please. All this singing you know.' He touched his throat and smiled, crinkling his round face that was smudged with dirt from Fisher's factory. For the first time Annie noticed his dark blue eyes twinkled when he smiled. 'I saw Lil at the corner. She tells me she was singing at a club last Saturday.'

'Yes, she's got a nice voice.'

'Could do with her in our group, and you. Have you ever thought about joining us, Annie?'

She laughed. 'Sorry, Will. But could you honestly see me and Lil standing there waving our tambourines?'

He picked up the Zubes. 'We could do with someone with a bit of life in them.' He put his money on the counter, and the shop bell rang again. He stood to one side as one of the ironmonger's girls came in for her dad's tobacco.

'Why don't you think about it?' asked Will when the girl left.

Annie put Will's and the girl's money in the till. 'I don't think so.'

'Well, if you ever change your mind, I'd be very happy to show you how to play a tambourine.'

'Thanks.'

As he left the shop, Annie thought how kind he was, so different to the other boys at the factory. But at that moment the last thing in her mind was joining the Salvation Army.

At seven o'clock her parents returned from the pictures and they shut the shop. When the evening meal was on the table, Annie sat down and began picking at her food.

'What's up with you?' asked her mother.

'Nothing. I'm not very hungry.'

'You look a bit peakish, love,' said her father.

Her mother eyed her suspiciously. 'Are you sure you're all right?'

'Course – stop making a fuss. I just feel a bit off, that's all.'

'She could be coming down with a cold or something.'

Mrs Rodgers shot her husband a glance of disapproval, then turned to Annie. 'I think we'd better have a little talk later, young lady.'

'What about?'

Her mother shifted uneasily on her chair. 'About, you know – things.'

Annie laughed. 'You don't think . . .' She suddenly became serious. 'Thanks. Is that all you think of me?' She threw her fork on the table and stood up.

'Sit down, Annie,' said her father. 'Your mother didn't mean anything.'

'Yes she did.' Tears filled her eyes as she slowly sat down.

Her mother looked uncomfortable. 'I'll fill the teapot.' With her back to them she went on, 'I'm concerned about you, and I can't help worrying about you. You know I don't like you going out with that crowd, all this drinking and staying out late. How do we know what you get up to?'

'That don't say much for me. And, Mum, Dad likes . . .'

She sat down at the table again. 'Oh yes, we all know what your father likes. But I don't hold with it.'

'I'm sure young Peter's not like that – he's been well brought up,' said her father.

'He's a man, isn't he?' was her mother's curt response.

Annie stood up and left the room. She knew there was no point in staying to listen to the arguments for and against Peter. At this moment she didn't even know her own mind.

Tuesday came and went, and there was still no sign of Peter. Lil only popped her head round the door to tell her her mother's frock had turned out fine, so she wouldn't be borrowing one of Annie's.

At six-thirty on Wednesday, Lil burst in again. 'Peter been in?'

Annie shook her head.

'That's a shame, I was looking forward to us all going out again ternight. Still, we'll all be tergever on Saturday.'

'That's if he turns up.'

'Can't stop, got ter get ready fer me big night. I'll tell yer all about it termorrer.' She left, as she had come in, in a hurry.

All evening Annie was on tenterhooks, worrying about Lil and wanting to be with her. She couldn't concentrate on her book or listen to the wireless for very long before her mind wandered to her friend. She felt responsible for her – after all it was through Annie that Lil had met Julian. What if he tried something on . . . ? She quickly dismissed that thought. Lil would know how to deal with anything like that. Annie was glad when it was finally time to make the cocoa and go to bed. That night her sleep was fitful and restless.

Annie kept looking up at the clock. It was almost six-thirty. 'Dad. Could I go and wait outside for Lil?'

Lil always had to walk through the Mews and pass Rodgers' grocer's on her way home from work.

'Why's that? Don't want me to hear all the girl talk?'

'Well, you do tell us to be quiet when we get a fit of the giggles.'

'I should think so – when you two start you don't know when to stop. Go on with you, we've got nobody to serve. Wrap up mind, it's a bit nippy out.'

Annie pulled on her blue woolly beret and brown coat and stood at the doorway. She pulled the fake fur collar up round her ears. It was a dark night, and the lights in the few shops that were still open looked warm and inviting.

Old Ted in the butcher's opposite gave her a wave when she stepped outside, then he continued to scrub his chopping block vigorously. Only Ted and his wife lived above the shop now that all four of his daughters had married and moved away.

Annie looked up the Mews to Fisher's tall chimneys belching out thick black smoke. In the night sky they seemed to dominate the view, towering over that end of the Mews like tall, fat, still fingers reaching upwards. Even in the summer, the late evening sun could only just filter through the smoke.

A few of the girls who she knew worked with Lil walked past and called out her name. Annie waved back at them, slowly moving on a few steps and looking in the window of the haberdashery and wool shop next door to her father's. It was closed and dark. Like all the shops in the Mews the door to the flat above stood next to the attractive bow window. The window was always neat and well laid out. Annie loved going in there to buy ribbons and the like. The shop had a dusty, old feel about it, and always smelt of lavender. Annie had known the two Miss Pages, two elderly spinsters who always had a kind word and a smile for everyone, all her life. Her father once told her they had both lost their fiancés in the First World War. To Annie it seemed sad that their lives and style of clothes had never moved on from that time.

She ambled on past the baker's. That too was locked and in darkness. Later, in the evening, Mr Jones and his two sons would be coming down to work. After the baking was finished, the boys, Len and Ron, would go off on their large black bikes with the huge wickerwork basket filled with bread and cakes, delivering to the local shops and even to some of the posh restaurants over the other side of the water. If the wind was in the right direction and blowing the clouds of smoke from the factory away from the Mews, the lovely mouthwatering smell of fresh bread and cakes would fill the air. Mrs Jones was a small woman who served in the shop till after lunchtime, and the last bun had been sold. She would shout up at her tall, strapping sons, and threaten them with a clip round the ear if they ever answered her back. Annie often wondered if she had to stand on a chair to wallop them.

On the other side across the old cobbles the greengrocer's was still open.

'All right, Annie love?' shouted Mr Day as he carefully took an apple from the display neatly piled up outside under his window. He polished it on his white apron then, after admiring the shine, put it back in its little paper nest.

'Yes thank you,' she replied with a smile, remembering how fat, busybodying Mrs Day still told everybody her Amy had been taken away by the white slave traders. The eldest daughter, Molly, was a well-built girl, aged about thirty and unmarried, and she helped Mr Day in the shop.

A group of young boys rushed past her on a home-made wooden cart. The ball-bearing wheels were deafening as they rumbled over the cobbles. 'Got any mouldies, mister?' they shouted.

'Get out a 'ere,' shouted Mr Day back at them. 'Little perishers.'

He waved his fist in the air. 'Soon as I turn me back they'll 'ave me apples.'

Annie laughed, thinking how happy she was living here, surrounded by people she knew. By now she had wandered to the other end of the short Mews in which there were only six shops with beautiful bow windows. They always reminded her of the old-fashioned pictures on Christmas cards. She could almost imagine ladies in crinolines, with white fur muffs and matching trim on their bonnets, looking in the windows.

A screeching cat brought her back to reality. At this end there was a lamp-post in the middle of the Mews and Annie walked over to lean against it. The hissing sound from the gas light no longer frightened her as it had done when she was a child. She looked up at the arm sticking out, remembering when they used to throw a rope over it and swing round and round. The shop had been her father's for years. Her dad didn't have any family since his dad had been killed in the war, and his mother had died in the 'flu epidemic. The former owner of the shop, kind Mr Williams, had taken a liking to her father who had worked for him since he was fourteen, and left him the shop and, it seemed, a lot of debts. Her mother and father had met when her mother would come in from the biscuit factory where she once worked. But all that, Annie reflected, was a long while ago.

Annie looked at her watch. It was almost seven, and Lil was late. Where was she? Perhaps she hadn't gone to work today, perhaps she was ill. But then her mother would have sent one of the kids round to tell her – perhaps her mother was ill.

Annie peered down the long wide alley which had a high fence each side and gates that led into the back yards of the two rows of terraced houses. The alley was empty and looked eerie, full of shadows. The banging of a dustbin lid, as someone threw a bottle away, made her jump. In the distance the doleful sound of a ship's hooter on the Thames drifted through the damp air. Annie shivered. She suddenly felt cold and decided to go back to the shop. The barking of dogs made her look round, and the sound of someone's footsteps hurrying along the alley caused her to pause.

'Annie. What yer doing out 'ere?' Suddenly Lil came into view.

'You're late, I've been waiting for you. Where've you been? And what have you got there?' Annie pointed to the brown paper carrier bag Lil was carrying.

Lil grinned. 'It's me new frock.'

'A new frock. Where did you get the money from for a new frock? Why didn't you tell me? And why didn't you let me come with you to buy it?' She was cold, and very angry with Lil.

'Look, I'm already late, I'll come round ternight and tell yer all about last night.' She hurried on, but at the bottom of the Mews Lil turned and waved.

Annie stood for a while staring at the two black metal bollards that had been erected that end. She felt totally rejected.

All through tea Annie wondered whether Lil would bother to come round that evening. As soon as she heard the knock, she raced down the stairs and threw open the door. Lil was standing holding the carrier bag. Instantly Annie forgave her.

'Brought me frock round ter show yer,' Lil chirruped.

They went into Annie's bedroom and closed the door.

'Well,' said Annie eagerly. 'Where did you go last night? What was it like? Was you good? What did you sing?'

''Ang on. One question at a time.'

'Sorry, but I can't help being excited for you. I wish I'd been there. Did your mum's frock look all right?'

'Yer, it didn't turn out too bad. I got a note for yer.'

'Is it from Peter?'

'Fink so. Julian gave it to me.'

Annie quickly opened the envelope and read the short letter.

Dear Annie,
Sorry, I won't be able to see you on Saturday.
Something has cropped up.

Love, Peter

It was so impersonal. There wasn't any hint of when he would get in touch with her again, or any kisses.

'It was a shame he didn't ask yer ter come last night. Yer seeing
'im Saturday?'

'Was he there?' Annie was still shocked.

'No. What's 'e 'ave ter say?'

'He can't make it on Saturday.'

'That's a shame,' said Lil, quickly dismissing it. 'Last night was
good, a bit like the other pub. The manager liked me.'

'Well, you've got a smashing voice.' Annie was trying to keep
her voice steady. 'What did you sing?'

Lil sat on the bed and removed a bright red satin dress from the
bag. Annie gasped. 'That's a bit bright.'

'Don't yer like it?'

'Well. I don't know. Try it on.'

'Julian said I've got ter stand out.'

Annie was still put out over Peter's letter. 'It's your frock, why
should he tell you what to wear?'

Lil looked a little flustered. 'Well, yer see . . .'E bought it for
me.'

Annie sat next to Lil and lifted up the dress. She let the satin
slip through her fingers. 'What did he do that for?' Annie's voice
was low.

''E just wants me ter look nice, that's all.'

'What did you have to do to get it?'

'Annie Rodgers, that's not a nice fing ter say. I told yer 'e wants
me ter look nice, and 'e's got me this other pub to sing in, and
guess what? I gits five bob in this one cos it's a lot bigger.' There
was an edge to her voice as she stood up and rammed the dress
back in the bag. ''Sides, 'e's not like that.'

Annie jumped to her feet. 'Course he's like that. Oh, Lil, can't
you see he's using you, gaining your confidence. I bet before long
he wants you to . . . You know.'

Lil looked at Annie, her hazel eyes wide and full of anger. Annie
thought she was going to shout at her, but her voice was very even.
'Annie, for the first time in me life somebody's taking an interest
in me, and likes me, and if 'e gives me a quid ter buy a new frock
I ain't going ter turn it down. It's all right for you ter be a Miss

'igh and mighty, you've never 'ad ter go without.' She walked towards the door. 'And if 'e wants somefink else, well . . .'

Annie felt guilty. 'Lil, you can't let him . . .'

'I ain't got the same sort a conscience as you.'

'But . . . But, what if you end up having a baby?'

'I'll worry about that if and when the time comes. 'Sides, 'e ain't done nuffink yet.' Lil walked to the door.

'Lil, don't go. I'm sorry. It's just that I don't want to see you get hurt. Come on, show me your frock.'

Slowly Lil turned. A huge grin spread across her face. 'I told me mum I only got 'alf-a-crown like before. She said she'd let me keep sixpence, so this way I'll be 'aving three and six a week all to meself, just fer singing.'

'What did your mum say about the frock?'

'I told 'er one of the other girls lent it to me. I'm not sure if she believed me or not, but with another four bob a week coming in, she didn't argue.'

Lil slipped on the dress. It was sleeveless and made her arms look long and gangly. Low at the front, it had sequins cascading over one shoulder and, since Lil was so thin, it really didn't do much for her except show off her tiny waist.

'It's very nice,' said Annie, 'but I think you could do with a bangle or something up your arm.'

'I've got some money left out of the pound,' Lil said eagerly. 'This was nine and eleven down Brick Lane. Not bad, eh?'

'Are you giving him the change?'

'No fear, I'm going ter get me 'air done proper first, and I fought I'd get a feather or somefink ter wear in it.' She patted her hair and preened in front of Annie's long mirror, then, self-consciously touching the top of her arm, said, 'I fought a wide bangle would look good and I can put a silk scarf frough it and waft it about all film star like. What d'yer think?'

'Should look very nice,' Annie said, but her real thoughts were, what did Julian really want from Lil; and when was Peter going to call on her again?

Chapter 7

A month had passed, and Annie had seen nothing of Peter. Lil was still singing at the two pubs and, full of enthusiasm, she would tell Annie all about it. Annie was upset for she knew that after all these years they were drifting apart. The only time they spent together now was Sundays, and at the pictures on Friday night. Lil was besotted with Julian, and talked about him constantly.

Today was Thursday, and Annie was gazing out at the rain that everybody was predicting would soon turn to snow. It had been falling steadily all day and she was bored: not many people had been in the shop. Thursday was one of the days Lil had time to call in on her way home from work. Annie glanced up at the clock, eagerly awaiting six-thirty when Lil would rush in to tell her about her singing last night. Lil had said it was a big pub, and it sounded as if she was very popular there, and always had to do a few songs. Lil was changing, Annie could see. She appeared more self-assured, confident, and was beginning to look better dressed. She also wore a lot of make-up.

The door opened and one of the men from the factory came in, wanting his cigarettes. 'Only five, Annie. How much do I owe now, love?'

Annie took the black book from off the shelf behind her. 'Not so much this week, Mr Harrison, only a shilling.'

'I'll be able ter pay yer tomorrow. Been trying ter cut down on me fags,' he said, putting his packet of five Woodbines in his boiler-suit pocket. 'Got another one on the way.'

The bell went again, and Lil came scurrying in, shook the rain from her coat and stood to one side while Annie finished serving Mr Harrison.

When he left Annie asked, 'Was you good last night?'

"Bout the same – 'ad quite a few drinks bought me though.'

'You want to watch out you don't finish up a right old boozer like some of them round here.'

Lil laughed. 'Is yer dad around?'

'No, he's gone upstairs for a cup of tea. What d'you want me dad for?'

Lil looked anxiously about her. 'I don't want yer dad, I just want ter know if yer can 'ave Saturday afternoon off.'

'Why?' asked Annie suspiciously.

'I'm going to buy meself a new frock.'

'What, another one? You only got one a couple of weeks ago,' said Annie brusquely.

'Well, yer I know, but I want another.'

'You come into a fortune or something?'

Lil looked sheepish. 'No, but I've gotter look nice for Julian.'

'He paying again?' asked Annie sharply.

'No, this is my money. Well, yer coming with me or not?'

'I'll have to ask me dad. We going to the pictures tomorrow?'

Lil wandered round the shop. Finally she picked up a jar of pickles from the far end of the counter, and examined it. With her back to Annie she said, 'I can't – I'm going out with Julian.'

'What?' Annie banged down the scissors she'd been using to cut up small pieces of greaseproof paper for the bacon. 'We always go to the pictures on a Friday.'

'I'm sorry, Annie.'

'No you're not. You could go with him another night. Why did you say Friday?' Annie was finding it hard to control her temper.

'We'll go next week, I promise. Anyway, what about Saturday?'

'I don't know.' Annie was angry.

'Please, Annie. Yer got much better taste than me and, well, it'll be nice ter browse round the shops together.'

Annie looked at the hurt expression on Lil's face. 'All right. Stay here, I'll go up and ask him.' On her way out she had to slam the door behind the counter, just to show Lil her feelings.

Annie returned a few minutes later. 'Yes, he said that's all right. What time will you be round?'

'About two – that OK?'

Annie only nodded her reply, and Lil left the shop.

Annie couldn't believe how things had changed between them since Christmas. Was it only three months ago when she first went out with Peter? Where was he? And why had he stopped taking her out? If he really liked her, as he said he did, why didn't he come round? It was his fault Lil was going out with Julian, and because of him, she and Lil were falling out. Her head was full of all these thoughts as she idly stared into space. The next time Mr Barrett came in for the rent she would make sure she was here, and she could ask him, casually of course, about Peter.

She was still feeling miserable and sorry for herself when Will Hobbs came into the shop.

'Hello, Annie. Cheer up, it might never happen.'

She smiled. 'I'm all right. I'll be glad when this weather gets better. I'm fed up with looking out on this rain.'

'They say it's going to snow. It does get you down after a while, especially when you're standing on street corners banging a drum.' He smiled. 'Just seen Lil, she looked pleased with herself.'

'Yes, she's doing all right with her singing job.'

'Do you still go with her?'

'No, not now.'

The door behind the counter opened and Mr Rodgers came in. 'Hello there, Will. How are you?'

'I'm fine thank you, sir.'

'Annie, your tea's poured out, go on up before it gets cold.'

As Annie walked towards the door, Will called her name. She turned. 'Yes, Will?'

He twisted his cloth cap round in his hands and looked at Mr Rodgers. 'It doesn't matter,' he said quietly.

It was two-thirty on Saturday afternoon. Lil was late and Annie was getting more and more impatient.

'Why don't you go and meet her?' said her father. 'It'll do you good to get outside, even if it's only for an extra few minutes.

65

You've been a right little misery these last few days. What's up, love?'

'Nothing really.' Annie shrugged off his concern. 'I'll get me coat.'

Annie was walking past the Eagle when Lil turned the corner looking flustered. 'Sorry I'm late. Me old man's being awkward again.'

'What over?'

'One of the boys came 'ome with 'is trousers torn. I 'ad ter git between 'em – I'm sure 'e would 'ave killed 'im. 'E's been in the pub all morning. 'E won a few bob on the dogs last night.'

'What did your mum say?'

'Not a lot. She's a poor thing, waddling around, puffing and blowing.'

'When's the baby due?'

'Dunno, in a couple of weeks I think. I thought we'd go to Peckham, and 'ave a look over there.'

'All right. Not much point going to Brick Lane. Most of the shops there shut on Saturday, them being Jews.'

'Look there's a tram – run.'

Ambling round the shops they laughed and giggled like old times – only now it was Lil who was doing the spending. Annie was amazed at the amount of money she had.

'Where did you get all that?' whispered Annie when Lil opened her purse in the shoe shop.

'Worked fer it.' She paid the three and eleven for her shoes and they left the shop. 'Right, if I can git a really posh frock for under ten bob I can treat you to a cuppa tea for a change.'

Lil found a blue silk frock that she liked. It wasn't to Annie's taste but, as Lil said, it would look all right on the stage. She then bought some make-up and a pair of silk stockings.

'That's me lot,' said Lil, bustling her way through the crowds. 'Let's go ter Lyon's now fer our cuppa and a bun.'

They settled at a table and gave their order to the nippy as Lil put her paper carrier bags on the empty seat next to her. Her eyes were shining as she patted them. 'Cor, I've never been shopping like this before in me life. And it's all fanks to you.'

'Me, why?'

'Well, if I 'adn't gone out with yer that first time I'd 'ave never met old Julian.' She laughed. 'I still can't 'elp laughing at 'is poncy name – and, well, I wouldn't 'ave been singing and able ter buy all this.'

Annie smiled. Deep down she was really pleased for her friend.

Lil continued. 'I didn't say anyfink before, but . . .'

The waitress came back and placed a tray tea and buns in front of her. 'Ta,' said Lil. 'I 'ad a word with Ju last night, and 'e said to ask you if yer'd like ter come with us ternight?'

Annie stared at Lil, speechless, her bun frozen midway between her plate and her mouth.

'Well, say somefink.'

Annie put the bun back on the plate. 'Will Peter be there?'

'Shouldn't fink so. Well?'

'I don't know. It's very nice of you but . . .'

'But what? It'll do yer good to 'ave a night out.' Lil stirred the tea in the pot, put the strainer on the cup and poured it out. 'You've been a bit of a misery lately since yer stopped seeing Peter.'

'I didn't stop seeing him . . . He stopped seeing me.'

'You liked 'im didn't yer?'

Annie blushed. 'Yes.'

'Well, yer shouldn't 'ave been in such a 'urry ter give 'im the elbow. Those sort a blokes don't 'ang around waiting fer another chance yer know.'

'I know that now, don't I?'

'Well anyway, what d'yer say about tonight?'

Annie sat back and smiled. 'Things have certainly changed around between us. I'd love to come.'

'Good, come round about seven.' Lil sat back as well and began drinking her tea. Annie noted Lil didn't clasp the cup with both hands any more – she used the handle.

Sharp at seven Annie was at Lil's front door – Julian was already waiting.

'Hello there, Annie. Haven't seen you for a while. How are you?'

'I'm all right.' Annie was still finding it hard to be polite to him.

Lil, as usual, came racing out of the door, flustered. 'Sorry about that.' She held up her face and Julian kissed her full on the lips.

"Allo, Annie.'

Annie nodded, taken aback at the amount of make-up Lil had on.

Lil put her arm through Julian's and they walked to Jamaica Road, where he whistled for a taxi.

Annie sat opposite them, truly amazed at the way Lil fawned and fussed over him. She was also embarrassed, and glad when they arrived at their destination.

It was the pub that Lil had first sang in and, much to Annie's surprise, they were greeted with great enthusiasm when they walked in, and were quickly ushered to an empty table right at the front.

'What would you like to drink, Annie?' asked Julian after taking Lil's coat and pushing her chair in.

'I'll have a small shandy please.'

'Usual, my love?' He bent down and kissed Lil's long white bare neck. She was wearing the new blue dress, low-cut and sleeveless with beads sewn on the shoulder and a wide frill round the bottom.

The pub was crowded, and there was plenty of noise from people laughing and chatting. Annie looked around the smoke-filled room half hoping to see Peter somewhere in the throng.

A few men came up to Lil and kissed her cheek. Annie couldn't make out their conversation as Lil was laughing very loudly most of the time. After a while she turned to Annie. 'I love this place.' Her eyes, under the heavy make-up, were dancing. She pushed her wide red bangle, with a red silk scarf threaded through it further up her pale, thin arm. She leaned forward and whispered to Annie. 'Should 'ave got meself a blue one ter match me frock.' Glancing round she added, 'They always make me feel ser welcome 'ere.'

Annie could only sit and stare. She couldn't believe this was little Lily Grant – who only a few months ago was a shy, mousy sort of person, who never went out unless Annie took her, and was reliant on her for money.

Julian returned with the drinks, and as the band came on to the small stage they waved to Lil, who in turn enthusiastically blew them all kisses before they settled down and began warming up.

When the announcer walked on the stamping and chanting began. 'We want Lil. We want Lil.'

Lil stood up and bowed to the whistles and tumultuous applause. Annie knew her mouth had fallen open but she didn't have the strength to close it.

Lil walked on to the stage and they quietened down. She started singing with so much verve and vitality, everybody joined in the choruses. She strutted and swaggered up and down the stage – she had the audience in her hand as she went from one song to another. There was nothing amateur about her, she looked like a true professional. Annie knew Lil had found her vocation, and things would never be the same between them again.

Many times throughout Lil's performance Annie looked over at Julian. Between each song he jumped to his feet and applauded with tremendous fervour; the huge grin on his round pasty face made his squinty eyes almost disappear.

When Lil finally returned to her seat, flushed and glowing, drinks began to fill the table, all of which were downed very quickly. As the evening wore on, Annie looked for the opportunity to ask Julian about Peter – but it never came.

Lil didn't stop laughing and talking all the way home. She and Julian insisted on taking Annie back, and she was thankful when at last they reached Albert Mews.

'Thanks,' she called over her shoulder as she ran the last few yards to her door.

'See yer in the morning,' yelled Lil after her.

The following morning Annie waited for Lil. By the afternoon she still hadn't arrived.

'Stop moping around here,' said her father. 'Why don't you go and find out where Lil's got to.'

'Don't want to go round to their house, not with her dad.' Annie tossed her head and went to her bedroom. She knew she was being silly, but she didn't really want to confront Lil. She was much too unhappy, and jealous. When she went to bed that night Annie still hadn't seen Lil.

On Monday lunchtime the boys from Fisher's came in, full of high spirits, since most of them had just been given the promise of a pay rise.

'Fancy the pictures ternight, Annie?' yelled Georgie Bates. 'Can afford ter take yer upstairs in the shilling seats now, that's if you brings the sweets.'

'I wouldn't go out with you, Georgie Bates, even if you paid me,' she said and laughed at the chorus of whistles and shouts that followed.

George pulled his cap round back to front and, getting down on one knee, put his hands together. 'Annie, you've really 'urt me feelings,' he announced and, struggling to his feet, said to his audience, 'guess I'll 'ave ter go back ter me missis now.'

'You're not married,' said Annie as she handed Eddie Finch, one of his mates, a packet of Woodbines.

He crept up to the counter. 'No, but I've got a secret harem I 'ave, so yer better watch out.'

Everybody in the shop burst out laughing – they all knew Georgie was a joker, and very sweet on Annie. One by one they left the shop until only Will Hobbs was left.

'What can I get you, Will?' asked Annie.

'Don't 'ang about Will,' shouted Mr Harrison, poking his head back round the door. 'The foreman ain't very 'appy.'

Will looked nervously about him. 'I was going to ask you if you'd like to come to the pictures with me one night?' Annie smiled and he looked embarrassed. 'But . . . well, now you've turned Georgie down . . .'

Annie walked round the counter. 'I wouldn't mind going to the Regal this week.'

His face broke into a grin. 'Would you? With me? Would Thursday be all right?'

She nodded. 'I'll bring the sweets.'

'You don't have to, I could get you a box of chocolates. Would you like that?'

70

'You don't have to. Can you be round about seven?'

The long moan of the factory hooter calling the men back to work, sounded. 'OK. Got to rush.' With that he was gone and the Mews settled down to its usual peace and quiet again.

At six-thirty Lil finally came in. 'Sorry I didn't come round yesterday but me mum wasn't none too well.'

Annie suddenly felt guilty. All her life things had gone easy for her but now her emotions were all mixed up, like the scenic railway, up one minute and down the next. Tears so often seemed to be followed by laughter – what was happening to her? 'That's all right,' she said. 'I was going to come over to your house, but I had a bit of a throat, and it was so cold.' She cleared her throat to convince both herself and Lil. 'Is your mum all right now?'

'Yer. Mind you, I don't fink it'll be long before this one's born.' Lil perched herself on the seat. She looked sad, Annie noticed with another pang of guilt. 'Poor old Mum. It ain't much fun being married and 'aving lots o' kids. I'll take 'er a small bar of chocolate, that'll 'elp cheer 'er up.' She dived in her handbag and brought out her purse. 'How much?'

Annie handed Lil the chocolate. 'I'll treat her to this.'

'You don't 'ave ter,' Lil was a little tetchy. 'I can afford it, yer know.'

'Yes I know. You can buy her one tomorrow.'

'All right. Anyway, did you enjoy yerself Saturday?'

'Yes. You certainly know how to belt out a song now.'

'Yer.' Lil smiled. 'Julian's been showing me how to stand, and breathe.' Her eyes sparkled. ''E's been ever so good ter me. I'll never be able ter fank yer enough for taking me on that first date.'

Annie took the feather duster from under the counter. 'Yes, well, a lot of water has flowed under the bridge since then.'

'Yer, it's a pity you don't see Peter any more.'

With her back to Lil, Annie casually flicked the duster over the shelf and, trying to keep her voice even, asked, 'Does Julian ever talk about him?'

'Not a lot. 'E did say 'e's going out with someone, she's got a posh name.'

'Belinda,' volunteered Annie.

'Yer that's right. D'yer know 'er?'

'We have met.'

Lil looked up at the large clock and slid off the chair. 'I'll 'ave ter go. We still going ter the pictures Friday?'

'I don't think so.'

The bell over the door was still jingling as Lil stood in the doorway. 'Why not?'

'I'm going on Thursday.'

'Who with?'

'Will Hobbs,' whispered Annie.

'Who?' shouted Lil pushing the door shut.

'You know, Will . . .'

'Course I know 'im. What yer going out with 'im for?'

'He asked me, and he's nice and polite.'

'And a bloody bore.' Lil pulled the door open again and the bell jangled incessantly. 'S'pose we'll 'ave yer joining the Sally Army next.' Lil slammed the door behind her. It was her turn to be angry now.

Chapter 8

It was almost seven o'clock and Annie was sitting in the kitchen patiently waiting for Will to call for her.

'You look very nice, dear,' said her mother looking up from her knitting.

'Thank you.'

'I'm glad to see you haven't put too much stuff on your face. Will wouldn't like that.'

Annie didn't answer. She had deliberately put on only a small amount of pale pink lipstick, and she still felt she might well be overdressed for him. It had occurred to her as she was getting ready that she had never seen him in his going-out clothes: he was always in work overalls, or his Salvation Army uniform, and she was a little worried as to what he would turn up in.

'I think Will is a nice lad,' Annie's mother was smiling. 'His sister and father are always very polite.' She sat back in the arm chair. 'They're a very nice family.'

'Don't start, Mum. Don't start trying to get me married off.'

Annie's father walked in with his newspaper tucked under his arm. 'Right, that's another day over. Who's trying to get you married off?'

Mrs Rodgers laughed. 'Silly girl. I was only expressing an opinion.'

'What's all this about?' asked Mr Rodgers, looking along the mantelpiece for his glasses as usual.

'Mum was talking about Will Hobbs.'

'He's a nice enough boy. Ah, here they are. Mother, why do you always have to hide them?' He put on his glasses and sat in his chair. 'What do you think of the girl old Day's got working for him?'

His wife tutted. 'She's not a girl, she's a woman. Done up like a dog's dinner, she was. Talk about mutton dressed up as lamb.' She put her knitting in her lap. 'Ted's wife and me was watching her. Giving all those factory men the glad-eye she was.'

Mr Rodgers glanced over his glasses. 'I bet old Day's chuffed. She must be good for business.'

'You would say that. Why couldn't he have got a young lad? He would have been more useful, especially lifting those heavy boxes.'

He laughed. 'Perhaps old Day fancies a bit on the side.'

'Ben. That's not a nice thing to say, and in front of Annie as well.'

'He wouldn't need to pay for staff if his missis was a bit more helpful,' said Mr Rodgers. 'Still, she'd have to lose a bit of weight. Couldn't see her bending down sorting out the veg.'

Annie smiled at the thought of Mrs Day bending over and showing her big pink knickers. As kids, they'd all laughed at them blowing on the washing line like ships in full sail.

'She can't help being big, poor woman.' Mrs Rodgers continued knitting. 'She's still very upset at her Amy running off with that sailor, and he's only got help because her Molly's getting married and moving out to one of these new estates.'

Mr Rodgers opened his newspaper. 'That Amy affair was over a year ago. The poor old girl can't cope with her wayward daughters. I was surprised to hear her Molly's getting married. Didn't think she was the type.'

'Yes, well.' His wife leaned forward. 'He's a bit older than her. A widower with three boys, so I heard.'

'There's the knocker,' interrupted Annie. 'Bye.' She quickly kissed her parents on the cheek and hurriedly left the room.

Annie was taken back by Will's smart appearance. He was wearing a neat brown suit and shiny brown shoes. He raised his brown trilby and revealed his light-brown slicked-down hair.

'You look very nice, Annie,' he said when she stepped outside.

'So do you, Will,' she smiled at him. 'I've got some sweets, so shall we go?'

He behaved just as Annie thought he would, although he did try to hold her hand in the pictures. She was surprised at his sense of humour, and she soon found she was laughing a lot and enjoying his company. At the end of the evening when they arrived at her door he asked if he could take her out the following Thursday. Annie readily agreed, and when it was time for him to leave, he only pecked her cheek.

Although Lil was annoyed, on the next two Thursdays Annie went to the pictures with Will. She was surprised how different he was away from his workmates. She liked him, and he certainly wasn't shy or boring, and each week she looked forward to their night at the pictures.

It was six-thirty on Monday when Lil, as usual after work, called into the shop. Today she looked drawn, her eyes dull and lifeless through lack of sleep.

'You look terrible – you had a night out on the tiles?' Annie was curt, guessing she'd been out with Julian without telling her.

Lil shook her head. 'Guess what? Been up all night with me mum. She's 'ad another girl.' She looked sad as she slumped on the chair next to the counter.

'You've been up all night and then had to go into work this morning?' Once again guilt crept over Annie for jumping to the wrong conclusions.

'Don't get paid if we don't turn up, do we?'

'Is your mum all right?' asked Annie with genuine concern.

'Yer, but the baby was dead. Oh, Annie, you should 'ave seen the scrawny little fing.' Tears filled Lil's eyes. 'I 'ad ter 'elp deliver it as the doctor was busy with someone else.'

Annie gasped in horror. 'You didn't?' As it was Monday she was alone in the shop, and she quickly hurried round to the front of the counter. 'Why didn't a neighbour come in and help?' Annie's big brown eyes were wide open as she stared at Lil in amazement.

'She didn't want any of them nosy old cows in; she only wanted me.'

'Was it horrible?' asked Annie, filled with curiosity.

Lil nodded, and a tear began slowly trickling down her face.

Annie shuddered. 'Was she all bloody and . . . ?'

'Course she was.'

'What did you have to do? Did you have to cut the cord?'

'No, fank gawd, the doctor arrived just after she was born.' She looked up at Annie. 'There I was, just me, 'olding this dear . . .' Her voice broke with emotion. 'She was still attached to me mum – I knew she was dead, bless 'er. You should 'ave 'eard me mum's screams. Annie, it was awful.'

'Where was your dad?'

'Up the pub. He was there till well past closing. I fink 'e was too scared ter come 'ome.'

Annie gently patted her shoulder. 'Is your mum all right now?'

Again Lil nodded. 'You should 'ave seen this poor little fing. She was all blue when she came out. She was only this big.' She held her hands apart to indicate the baby's size. Lil sniffed as the tears began to flow. 'The doctor said it wasn't my fault, she was dead before she was born.' Lil gave way to her pent-up emotion.

Annie put her arm round her.

'I tell yer something, Annie,' she sobbed. 'After seeing me mum like that – I'm never gonner 'ave any kids. She said they bring yer nuffink but grief.'

'What happened to the baby?'

''E took her away. She can't be buried proper in a cemetery, as she was never christened. Poor little bugger.' Lil looked up, and a faint smile lifted her mouth. 'She was a pretty little fing. She 'ad a mass of black 'air.'

'What will they do with her?' whispered Annie.

'I don't know. I didn't ask in case it's something 'orrible.'

Annie looked up at the clock. 'Look, it's nearly seven and me mum and dad's not home from the pictures yet. You go on upstairs, I'll close the shop.' Annie locked and bolted the front door and pulled down the green blind. 'Go upstairs and put the kettle on,' she called over her shoulder, 'I'll be up in a minute when I've turned the lights out.'

Lil sniffed and wiped her nose as Annie walked round the back of the counter. 'No, fanks all the same, but I've got ter git the kids' tea. I'd better 'ave a couple of eggs. I told young Elsie to git a loaf at lunch time on 'er way 'ome from school: they can 'ave an egg sandwich ternight. I 'ope she remembered.'

'You sure you don't want a cup of tea or something?'

'No fanks.'

Annie took two eggs from the wicker basket on the counter, brushed the straw from them, and put them in a blue paper bag. Lil picked up the bag. 'I'll pay fer these at the end of the week, that all right?'

As Annie nodded, someone rattled the shop's doorhandle.

'Shouldn't you open the door?' asked Lil.

'No, don't worry, they can come back tomorrow.'

'I best be going. Fanks for the sympathy.'

'Look, I'll come round after tea. That's if I won't be in the way?'

'Course you won't. Mum'll be pleased to see yer. Annie? What's wrong? You've gone as white as a sheet, you just seen a ghost or somefink?'

Annie didn't answer. She raced round the counter and began feverishly fumbling with the key in the lock, and pulling at the bolts. When she finally flung open the door she ran out into the Mews. After a few minutes she slowly returned to Lil who was standing on the doorstep.

'What was all that about?'

'That was Peter. I saw him passing the window. I was too late, he'd gone.'

'Yer still sweet on 'im, ain't yer?'

'I don't know.' Annie looked up at the calendar. 'I expect he was on his way to his club – it's the last Monday in the month.'

'I'll 'ave ter ask Ju ter 'ave a word with 'im.'

'Would you?'

Lil nodded. 'See yer later.'

The following Saturday it was Mr Barrett who came for the month's rent, and he confirmed what Lil had already told her, that Peter had gone away on a course and he would be away for a few months. Lil had also said that Peter had come to the shop to tell her, but the shop was shut.

As the winter slipped into spring, Annie continued to go out with

Will. Gradually she realized how important their one night out a week was to her. He was kind, and had everything she looked for in a boyfriend. He had a lively sense of humour and she found herself laughing at so many of the things he said, and he would often bring her little surprise gifts. On some Saturday afternoons, if her father wasn't busy, and she wasn't shopping with Lil, they would go to a museum, or just walk and talk. They enjoyed the same things, but to her relief he never tried to persuade her to join the Salvation Army. In fact that was one part of his life they rarely talked about.

Lil continued to pop in on her way home from work whenever she wasn't singing or going out with Julian. She was now singing three nights a week. Every Sunday morning would find Annie eagerly listening to Lil's description of her own performance and that of the others with whom she had shared the limelight the night before. They would pore over magazines looking at the latest fashions, trying to make Lil glamorous like a film star. Lil was changing, filling out, and beginning to look very different. They no longer went to the pictures together as Annie was going with Will and when they did go shopping together, it was always Lil who did the buying. They were growing up, and were happy with the way their new lives were progressing.

Every Saturday and Sunday evening throughout the long hot summer of 1936, Annie and Will went for walks in the park after he had finished playing on the bandstand. They found they had a lot in common; Annie really enjoyed his company, and knew she wanted to be with him more and more. One evening they were sitting on the grass. Will moved closer to her and put his arm round her shoulders.

'Annie, I'm very fond of you. Would you mind if . . . ?'

She looked up at him, her eyes shining. 'I'm very fond of you, Will.'

He kissed her, a long romantic kiss, with nothing demanding in it. She nestled against him, and he gently kissed the back of her neck. She was so very content and happy.

They were watching the children playing about in the rowing

boats, when suddenly there was a commotion at the edge of the lake. A woman was screaming.

Will jumped up and looked towards the lake. 'Quick, Annie, a child's fallen in the pond.' He raced away from her.

She quickly followed, and was in time to see him wading through the water to his waist. He was heading towards a very frightened little girl who had fallen out of a boat, and was splashing about desperately in the middle of the lake; her brother was frozen in horror in the boat. He managed to gather the gasping child up in his arms and made his way calmly back to the bank. The crowd that had gathered helped him ashore and someone took the child from him. All at once people were slapping him on the back and singing his praises, whilst the mother began shouting at her son as he brought the boat into the bank.

'Don't shout at him, Missis. It was an accident,' said Will, wringing the water from the bottom of his trousers. 'Besides, I think he's in enough shock.'

Annie stood back proudly. Only Will would do something like that, so quietly, with so much kindness and dignity. He had a lot of love for his fellow men, and she knew she wanted to share some of it.

That evening she was busy telling her parents about the incident.

'I always said he was a nice boy.' Mrs Rodgers had a big smile on her face as she put her knitting to one side. 'And he don't keep you out half the night.'

'Was the kiddy all right?' asked her father.

'A bit shocked and a bit wet, but she was fine. Will was a bit wet too,' she laughed. 'Someone lent him a jacket, but he had to take his shoes off to walk home: the water was squelching out of them.'

'What? He walked home barefoot?' Her mother was shocked.

'He didn't have a lot of choice. He kept his socks on. Good job it's not too far.'

'Well, I think that it was a very brave thing for him to do.'

'That lake's not that deep, Mother,' said her father.

'I still say he's a nice boy.' She picked up her knitting again.

As Annie lay in bed that night her thoughts were full of Will. He *was* nice, and she knew she was falling in love with him.

Soon it was winter once more, and the scandal of the King's abdication broke. Seeing him and Mrs Simpson together on the newsreels made Annie feel sad.

'That's what I call real love,' she said as she and Will walked home. 'Fancy giving everything up for the woman you love.' She sighed romantically.

'You are a real old softy.' He gently kissed her cheek. 'But I love you.'

'Would you give up everything for me?'

He laughed. 'And what would we live on?'

She laughed and cuddled closer. 'Love.'

Christmas came and, as usual after dinner, the family were sitting listening to the new King's speech.

'It's a shame,' said Annie's mother. 'I was reading somewhere that he didn't want to be King.'

'Well, he wasn't really educated for it,' said Mr Rodgers. 'A lot has certainly happened in this last year.'

Annie too was remembering all that had happened in the past year, and how it had all started with the party at the Barretts'. They hadn't got an invitation to one this year. What would have happened if she had behaved differently towards Peter? Would they still be going out? Annie knew that any real feelings she'd had for Peter had faded away. According to Lil he was now going steady with Belinda. Annie's thoughts went to Will. His sister Rose had invited her to tea on Boxing Day, one of the few nights they had off over Christmas. Annie wondered what that evening – or for that matter the coming year – held in store for both her and Will.

'Why don't you come with us on New Year's Eve?' Rose was pouring out the tea.

'I told you, Rose, Annie doesn't want to be involved.' Will looked anxiously at Annie. 'I promised her we wouldn't talk about . . .'

'That's all right, Will,' interrupted Annie.

'It's not all singing, selling *War Cry*s and bible-punching you know,' said Mr Hobbs, smiling. 'I expect William has told you that we do a lot of good work. Pass the cake please, Rose.'

'Yes, he has. He was telling me about the homeless in the hostel at Whitechapel.'

'I was passing out dinners all Christmas Day. They must have cooked hundreds,' said Will. 'But you have to watch some of the old regulars, they try to creep up again and get seconds.' He laughed, 'Some of them get up to all sorts of tricks, like taking their coats off, or pulling someone's trilby down over their eyes.' His chuckle was deep and warm.

'Still, it's all very rewarding,' said Rose. 'I'll refill the pot.'

After her nervousness about having tea with the Hobbses, Annie was surprised how much she had enjoyed the evening. She was telling Will her feelings as he walked her home. 'Rose is quite nice. She always used to frighten me when she came in the shop.'

'Why?' he asked.

'I don't know, I think it's the uniform, although the bonnet's very pretty.'

'It'd suit you, Annie.'

She laughed. 'Now, you promised.'

'Yes, I know.' When they reached her door, he took her in his arms. 'I love you, Annie,' he said softly.

She looked up at him, for he was a head taller than her, feeling safe as he held her close. 'And I love you,' she whispered, settling in his arms.

'I used to be very jealous when I saw you with that posh bloke.' He kissed her forehead.

'That's all over now,' Annie said quietly.

'Annie. I never thought you could love me.' He kissed her long and hard. His arms crushed her to him and, burying his head in her neck he whispered, 'I can't believe this. I've loved you for a long while but I never thought I was good enough for you.'

Annie smiled and gently pushed him away. 'You're very special to me, Will.'

'We've been going out together for a while now.' He stood back and kicked a stone which rattled along the Mews, making a dog bark.

'Shh,' said Annie.

'Sorry. Annie, could you . . . ? Would . . . ? Do you think you could see yourself getting married one day?'

Annie paused. 'I hope so. But not for a while yet. After all, I'm still only eighteen.'

'Yes, I know. D'you think I would stand a chance?'

She smiled. 'I should think so.'

He swept her off her feet. 'Annie, please say you'll marry me.'

'Careful,' she laughed. 'You'll have me over. I'm not rushing into anything, Will, and what about the Salvation Army. Would you expect me to join?'

In the lamplight she could see his expression change. 'I've been giving that a lot of thought. And I know that if you ever said yes I would give it up, give up Fisher's and start a new life on one of these new estates that are springing up outside London. That is, if it's what you'd want . . .'

Annie was taken back. 'You'd do all that for me? But what about work?'

'There's plenty of firms moving out.' He held her hands and added, '*Would* you like to move away? Get away from London? You can always come back for a visit.'

'My auntie lives in the country, I had a holiday there once – it was smashing.' Annie was getting excited at the prospect.

'Perhaps one day we could get a car. I've got quite a bit saved.'

Annie kissed his cheek. 'We could be very happy together, Will.'

He gently kissed her lips. 'I'll speak to your mum and dad about us getting engaged.'

She giggled. 'They're going to be surprised.'

He took her in his arms. 'As long as they don't object.'

'I don't think they will, but don't tell them about moving away just yet. They might not like the idea.'

He kissed her.

'Will,' she whispered. 'I think I'd like to come to the hostel with you on New Year's Eve.'

'Would you?' He held her close. 'We could see the New Year in together then. It's going to be our year, Annie,' he said, kissing her again.

Chapter 9

On Sunday at ten o'clock, Lil came bursting into Annie's bedroom. 'Annie, Annie, guess what?'

'Lil. I didn't hear you knock.'

'No, yer dad let me in, 'e'd just got 'is paper.' She sat on the bed, her face flushed, and her eyes shining.

'Annie, yer never gonner guess, not in a million years.'

Annie was getting cross. 'Just get on with it then.'

'Guess where I'm going on New Year's Eve?'

Annie stopped folding her cream winceyette nightdress and looked long and thoughtfully at Lil. 'Julian's club,' she whispered.

Lil looked deflated. 'Yer, ow did yer guess?'

'I thought he would ask you.'

'Well, what d'yer fink of that?'

'I think it's very nice.' Annie tucked her nightdress under her pillow. 'You'll enjoy yourself there.'

Lil hugged her knees and rocked back and forth. 'I remember when yer told me all about it last year. I never fought in me wildest dreams I'd ever be going there.'

'Will you be singing?'

'Ju reckons I should. There could be lots of interesting people there and, who knows, I might even get a job in a band.'

'Would you like that?'

'Not 'alf.' She stood up and looked in the mirror. She patted her permanently waved hair and ran her little finger with its scarlet-painted nail over her bright red lips. 'Anyway, I'm finking of giving up the factory.'

Annie's head shot up. 'Why?'

'Well, I'm getting more fer me singing than in the tea factory, and I'm going ter get a job as a barmaid as well.'

Annie sat on the bed. 'Where?'

'At old Bill's place. You know, the big pub I sings in. The Castle.'

Annie nodded; she knew of it.

'We went there last night. I wore me new necklace, and your earrings. I still can't believe Julian would buy me sumfink ser lovely fer Christmas.'

Lil had been wearing the necklace when she had come to tea on Christmas night. 'It is very pretty,' said Annie.

'I've got ter get meself a long frock before Thursday. Can yer come with me termorrer night?'

'Is he buying this one?' Annie's tone was curt.

'No 'e ain't. Annie, why don't you like 'im?'

'I'm sorry, Lil.'

''E's been ever ser good to me.'

'But why?'

'Yer don't always 'ave ter 'ave a reason ter be nice ter someone, do yer?'

'No, of course not.' Annie was annoyed with herself for being so unreasonable. 'Look, you can borrow my long frock if you like, I don't suppose I'll wear it again.'

Lil looked uneasy. 'If yer don't mind, I'd rather buy me own. Yer see I fancy sumfink black and all slinky.'

'Course I don't mind.'

'I'll call in straight from work,' said Lil quickly. 'It's a good job the shops don't close till after eight over Brick Lane.'

'You'll have to wait till me mum and dad get back from the pictures, but I should think it'll be all right.'

'I forgot ter ask, what was it like the other night, 'aving tea with the Hobbses?'

'Very nice, thank you.'

'Is that it? That all yer going ter say? Very nice thank you,' imitated Lil.

'Well, there's not a lot to say about it, is there? We had tea and cake and sandwiches. What else is there?' Annie didn't feel she wanted to tell Lil just yet that she was going to get engaged.

'Nothing I s'pose. Did yer 'ave ter say grace?'

'Yes.'

Lil giggled. 'Bet you fought you were back in Sunday school. 'Ere, d'yer remember how we used ter play noughts and crosses when we was supposed to be saying our prayers?'

Annie smiled and nodded. 'And what about the time you pinched that apple at the harvest festival?'

'Didn't get caught though, did I? Fancy expecting us kids to sit and look at a plate of apples.' Lil stood looking at herself in Annie's long mirror. 'What yer going ter do this New Year's Eve?' she asked.

'I'm going out with Will.'

'That's good. 'E taking yer somewhere nice?'

Annie smoothed out the dents in her pale green bedspread where Lil had been sitting and, with her head bent, she mumbled, 'I'm going with him to the hostel in Whitechapel.'

'What? The down-and-outs' gaff?'

Annie nodded.

''Ere, yer ain't joined that lot, 'ave yer?'

'No.'

'I don't believe it. You going with the Hobbses. It'll be an all-singing, all-dancing night out, will it?'

'Don't talk daft, Lil.'

''Ee taking 'is drum? And 'is sister 'er tambourine?' Lil laughed.

'Shouldn't think so,' Annie replied stiffly.

'Well, that's a turn up fer the book, ain't it? Last year there was me jealous of you going out with Peter, and this year I expect you're narked at me going to that club with Julian.'

'No I'm not,' replied Annie quickly. 'It was at that dance I found out the truth about Peter, remember.' Annie was beginning to get angry. 'You want to watch yourself. In fact I'm surprised he hasn't tried to . . . You know. Before now.'

It was Lil's turn to look away. 'Well, I wouldn't tell you even if 'e 'ad.'

'Lil. He hasn't? Has he?' asked Annie in a shocked voice.

Lil quickly glanced at Annie. 'What if 'e 'as? It ain't none of your business. 'E's been very good ter me.'

Annie sat on the bed. 'Has he?'

Lil didn't answer.

'He has. The dirty . . .'

'It takes two yer know,' said Lil quickly, her face flushed.

'Lil. You didn't let him? Did you? Was you scared?'

'No,' said Lil confidently.

'Not even when he first . . . you know?'

'No. Well, the first time I was drunk anyway.'

Annie's anger was quickly overwhelmed by her curiosity. 'Where did you . . . ?'

Lil sat next to Annie, looking smug as she smoothed her dress down. 'I don't remember much about the first time. It was in the summer round the back of the pub.'

'All that time ago and you didn't tell me?'

'Didn't see the point. Not the way you used to go on about Peter wanting his oats.'

'He didn't want it, it was your Julian and a bet they had.'

'Well, anyway, I knew yer wouldn't approve.'

'What's it like?'

'All right, I s'pose.'

'What if you end up having a baby?'

'Then 'e'll 'ave ter marry me, won't 'e?'

'But I thought that after your mother . . .'

'Yer, well, fings change.'

Annie's brown eyes widened. 'Would you marry him?'

'Not 'alf. Just fink of the place we'd live in. It's a good way ter get away from 'ome, ain't it?'

'Yes, if that's what you want,' said Annie doubtfully.

'Wouldn't you if yer lived like us?'

'I suppose so.' Annie was unable to put her real thoughts into words, words like, Yes, but would he want to marry you? 'Do you love him, Lil?'

'Yer, funny enough I do.'

'Annie, give me a hand with dinner can you?' shouted her mother.

'Coming,' she called back.

As they walked down the stairs together, Lil promised to call round the next day after work. Annie nodded distractedly, her thoughts still on Lil and Julian, and what the outcome would be.

On New Year's Eve Annie sat at her dressing-table, still in her dressing-gown, trying to decide what to wear. She began to visualize what Lil would look like in her slinky black satin evening gown. It had thin shoestring straps with a huge silver bow covering the left shoulder, and now Lil had filled out a bit she had quite a nice figure. The shop owner had wanted twenty-four shillings and eleven pence for the dress – over one week's wages for Lil – but after a lot of haggling, she managed to get it for nineteen and eleven. She had bought silver shoes to go with it, and a wide silver belt. She was going to wear the sparkling necklace Julian had given her for Christmas, and the earrings which had been Annie's present to her. She now used a lot of make-up, had permed hair, and painted nails. Annie knew Lil was really going to enjoy herself tonight.

Annie sighed and, as her thoughts went to Will, a wide smile lifted her face. She did love him, he was never demanding, and deep down she didn't envy Lil one little bit.

She finally settled for her navy blue wool frock with the long sleeves and large collar – so very different from Lil's outfit.

When Will knocked on the door, Annie kissed her mother and father goodbye and hurried down the stairs.

He kissed her cheek and, as they walked through the Mews, he pulled her arm through his and, patting her hand said, 'This is a big night for me, Annie. I'm going to show you off to all my fellow officers.'

Annie giggled. 'I'm glad you didn't bring your drum, it might have got in the way.'

He stopped and turned her to face him, kissing her again. 'I do love you, and tonight I told Rose and Father I was going to marry you.'

'What did they say? You didn't tell them we want to move away, did you?'

'No, I thought we'd take one step at a time. They were pleased. You know they thoroughly approve of you. Father was a bit upset that you don't want to join us, but I told him to give you time.'

'I haven't said anything to anyone yet.'

'Not even to Lil?'

'No, not even to Lil. I want to do this all properly and tell Mum and Dad first. Now come on, let's get the tram.'

When they arrived at the hostel, Annie was surprised at the number of men hanging around outside. As they pushed their way through the crowd she noticed some women with small children sitting in the kerb. 'Will,' she tugged at his sleeve. 'Why are those women sitting there?'

'Some of them are waiting for their husbands or men friends. They're hoping they'll get something to eat if there's any over. They should really go to the women's mission, there's one not too far from here. But I expect they're frightened of leaving their husbands. As soon as their backs are turned, they go off to the pub.'

Annie was appalled. 'Fancy hanging around out here in the cold. Some of them are only kids themselves.' She stood staring at them.

A young girl of about twelve was sitting with her back to the wall. Her eyes were closed and she looked dejected. In her arms was a small bundle wrapped in a grubby old blanket. Suddenly the bundle moved and a baby began to cry. As Annie stood in front of her the young girl opened her eyes and looked up, her dark eyes sunk into her thin pale face. Her long dark hair was matted and Annie could see she was wearing a thin coat that was much too small for her.

Tears welled up in Annie's eyes. She had seen poverty and poor people before – there were plenty round where she lived – but these seemed to have given up, lost all hope.

'Got a penny, miss?' whispered the girl holding out her hand. It was red and bony like that of an old woman. 'Little Becky 'ere ain't 'ad any milk terday.' She gently rocked her baby.

'Yes, yes.' Annie fumbled in her bag for her purse. She took out sixpence and, bending down, gave it to the eager outstretched hand.

'Cor, fanks, Miss, you're a toff.' The girl scrambled to her feet. Her clothes were torn and tattered and her filthy white plimsolls had no laces.

'Where are you going?' asked Annie.

'Ter the coffee stall round the corner. 'E'll give me some milk now.' With her shoulders bent like an old woman, she quietly shuffled away.

Annie wanted to cry. She was angry. She was angry with the way these people were being treated. She was angry with herself for not being aware of the trouble they were in. And she was angry with people like Peter, Julian, and now Lil, who would be drinking, dancing, and not caring about anyone else but themselves. Just as she had done a year ago.

'Come on, Annie love.' Will's soft voice brought her back.

She wanted to hold him and kiss him. He was concerned about all these people, and he and his family were at least trying to help them. If they had nothing else, they were giving them their time. Suddenly the Salvation Army didn't seem quite so silly as she'd once thought it was. 'Will, what's going to happen to all these people?'

'Those that got here early enough have got a bed for the night, and we will feed as many of the others that we can, but when it runs out, well . . .' He shrugged his shoulders. 'We can't perform miracles. We have to rely on people's generosity. That's why we go round the pubs on a Saturday night selling our *War Cry* and rattling the tin under their noses. When they've had a few drinks they part with their money a little easier, and it looks good in front of their friends.'

Annie didn't speak as she followed him inside. She was taken aback at seeing Christmas decorations hanging from the high ceiling. There were rows of long tables, and chairs which were quickly being filled. Rose, with some other women, was behind a trestle table that had been pushed against a wall, and was diligently ladling out soup from a large urn into a variety of containers.

'Hello, Annie. I'm glad you've come to give us a hand. Looks like we're going to be kept pretty busy tonight.'

Annie quickly took off her coat. 'What do you want me to do, Rose?'

'Get behind there and take my place. And bring your coat round the back here. Things have an odd habit of going astray.'

Annie looked at the old man who was standing in front of Rose holding out a dish. 'Well, yer gotter look after yerself, ain't yer, miss?' he said wickedly.

Annie knew he was smiling under the full set of unkempt white whiskers, as his twinkling pale blue eyes crinkled.

'Yer new 'ere, ain't yer?'

'Yes,' she whispered.

He leaned forward. 'Well, make sure yer fills me bowl up then.'

As he moved away, Annie smiled. His trousers were very short, and she could see he was having a great deal of difficulty keeping his old battered boots on. They must have been at least three sizes too big, and had string threaded through the top laceholes. Tied round the waist of his dirty old ragged raincoat was a thick piece of string.

''Ere ducks, yer gonner stand there all night wiv that there spoon in yer 'and, or yer gonner give us some soup?'

'Sorry,' she said, returning to her task.

Annie was happy talking and laughing with the men. Some of them wanted to tell her their life story, but they were soon pushed on by others in the line. Gradually the soup in the large urn got lower and lower.

'Have we any more, Rose?' she asked.

'Sorry, 'fraid not. That's it for the night.'

'But what about all these others?' She looked along the line.

Rose, like Will, shrugged her shoulders. 'Not a lot we can do about that, I'm afraid. I'll give you a hand to take the urn into the kitchen. Someone there will wash it out.'

Annie had seen very little of Will all evening. Once or twice he came up and asked her if everything was all right, then he went off and busied himself with other duties.

It was almost half-past ten. Annie couldn't believe how quickly time had flown. She put on her coat and went outside to see if she could find the young girl with the baby. It was still worrying her. She glanced up and down the road, but it was almost deserted, just pockets of men talking. There was no sign of her. Annie shivered. A mist of fine drizzle was falling and it looked almost magical in the lamplight as it slowly drifted down, cleaning the streets, making them glisten, defying the dirt and poverty that was all around them.

'What are you doing out here?' Will wrapped his arms round her.

'I was looking for that young girl I saw when we came in – she had a baby with her.'

'She's probably hanging around outside the pub now, either waiting for the father or for money. Come on inside, you're freezing.' He rubbed her hands. 'What did you think of it here tonight?'

'It makes me feel very humble. I didn't realize so many people were homeless.'

'This is only the tip of the iceberg. There are lots of hostels like this in all the big cities.'

'I'd like to come with you again one night.'

'Would you? Would you really?'

Annie nodded. 'I enjoyed it. Some of the old men are really charming, right old flatterers some are. A few of them are very well spoken, too.'

'Yes, well, unfortunately all kinds of people fall on hard times. We all take turns to come here, but if you come again I'll have to keep my eye on you. I don't want to lose you.'

She gently kissed his cheek. 'There's no chance of that, not now.'

He held her close. 'I could stay all night out here with you.' Annie shivered. 'But you'd soon freeze to death. Come on, I can hear Sergeant Walsh playing his concertina. We'll sing a few hymns with them, and then be off.'

'Do you want to come back to my house? We can toast the New Year in with my mum and dad.'

'Will they still be up?'

'I should think so.'

'Why not?' He took her hand and led her inside.

Chapter 10

Annie was so happy. All day she eagerly waited for six-thirty and for Lil to come in on her way home from work. She had so much to tell her. First that she was going to get engaged to Will, and that her mum and dad were really pleased about it, although they hadn't yet told the family they hoped to get married the following year, or that they would be moving out of London. But she also wanted to tell Lil how she spent her New Year's Eve, and how much all those poor people had stuck in her mind. She was going to the hostel with Will again; it made her feel she was really doing something worthwhile. The sad face of the young girl with the baby was still on her mind. She was even thinking about joining the Salvation Army – at least she would see more of Will that way. But she wouldn't tell Lil that just yet, not till she was really sure herself. And she wanted to hear all about Lil's New Year's Eve.

But at seven o 'clock Annie's father said, 'Lock the door, love. I'm surprised Lil's not come in to tell you about what she got up to last night.'

Annie too was anxious, and a little annoyed. She had been looking forward to hearing all about Lil's New Year, and felt let down, especially after telling her parents that Lil was going to the same party as the one she had been to last year. Annie knew her father had been disappointed that she wasn't seeing Peter, but he didn't make too much of it, and her mother was more than pleased she was going out with Will.

After they had finished tea, Annie looked at the kitchen clock. 'Mum, is it all right if I go round to Lil's?'

'Of course. You're not seeing Will tonight then?'

'No, he has a meeting.'

'Wrap up well, it looks like snow.'

Annie pulled on her blue beret and, wrapping her long scarf round her neck, hurried down the stairs. Outside she blew on her hands before pulling on her woollen gloves.

It was dark and eerie as Annie made her way through Victoria Gardens, and she held her nose as the smell of vomit and urine mixed with the reek from Mr Reeves, the rag-and-bone man's horse. His cart was leaning on its end against the wall, with a pile of old rags next to it. Many a time Lil had told Annie of the commotion round their way on a Saturday night: the fights and shouting that made all the dogs bark, the objects that were thrown from the bedroom windows, women screaming at their husbands and blokes bringing up their boots. She guessed New Year's Eve must have been like a Saturday.

Carefully, in the dim gas light, she picked her way over the mess and made her way up the stone stairs and along the landing to the Grants' flat. She banged on the front door and it was opened by Lil's youngest brother, Ernie.

'Allo, Annie, our Lil's still in bed.'

'What still? Didn't she go to work?' She suddenly felt very uneasy. 'Is she all right?'

'Yer, she's only got a 'angover. Yer best come in.' Annie relaxed and smiled, as she saw he was excited and pleased to see her. She liked all the Grant children, they were always such a happy bunch despite the poverty they lived in. She followed Ernie along the dingy passage. 'Yer should 'ave 'eard the racket when that posh bloke brought 'er 'ome last night – well s'morning really. Woke up all the 'ole blooming flats.'

''Allo, Annie,' shouted another of the children. 'Mum's in the scullery.'

'Thank you, Sally,' called Annie. 'What happened, Ernie?' she asked, intrigued.

He stopped. 'Well, Mrs Wilson two doors up saw it. She said our Lil was so drunk 'e 'ad 'er on 'is shoulder, and it seems 'e just chucked 'er in the yard. She shouted after 'im, waking up 'alf the flats. Me mum went after 'im but 'e'd gone. Good job me dad was

94

drunk as well. Yer should 'ave seen the state of our Lil. Been sick all over 'er nice new frock.'

'Annie, is that you?' Mrs Grant was calling from the scullery.

'Yes.'

'Yer better come in 'ere first.'

Ernie was still jumping up and down in front of Annie.

'Let Annie come frew,' said Sally. Lil's young sister was growing into a lovely girl, Annie noticed.

'Sit yerself down, love,' said Mrs Grant. 'Fancy a cup o' tea?'

'No thank you.' Annie sat at the table and tried not to look round the scullery. It was damp and cold. Big black patches of mould clung to the walls. A small dark room, it only had one tiny window, and during the day it let in very little light. There was a cupboard, a table and four chairs, and all the cooking had to be done on the fire in the kitchen with an oven at the side. Before the gas light began to flicker and pop and Mrs Grant turned it out, Annie noted that on the wooden draining-board next to the sink was a galvanized bucket that contained a mass of black material. It had a limp silver bow hanging over the side.

'Got ter git a new mantle,' said Mrs Grant. 'Come inter the kitchen, it's a bit cosier in there.'

In the kitchen were two tatty armchairs, one each side of the fireplace. Annie often wondered where they all sat.

'Our Lil got 'erself in a bit of a state last night. She looked really smashing when she went out as well. You should see the mess that frock's in. Sit down, love.' Annie sat in one chair, Mrs Grant in the other, and she continued, 'I've 'ad ter put it in soak. Don't like doing washing on New Year's Day, cos yer knows what they say?'

Annie shook her head.

Mrs Grant leaned forward. 'If yer washes on New Year's Day yer'll be washing all year round.'

Annie smiled at another old wives' tale.

Mrs Grant sat back. 'Dunno that I'll be able ter git it all out.'

'Will it be all right?'

'Dunno, that satin's funny stuff.'

Annie felt very sad. Lil was so proud of her new clothes. She could understand now why she would be willing to trap Julian into marrying her to get away from all this. 'Is she all right?'

'She will be till 'er dad gits 'ome. 'E ain't none too pleased at all the neighbours 'earing it, I can tell yer. That's why she stayed in bed this morning, ter keep out o 'is way. And I reckon 'e'll go mad when he gits in and finds she ain't been ter work. She don't git paid, yer know. You should 'ave heard the scuffle that went on, must 'ave been about two this morning. That Julian's a right one. I fink yer did yerself a favour when yer chucked that Peter. Those bloody toffs fink they can do what they like.'

'He did get Lil her singing jobs.'

'Yer,' a smile filled Mrs Grant's face. 'She's got a lovely voice. S'pose we should be grateful for 'im gitting 'er the jobs, and the extra money. Did yer know she's leaving the factory and going to work at the Castle?'

'She did tell me.'

'Gitting good money there, and a chance ter do more singing.'

'Can I go and see her?' asked Annie, standing up.

'Course love. Tell 'er she's gotter git up, she can't stay there fer ever.'

Annie pushed open the door to the front room. The thin thread-bare curtains were drawn, and a meagre amount of light filtered through from the streetlamp down the road. Annie had been in the room before, and knew her friend shared it with all the other children. Lil was in the bed that all three girls slept in, with bundles of bedding on the floor for the boys. Hanging from the picture rail were the dresses Lil had bought herself since she started singing. There was no dressing-table or cupboards in the room. Tears began to sting Annie's eyes. Lil'd go mad when she found out that the most expensive dress she had ever bought had finished up in a bucket.

'Lil, Lil.' Annie gently shook the mound.

'Go away.' Lil turned over, clutching the blanket to her throat, revealing that she had slept in her underwear.

'Lil, it's me.' Annie sat on the bed.

Slowly she turned her head and opened her eyes. 'What yer doing 'ere?' she croaked, her voice thick with sleep. The heavy make-up she now wore was smeared all over her face, and her eyes had almost disappeared into two black craters.

'My God, you look a mess.'

'Fanks. I don't need you ter tell me.'

'What happened?'

''Ad a drop too much, that's what.' She slowly sat up. 'What time is it?'

'Eight.'

'Eight? Christ, me old man must 'ave gone straight to the pub. Been waiting for 'im ter come in and give me a pasting.'

'Come on, get up. Come out for a walk, it might do you good.'

'I dunno. Oooh, me 'ead.'

Annie stood up. 'Come on, before your dad gets back.'

''E won't be in till chucking-out time.'

'Well then, on your feet.'

'I 'ate you when yer so bloody cheerful. Pass me skirt and jumper, they're in that corner.'

Annie found them and threw them on the bed. 'I'll wait for you in the kitchen. You'd better wash your face before you go out.'

'I'm in fer a bloody good 'iding when me dad gits 'is 'ands on me,' Lil muttered, gently sliding off the bed. She looked small and vulnerable. Annie wanted to hold her and take her away, for she knew all too well about Mr Grant's temper.

'Did you enjoy yourself last night?' asked Annie.

'Yer, it's a smashing place ain't it?'

'Yes.'

'Peter was there with that Belinda. She's a right posy tart. Tried ter make me look small, but when I got up and started singing, and everyone started buying me drinks, she soon changed 'er tune.'

Annie sat on the bed. 'Did he ask after me?'

Lil pulled her jumper over her head. 'Yer. I told 'im you was going out with Will. They're suppose ter be gitting married soon, so she reckons.' Lil smoothed down her hair and pushed her permed waves into position. 'I'll just go in the scullery and give me face a quick licky-spit, then I'll be ready. Did you 'ave a good time last night?'

'Yes. Yes I did.' Annie was deep in thought as she followed Lil into the kitchen. 'Very different from yours though,' she added.

'Yer, well, some of it I could 'ave done without, but I'll tell yer all about that when we're outside. Come on, walls 'ave ears in this place.'

As they walked down the concrete steps, Lil pulled at her coat. 'Christ, it's cold.'

'It'll bring a healthy glow to your face. Now tell me about last night.'

'Well, there's not a lot ter tell really. We got there and 'e went . . .'

'You mean Julian?' interrupted Annie.

'Yer. Well 'e said I 'ad ter sing. I don't fink 'e took me there just ter see 'is mates, and I don't know what sorta bargain 'e struck with the manager, but I was singing most of the time. Not that I mind, and when I asked 'im how much was I gitting, d'yer know what the saucy bugger said?'

Annie shook her head.

''E reckoned I owed 'im that fer all the favours 'e'd done me. I tell yer, Annie, I nearly went mad. What about all the favours I've done 'im, including you know what . . . And now when I fink about it, I reckon 'e got money from all my singing.'

'What makes you say that?'

'Well, the managers always gave it to 'im, and they never told me what I was getting. Only the first bloke told me, after that Julian used to see to all that. Crafty sod.'

'Where were you when all this was going on?'

'Outside. I was 'aving a quiet smoke, trying ter clear me 'ead. I'd sunk quite a few.'

'What happened then?'

'Well, we 'ad a row and I stormed off inside and 'ad a few more drinks.'

'I'm surprised he brought you home.'

''E didn't 'ave a lot of choice: there was four of us in the cab going, so it would've looked a bit funny if 'e'd left me behind. Anyway when I got out the taxi I passed out. That was after I was sick all over 'im,' she laughed.

'Oh, Lil, will you see him again?'

'Dunno. Funny ain't it, last New Year's Eve you packed up with

Peter, now this time it's me what's been given the elbow.' There was a sob in Lil's voice. 'I liked 'im, Annie, I really did.' She sniffed. 'This cold's making me eyes water.'

'I don't want to sound, you know, nasty. But did you honestly think Julian would marry . . .' Annie hesitated, she needed to choose her words carefully, but Lil interrupted.

'Yer mean the likes of me?'

'Well, yes, in a way. Well, any of us, really. When they've got the pick of all those other girls.'

''S'pose yer right. It would 'ave been a right turn-up for the book if I'd been up the spout though.' Lil pulled her scarf tighter at her neck. 'I 'spect 'e would 'ave said it wasn't 'is.'

'Well, thank goodness you're not, and try and cheer up.'

'That's easy fer you ter say.'

'Look, d'you want to go back?'

'Ain't got a lot of choice 'ave I? Got ter face the music sooner or later.'

'Perhaps things will turn out all right.'

'I 'ope so.' She wiped her eyes. 'See yer termorrer after work. That should be a laugh. Gotter give me notice in, in the morning.' Lil turned and headed for home.

Annie hastened her step. She wouldn't be seeing Will until tomorrow, but at this moment she wanted to hold him and tell him how much she loved him. She was never more sure of anything now, and she felt a deep pity for Lil, who had only had a few months of happiness, while she had a whole lifetime in front of her.

'Well, what do you think of the news, Lil?' Mr Rodgers was smiling as she walked into the shop on Saturday afternoon.

'What news?' asked Lil with a bewildered look on her face.

'Didn't Annie tell you last night?'

'No, she didn't tell me nuffink.'

Annie blushed. 'Well, I didn't get much of a chance, you were so busy telling me about your night out.'

'Well, don't keep me dangling, what is it?'

'Her and Will are getting engaged,' said Mr Rodgers.

'No. When?'

'Not yet,' said Annie. 'Perhaps in a few weeks' time.'

'Well, I never fought I'd 'ear that.'

'What a night,' said Mr Rodgers. 'Didn't get to bed till well after twelve.'

'Dad, you make it sound as if we were living it up.' Annie turned to Lil. 'We came back from the hostel and decided to see the New Year in with Mum and Dad – it was then Will asked their permission. They said yes, and we had a drink to celebrate, then Will left, that's all.'

'You dark old 'orse.'

'Have you got time to come up?'

'Yer.'

'What happened with your dad?' asked Annie over her shoulder as they made their way up the stairs.

'I'll tell yer later.'

As soon as the door was shut Lil turned to Annie. 'Yer not just doing this ter spite Peter are yer?'

'No, of course not.' Annie's tone was one of anger.

'All right, don't git uppity.'

'I'm very fond of Will.'

'Yer but do yer love 'im?'

Annie blushed. 'Yes I do,' she whispered.

Lil threw herself back on the bed and laughed. 'Yer gonner join the Sally Army?'

'I may do.' Annie was feeling put out.

'I can just see you waving yer tambourine. This I gotter see. Anyway, when yer gitting married?'

'Not for a few years yet.'

Lil sat up, and her mood changed. 'Yer, well, a lot can 'appen in a few years. Just fink of all what's 'appened this past year.'

'Yes, but what about last night and your dad?' Annie was determined to change the subject.

Lil moved to the edge of the bed and let her legs dangle. She looked sad. 'Well, 'e tried ter 'it me, but me mum and Ernie got between us and made 'im stop. Anyway, when I told 'im I was going to work at the Castle, and promised 'im a free pint, it calmed 'im down a bit.' She laughed. 'I tell yer, Annie, I was scared stiff.

I've 'ad a belting off 'im before, the wicked old bugger.'

'I remember the time you came to school with a bruised face, and you told Miss French you'd walked into the door.'

Lil nodded. 'Yer, I fink she guessed it was me dad.'

'What about your frock?'

'Oh Annie, I could 'ave cried when I saw it all screwed up in a bucket. Me mum 'ung it on the line this morning but I fink it's 'ad it. I loved that frock.'

'That was a shame.'

'Still, don't s'pose I'll need another long frock.'

'Why not? You could always wear it on the stage.'

'Yer, s'pose I could.' Lil sat on her hands.

'You will still be singing at those other places, won't you?'

'I 'ope so. But it looks like I've blown me chances of moving up with the posh lot. Don't suppose I'll be seeing Julian again.'

'I'm really sorry about that. Still, cheer up. Working in a pub, and all that singing, you're sure to meet someone nice soon.'

'Yer. I 'ope so. I've really 'ad enough of living at 'ome.'

Chapter 11

Over the next few months Annie saw very little of Lil. When she did it was only for short periods during the odd days she was off, as most evenings she was either working in the pub or singing. They no longer had Sundays together: Lil had to do the lunch time shift, clear up, and be back behind the bar then sing in the evening. She told Annie many times how much she loved it, but Annie missed her, and their chats.

She was seeing a lot more of Will though, going to some of the Salvation Army meetings with him. She particularly enjoyed helping out when they went to the Whitechapel mission, but although she always kept a look-out, she had never seen that young girl again.

One Thursday morning, when Annie was helping her mother wash up she said, 'Mum, me and Will are going to the country for the day.' She tried to make it sound casual.

'That's nice, when?'

'Next Saturday, that's if Dad don't mind.'

'Don't worry, I can go down and give him a hand.'

Annie kissed her mother's cheek. 'Thanks, I'll tell Will tonight.'

'Whereabouts in the country are you going?'

Annie folded the tea-towel and began putting the clean crocks in the dresser, making sure her mother didn't see how excited she was. 'We're going to Carshalton.'

'Where's that?'

'It's in Surrey.'

'What are you going there for?'

'Someone Will knows has moved to the new estate that's being built there.'

'That's nice,' said Mrs Rodgers, wiping her hands and removing her apron. 'Is it someone from the Salvation Army?'

'No, it's a fellow that used to be an apprentice with him at Fisher's.'

'Oh. What made him move there? Has he got a job?'

'Yes. Well, it was his dad really, his factory moved. It seems a lot of new factories are opening down there.'

Mrs Rodgers looked up. 'You're not thinking of going to one of these new estates, are you?'

Annie blushed and looked away. She wasn't very good at telling lies. 'No. We're only going to see his friend,' she said lightly.

'Who is it? Anyone we know?'

'I don't think so. He used to live over the other side.'

'Well, I hope you two haven't got any ideas about moving away. Your dad would be very upset.'

'We're only going for an outing, Mum.'

'That's as may be, but you could get carried away with all those nice new houses. Mrs Day was telling me only the other day about her Molly. It seems she loves it at Downham, and keeps going on about all the open fields there are for her boys to play in. Never wants to come back up here to see her mum.'

'Yes, well, we're not going to Downham.'

'Mrs Day's very upset that she doesn't see a lot of her now.'

'Well, that's up to Molly,' said Annie firmly, and went down into the shop to help her father.

It was a bright sunny spring morning when Will called for Annie, and they set off on the underground to Morden.

She clung to his arm. 'I'm ever so excited,' she said as they sat on the train and studied the map above their heads. 'Look, Morden is right at the end of the line. Will it take long?'

'I don't know. Never been that far before.'

'I went to my Aunt Ivy's once. She lives in Sussex, and I remember it took me and mum ages to get there.'

'Did you like the country?'

'Yes, I did. You'd like my cousin Roy. He's a real country boy.'

At Morden they caught the bus Bobby Wilks had told them to;

as it made its way up the hill, Annie was amazed at the wide roads with neat grass verges beside the pavements, and the new red-brick houses. Everything looked so clean and fresh.

They had told the conductor where they wanted to get off and after a short while he called out, 'This is it, mate. And yer go up that road over there.' He pointed the way. 'It's quite a walk.' He rang the bell and they stood and watched as the bus moved off.

When they finally arrived at Bobby's house, Annie stood for a while gazing at it. 'It's lovely. Look at the garden. It'll be so nice when the grass grows.'

The front door opened and Bobby came out and shook Will's hand. ''Allo, you two, come on in. Me mum's got the kettle on. You found us all right then?'

'No bother.'

'Dad's still at work. 'E's 'elping 'em set the machine shop up.'

'What's it like working down here?' asked Will as they stepped into a large bright room.

'Smashing. It's so clean. You're not up ter yer ankles in grease and dirt like at Fisher's. I tell yer, Will, yer'd be daft if yer didn't come down 'ere. There's plenty of really good prospects, and yer'd git a 'ouse as well.'

'I've done a few sandwiches, love,' said Mrs Wilks, coming in from the kitchen. 'Sit yerselves down. I 's'pect you're starving.'

'Thank you,' said Annie. 'Do you like it down here, Mrs Wilks?'

'Takes a bit o' getting used to. Shops ain't just round the corner like back 'ome, but they say they're gonner build some nearby. It's nice for the little 'ens though, all this grass and the building site ter play on, but they 'ave a long way ter go fer school.'

'After yer've 'ad yer sandwiches I'll give yer a bit of a tour round. It's gonner be a big estate when it's finished.' Bobby sank his teeth into the bread and cheese with gusto.

They spent the afternoon clambering over rubble, going into half-finished houses, balancing on wooden joists that were waiting for floorboards, and walking over bare foundations. They stood gazing in awe at bathrooms and kitchens. All this was accompanied by Annie's oohs and ahhs as she giggled with excitement, exclaiming how much she loved each new house she saw.

All too soon their day ended and they were on their way home. 'Well, Annie,' Will asked once they were settled on the bus, 'what do you think? Would you like to live there?'

She squeezed his hand and smiled at him. 'I can't think of anything better. I loved those houses. Do you really think we could have one?'

'We'll have to drop our bombshell very gently. I don't think your mum and dad will be too pleased.'

'We'll give it a while before we say anything. After all, we've got at least a year before we get married, and I'm not going to live in sin with you before that.' She laughed and snuggled against him, knowing she couldn't be happier.

A month later everybody was busy and looking forward to King George VI and Queen Elizabeth's Coronation. Excitement was running high as the great day was almost on them.

'You know, Mum, you could go to your usual pictures this afternoon,' said Annie, 'I'll be able to manage.'

'That's all right, love,' said her mother, clearing the table. 'I know your dad's busy. Besides, I've still got to string the last of this bunting together. I know all the men want to finish putting them up tonight. Take dad's tea down before it gets cold, will you?'

Annie walked in the shop. 'Here's a cup of tea, Dad,' she offered cheerfully.

'Thanks. If you could carry on packing all that stuff in those boxes, I'll finish off this list. I'll have to go to the wholesaler's again in the morning.' Mr Rodgers was studying a list that one of the children from Paradise Street had brought in earlier. 'Seems they want about the same as the others. Ron's going to be kept busy Tuesday night baking all the bread for the sandwiches this lot are making, if all these pots of fishpaste are anything to go by.'

Annie smiled, as she continued to pack yet another order for another street party. Everybody was getting prepared for the big day on Wednesday.

Both she and her father looked up when the bell tinkled. ''Allo there, Annie. Mr Rodgers.' Bessie, who worked at Day's, the green-grocer's, pushed the door shut behind her. 'I'll 'ave me fags now while we've got a quiet moment. 'Ave all the boys from Fisher's in shortly.' She patted the back of her blonde hair. 'And you know what little devils some of 'em can be. Get me running around all over the place they do. Making me weigh up apples, then saying they don't want 'em. Saucy buggers some of 'em are, especially that Georgie Bates and his mate Eddie Finch.'

Annie handed her a packet of Park Drive. 'To go on your slate, Bessie?'

'Ta, love.' With that she sauntered over to the door wiggling her behind which was encased in a tight skirt. 'Bye.' She turned and, with just her fingers, gave them a little wave.

'I know why they make her weigh out the apples,' said Annie tersely. 'It's so they can look down her blouse when she's bending over the boxes. She knows that as well – you never see her in an overall.'

'Don't be such a spoilsport. There's no harm done, and at least she enjoys a laugh.'

Annie looked at her father. 'Don't you let Mum hear you say that.'

Mr Rodgers was grinning. 'And don't *you* go saying anything in front of Mrs James.' He carried on packing the cardboard box.

'Why?' asked Annie, curious.

'I think her old man's got a soft spot for our Bessie.'

'No. Why do you say that?'

'He's always hanging round her in the pub.' Mr Rodgers wrote the name of the road on the side of the box and placed it on the floor beside the others, just as the boys from Fisher's walked in.

Will was, as usual, with them. Annie smiled. He always popped in during his lunchtime.

'Are you still coming to the meeting tonight?' he asked, squeezing to the front of the counter.

'Yes, pick me up about half-past seven.'

Will stood back while Annie served George Bates and the others.

'Still can't see what yer see in 'im.' Georgie flicked his thumb over his shoulder. 'I'm much better looking.'

Annie laughed. 'Well, I don't think so.'

He began to walk out. 'Don't be long, mate,' Georgie called.

Gradually the shop emptied and Annie went and stood with Will.
'Rose said, would you like to come to tea?'

'I'd love to. When?'

'I'll let you know tonight.'

The sound of the hooter calling them back to work filled the air.
'See you tonight,' said Will, and waved goodbye. He never kissed
Annie in company.

The Mews was quiet again, the children back in school, the men
at work, but suddenly a familiar noise filled the air. Annie quickly
looked at the clock. It was half-past four. 'That's Fisher's hooter,'
she said. 'It shouldn't be going off now.' A bewildered look flitted
across her face.

Mr Rodgers hurried to the door with Annie close on his heels.
Everybody in the Mews had come out of their shops.

'What d'yer think's up, Ted?' asked Mr Day, coming towards
them with his hands tucked under his white apron, Bessie tripping
by his side.

Ted the butcher looked up at the factory chimneys. The smoke
was still belching out. 'Dunno. Could be some joker turned it on
for a laugh and it's got stuck.'

The noise was incessant. 'I do wish they would hurry and turn it
off,' said the thin Miss Page, who everybody assumed was the
younger of the two. 'It goes right through you.'

The other Miss Page tutted and fiddled with the long knotted
amber beads that rested on her ample bosom. 'Do stop moaning,
Dorothy. I'm sure they will turn it off as soon as they can.' She
turned and studied her reflection. 'You've made a really good job
of this window.'

Her sister smiled. 'Thank you. It's always such a joy dressing
such a lovely shaped window.'

'I love the way you've twirled those red, white and blue ribbons
round,' commented Annie, putting her hands over her ears. 'I do
wish they'd stop this racket.'

'Well, I reckon it's got stuck,' said Bill Armstrong coming from
his ironmonger's shop to join the others for a short while before
turning and slowly ambling back to his shop.

Gradually the small gathering began to disperse. Annie wandered to the end of the Mews and peered down the alley apprehensively.

'Come on, love,' shouted her father. 'Still got a lot of orders to get packed.'

'What time shall we start putting up the rest of these decorations, Ben?' Ted asked her father.

'About eight, that all right? Give me time to have me bit of tea first.'

Suddenly the rush of heavy booted footsteps stomping up the alley stopped everybody in their tracks. Two men covered in dust and dirt pushed Annie to one side.

'What's up, mate?' called Ted.

'Been a bloody accident at Fisher's. Gotter git ter Doc Bains,' panted one.

'Is it bad?' asked Mr Rodgers as they ran past.

'A machine's collapsed,' yelled one of the men over his shoulder as he rushed past.

Annie hurried to her father, her face ashen. He put his arm round her. 'Don't worry. I shouldn't think for one minute it's anywhere near where Will works.' The hooter wailed to an end. 'Thank goodness that's stopped. Remember, it's a big factory.'

She nodded. 'Could I go to the gate and see if I can find out more?'

'You'd probably be in the way,' her father said sensibly. 'Best wait till Will comes in tonight then he'll tell you all about it.'

As they wandered into the shop the urgent sound of the ambulance bells as they raced along the main road brought Annie and her father to a halt.

'I think I'll go along and have a look, Dad, if you don't mind – just to put my mind at rest.'

'Yes, all right, love,' he nodded. 'I'll call up and let your mum know.'

Annie hurried along the alley, her thoughts full of Will. 'Please God,' she whispered to herself, 'don't let anything happen to him.'

At the end of the alley she was joined by many others, all heading towards Fisher's. She found herself trying to pass two women who took up most of the path.

'I 'eard 'alf the factory's gorn,' panted one women as she shuffled along in her tattered carpet slippers.

'Christ, I 'ope my Fred's all right,' said her companion, pulling her shawl round her shoulders. 'D'yer know what 'appened?'

'Seems one of the great big machines toppled over and took the wall out.'

'Many 'urt?'

'Dunno.'

When Annie reached the outside of the factory she could see a lot of activity behind the tall iron railings. Dozens of men were rushing about, some carrying their fellow workers and gently laying them on the ground while others stood around with a dazed look on their faces, gazing at the factory with disbelief. From where they were standing the building looked normal but there were police and ambulances everywhere, and a lot of women had joined the men in the yard.

Annie knew quite a few of the men who worked at the factory, and she desperately scanned the crowd, looking for someone she recognized. Suddenly she caught sight of Mr Harrison leaning against the wall, wiping his hand over his dirty face, his navy overalls covered with dust.

Annie began pushing her way through the horde of people. 'Mr Harrison!' she called, trying to make her small voice heard above all the chaos. 'Mr Harrison!' He turned and said something to a man who had just staggered out with someone slung over his shoulder, but she couldn't get to him before he disappeared inside. She knew Mr Harrison worked in the same area as Will.

In panic, she pushed and shoved her way nearer to the building. As she managed to get closer, she could see ambulance men attending to the wounded. Many were bloodied and dirty, lying or sitting on the floor. Frantically she searched for a familiar face.

'Annie.' A soft voice called her, and she could have cried when she turned and saw Eddie Finch, another of Will's workmates. He was sitting on the ground, his back against a wall. Blood was pouring from a long cut on his face, his left arm was twisted at a funny angle.

She dropped to her knees. 'Eddie, what happened?'

'I don't know. Oh, Annie, it was awful. All that metal crashing down, the noise and dust.' He hung his head.

'Is Will all right?' she asked.

'I don't know.'

'Can I get you anything?'

He shook his head. 'I've been told to sit 'ere and wait till an ambulance comes back. I've got to go to hospital. Could you let me mum know?'

Annie nodded, tears streaming down her cheeks. She took her handkerchief from her pocket and gently dabbed the blood from Eddie's face. He closed his eyes and rested his head against the wall.

'I must go and see if I can find Will,' she whispered to him. 'I'll be back soon.'

He didn't open his eyes.

She moved amongst the injured, anxiously looking all round her. Gentle moans were coming from some of the men, about fifteen of them lying near her. Some were being comforted by doctors, others by their workmates and the local womenfolk, some of whom were wiping the faces of the victims while others brought tea for the injured and their rescuers. A number were being lifted on to stretchers and carried to one of the four ambulances. When they were full, Annie guessed they would be racing off to St Olave's, the nearest hospital.

When Mr Harrison emerged from the building again, Annie pushed her way to him.

''Allo, Annie love.'

'Is Will all right?' she asked.

He took a packet of cigarettes from his overall pocket and, after lighting one, leaned against the wall and drew heavily on it. 'I ain't seen 'im,' he said at long last. 'They're all out now. Can't yer find 'im?'

She shook her head, and tears rolled down her face.

'There, there, love.' Mr Harrison put his arm round her shoulder. 'P'raps 'e was one of the first out. Yer could 'ave missed 'im. 'E could be in the 'ospital.'

'Could he be all right?'

111

'Wouldn't like ter say. It was in his machine shop the accident 'appened. Did see young Georgie Bates though. 'E was OK, though 'is leg was a bit of a mess.'

'Georgie works with Will. You've been getting them out, are you sure you didn't see him?' Her voice was rising with emotion.

'There was a lot of us in there, and there was a lot of dust and muck flying about. Could hardly see yer 'and in front of yer, so I didn't see 'em all. Git yer dad ter take yer along ter the 'ospital. 'E could be in there.'

'Mr Harrison,' Annie's voice was low and trembling. 'Has anybody—' she hesitated – 'is anyone dead?'

He shook his head. 'Don't fink so.'

'Annie, Annie, are you all right?'

She looked up to see her father running towards her. 'We've just heard all about it. How's Will?'

Annie threw her arms round her father and cried.

'Oh my God, is he . . . ?' He hesitated, gently patting her back.

'We don't know,' said Mr Harrison. 'P'raps you could take 'er along to the 'ospital to see if 'e's there?'

'Of course. Are you all right?'

'Yer,' Mr Harrison smiled. 'It'll take more than a bleeding machine and a wall ter stop me.'

Mr Rodgers gripped his shoulder. 'I think you should go on home now, you'll have your missis worried sick.'

'Yer, suppose so. They fink everybody's out now, so there's not much point in 'anging about.'

When the last victim was taken to the hospital, the crowds gradually began to move away.

'Come on, love, let's go home and get the van.'

'I promised Eddie Finch I'd tell his mum that he's in hospital, and I'd better tell Mrs Bates as well.'

'OK,' nodded her father, 'we can do that on the way home.'

Chapter 12

'D'you think we should go round to Rose first to tell her what's happened?' Annie was shaking as she climbed into the van. She sat upright beside her father, her eyes staring.

'Will she be home?'

'Yes, she finishes teaching school at half-past three.'

Annie didn't speak, her thoughts were of Will. Her mind was turning over and over, trying to piece together every snatch of conversation, trying to remember if anyone had mentioned his name.

'Hello, Annie, this is a pleasant surprise,' said Rose on opening the front door. 'Mr Rodgers. What do . . .' her voice trailed off when she saw the look of anxiety on Annie's pale face. 'Come in. What's wrong?'

'Rose, there's been an accident at Fisher's.' Mr Rodgers was speaking very calmly.

'William, William, is he all right?' Rose quickly looked from one to the other.

'We don't know yet,' replied Mr Rodgers.

Annie remained silent.

Mr Rodgers continued. 'Annie's been to the factory, but she didn't see him. It seems they have taken a lot of the boys to St Olave's. We're on our way there now. Would you like to join us?'

'Yes, yes of course. I'll just get my coat.'

On the journey Mr Rodgers briefly told Rose what had happened, and when they arrived at the hospital, all three hurried inside.

'We're looking for the boys who were in the Fisher's accident,' said Mr Rodgers to a young nurse.

113

'What name?'

'Hobbs, William,' volunteered Rose.

'If you just take a seat I'll find out which ward they've been taken to.'

'I'm sure he's fine,' said Rose, putting a comforting arm round Annie. 'If he was one of the first out, then he must have been walking.'

'Do you really think so?' asked Annie. Tears had made clean runs down her dirty face.

They sat on the hard wooden seats, watching the comings and goings all around them closely, hoping to recognize someone.

'Do you know how many were hurt?' asked Rose.

Annie shook her head. 'There was a lot lying on the ground outside the factory, but Mr Harrison told me that no one had been . . .'

'Cheer up,' said Mr Rodgers. 'We'll have him coming round that corner soon, and he'll be wondering what all the fuss was about.'

Annie tried to smile at her father's optimism.

Finally, after what seemed a lifetime, the young nurse returned and they all jumped to their feet.

'Would you follow me, please?' she said politely.

They started to fall in behind her.

The nurse stopped. 'Who is the next of kin?'

Annie gasped. 'Is he . . . ?'

'I'm sorry,' she said kindly. 'I'm not in a position to tell you anything. You have to go along to the sister's office, and I'm afraid it's only the next of kin she will speak to. Are you his wife?'

Annie shook her head.

'Annie is William's fiancée, and I'm his sister,' said Rose.

The nurse looked at Mr Rodgers.

'This is my daughter.' He put his arm round Annie's shoulders.

'I see. Perhaps, Miss Hobbs, you would like to follow me.'

Annie and her father returned to the hard wooden chairs. She slumped down. 'She said next of kin. Dad, you don't think . . . ?'

'That's what they always ask.'

Annie sat wide-eyed, bewildered. Her father didn't speak, just put his head down and, his trilby hat in his hands, began twirling it round and round between his knees.

After a while the nurse came towards them again, and again they jumped up. 'Would you like a cup of tea?' she asked.

'That would be very nice, thank you,' said Mr Rodgers as they sat down again. 'How about you, Annie?'

She shook her head. 'No, thank you.' She looked up at the clock. 'Will Mum lock the shop up?'

'Course.'

'What about Ted, he'll want you to help put up the rest of those decorations.'

Her father patted her hand. 'Don't worry about that. We'll get all that sorted out when we find out how Will is.'

Much later, Rose turned the corner at the end of the corridor. Annie leapt up and ran to meet her but she reeled back when she saw Rose's gaunt white face. She was carrying a brown paper carrier bag, and Annie could see Will's navy blue overalls on top.

Mr Rodgers was on his feet. 'How is he? Is he badly hurt?'

Rose gently lowered herself on to the chair. She raised her eyes to Annie's. 'He's dead.'

Annie too sat down. She gave a muffled sob. 'Will's gone. But how?'

'It seems he was nearest the wall,' whispered Rose.

'I can't believe it . . . Mr Harrison said . . . He can't have, oh, Dad, we . . .' Every sentence was left unfinished, and the tears began to fall.

'I'm so sorry. There, there, love.' Her father sat with his arm round her.

'I want to see him. What if they're wrong and it's not Will?'

Rose whispered. 'I have seen him, Annie.'

Annie buried her head in her father's chest and cried.

On Wednesday 12 May, 1937, Coronation Day, there wasn't a lot to celebrate in Rodgers' grocer's shop, or indeed Albert Mews. With a heavy heart Mr Rodgers opened his shop as usual.

'Wasn't sure what yer'd be doing terday,' said Ted tentatively as he came in, obviously ill at east with the situation.

'Well, a lot of people will be waiting for this lot.' Mr Rodgers

115

nodded towards the cardboard boxes squatting on the floor.

'I'll give yer 'and if yer like.'

'Thanks, a lot of hard-earned cash has gone into these pre-parations, and besides, we can't let the kids down, Will wouldn't like that.'

'No, course not. 'Ow's Annie?'

'Very quiet.'

'It's ter be expected.' Ted bent down and picked up a box of groceries. 'Where to?'

'Paradise Street.'

During the day many people came into offer their condolences but Annie didn't go down to see them. The following Monday was the day the world saw Annie's grief. Up until now it had been very private. At night her dreams, when she finally fell asleep, were of Will, but every time she tried to hold him, he disappeared. She was standing in the kitchen staring into space when her mother's voice invaded her thoughts.

'That was kind of Rose wanting you to go in their carriage with them.' Mrs Rodgers was standing in front of the mirror adjusting her black straw hat.

'Do you mind?'

'Course not, love. Are you all right?'

Annie nodded. 'I told Lil you would take her to the cemetery.'

Her father pushed open the kitchen door. 'Ready, love. Lil's downstairs. She looks very nice.'

Annie gave a deep sigh and picked up her handbag. Ever since the accident she had been dreading this day. The day when she would be saying goodbye to her beloved for ever. All the time they had wasted when they could have been together. All the plans they had made for their future. Now it was all over; he had gone from her life. But he would never go from her memory. She had been through all the emotions over this past week. At first she had been sad, and tearful, then angry; angry with God for taking him from her. He was a good kind person. Why was he the only one to die? Why? Why? Why? She began to hate the Salvation Army, and all those who said it was God's will. At first she said she wanted nothing to do with them, although the look of despair on that young

116

girl's face still haunted her. But today she was numb.

''Allo, Annie.' Lil kissed her cheek.

'That's a nice hat, Lil.'

Lil knew of Annie's innermost feelings, for she had already cried with Annie when she was first told the news. She pulled at the eye veil of her small black hat. 'It's not bad. Yer ready then?'

Annie nodded.

They rode in silence to Rose's house. Annie was surprised at the number of people waiting outside. The day was bright and sunny, but as the cortège set out on its ponderous way, the slow beat of a Salvation Army drum accompanied them, seeming to make the very air oppressive.

Annie had never been to a funeral before. When her brother died she'd been only seven, and on the day of his funeral she'd stayed with Ted the butcher and his wife. She suddenly remembered, they'd had jelly for tea, and it hadn't been a Sunday. Today, sitting in the darkened carriage with the horses bowing and shaking their black plumed heads in front, all kind of random thoughts were flitting through her mind. What sort of house would they have had if they had moved to the new estate? Ahead of them was the hearse carrying the coffin – could Will really be in there? But she knew he was; only last night she had said a last goodbye and kissed his cold cheek. Perhaps this was all just a bad dream? The wreaths were lovely, she noticed dreamily, May was a good month for flowers. She quickly looked across at Mr Hobbs, sitting very stiff and upright. He caught her gaze and gave her a faint smile.

'Soon be all over, my dear.' He leant across the carriage and gently patted her hand.

Rose too managed a smile, but it was very weak. She looked sad and vulnerable, so different from when she used to come into the shop for her cough drops. It was only a few years since they'd buried her mother. Rose must be a very brave person, Annie thought, for she hadn't seen her cry at all.

At the graveside, Annie held on to Lil's arm as she watched Will's coffin being slowly lowered into the ground. She couldn't cry any more, all her tears were spent.

Glancing round she was surprised that so many people had come to pay their last respects. There were some she knew from the factory, some were from the Salvation Army, and there were many others who'd known him, had watched him grow up. William Hobbs had been a well-liked young man. In all his twenty-two years he had made nothing but friends.

One morning, a few weeks after the funeral, Mrs Rodgers came into the kitchen holding an envelope. 'Look, I've got a letter from Ivy. She's very sorry about Will.'

Annie looked up from the table. Her eyes no longer had their sparkle, and she seemed to have lost interest in most things. Last Saturday Rose had persuaded her to go to the mission, and she was still toying with the idea of joining the Salvation Army. She knew Will would have liked that.

Her mother was still reading the letter. 'Ivy says she'd be very pleased to have you stay for a while.' She sat beside Annie. 'Why don't you go, love. It'd do you good to have a holiday, it'd cheer you up. You're too young to sit around and mope.'

'What about you after John died. You sat around for months.'

'Annie.' Her mother's voice was sharp. 'He was my son, my only son, and only ten years old.'

'Sorry,' she mumbled, 'that was a bit thoughtless of me.'

'That's all right, dear,' her mother's voice softened. 'We all need time for the pain to heal.' Mrs Rodgers began filling the kettle. 'I'll make another cup of tea, then you can take it down to your father.'

Annie smiled. She knew her mother was well meaning, and had grieved with her. 'Would you and Dad mind if I went to Aunt Ivy's for a week?' she asked after a moment.

'We'd be only too pleased – I'll drop her a line later to find out when it's convenient.'

Annie walked into the shop, carefully balancing the cup on the saucer. Mrs Bates was at the counter. 'Hello, Mrs Bates,' Annie greeted her, 'how's Georgie?'

'Not ser good, love. Yer knows they 'ad ter take that leg orf?'

'Yes, I did hear. I'm very sorry. If there's anything I can . . .'

A feeble smile lifted her pale drawn face. 'If yer could go and

118

see 'im in 'ospital 'e'd be very pleased. And I'd be most obliged to yer.'

'Yes, I'll go, when will it suit you?'

'Any Monday. I 'ave a job ter git there on a Monday, and I always feels guilty if no one's going in ter see 'im. 'E 'ates being the only one with no visitors.'

'That's settled then. I'll go Monday. It's a pity we only get half an hour but I'll see if Lil can come with me. She can cheer anybody up.'

'Ta ever so. I'll tell 'im ternight. 'E'll be ever ser pleased.' The thin woman hurried from the shop.

'You've just made a little old lady very happy, Annie,' said her father.

'I bet she's not all that old,' she said, still looking at the door. 'And I think she's done a lot to cheer me up as well.'

'That's good, love,' smiled her father. 'I don't like to see you so unhappy.'

The following Monday evening Annie met Lil and they went off to the hospital with plenty of sweets and cigarettes. When they saw Georgie, they were surprised to see him looking so well.

'Fanks fer coming. See,' he shouted to his bedfellows. 'I told yer I was 'aving two of the prettiest girls round 'ere coming in ter see me.' He laughed. 'It's good ter see yer both.'

'And it's good to see you,' said Annie sincerely.

'I was sorry ter 'ear about Will. Wish I could 'ave shown me last respects.'

'That's all right. Anyway, how are you?'

'Not ser bad. And look at you, Lil – cor, yer looks a real smasher.'

Lil laughed. 'Go on, I bet yer say that ter all the nurses.'

'Got some right little darlings in 'ere, we 'ave. I'll be glad when I can git up, though.'

'Why's that, so you can chase 'em round the room?'

'Not 'arf.'

'How . . . How will you manage?' Annie put her handbag on the bed. 'I'm not hurting you, am I?'

'Na, me leg ends 'ere.' He pointed to below his knee.

119

Lil sat on a chair. 'Well, yer better not enter any three-legged races. You'll fall over.'

'Lil,' said Annie sharply.

Georgie laughed. 'That's all right. Yer wonner 'ear some of the remarks that fly round these wards. Still singing in the Castle, Lil?'

'Yer, and I work behind the bar as well now. You'll 'ave ter come over fer a drink when they let yer out.'

'Christ, I better not get plastered, I'll fall off me crutches. 'Ere, yer still going out with that posh bloke?'

'Na. We 'ad a big row and I decided ter chuck 'im.'

Annie quickly glanced at Lil, for she knew she still saw Julian at the clubs she sang in, but Lil had told her that he kept his distance and almost ignored her and, besides, he was with a new crowd now.

Georgie was rubbing his chin. 'So, there could be a chance fer me then?' he laughed.

'Could be, but only if yer play yer cards right.'

'What d'yer mean, only if I park me Rolls outside yer 'ouse.'

'Or yer crutches,' Lil laughed.

Soon all three were laughing and chatting; all too quickly the bell was ringing for the visitors to go.

'Lil, Annie, fanks fer coming, and fer the fags and sweets.'

'We'll come next Monday if you like,' said Lil.

'That'll be great.'

'I'd bring yer a book if I fought you could read,' laughed Lil.

'Go on with yer, yer saucy cow.'

They left Georgie laughing and waving.

'D'yer know I ain't seen Georgie Bates fer years. Not since we were at school and 'e used ter chase us.'

'He won't be chasing anyone now.'

'No, it's a shame.'

'Still, at least he's still alive.'

'Yer.' Lil put her arms through Annie's. ''E ain't turned out ser bad though, as 'e?'

'No, him and Will were good workmates.'

'Seriously though, Annie, thanks fer asking me ter come with

120

yer. It makes yer stop and fink, don't it, when yer see some people worse off than yerself?'

'Yes, and seeing him has done me a lot of good.' Annie nudged her friend. 'Here, I didn't know you could be such a sensitive old thing.'

'I 'ave me moments, and not ser much of the old.'

'Now you know why I'm thinking of joining the Salvation Army. It makes me feel better to think I'm trying to help people.'

'I still dunno why yer wonner join *that* lot.'

'Oh Lil, if you could have seen the look on that young girl's face that night.'

Lil looked at her. 'She really did upset you, didn't she?'

'Yes. And I really would like to help some of these people. Just like Will did. He was so good.'

'Just ser long as yer knows what yer doing? Christ, who'd 'ad fought a while back that you'd be finking of joining the Sally Army, and I'd be working in a pub.'

'Yes, well a lot of things change. I'm glad you have Mondays off now, at least we'll be able to go out together again.'

'Yer,' said Lil thoughtfully.

As they continued strolling back home, a crowd of men came round the corner, laughing and shouting. They were pushing and shoving each other and kicking a ball of newspaper along the road, almost bumping into Annie and Lil. Shocked, Annie realized she recognized one of them.

'Why, hello there, it's my little Annie, and my darling Lil.' Julian flicked his grey trilby back with his finger and, pushing between them, put his arms round both the girls' shoulders.

'Who're the little darlings, Jules old chap?' asked another of the crowd as he came towards them.

Annie quickly brushed Julian's arm away. At the back of the group she spotted Peter. He had scooped up the ball of newspaper and was trying to balance it on his nose.

'Hi, Annie, long time no see,' he called out. 'I must say you look well.'

It was the last Monday in the month, Annie remembered, so

they must have been to their club. 'Hello, Peter,' she said softly.

'Sorry to hear about your boyfriend.' Peter was still playing with the newspaper ball. 'Still, they say the good die young, so in that case – I should last for ever.' He laughed.

How could he be so heartless? Tears were beginning to fill Annie's eyes. She tried to walk away but Peter jumped in front of her and blocked her path. She could see Lil was getting cross with Julian, who was trying to kiss her. When she pushed him away he laughed in her face.

'Come on, Annie,' said Lil, grabbing her arm and marching her away. 'This lot's worse than the silly sods we gits in the pub.'

'Please, Lil, mind your language.' Julian held his forehead in mock horror.

All the men laughed, and stood to one side as Annie and Lil hastily continued their journey.

'Bye-bye, Annie,' said Peter, waving after her in a stupid fashion.

She didn't acknowledge him. How could she ever have thought that she liked him, she asked herself, the question filling her out-raged mind.

'Act like a bloody load of kids they do when they've 'ad a few.' Lil was still flushed with anger.

Annie nodded in agreement. She could never imagine Will saying anything like that, or behaving like that. Even Georgie, who only wanted to make people laugh, was a million times better than that sort. She was glad Peter Barrett was Belinda's problem now and had only, for a short time, ever been hers.

'I'll need another reel of black cotton please.'

'How long are you going for, Annie?' asked Miss Dorothy Page.

'Only a week.' Annie wandered round the shop.

'That'll do you good. Let's hope the weather stays nice.' She paused. 'Annie.' Miss Page looked around her. 'I hope you don't think I'm being . . . Well, interfering. But you know both Maud and myself lost our fiancés in the war.'

Annie felt embarrassed. Miss Page had never mentioned this before.

'Well,' she began rewinding a reel of pink ribbon, 'what I'm trying to say is that you are young and very pretty, and I would hate you to go through life bitter and hard, and become a miserable old spinster.'

'But you're not, you're very . . .'

Miss Page put up her hand to silence her. 'William was a well-liked young man, and I know you'll never forget him, and I'm not suggesting for one moment that you should; but remember life goes on. And who knows, one day you may meet someone else – time is a great healer.'

Annie didn't have time to respond, for the door tinkled open and Maud Page walked purposefully into the shop carrying a paper bag. 'Hello, Annie.' She sniffed the air. 'These buns are delicious. We are so lucky to have such a good baker's close at hand. I hear you are going off to your aunt's for a week's holiday? Do you good. When are you off then?'

'In the morning,' mumbled Annie, still a little embarrassed. 'I best be going back, Mum's waiting for this cotton.'

Chapter 13

When Annie arrived at Horsham station, she was pleased to see her cousin Roy waiting for her. She had been a little apprehensive as to whether she would recognize him after all these years, but the minute she stepped off the train he ran to meet her.

'It's so good to see you again, Annie, after all this time. How are you?' Roy kissed her cheek. 'You remember Matt?'

'I'm all right thanks. Hello, Matt.'

Roy's friend Matthew had been striding behind her cousin. 'Hello, Annie,' he said shyly, snatching off his cloth cap to reveal his blond hair.

'Going to take you home in style; managed to get a car,' said Roy. 'Here, give me your case.'

'A car, you've bought a car?'

'No, I work in a garage, and the boss said I could borrow one to meet you.'

'That's very good of him. What do you do now, Matthew?'

He looked down at her, for he was a head and shoulders taller than her, and smiled. 'I'm working on Dad's farm.' He had bright blue eyes that were wide apart, and set in a brown rugged face. He had grown up since she had seen him last, and she was surprised at how handsome he was.

Roy bundled her and the case into the back of the car, and with Matt sitting in front, they set off for Aunt Ivy's.

'Sorry to hear about Will,' said Roy quickly, glancing over his shoulder.

Annie smiled bravely. 'Yes, it was very sad. He was a lovely person. You would have liked him.'

Annie settled back, and for a while there was an uncomfortable silence.

Then Matt asked, 'How long are you staying for, Annie?'

'Only a week.'

'That's a shame. Couldn't you get more time off from the shop?'

'Well, I don't like to be away for too long.'

'Why's that? Frightened you'll miss the bright lights? Do you live it up in London then?'

She laughed. 'No.'

'Don't you go to lots of dances? And what about all the latest pictures?' asked Matt enthusiastically.

'We go to the pictures, but Will didn't dance.' She leaned forward. 'My friend Lil and me used to go to dances. Been to some real posh places, we have.'

'Is Lil good-looking?' asked Roy.

'Yes, she is. She's a good singer as well.'

Matt half turned. 'We could do with her down here, especially tonight.'

'Why tonight?'

'Got a dance on in the village hall.'

'Hope you brought some glad rags with you,' said Roy.

'Well, I did put in quite a nice frock.'

'I reckon you'll be the belle of the ball,' said Matt.

'She's not got a lot of competition, has she?' laughed Roy. 'Only June Markem.'

They passed through the village, and Roy sounded his hooter and waved to a couple of girls. 'Look, there's June. You watch Matt blush.'

'Who's June?' asked Annie.

'A girl Matt's keen on.'

Annie could see the back of his neck suddenly turn very pink. 'No I'm not,' he said quickly.

Roy carefully manoeuvred the car into a narrow side road, then turned off, and bumped along a dirt track.

'Look, your auntie's waiting at the gate,' said Matthew.

Annie waved. 'Where's Uncle Fred?'

'Probably putting the kettle on.' Roy brought the car to a halt, and Annie ran down the path to her aunt and hugged her.

'Get down, Nell.' Aunt Ivy pushed a lolloping black dog, with a long wagging tail out of the way and held Annie at arm's length. 'Let me look at you. My, how you've grown. And grown very pretty as well.' She linked her arm through Annie's and patted the back of her hand. 'Right, let's have a nice cup of tea, then you can tell me all your news.' She stopped. 'We were all very sorry to hear about your young man. Your mother said he was a real gentleman.'

'Yes,' said Annie, 'he was.' As she bent down to pat Nell, the smell of flowers was all around her.

'Your garden looks lovely. Look at all those beautiful roses.'

'It's been a good year for the flowers, and the veg. I must give you a nice bunch to take home to your mother. Fred, here's young Annie.'

Inside the cottage Annie kissed and hugged Uncle Fred, the farmer her aunt had met as a soldier all those years ago in London, then she was taken up to her room. It was sparsely furnished, just a bed, wardrobe and chest of drawers, but it was bright and sunny and overlooked the back garden. The cottage was on a hill, so the view was lovely. All the open fields had hedgerows bordering them and, with her elbows resting on the windowsill, she idly watched the cattle grazing contentedly. Far beyond in the distance were some very tall trees, and she could just make out the birds flying high above them – it was all so peaceful. After a while Annie began unpacking, sensing with relief that this week she was going to feel happy and relaxed. Roy and Matthew had already told her they were going to see she had a good time: it felt comforting to have those two gentle young men looking after her. Suddenly the door was pushed open and Nell wandered in, still wagging her long hairy tail. With a large sigh she flopped down beside Annie and looked up at her with big brown doleful eyes.

'You were just a puppy when I was last here,' said Annie, patting her head.

That evening Roy took her to the local dance, looking very smart. It was a lively affair, where everybody knew everybody else, and Annie was introduced to Matthew's friend June, who was shorter than Annie, slim and with an elfin face. Her dark curly hair had a fringe that was always falling forward, her wide dark brown eyes sparkled, and Annie felt at ease with her immediately. They were soon talking and laughing as though they had known each other for years. June was a lovely girl, Annie thought warmly, and so obviously in love with Matthew.

At the end of the evening, Annie realized she'd had a really good time. She had had many dances, and laughed a lot and now, for the first time in weeks, she felt happy.

'I didn't know you country bumpkins enjoyed yourselves so much,' said Annie, walking home with Roy through the clear, warm night.

'We've not all got straw and hayseed for brains, you know,' Roy laughed. 'But it's good to see you having a good time.' He gave her a brotherly kiss on the cheek. 'Shh, we don't want to wake up the old 'ens. In you go, and you can make the cocoa.'

Every day, Annie woke up to the sun streaming through the window. She went with Aunt Ivy to the village in the mornings, and every afternoon she took Nell for long walks over the fields. In the evening, June and Matt joined her and Roy and they went to a pub or for walks. With rosy cheeks, and the sparkle back in her eyes, she was beginning to look well, and she didn't want this week to end.

But end it did and, after all the hugs and kisses and frantic waving from the train window, Annie settled herself in a corner seat with her thoughts. She now really felt she knew her cousin Roy and that she'd made friends of June and Matt. One day, she hoped, she would be invited to their wedding. She refused to feel jealous of their happiness and she inwardly smiled that the thought of someone else's wedding couldn't hurt her. Now she was going back to her memories, and she knew she was ready to start her life again.

The following Friday Annie was having tea with the Hobbs.

'Are you sure it is what you really want?' asked Rose.

'Yes,' said Annie determinedly.

Mr Hobbs stood up. He was a tall man and Annie had to strain her neck to look up at him. 'We are pleased, very pleased.' He tenderly put his arm round Annie's shoulders. 'And I know William would also have been delighted. Many times he said he would have liked you to join us.'

'I must admit I'm more interested in the good work you do, especially in the mission, than the religious side.' Annie felt she had to point this out quite strongly to them.

Mr Hobbs tried to hide his surprise. 'That's all right, my dear. When you realize the good Lord must have sent you to us, you will come round, I'm sure.' His arm tightened around her shoulder and he pulled her closer.

'Oh, I do believe in God,' said Annie, quickly moving away. 'But I couldn't devote my life to him.'

'We don't expect you to,' said Rose, quickly standing up. 'Now help me lay the table, tea is all ready. I must say you look very well after your holiday. Where was it you went to?'

'Downfold. It's a little village in Sussex.' Annie smiled at her memories of her holiday. She hoped one day she'd return there, but life in London, she was determined, was going to hold a lot for her too. If she felt she was doing something worthwhile then her life would feel worthwhile.

That evening, when Annie arrived home, she was full of high spirits. She sat on the arm of her mother's chair and broke her news to her parents.

'Are you sure this is what you want?' asked her mother when she had finished telling them.

'That's what Rose asked me. Yes, I am sure. They do some wonderful work at the mission.'

'Well, I don't approve.' Her father looked angry and he turned on his wife. 'This is all your fault.'

'Mine? What did I have to do with it?'

'You wanted her to go out with Will, while I was all for her going out with someone like Peter Barrett, but oh no, you didn't like her using make-up and dressing up.'

'But, Dad . . .'

Annie was ignored as her father continued his tirade. 'And now look what's happened. She ends up joining the Sally Army.'

'But, Dad,' cried Annie again, 'I thought you liked Will.'

'I did. He was a pleasant enough boy.'

'Well, he was in the Army.'

'Yes, and he told me he was giving it up. Now you come home with this damn fool notion. I wanted something better for you.' Standing up he threw his newspaper to the floor and stormed across the room. At the door he turned and wagged his finger at them both. 'I don't want any part of this, and you, young lady, don't you come home here preaching to us. Now I'm going to the pub.' He slammed the kitchen door.

Annie jumped to her feet. 'Oh, Mum, I'm sorry. I didn't think it would make him this unhappy. Why is he so against it?'

Mrs Rodgers picked up the newspaper and began folding it carefully. 'I think it's because he wanted you to marry above us. He's always talked about you marrying some toff. He loves you and wants you to be happy.'

'I know that. But I wouldn't have been happy with Peter.' She hung her head. 'And I *would* have been happy with Will, I know that.'

'Don't let your father upset you.' Her mother reached out and patted her arm.

'Can't he see that so many other people are poor and unhappy, and they need help?'

'He knows all about that. But that's not his worry, you are.'

Annie hugged her mother. 'Just give me time. I may get fed up with it. It's just that I want to do something useful.'

'I think you'll make a very caring Salvationist, and you'll look lovely in the bonnet.'

Annie smiled. 'If you like I'll wait up for Dad to come back from the pub. Perhaps I could have a little talk with him.'

'Don't worry about him, he'll be all right. Now you go on to bed – I'm going up soon.'

Annie kissed her mother. 'Goodnight.'

'It's good to have you home, love. We really missed you last week.'

Annie smiled and closed the door.

* * *

130

Annie was in a deep sleep when the sound of loud screams and hysterical laughter woke her. It was a hot night, and her bedroom was at the front overlooking the Mews. She sat up and looked out of the open window, and was shocked to see her father trying to climb the lamp-post. At the bottom stood Bessie who worked in the greengrocer's, giving him a push up. He would get so far then gently slide down again, and all this was accompanied by Bessie's high-pitched laugh. Annie hoped and prayed that most of the Mews slept in the back room like her mother, and were out of earshot.

She lay back on her pillow. This was her fault. What was her father doing with Bessie? Had he known she would be in the pub? Annie tossed and turned. Bessie had a bit of a reputation as a man-eater. It had been the talk of the Mews when Mrs James had had a go at her only the other week.

Why did he go to the pub and get so tipsy? And why was he so against her decision? Could it upset their wonderful relationship? But Annie knew he didn't hold grudges for long. Tomorrow he'd be his old self again.

The giggling had stopped and Annie looked out again – the Mews was empty and she heard her father's key in the door. Annie plumped up her pillow and smiled. 'Mum'll have a right go at him in the morning,' she said to herself.

'Good morning,' said Annie, walking into the kitchen.

Her father looked up from his plate of bacon and eggs. 'Is it?'

Annie looked across at her mother who quickly shook her head.

'Are we a little grumpy then?' teased Annie.

'Sit down, Annie, your breakfast is ready,' said her mother.

'Don't forget on Monday I'll be going to the hospital with Lil,' said Annie cheerfully.

'How long will Georgie be in there?' asked her mother, putting a plate of egg and bacon in front of her.

'I don't know, but he was saying the other week that he should be going to a convalescent home soon.'

'Wonder where he'll go?'

'The seaside, I reckon. If he does I think Lil would like to go and see him.'

'She sounds sweet on Georgie,' her mother smiled.

'No, not really,' said Annie. 'She likes him, he's good company. But I think she's got her heart set on someone with plenty of money.'

'Well, you can't blame her, after all she's had a pretty rough time of it up to now,' said her father, stirring his tea.

'Do you know she's never seen the sea?' Annie continued eating her breakfast.

'Well, you've only seen it twice,' said her mother. 'And that was when we went those two times with the pub outing to Margate.'

'Lil seems to have a few bob to spend now,' said her father, pushing his plate away.

'Well, now she gets all that money from her singing, and the bar work.' She looked at her father. 'D'you know that Julian used to take half?' Annie chewed her bacon thoughtfully. 'I reckon she'll be leaving home soon.'

'Oh, where will she go?' asked her mother.

'It seems the owner of the pub's got a spare room, and she's thinking of taking it. I think she'll be moving in there before long.' She paused. 'I'm sorry if I upset you last night, Dad.'

'That's all right. Just forget it.' He stood up quickly. 'I'm off downstairs. Come down when you're ready, I've got to go and see someone later.'

'Was Dad all right when he got in?' asked Annie when he'd gone.

'I don't know, I was asleep. I think he'd had a bit too much to drink, but he didn't wake me.'

'That's good,' said Annie sipping her tea, hoping that she wouldn't find out about Bessie and the lamp-post incident.

Chapter 14

On Monday evening Annie and Lil went to the hospital as usual. Georgie told them he should be going to a convalescent home very soon: he was very excited about it.

Lil was upset at the news, and, on the way home said to Annie, 'Yer know, it's funny, but I really look forward ter coming up 'ere ter see 'im.'

'Don't worry,' Annie reassured her. 'He said he would write when he gets settled. Then perhaps, if it's not too far away, we could go and see him.'

'I'd like that, that'll be smashing. Would yer really come with me if 'e went ter the seaside?'

'Course.'

'What about yer Sally Army fing?'

'I'm sure we can come to some arrangements, and Dad don't mind me having a day off.'

'I've made me mind up ter leave 'ome,' said Lil, stopping to look in a shop window.

'When?'

'Next week. Look at that nice frock. One fing, it won't take me long ter pack.'

'You're going to miss your family.'

'Yer, but now I gits the whole o' Monday off I can spend all day with me mum and all evening with you. That way I don't 'ave ter see me dad.'

'He still giving you a hard time?'

'It ain't ser bad now I'm earning a few bob.'

'What shall we do next Monday night?' Annie asked. She thought for a minute and then said, 'We could go to the pictures.'

'Why not, it'll be my treat,' said Lil grinning.

'Times have certainly changed,' laughed Annie. Nowadays she was just happy for Lil that she was earning so much money.

'Yer, fank god.'

Annie was pleased Rose had asked her to go along to the mission on Saturday evening and, as she approached the building, she looked anxiously once more for the young girl who had made such a deep impression on her on New Year's Eve.

'Annie, could you help Sister Harris peel some more potatoes?' asked one of the older women as soon as she walked in. 'She seems to be having trouble.'

'Of course.' Annie liked Sister Harris, who was in her late thirties, unmarried, and so devoted to the Army that she was thinking of becoming a missionary in Africa.

'You'll have to learn to be a lot quicker than that when you get to Africa,' said Annie, walking into the large kitchen.

'Providing, of course, that they have potatoes,' said Sister Harris. 'It's only because of my hand that I'm so slow.' She held out her heavily bandaged left hand. 'I cut it being careless.'

Annie busied herself all evening, and between her chores she popped outside, still hoping to see the girl.

'We'll have to look after you when you go round the public houses,' said Sister Harris as she was wiping a table down.

Annie smiled, thinking of Mrs Day's daughter. 'Why's that, frightened somebody's going to whisk me away?'

'Some of the pubs round here can be very rough, and some of the men can be very naughty when they've had a drink or two, especially with pretty new recruits.'

'I'll worry about that when the time comes.' Annie thought of some of the things Lil had told her about. How, when she was collecting the empty glasses she had to make out she was enjoying herself even when men were touching her and breathing their smelly beery breath all over her.

'Have we nearly finished?'

'Yes, it's just time for prayers, then you can go off. You'll be in plenty of time to catch your tram.'

Outside, as Annie said her goodnights, she wished Will was by her side. Tonight she was on her own, there were none of the Hobbs to walk with her, and nobody was going in her direction. Walking alone gave her time to think about Will, and how much she missed him. It was a cloudy night, and as the clouds drifted across the moon it created dark, scurrying shadows. There were men lying in shop doorways, covered with old newspapers. Some were drunk and, hardly able to stand, were lolling around their friends' necks, and one was draped round a lamp-post being sick. Annie quickly crossed the road to avoid any direct confrontation with them. Others were singing and shouting, and once or twice a scuffle broke out, with a lot of pushing and shoving till somebody parted the offenders. There were tarty women, laughing loudly and waiting on street corners for men. She was reminded of Bessie. The sudden barking of a dog behind a fence made her jump. She pulled her cardigan round her shoulders and quickened her pace, giving a loud sigh of relief when she saw two other people waiting at the stop.

As the tram came into view, Annie casually glanced around her. Then, to her joy, she noticed on the other side of the road a young girl hurrying along. She was carrying a baby and wearing dirty white plimsolls. Annie was just about to raise her hand to wave, when suddenly she saw the look of fear on the girl's face. The girl looked behind her and held the baby closer. She turned the corner, and was out of sight.

Annie looked up the road at the tram coming towards her. Would she have time to run after her? This was the last tram tonight. What would she say to her? The tram was getting nearer. She had to know if the girl and the baby were all right. But how would she get home if she missed this tram? Four drunks were reeling along the road, two holding another between them, his feet being dragged along the road. Suddenly he stood up, and with a lot of shouting and abuse, brushed them off. ''Ere, mate, where's that little darling gone ter?' he yelled.

135

The woman waiting at the stop with her arm tucked through her young man's tutted loudly. 'It's disgusting the way some people behave when they've had a few.'

To Annie's horror the men turned the same corner as the girl had done.

'I hope that young girl knows them,' said the young man.

'It's probably the father,' said the woman. 'Ah, here's our tram at last.'

Annie knew she had to make a decision, now. Turning from the tram stop, she set off at a run in the direction in which the girl – and the four drunks – had disappeared.

She quickly overtook the four drunks as she turned the corner and, as she ran past them, one called out, 'What's yer rush, gel? Come and 'ave a drink wiv us.'

She hurried on, not knowing where she was going. She heard the tram's bell as it trundled away. It was quiet, apart from the shouts of the drunks and her feet echoing on the cobbles. The road was full of tall, dark warehouses, which hung over her menacingly. There were no streetlamps burning down here, and as she looked up she realized the street was a dead end. Where had the girl gone? There were windows on the other side, but they looked as if they were boarded up. She stood frantically looking around for a way out, a door, an opening, or an alley. She began to panic. The drunks were now singing very loudly and getting closer. She looked for a doorway in which to hide. Tears were stinging her eyes. She pressed herself against the wall and tried to make herself as small as possible. She closed her eyes and offered up a prayer. 'Please help me,' she said out loud.

When she opened her eyes the men were standing in front of her. They moved forward and, horrified, she slowly slid along the wall as they forced her into a corner. Before another cloud blotted out the moon, Annie caught sight in the half light of the tattoos which covered one of the men's arms. He was a large man with thick arms and he stepped in front of the others, grabbing her. 'Where're yer going, darling?'

'You're hurting me. Let go. Leave me alone.' She tried to sound confident.

'Don't you git stroppy wiv me. Come and 'ave a drink.'

'No, thank you.' She was trying to appear calm, even though she was sweating with fear.

'What yer doing down 'ere?' asked another.

'Looking for a friend,' she stammered. Annie ran her fingers along the wall behind her, hoping to find a loose brick, or something she could defend herself with.

The man with the tattoos threw his head back and laughed. ''Ere, Curly, she's looking for a friend. Go on, show 'er how friendly yer can be.'

Curly, who was reeling about, came up close to her and put his arm round her shoulder. The smell of his unwashed body almost took her breath away. 'Is this friendly enough?' His beery mouth came down on hers and his unshaven face rasped against hers. She felt sick as his tongue forced her mouth open. She tried to push him away but she might as well have tried to move a mountain.

At last he let her go. 'Leave me alone,' she whimpered, and feverishly rubbed her mouth with the back of her hand. She wanted to cry.

A fat, short, bald man, holding a bottle, was grinning. 'I can be even more friendly than Curly 'ere. 'Ere, 'ave a drink.' He put the bottle to her mouth and tipped it up, the smell of whisky filling the air as she spluttered and coughed. It ran over her face and mingled with her tears. Her cardigan fell from her shoulders.

Curly picked it up and draped it over his head. 'How do I look?' He started to dance in front of her. 'Go on, yer must fancy me now.' He gave her a shove.

The men were bent over laughing. 'Out the way. Now it's my turn ter be friendly,' said the fourth. He had dark, greasy, slicked-down hair and as he stood in front of her he ran his fingers over his thin dark moustache.

'This I gotter see,' said the tattooed man.

The dark-haired man put one arm on the wall and the other across her throat, stopping her from escaping. Frantically she started trying to push him away, but he was too strong. Fear was pounding in her head.

'Now stop struggling, darling. I can be ever so nice if yer let me,' he whispered loudly. 'And I'm very good at it. Yer see I've 'ad a lotta practice, and I don't git a lot of complaints.'

'Come on,' yelled Curly. 'Git on wiv it.'

'Shut up,' he yelled over his shoulder to his audience. 'They like this fancy stuff. I'm not an animal like you lot.' He roughly pushed his knee between her legs and put his hand up her skirt, to the laughter and amusement of the others.

Annie thought she would die. She began screaming. 'Let me go, leave me alone.' She was writhing, fighting, and hitting him to get away. 'She likes me,' he announced again over his shoulder. 'Cor, this whisky smells nice. Let me lick yer all over.'

The fat man with the bottle grabbed his arm. ''Ere, that's my whisky, so I should do the licking. Gotter 'ave a jimmy first though.'

'Gis a drink then.' Curly took the bottle from the fat man.

'I gotter 'ave a jimmy as well,' said the one with the moustache. 'Don't go away.'

Annie slid down the wall. 'Please let me go,' she pleaded.

'Get up, yer silly cow.' The man with the tattoos roughly grabbed her arms and pulled her to her feet, his fingers digging into her bare flesh. 'Come on, on yer feet, it's Saturday night, and this is the night we all like ter 'ave a bit o' fun.'

Annie screamed out again; her screams echoed round the empty buildings.

'Shut up.' He brought the back of his hand across her face. She felt numb with fear and pain. He took hold of her hair and forced her head back, hitting it against the wall. As he kissed her mouth hard, she could feel herself slipping away.

'I mustn't pass out,' she murmured. 'I've got to get away.'

'You ain't going nowhere till we've 'ad our bit o' fun.'

''Ere, 'old this,' said Curly, handing the tattooed man the whisky bottle. 'I'm going first. Gotta while I can.' He laughed. 'Me old woman don't fink I got it in me.'

Curly came reeling towards her again. The tattooed man had the whisky bottle to his mouth while the other two peed against the wall. Curly came closer, closing his eyes as he fumbled with his trousers. Annie was desperate. This would be her only chance.

138

Quickly she pushed him to one side and started to run. Behind her she heard a loud crash as the tattooed man threw the bottle to the ground. He moved swiftly across the road, snatching roughly at her arm as she struggled to break free. A shout distracted her attacker.

'Yer broke me bottle,' yelled Curly.

The tattooed man turned. 'Shut yer noise.'

Annie squirmed and wriggled till she managed to escape for a moment, but the tattooed man put his foot out and she crashed to the ground. She could hear shouting and yelling, and guessed a scuffle was taking place, but bit by bit it faded away . . .

Her body ached. The pain in her head was blinding. She could hear herself moaning, then felt someone wiping her face. There was a damp, dirty smell mingled with whisky. Fear was gripping her. Someone was coughing. She didn't want to open her eyes. Where had those men brought her? And what had they done to her?

'Yer all right now, gel,' came a woman's soft whisper. 'Yer safe wiv us.'

Slowly Annie opened her eyes. It was dark. Gradually, as she became accustomed to the light from a small candle sitting in a tin lid in the far corner of the room, she managed to make out a scruffy white-haired old woman bending over her.

'Where am I?'

'Shh, don't worry. Yer all right now.' The old woman pushed her hair from her eyes.

Annie realized she was lying on the floor. She tried to sit up, but her head felt as if it would explode, and it forced her down again. 'Me head.' She put her hand to the back of her head. It felt warm and sticky.

'Yer've 'ad a nasty fall,' came the voice again.

Annie was frightened and began to cry.

'Don't cry. I told yer, yer going to be all right. Me gel's gorn ter git 'elp.'

'Where am I?'

'At our place.'

'Where's that?' She lay back trying to recall earlier events. Suddenly it came back to her and she quickly sat up. 'Those men,' she screamed.

'Shh, yer'll wake the kids.'

Annie took her arm and shook it. 'Those men. They tried to . . . Did they . . . ?'

'Na. Me boy stopped 'em. Bloody dirty toe-rags. Worse 'en animals some men are.'

Annie laid back and began to cry. Despite the warmth of the night she was shivering.

'Just you lay still till Daisy gits back.'

'I've got to get home. Me mum and dad will be worried stiff.'

'Yer, well Daisy's gorn ter see if she can git someone ter 'elp yer. She's gorn ter the pub. She should be back soon.'

Annie lay back feeling weak and exhausted. At the moment she didn't have the strength to argue. She began fingering the bedclothes and discovered they were sacking. She glanced round the room. There wasn't much furniture, just a couple of wooden boxes and two chairs. As her eyes became accustomed to the feeble light she could see two small bundles in the corner. One of the bundles moved and began to whimper.

The old woman went over and picked it up. She gently rocked and soothed it with soft words. 'Ain't 'ad much ter eat terday,' she said to Annie.

Annie sat up. 'Where is this place?'

'The basement in the warehouse. It's empty, so nobody bothers us.'

'How long have you lived here?'

'Months. Before little Becky was born.' She sat on one of the chairs.

'Months, in here?' Despite feeling so forlorn, Annie was beginning to be intrigued. 'How many children have you got?'

'Four in all. There's Joey, that's me boy, 'e's the eldest,' she said with a smile. 'Then there's Daisy, then Joan, and last ter come was Becky.' She tried to stifle a cough.

'Have you got a husband?'

'Na, the sod left me when 'e found out Becky was on the way.'

Suddenly the light from the candle flickered as a draught from the door being pushed open caught it and two men walked in. Annie could see the outline of a third person behind them. She shuddered, involuntarily backing away.

''Allo, Grace,' said the first man. He was the older of the two. 'This is a right turn-up fer the books, ain't it? I'd like ter git me 'ands on those buggers, I'd cut their bleeding cobblers off.' He turned to Annie. 'All right, love. Me name's Chalky, Chalky White.'

''E'll look after yer,' said the other man, who Annie realized was still only a boy. She guessed he must be Joey. He giggled and screwed up his round, shiny face. 'Me and Daisy bashed those blokes. We 'ad big sticks, then I picked yer up and brought yer 'ome. Yer ever ser light.' He looked down shyly at his overlarge boots, and gently kicked one against the other.

'Thank you,' whispered Annie.

'What's yer name?' asked Joey.

'Annie.' She looked up at Chalky White. 'Can you help me get home?'

'Course, love, that's what I'm 'ere for. Got me car outside. Where d'yer live?'

'Albert Mews.'

'Where's that?'

'Near Jamaica Road.'

'I told Chalky I fort yer was looking fer me.' A young girl wearing dirty white plimsolls moved from behind the others. 'I remembered you, you gave me sixpence once. Don't often git sixpence.'

'Yes I did.' Annie began to cry.

'Don't cry, miss, yer all right now.' The young girl crouched down beside Annie.

'It's shock,' said Chalky. He turned to Grace. 'They didn't . . . Did they?'

'Na. When Daisy and Joey 'eard 'er screaming they rushed out just as the big one tripped 'er up. Be all accounts she fell and 'it 'er 'ead.' Grace began coughing again.

The young girl got up and went to her mother. 'Don't get yourself in a state, Mum. It always makes yer cough.'

Her mother pushed her away. 'Leave me be. I'll be all right.'

'Yer,' said Joey. 'We bashed those blokes and made 'em run. Then I picked 'er up. She's as light as a fevver.'

'Good job we've got some big sticks,' said Daisy.

'Right, come on, love, I'll give yer 'and.'

Daisy and Chalky White helped Annie to her feet. She began crying again. 'I don't know what me mum and dad's going to say.'

'I'll come in and tell 'em what 'appened, if yer like.'

'Would you, would you mind?' she sniffed.

'Course not.'

When they reached the door Annie turned. 'Thank you, Joey.' She brushed her tears away with her hand. 'I'm sure my dad will be over to thank you as well.'

Joey grinned.

Annie was still crying as they made their way along a dark passage.

'Mind, there's six steps 'ere,' said Daisy.

Annie gripped Chalky White's hand as she inched her way up the dark steps. She quickly looked around her when they were outside, half expecting the four drunks to pounce on them. Joey, who was following them as they made their way to the car, sensed her reaction. 'Don't worry, they've gorn. Annie, will yer be coming to see our Daisy again?'

'I don't know.'

'I won't let 'em 'it yer again, Annie.' He laughed. 'It was me what picked yer up and carried yer indoors.'

'Yes. Thank you, Joey,' she said as Chalky helped her into the car.

'Don't mind Joey, miss,' said Daisy, ''E's a little bit—' she put her finger to her forehead – 'you know?'

Annie looked at Chalky White as he started the engine. 'He's a good lad, though, finks the world of the family. See yer later, Daisy,' he called to her through the car window.

Annie waved as they set off for home, and her father's wrath. She would never be able to make him see things her way now about joining Rose and Mr Hobbs.

'Have you known that family long?' asked Annie.

142

'Yer. D'yer know they ain't got nuffink, but they're as good as gold. Wouldn't 'arm a flea, or pinch anyfink. They just about manage ter live. Joey gives me a 'and with the glasses, and little Daisy looks after the kids. Their mother Grace is dying yer know. She's got consumption, poor cow. I do what I can, but they're a proud lot. Don't like charity.'

Annie felt the tears well up inside her again. 'I'd like to come back to see them, but how do I get in?'

'If you call in one of the broken windows, someone will 'ear you. There's a few families down there. All of 'em 'ard up.'

'Why are you so kind to them?'

'Grace's old man was a distant cousin of mine. 'E's run off with another woman. I'd do more if I could, but me old woman can't stand 'em, and it's 'er pub.'

Annie couldn't believe relations could act this way to each other, and she thought of Aunt Ivy and Roy. 'You've got to stop here. We have to walk down the Mews.'

He helped her from the car, and they silently made their way along the dark Mews to Rodgers' grocer's, and to her parents.

Chapter 15

It wasn't until Annie reached her door that she realized she had lost her handbag.

'Don't worry,' said Chalky when she told him. 'If Daisy or Joey find it, they'll git it back ter yer.'

'I'll have to knock, I haven't got a key.' With a trembling hand she reached up for the knocker, and almost immediately the door was flung open.

'Where the hell have you been? Do you know what time it is, young lady?'

Annie flung herself into her father's arms and wept.

'Annie, oh, Annie, we've been so worried about you.' Her mother was close behind and trying to put her arms round her daughter. They were a tight group locked together on the doorstep.

'Is that whisky I can smell?' asked her father, pushing her away. 'You been out drinking?'

'If you let me come in, I fink I can explain,' said Chalky White, moving tentatively into view.

'Who the bloody hell are you? And what do you mean keeping my daughter out till this hour?' shouted Mr Rodgers.

'Shh, Ben, keep your voice down,' said his wife.

'Dad, it wasn't Mr White,' sobbed Annie.

'Let them get in, Ben. We were just about to go round to the police station,' Mrs Rodgers said over her shoulder as they made their way up the stairs.

In the light of the kitchen her parents couldn't disguise the look of horror when they saw Annie.

'My God. Have you seen yourself? Look at the state you're in.

Who did this to you? Just let me get my hands on them,' said her father, shooting Chalky a filthy look.

'What happened, love?' asked her mother, her voice faltering.

'I'll just get a hankie,' sniffed Annie as she went to her bedroom.

'Would you like a cup of tea?' called her mother after her.

'Please.' Annie sat on the bed and studied herself in the long mirror on the wardrobe door. Her face and clothes were dirty, her stockings torn, and her knee grazed. She had lost her cardigan and her handbag, and the smell of whisky made her feel sick. She gently touched her face; the bruise was just beginning to show. Her hair was a mess. She went to her dressing-table and, picking up a comb, winced as she gently tried to pull it through the tangles. Her head was sore, and the hair at the back was matted with blood. She didn't want them to see her like this. She would stay here till the morning. How could she tell them what had happened? Her father would go mad. What if those men had . . . ? How would she know? Would she feel any different? As the tears began to flow, her father's angry voice carried up the stairs.

'Now I want an explanation – fast.'

Annie moved closer to the door. She didn't want Mr White to be involved: he had been kind enough to bring her home and now he was getting the blame. She had to go down and face them.

'What d'you mean . . . ?'

'Dad, it wasn't anything to do with Mr White,' she said, pushing open the kitchen door.

'He was there, wasn't he?' he snapped.

Annie slumped in the chair, almost too weary to argue.

The kettle began whistling loudly. 'Ben, can't this wait till the morning?' Mrs Rodgers asked her husband, her voice tense.

'No, it can't. Well, I'm waiting.' He looked from one to the other as he angrily paced the room.

Chalky White sat on the edge of the chair and twirled his cloth cap round. 'I wasn't there when it 'appened, I only brought yer daughter 'ome. It seems a lot o' drunks set about 'er.'

'What?' Mrs Rodgers spun round from the sink. She put the teapot she was filling on the wooden draining-board and rushed across to where Annie was sitting. She fell to her knees. 'Did they hurt you, love?'

Annie had her nose buried in her handkerchief. 'Not really, Mum,' she sniffed. 'But I was ever so frightened.'

'And where did all this take place?' asked Mr Rodgers quietly. He had stopped pacing, and now stood with his back to them, staring at the brass fire-screen.

'Off Whitechapel Road,' said Chalky.

He turned round. 'The bloody Salvation Army,' he said slowly. 'I knew it. I knew something like this would happen. What did I tell you, young lady? Trying to look after those down-and-outs, and that's all the thanks you get.'

'But Dad, it wasn't any of them.'

'Ah, so you know them all, do you?' Her father sank into his chair. 'That's it, my girl. That's the last time you go over there, and I forbid you to see the Hobbs again. It's their fault this has happened.'

Annie's head shot up. 'But, Dad . . .'

'How come you found Annie?' he asked Chalky.

'It was the Murphys. They 'eard 'er screaming and they rushed out and 'elped 'er.'

'What else did they help themselves to? I see you've lost your handbag.'

'Dad, they didn't take it. I dropped it. They are very kind people.' Annie began crying again.

'Look, I know it ain't none a my business, but she's 'ad a rough time. Why don't yer let 'er git ter bed and let 'er tell yer all about it in the morning?'

'I think that's a good idea, Mr White. Thank you for bringing Annie home. Ben. See Mr White to the door.' Mrs Rodgers' tone was forceful.

Mr Rodgers opened the kitchen door. 'I'll see you out. Sorry if . . .'

'That's all right, mate. If I 'ad a daughter, I'd be upset. Bye, Annie.' He gave her a slight wave.

'Bye, and thank you,' she replied.

'Come on now, love,' her mum said gently. 'Off to bed with you. We can sort your father out in the morning.'

'Thanks, Mum.'

In the peace and quiet of her bedroom, Annie lay thinking of the evening's events. If only she hadn't been so stupid, none of this would have happened. Would her father stop her from joining the Salvation Army? She knew more and more now that she wanted to help people like the Murphys. Despite all their problems they seemed . . . Her mind was wandering and her eyes became heavy.

'Cup of tea, love?' Annie opened her eyes as her mother pulled back the curtains. 'It's a lovely day.'

The sound of church bells ringing loud and clear came through the open window.

'Dad up?'

'Yes. I'll bring you up a bowl and a kettle of hot water, then you can have a nice wash in private.'

Annie hated having to wash in the kitchen sink. If she and Will had got a house in Carshalton they would have had a bathroom. Annie sighed at those fond memories. And this wouldn't have happened if Will had been here. She sipped her tea. How much should she tell her parents? How would she know if she had been . . . ? Annie shuddered at the thought of those old men doing things like that to her. She must go over to see Daisy today, and find out what happened after she got knocked out. Tears began to well up again.

The door opened and her mother put the kettle and bowl on the floor. 'Come down when you're ready. Dad said that while I'm doing the dinner he'd take you for a ride. That's if you want to go out.'

'Thanks,' said Annie slipping out of bed. 'I won't be long.'

'That's a nasty bruise,' said her father as Annie sat at the break-fast table. 'How did that happen?'

Annie took a piece of toast. 'These drunks came up and wanted me to have a drink with them.' She looked up at her mother. 'They had a bottle of whisky.'

'We could smell that. Do you want the marmalade?' asked her mother.

Annie nodded. 'They tried to force me to drink it, and it went over my frock. Then they got mad and started to chase me.'

'I hope you didn't encourage them,' said Mr Rodgers.

'Ben, that's a dreadful thing to say,' her mother scolded.

'Well, you know what these young girls are like. Anyway, I want to know how come you didn't catch your tram? Where were you off to?'

Annie looked at him. 'I was trying to find a friend. A young girl – her name's Daisy. It was she and her brother who found me and looked after me. Oh, Mum, you should see the way they live. Her mother's got consumption, her husband's left her, and she's got four kids. Joey's a bit backward but ever so kind, and there's two babies.'

'Where do they live?' asked her mother.

'In a basement in an old warehouse, off Whitechapel. They've got nothing, but they're ever so proud. Dad, could we go over there this morning and take them a few bits.' Annie was beginning to get very enthusiastic. 'They haven't any furniture, and they all sleep on the floor. Mum, have we got any old blankets?'

'Well, I don't know. I'll have to have a look.'

'And who says I'm going over there?'

Annie looked at her father for a while, then stood up. As she pushed her chair under the table she said, 'Well, if you don't take me, I'll go by tram.' And walked defiantly out of the kitchen.

When Annie came back, she had her hat on. 'I'm going down to the shop to weigh out twopennorth of broken biscuits,' she announced, glancing at her father who was reading the newspaper. 'I don't suppose those little 'ens have ever had a biscuit in their lives. Don't worry, I'll pay for them,' she added. 'And I'm going to take a couple of candles as well.'

'How does the mother do her cooking and washing?' asked her mother.

'I don't know. I'll be able to tell you more after I've been in the daylight. Don't worry, Mum, I'll be home in time for dinner.'

'Annie.' Her father's voice was strong. He folded the newspaper. 'Looks like you've made up your mind. I'll take you, but only if you promise that this'll be the last we hear of it.'

Annie was across the room in one bound. She hugged her father. 'Thanks, Dad.'

He gently pushed her away. 'If I take you I may be able to find out more about last night's incident. You see, I don't think you've told us everything.'

Annie looked away.

'This doesn't change what I said last night. I still don't approve of you mixing with that Sally Army lot.'

'I'll get the biscuits.'

'While you're down there, get the kids some sweets from me,' called her father as she left the room.

A big smile spread across her face as she hurried down the stairs. She knew her father wouldn't be cross with her for long.

Annie was leaning forward in the van. 'It's down here, Dad.'

Mr Rodgers followed Annie's instructions as they bumped over the cobbles. 'It's a dead end!' he exclaimed, stopping the van.

'Yes, I know.' Annie looked around her. In the bright early morning sunlight everything looked different. She couldn't believe this was where she was trapped last night. There was nothing frightening about the tall buildings now, especially sitting next to her father. 'Look, there's a door.' Annie jumped out of the van.

'I don't know why you get yourself so involved,' grumbled her father, following her. 'Remember what I said last night?'

Annie ignored him and ran across the road. 'Daisy, Joey,' she called banging on the door. 'It's me, Annie.'

Her father came and stood beside her. 'It's a right dump down here, and what a stink. Bloody flies everywhere.' He waved his hand in the air. 'Spitalfields market's round here somewhere, and Petticoat Lane's over there. You sure someone lives here?' He looked up at some of the high, dirty windows that were still intact.

'Yes.'

'Looks as dead as the grave, filthy hole,' he said, walking away.

Annie looked at the rubbish heaped up against the wall. A gentle

150

breeze lifted a sheet of newspaper and blew it across the road.

'Can't see anybody. How much longer are we going to hang about here?' He put his shoulder to the door and pushed. 'It's stuck.'

A look of anguish flitted across her face. 'There should be some-one down there.' With the flat of her hand she rubbed a piece of glass that remained in a window, and peered in. Annie called through a broken window. 'Daisy, Joey, it's me.'

'Come on, let's get home.'

'No. We've got to wait a bit longer.' Annie was beginning to panic. She didn't want to lose this chance of finding them.

'You sure you've got the right place? They all look the same in the dark.'

'Yes, Dad.' Annie was very sure. She looked across the road, and could almost feel those men pushing her against that wall. Her hand knew every bump, and there was the broken whisky bottle lying in the gutter, a grim reminder of her ordeal.

Her father walked back to the van and climbed in. 'Come on, Annie, there's no point in hanging around here.'

'We could go and try to find the pub Mr White's wife owns,' said Annie, walking towards him.

'What's the point? If you ask me I reckon they've done a runner. Could be they're wanted by the police.'

'Don't talk daft, Dad.'

'Watch yourself. I don't want any cheek from you.' He started the engine. 'Come on, get in.'

Reluctantly Annie climbed in. Where were they? Why didn't they answer her? Her father turned the van round and they began to trundle down towards the main road.

'Stop, Dad. Quick, stop.'

He slammed on the brakes. 'What the . . . ? What's the matter?'

Annie was clambering out of the van. 'Look, look over there, it's Daisy and Joey.' Before she dashed across the road, Annie noted her father drape his arms over the steering wheel. She could almost hear him sigh as he watched her go off.

'Annie. Look, Dais, it's Annie.' Joey's face lit up as Annie ran towards them. 'What yer doing 'ere?'

'I've come to see you. I've been down there,' she pointed behind her. 'And I called, but nobody came. Where have you been?'

'I've bin to get Joey, 'e's been 'elping Chalky,' said Daisy. 'I likes 'im ter be out the missis' way before she comes down. She 'its 'im round the 'ead, and I don't like it.'

'Look, Annie, I gotta a penny, a whole penny.' He held out his open hand to reveal his treasure.

''E 'elps Chalky wiv the crates on Sunday mornings.'

Annie smiled. Daisy only came up to Joey's chest, yet here she was protecting him. 'How old are you, Daisy?'

'Twelve, I fink.'

'Do you go to school?'

'Na.'

'What about the school board man?'

She laughed. ''E ain't caught me yet. 'Ere, yer ain't gonner shop me, are yer?' There was a note of anxiety in her young voice.

Annie shook her head, at a loss for words. 'I've brought you some biscuits, and sweets.'

Joey began dancing up and down. 'Cor, fanks, Annie. Sweets, we don't git many of them, do we, Dais?'

'No. It's ever ser kind of yer, Annie.'

'That's all right. Are you going home now?'

'Yer. We've got some soup fer dinner. Chalky gave me mum a couple o' bob the other day, and she went over the market and got a lot a bones and some veg. It's good.'

'How does your mother cook?'

'She's got a primus, but sometimes she ain't got enough fer paraffin. It's the winter that's the worse, and now we've got little Becky . . .'

Annie looked anxious.

'Not ter worry, we manage,' she said cheerfully.

'What about water?'

'There's a tap we all use.'

'Can I walk with you?'

'If yer want.'

'I'll just tell me dad.' Annie hurried over and told her father she was going just a little way up the road with them.

152

'Well, don't be long.'

'Pass the bag please,' she instructed.

The brown paper bag of goodies, and the half-a-crown her father had put in an envelope, was duly handed through the window.

As they walked along Annie found herself asking Daisy and Joey all kinds of questions; she couldn't understand how they would survive in their hand-to-mouth existence. Daisy's biggest worry was her mother. She said she took the baby with her when she could, as she always managed to get more money that way. Her mother got angry with her for begging but, as she said, at least the kids didn't go hungry for long.

When they had nearly reached the place where she'd been attacked, Annie plucked up courage. 'Daisy. Were those men doing anything to me when you found me?'

'Na. The big one was just tripping yer up when we went fer 'im with our sticks.'

Annie felt her stomach lurch. She'd heard Joey tell Chalky White that was what had happened but until she heard it from Daisy she couldn't be sure. 'Thank you.'

'It was me what carried yer in, Annie,' said Joey.

'Yes, I know. Thank you, Joey. How do you get in? There's no handle on the door.'

'We go frough the winder, look.'

They stopped in front of a broken window. Daisy put her hand through and unlatched it.

'But I came out through a door,' said Annie, looking around her.

'Yer, well, the door's down there, but we keep it locked from the inside in case anybody tries ter frow us out,' said Daisy confidently.

Annie was amazed at this girl's worldliness. 'Whose place is it?'

'Dunno. Been empty fer years, so the others say.'

'How many of you live here?'

'Dunno. We all keep to our own bit. Don't like some of 'em we've got 'ere. Bloody robbers some of 'em are. We've gotter go now,' she said hurriedly. 'Fanks fer these.' Daisy waved the bag above her head and, climbing through the window, disappeared inside.

'Bye, Annie,' said Joey.

153

'I'll come again,' Annie called after them. She stood for a while looking at the empty window. She wanted to follow them but somehow had the feeling she wouldn't be very welcome.

Chapter 16

All the way home, Annie was deep in thought. She needed someone to talk to, someone to get advice from. If only Will was here – or even Lil: she'd know what to do and say.

'You're quiet,' said her father.

'I was thinking.'

'Well, I hope you're satisfied now that you've seen them again. If you ask me,' he added smugly, 'they didn't seem all that pleased to see you.'

'Oh, but they were. Dad? Do you think the Salvation Army could help them?'

'How should I know?'

'I'll have to ask Rose when I see her next.'

'What did I say last night about that? I don't want you to have anything more to do with them.'

Annie stared out of the van window – there was no point in arguing with her father at this stage. But her mind was made up; she knew she was going to join them. She knew this was what she wanted to do, to help people, to feel needed.

'Everything all right?' asked her mother as they walked in.

'Yes, we found them,' said Annie.

'Well, what did they say?'

'Not a lot really.'

'Oh,' said her mother. 'Did they like the things you gave them?'

'They didn't say.'

'That's not very grateful of them.'

'They didn't get a chance to open the bag.'

'Oh, I see. Sit down, dinner's ready. Did you find out any more about last night, Ben?'

'No. It's a right dump round there, and there wasn't anybody around to ask. I'll just wash me hands, then I'll be ready to carve.'

Dinner was a quiet affair for a change, and when it was finished Annie told them she was going for a walk.

Outside, she wandered along with her thoughts. It was a warm sunny afternoon and she felt at ease; the events of last night seemed years away. If only Will could have been there. She sighed. She missed him so much. She could have done with Lil being around now: they could have had a good old chat. But now Lil was living permanently in the pub and always working on a Sunday there was no one Annie could talk to. She felt sad and alone. She knew she had made the right decision. She had to do something with her life. She looked at her watch. Rose would still be in Sunday school, but that didn't stop Annie from going in that direction.

'Hello, Annie,' Rose greeted her as she walked in.

''Ere, miss, yer missed it,' said one young boy as he raced past Annie.

She quickly stepped to one side as the rest of the children lost no time in trying to get out, pushing and shoving each other in order to get through the mission's small door as fast as possible. 'They seem in a hurry to leave,' Annie remarked.

'Yes. Most of them are here under protest. They are sent here to be out the way while dad has his after-dinner sleep. Of course he's probably been in the pub right up till lunch-time. What can I do for you?' Rose was busy collecting books all the while she was talking. 'Was everything all right last night?'

Annie sat down on the hard wooden chair. 'Rose. I need to talk to you.'

'Carry on, then. You don't mind if I finish this, do you?'

'I'd rather have your full attention.'

'Oh dear, that sounds rather ominous.' She sat beside Annie, still clutching the books to her chest.

'I met that young girl again, the one I saw outside the mission on New Year's Eve.'

'Oh yes. That was nice for you.'

156

'Rose, last night – on my way home – I was attacked by some drunks.'

Rose put the books on the chair next to her. 'Oh, Annie, I'm very sorry to hear that. What did they do? Are you all right?'

Annie nodded.

'I did notice the bruise on your face, and I didn't like to ask. Where did this happen?'

'Down a road off of Whitechapel.'

'What on earth were you doing down there?'

'While I was waiting for my tram, I saw Daisy, that's the girl's name, carrying Becky. She went down this road, and these drunks went down there as well, and I thought she might be in danger, so I ran after her.'

'You had better tell me all about it.'

Annie went into detail about what had happened, and about the Murphys, and how she had been back this morning, and her father's reaction to it all.

When Annie finished, Rose sat back. 'I think you are very brave and, I might add, a little foolish. Fancy going to a place like that late at night, and in the dark, and on your own. Especially knowing you would miss your last tram.'

'I must admit it does seem daft now. But at least I found out about Daisy and the rest of the family. Rose,' she said eagerly, 'do you think the Salvation Army could help them?'

'Would they want to be helped?'

Annie too sat back. 'I don't know. I think so.'

'You would be surprised how many don't. Even those in really dire straits.'

'But I thought . . .'

'They are always afraid the family will be split up, and for some that is too much of a price to pay for being made comfortable. Some are proud too, and don't want charity.'

Annie was stunned. 'I don't believe they would turn help away.'

'Well, the best thing we can do is find them, and try to persuade them.'

'Would you come with me?'

'Yes, of course. I can see you are going to be a very caring

157

member. Now come along, I must get on. We have a service tonight.'

'I'm sorry to have taken up a lot of your time, but now Will's gone I don't have anyone to talk to.'

Rose patted her hand. 'I will always be a sister to you, and any time you feel you want a chat, just turn up.'

'Thank you, Rose.'

Annie's steps were a lot lighter as she made her way home.

'I'm going to a meeting tonight,' she said, clearing away the tea things.

'Annie, what did I say?' Her father's voice was loud.

'Don't start on that again, Ben,' said Mrs Rodgers. 'If she wants to go, let her.'

Annie felt angry and stifled. Was this going to be the pattern of her life now? She knew she had to make a stand. 'I don't have anywhere else to go, or anyone to go out with now. Perhaps you'd rather I went and found Lil in the pub?'

'Ben,' said her mother. 'Just leave her alone.'

'That's what you say now. It would have been a very different story if she had been out with . . .'

'Dad, please let me try and live my life.'

Her father looked sad. 'It's just that I don't want . . . Well, anything to happen to you.'

'It won't,' she promised and, knowing she had won that argument, left the room.

After the meeting, Rose told her they were going to help the Murphys. Annie was overjoyed.

'When are you going to see them?'

'I've got to arrange it. It will probably be sometime in the week.'

'I'll go over tomorrow evening and tell them. I'll take Lil with me.'

'What about your father? We don't want to upset him.'

'He won't mind if Lil's with me.'

Annie felt like skipping all the way home, she was so happy.

Lil wasn't too pleased at the thought of missing their pictures, but quickly agreed to go along with Annie after she told her what had happened on Saturday night, and how the Murphys had looked after her. So, armed with another bag of food and titbits, they set off for Whitechapel.

Annie looked about her as they made their way to where she knew the Murphys lived.

'In there?' said Lil in disgust as Annie shouted through the window. 'They live in there?'

'Yes.' She walked restlessly up and down.'They should answer. I'm going to go through the window.' She put her arm through the broken pane and undid the latch.

Lil laughed. 'Yer ain't gonner climb frew there? Christ, it looks worse than our place, and that's saying somefink.'

Annie pushed open the window. 'Give me a push up.'

''Ere, Annie, I don't fink yer better. What if there's a lot a dirty old men in there?'

Annie too looked a little apprehensive. 'Daisy! Joey!' she called again.

'What d'yer want?' A voice came from out of the dark.

'Joey, it's me, Annie.'

Joey leapt forward. 'Annie, I told Dais it was you. Can yer git frew?'

'Yes, give me a hand.'

Annie turned to help Lil.

'Who's she?' asked Joey aggressively, and started backing away.

'It's all right, this is my friend Lil.'

''Allo, Joey,' said Lil with one leg through the window. 'Give us a 'and, mate.'

When she spoke the look on his face changed. ''Allo, Lil, yer come ter see us then?' he beamed.

'Yer, if I can git me leg frew this winder. Ain't yer got a door?'

Joey was jumping up and down laughing. 'Course we 'ave, but you can git frew that, yer only skinny.' He took her hand.

'Fanks, Joey.'

'Come on, this way.'

Despite the rays of bright evening sunlight touching the top of the building, inside the chinks of light cast eerie shadows. The dust danced merrily in the shafts of light as they strained through the boarded-up windows and hit the ground.

They stood for a while to let their eyes get accustomed to the gloom, then they fell in behind Joey who led them through a maze of dark corridors. Lil was hanging on to Annie's hand.

'What a stink. Smells like the lavs at the pub. Any rats down 'ere?'

'Yer. Sometimes we 'ear 'em squeaking and running away from us. It's their beady little eyes I don't like,' said Joey cheerfully.

Annie felt Lil shudder. 'I don't fink I like it down 'ere. We gotter go much further?'

'Na, just round this corner.' Joey pushed open a door. 'I told yer I 'eard Annie, didn't I?' he said, bounding into the room.

Annie immediately recognized the room they walked into. It was hot and stuffy. Her gaze wandered around, taking in a window high up which let in at least some light. In the far corner, which Annie guessed was used as the kitchen, stood a primus stove, a kettle on top. Next to it a wooden box doubled as a table and a cupboard and Annie could see a few crocks and a saucepan inside. The two youngest were sitting on the floor, Mrs Murphy on a chair behind them. 'Hello, Mrs Murphy, I've brought you some bits.'

'Fanks. That's real kind of yer, gel. The kids liked the biscuits yesterday. Who's she?' she asked as Lil followed Annie.

'My friend Lil.'

'Did Annie tell yer I was the one what picked 'er up and carried 'er indoors?' said Joey grinning. 'She's as light as a fevver.' He brushed his dark hair away from his eyes.

'Yes, she did,' said Lil.

'Dais said yer got 'ome all right then.' Mrs Murphy sat on the chair as her frail body was racked with a bout of coughing.

'Yes, thank you. Can I get you a drink of water?'

She ran her thin bony hands over her face which was wreathed in perspiration. She shook her head. 'I'll be all right in a tick,' she gasped.

'Mrs Murphy, I belong to the Salvation Army, and I've been having a word . . .'

Her head shot up. 'We don't want any of them poking their noses round 'ere. 'Ere, what did yer tell 'em?' Her face was full of anger.

160

'Well, nothing.'

'Did yer tell 'em where we live?'

'We . . . Not exactly.'

'I don't want 'em round 'ere. Yer know they'll take the kids away from me, and young Joey could finish up in some 'ome. Go on, git out o' 'ere!'

'I'm sure they wouldn't do anything like . . .'

Mrs Murphy gave a false laugh. 'I can see yer don't know nuffink about 'em.'

Daisy looked at Annie, her face full of hurt. 'I fought yer was our friend.'

'I am, Daisy.' Annie glanced across at Joey who was sitting on the stone floor playing with Joan. He quickly looked away. 'I'm sure you've got it all wrong,' Annie was getting upset. 'They only want to help.'

'We don't need their 'elp,' said Daisy, picking up Becky.

'I've got two young sisters,' said Lil, trying to ease the tension. 'How old is this one?'

'Becky's nearly a year.' A proud smile filled Daisy's face as Lil tickled the baby under her chin causing her pale face to break into a wide grin.

'Go on, shove orf, the pair of yer,' ordered Mrs Murphy.

Annie was distressed at their attitude. 'Please, let me help you. You can't spend another winter living here. Not with your chest.'

'We can manage.'

'What about Daisy and Joey's schooling? They should go to school.'

'Yer, well, I'm their mother and I'll do what I like.'

'But, Mrs Murphy, it's against the law.'

'I fink yer better mind yer own business, young lady, and don't go poking it inter other people's affairs. We can do without your sort round 'ere. Now go on, push off. Sling yer bleeding 'ook.'

'But, Mrs Murphy . . .'

Mrs Murphy began coughing again.

'I fink yer better go, Annie,' said Daisy in a concerned tone. 'Yer only upsetting Mum.'

'All right.'

'And don't go bringing any of those school board men back 'ere, or the bloody interfering Sally Army,' shouted Mrs Murphy as she fought for breath.

'Come on, Annie, yer ain't doing any good 'ere,' said Lil taking her arm and pulling her towards the door.

'But, Lil, they shouldn't be living like this.'

Lil edged her along the dark corridor. 'Well, they ain't gonner fank yer fer 'elping them. They're frightened ter death of being split up.'

'Why couldn't we go frew the door?' Lil grumbled as they climbed back through the broken window.

'I can't remember where it is, I was too upset. Do you really think they would split them up?'

'How the 'ell would I know. You're the so-called expert on those sorta fings.'

'But that woman's ill, and she needs help.'

'Yer, and I bet she ain't all that old.' Lil lent against the wall and took a packet of cigarettes from her handbag. 'Christ, I hope I don't ever finish up like that.'

Deep in thought, Annie didn't answer. 'I'll ask Rose tomorrow.'

'Come on, let's get a tram,' said Lil. 'I knew we should 'ave gorn ter the pictures ternight.'

The following evening Annie told Rose about her encounter with the Murphys. 'Would they take the children away from her?' she demanded.

'It depends how ill the mother is.'

Annie shrugged her shoulders in despair. 'I feel so helpless. All I wanted to do was help them.'

'Look, you can show me where they live. Perhaps if I have a word with them and try to reassure them, we may manage to get them round to our way of thinking.'

Annie brightened up. 'I hope so. When is the best time for you?'

'How about Friday after school. Would your father let you leave the shop early?'

Annie looked doubtful. 'Can't you make it before then?'

'No, not really.'

Annie resolved to persuade her father once more. 'All right then, I'll see you about four.'

'My father was asking about your uniform? He wants your measurements. You can pay for it weekly if you like.'

'That would be a help. I don't think I could ask Dad for the money, not after Saturday night.'

On Friday, sharp at four, Annie was waiting outside the school for Rose.

'What did your father have to say about this?'

'I told him you and Lil were the only people I had to talk to now. I think I made him feel sorry for me,' she laughed. 'Besides, I love going to the mission, and I promised him I would come straight home.'

'That's good, we don't want to lose someone like you.'

Annie was restlessly looking out of the tram's window. 'This is it,' she said when she spotted the stop in the distance at last. When they alighted, Annie found herself once more walking down that familiar road. 'We have to call through this window,' she said eagerly. 'Daisy, Joey.'

'Can they hear us?'

'Yes, all the sounds seem to echo when you're inside.'

Rose walked a way up the road and looked up at the old building. 'It's a disgrace. People shouldn't have to live in these conditions.'

Annie called again, then turning to Rose said, 'They may be out. We could get through the window.'

Rose looked a little apprehensive. 'Through there?'

Annie nodded.

'Well, all right, but you'll have to give me a hand.'

Annie smiled at Rose as she panted with exertion, hauling herself up on the windowsill and revealing the tops of her lisle stockings held up with white elastic garters. 'Is there a big drop the other side?' she asked tentatively over her shoulder, as she gingerly put one leg through.

'Not very,' said Annie.

Once inside, they made their way along to where Annie knew the Murphys lived. She tapped on the door. There was no answer.

She tapped again, and pushed open the door. The room was deserted. Annie ran to the corner: the primus had gone and the makeshift cupboard was empty. Annie turned on Rose. 'They've gone. They've gone, and it's all my fault.' Her tears began to fall. 'I've made them go away.'

Rose put her arm round Annie's shoulders. 'It's not your fault. Somebody would have made them move on at some time. This place must be due for demolition soon, and they would have had to go then.'

'Where could they have gone?'

'What about the other rooms in this place? Could they have moved into one of those?' asked Rose as she wandered around.

'I don't know. Daisy did say that a few people were living in some of them.'

'We could take a look.'

Carefully they made their way up the stairs, and began knocking on closed doors. In the rooms that were occupied they were either met with a mouthful of abuse from the occupants, or told politely to get out and mind their own business.

'Well, we're certainly not having any luck here,' said Rose. 'Do the Murphys have anyone they could go to?'

Annie shook her head.

'What about the man who brought you home, he might know where they've gone?'

Annie blew her nose. 'Chalky White, yes he might know. He could have helped them. His wife owns a pub near here,' said Annie with renewed enthusiasm.

'You don't know where?' asked Rose.

'No,' said Annie sadly. 'I saw them crossing the main road on Sunday. Joey used to work for him and was coming back from the pub.'

'It could have been round Petticoat Lane, then. We'll ask in a few of the local public houses. Most landlords seem to know one another, and what goes on.'

'There's a lot of pubs round here,' said Annie, doubtful again.

'Yes, I know, and standing around here won't get us any answers.

Now, you'll have to give me a leg-up to get through that confounded window again.'

'We'll go through the door, that's if I can find it,' said Annie, their feet echoing loudly as they hurried down the stairs.

Once they'd succeeded in making their way outside they headed in the direction of the nearest pub. Although the pubs had only just opened, inside there were plenty of men sitting around, and Annie could feel the eyes of some of them burning into her. She knew by the raucous laughter they were making comments about them and she hung back as Rose confidently walked up to the bar.

Rose made her way back to Annie a few minutes later. 'We're not going to get any help in here,' she said loudly, glancing over her shoulder at the landlord who was busy wiping down the bar.

"Ere, gel, come and 'ave one wiv us,' shouted a bearded man who was playing dominoes, leaning back in his chair and waving a glass.

'Some other time,' said Rose in a very self-assured manner. 'I should have my uniform on,' she said, as she closed the door. 'That always quietens them down.'

In the next two pubs they were met with the same lack of interest. Nobody knew, or was willing to say if they knew, Chalky White. Annie was beginning to get very despondent. 'What are we going to do?'

'If we don't have any luck tonight, I'll ask my father to inquire about him. That should bring in some sort of response. We'll try this one now, and if we don't have any luck here, we'll head on home.'

Hopefully Annie pushed open the next pub's door. The barman was a shifty-eyed man who wouldn't look them full in the face.

'Wot d'yer want ter drink?'

'Nothing, thank you,' said Rose. 'I would like to know if you know the whereabouts of a Mr White? I believe his friends call him Chalky.'

'Who wants ter know?'

'I do.'

'Why's that? She up the spout?' He nodded towards Annie.

165

'No. I believe his wife owns a public house round here somewhere.'

'Never 'eard of 'im.' He leaned forward. 'And if yer don't want a drink then piss off.'

'Very nice,' said Rose as she swept out the door.

'I'm sure he knows something,' said Annie. 'Is it worth asking him again?'

'No. His kind always ask for money in exchange for information.'

As they walked towards the tram stop, Annie felt more unhappy than ever. 'It's my fault for poking my nose in. The Murphys would never have left if they hadn't been afraid of being split up. All I wanted to do was help them and all I did was harm.'

'Come on, now. I'm sure we will find this Mr White, and then he'll be able to tell us where they are.'

Annie tried to smile. 'Here's our tram.'

Later on, as she related the evening's events to her parents, her father kept his nose buried in his newspaper.

Her mother, however, was concerned. 'I wonder where they've gone?'

'I only wish I knew,' said Annie. 'I'll make the cocoa and then I'm off to bed.'

'Annie.' Her father folded his newspaper and Annie looked at him warily. 'I'll make a few inquiries in our local about that Chalky White feller.'

'Oh, Dad, would you?' She hugged her father. 'I feel so guilty about all this.'

'Well, yes. But don't hold out any hopes. After all, it's the other side of the water, and there's a lot of pubs over there.'

'Yes I know. When you going, Dad?'

'Look, the kettle's boiling,' said her father. 'I've promised someone I'll meet them in the Eagle tomorrow night.'

'Oh yes, Ben, and who's that?'

'Not anyone you know, Mother.'

Annie glanced across at her father as she began stirring the cocoa and she thought he had a funny look on his face as he quickly put his head back in his paper. She couldn't help thinking back to that night when she'd seen him with Bessie.

Chapter 17

Over the next few weeks, and despite the efforts of Mr Hobbs, Rose, and Annie's father, nobody could find out what had happened to the Murphy family.

After a great deal of thought and, much to her father's distress, Annie joined the Salvation Army. But even he had to admit he was pleased at seeing her so happy. She went eagerly to the meetings and to the mission and on the nights she was at Whitechapel she always kept an eye out for Daisy and Joey, hoping that one day she would find them again. When she went into the pubs on a Saturday night to sell the *War Cry*, she constantly observed the men and the landladies, listening out for anything which might lead her to find Chalky White's wife, even hoping to find Chalky himself, but it seemed they had completely disappeared.

Once or twice on a quiet Sunday afternoon she would find herself wandering around outside the disused warehouse, hoping to find someone who lived in there and would help her, but all her efforts were in vain. She worried about the Murphys, and prayed they were safe and well. She felt guilty: She knew it was her fault they had moved on.

Summer was coming to an end, and when Annie stood on the street corner in Peckham on Saturday nights with her fellow officers, she was disturbed at the sight of so many of Oswald Mosley's supporters on the opposite corner, listening to his wild, compelling speeches.

One Sunday morning, Annie was telling her father about them, and how they attracted such large crowds, including a lot of hecklers.

'Bloody blackshirts,' her father muttered when Annie had finished.

'Ben,' said his wife. 'Watch your language.'

'Well, what do you expect? I tell you they're bringing nothing but trouble. Look at what happened over at Cable Street a couple of weeks ago. The paper said that over two thousand of them were on the march. What with him and this Hitler bloke.'

Mrs Rodgers sat at the table. 'You don't think there'll be another war do you, Ben?'

He shook his head. 'Wouldn't like to say. All the young men will have to go if there is another one.'

'What? Even the married ones?' asked Mrs Rodgers.

'I would think so. Oh, by the way, I forgot to tell you. Young Peter Barrett's getting married, so the rent collector told me yesterday.'

Annie looked up.

'That's nice,' said her mother. 'Did he know when?'

'Round about Christmas I think he said, wasn't really paying that much attention.'

'Do you know the girl, Annie?'

'Yes, Mum, her name's Belinda. I have met her.'

'I bet that'll be a posh do,' said her father pushing his chair back. 'I'm just going out to get me paper.'

Annie sat toying with the spoon in the sugar bowl. Although she knew Peter Barrett was engaged to Belinda she was still taken aback, she really didn't think he was the marrying kind. But he was part of her past and she felt nothing for him, him and his silly ways. Her thoughts were still on what her father had said, that there could be another war. She had read about the horrors of the last one and had seen on the newsreels some of the things that were happening in Europe. She didn't want anything like that to spoil her fragile happiness now.

On Monday as usual, Lil came into the shop to wait for Annie to go to the pictures. She looked a little down.

'You all right?' asked Annie as she turned off the lights.

'Yer, I'm OK.'

Lil had changed so much since she left home. Now she was always well dressed, very well made-up, and her hair had been permed and tinted. Her fingernails were long and scarlet, and she always seemed to have plenty of money. 'I 'ad another letter from Georgie terday,' Lil said.

'How is he?'

'Fine. I wish we could go ter Eastbourne and see 'im.'

'I told you I'd go. Just let me know when you can have a Sunday off.'

'That's the trouble – I can't.'

'Not even one?'

'Na, old Bill said no when I asked 'im.'

'Surely he could let you have one Sunday off.'

''E said it'll upset the punters, not 'aving me there.'

Annie smiled. 'It must be nice to be popular.'

'Yer, I suppose it is in a way.' But Lil didn't sound too enthusiastic about it.

They made their way upstairs and Annie began getting ready to go out.

'Annie, d'yer mind if we don't go ter the pictures ternight.'

'Why's that? I thought you liked . . .' Annie noted the look on Lil's face. 'What's wrong? Is your mother ill?'

'She's all right. Let's find a pub, then we can 'ave a good old natter. You can go in a pub, can't yer?'

'I'd rather go to Lyon's.'

'OK,' Lil agreed, surprisingly quietly.

Annie could see Lil wasn't in a chatty mood right now, and once outside they wandered along talking about things in general. They had both changed so much. They didn't laugh and giggle like they used to, and when they arrived at Lyon's they found a corner table and ordered a pot of tea.

'Well, what is it you want to talk about?' asked Annie as the tea arrived.

Lil looked apprehensive and was silent for a while. She took a packet of cigarettes from her handbag and offered Annie one. Annie shook her head. 'Sorry, I forgot,' said Lil, lighting the one that dangled from her full red lips. She puffed the smoke high in the air then looked straight at Annie. 'Annie,' she said in a hushed voice. 'I fink I'm 'aving a baby.'

Annie let the teapot fall from her hand, and as it clattered on to the table a large brown tea strain began spreading over the white cloth. The waitress came hurrying across. 'I'm so sorry,' said Annie. 'It slipped from my hand.'

'Not to worry, miss. I'll get a clean cloth and refill the pot.'

'Thank you. What did you say?' whispered Annie when the waitress was out of earshot.

'You 'eard. I'm 'aving a baby.' She stubbed out her cigarette in the ashtray.

'But . . . Whose is it? Will he marry you?'

The waitress arrived with a clean tablecloth, and began smoothing it out over the table. Lil took her tortoiseshell compact from her handbag, looked in the mirror, ran her tongue over her teeth to remove the lipstick that was on them, and began feverishly powdering her nose. The tray with the fresh tea was put on the table and the waitress walked away. Lil snapped her compact shut.

Annie leaned forward. 'Well, whose is it?'

'I don't know.'

'What?' Annie tried to keep her voice under control. 'You don't know? Lil, how many have you . . . ?' She couldn't finish the sentence.

'I know what yer gonner say. But it's an easy way ter make money.'

Annie's eyes were wide open. 'What?' she repeated. 'You do it for money . . . ?'

Lil smiled. 'I've been dying ter tell yer fer ages, but I knew yer wouldn't approve, specially now yer've gone and joined the Sally Army.'

Annie sat back. 'So why are you telling me now? You want me to get you into one of their homes for unmarried mothers?'

'No fanks! I'll manage. 'Sides, I reckon Georgie would marry me if I wanted 'im to.'

'You wouldn't burden him with someone else's child, would you?'

'Na. 'E's a nice chap but I'm still looking fer someone with a bit o' lolly. How's 'e gonner find work with only one leg?'

'I don't know.' Annie fingered the tea strainer, her thoughts racing.

'You gonner pour out that tea 'fore it gits cold?'

'Yes, sorry.'

'I'm sorry if I shocked yer.' Lil gently touched Annie's hand. 'But I couldn't fink of any other way ter tell yer.'

Annie quickly pulled her hand away. 'So, why are you telling me now?' she repeated.

''Cause I fought you was me friend. I ain't got no one else ter talk to.'

'Sorry.' Annie felt guilty, for she knew how it felt to have no one to confide in. 'How many months are you?'

'Only a couple, I fink.'

'Have you told your mother?'

'Not yet. She'll wonner send me round to that old quack Mrs Tracy, and I don't fancy that. I'll tell her nearer the time.'

'What are you going to do?'

'Look's like I'll be keeping it fer now.'

'You can't, not if you're working.' Annie moved round the table to the chair next to Lil. 'Lil, you must be sensible about this,' she said urgently. 'Let me find out about our home, then perhaps you could have it adopted.'

'I'll fink about it. I'll 'ave ter git meself some bigger frocks, or a wedding ring. I s'pose I could always say I married one of the sailors.'

'You've been with a sailor?'

'Well, they pay well, and they're not 'ere long.'

Annie sat back. 'I can't believe this. All this time I thought you were earning good money singing, instead of that you've been, well . . .'

'I do earn a lot singing,' said Lil tersely. 'But I'd like more, so when this first bloke asked me, and told me what 'e'd pay fer it I fought, why not? After all, Julian used ter git it fer free.'

Anger was beginning to rise in Annie. 'Lil, how could you? This makes you no better than a street-walker.'

'I don't 'ave ter go out looking fer it. It's the blokes that come in the pub.' Lil took another cigarette from the packet she'd left on the table and lit it.

'Oh Lil, how could you?' repeated Annie.

'Yer, well, we all know how you feel about that sorta fing.' She gently tapped the end of the cigarette with her finger.

Annie was staring at Lil. 'How long have you been . . . ?'

'Since I left 'ome. I've got me own key and Bill ain't fussy what time I gits in, just ser long as I'm in the bar at opening time.'

Annie was shaking her head. 'I still can't believe this.'

'Well, I knew yer wouldn't like it, that's why I ain't said nuffink before.'

Annie put her elbows on the table. 'Lil, what are you going to do? Will you lose your job?'

'Shouldn't fink so. I'll bind meself up so I don't show. I'll be able to keep it a secret fer a while anyway. Then, well, anyfink can 'appen. And, Annie, yer will keep it ter yerself, won't yer?'

Annie was still in a state of shock. 'Yes. Yes of course,' she said quickly. 'And you will ask me if you need any help, won't you?'

'Cheer up, Annie, I'll manage. Fancy another pot o' tea?'

Annie nodded, and Lil confidently raised her hand to attract the waitress.

That night sleep wouldn't come for Annie. Why did life have to have so many problems? Curled up in her bed, she gave a little sob. If only Will was alive she would be looking forward to their wedding now, she thought miserably, and instead she was worrying about Lil having a baby and no husband. She turned on her back and stared at the ceiling. Will I ever get married? She wondered hopelessly. Could she ever love anyone else? Other thoughts were milling chaotically around in her head too. Where were the Murphys? Were they all right? And, she wondered again, how would Lil ever manage? Gradually, despite her troubles, sleep overtook her.

The end of the year was almost upon them. On Christmas Eve, at breakfast, Annie upset her mother and father by announcing that she was going to help serve the dinners at Whitechapel on Christmas Day.

'How could you, Annie?' said her mother angrily. 'We always have Christmas dinner together.'

'I'll be home in time for tea,' Annie insisted. Now she thought about it, she didn't like the idea of not being with her family for the Christmas meal either.

'That's not the point. It's dinner I'm concerned with.' Her mother banged the toast on the table.

Her father looked up from his breakfast. 'You could have had the decency to tell us this before now – I've bought a big capon. We could have made do with a small chicken if I'd known.'

'I wasn't sure myself till last night. They asked for volunteers, and before I knew it, I said I'd go.'

'They've got too much of a hold on you, my girl. Pity you don't think as much of your family as you do of them.'

'But, Dad . . .'

Mr Rodgers ignored Annie and, waving a piece of toast at her, continued his tirade. 'I knew this would happen. Didn't I say so right at the beginning of all this nonsense?' He looked at his wife. 'And we know who we have to thank, don't we?'

'Don't start on that again Ben,' her mother said sharply.

'I'm sorry, Dad. I didn't think it would upset you so much.'

Her father ignored her. 'I'm going down to open up. Don't be long, we should be busy today.' Mr Rodgers slammed the kitchen door as he left the room.

Annie sat back and began sipping her tea. 'Mum. Could you make dinner a bit later? Then perhaps if Dad . . .' She leaned forward. 'If he could come and collect me, then I'd be back in time for dinner.'

Her mother gave her a long look. 'I can understand him getting upset, I'm not all that pleased about it. But I'll have a quiet word with him later.'

On Christmas Eve, Annie was out singing carols. The smell of chestnuts roasting on a nearby brazier made her mouth water, and she smiled at the chestnut seller who was singing out loud and strong with them. Although it was cold, her cheeks were flushed and tingling as she rattled her tin, wishing the last-minute shoppers, who were hurrying home laden down with trees and presents, a Merry Christmas. It was a heady, happy atmosphere, and she felt all the happier that her father had come round, and she was going to have her Christmas dinner at home after she'd been to the mission. But the black-shirts on the opposite corner still sent a chill down her back with their ranting and raving. It seemed Christmas made no difference to how they felt.

On Christmas morning, the paper chains and the men singing carols added to the festive atmosphere in the mission. Annie had been busy handing out dinners but now she was standing having a quiet cup of tea with Sister Harris and gazing out of the window. Suddenly all the misery of the world, her own included, seemed to catch up with her. 'I didn't realize so many people were homeless till I came here,' she sighed. 'That was almost a year ago. Last New Year's Eve.' The final words were said almost in a whisper.

'This is only one hostel. There are plenty of others round here, and in a lot of other cities, and they are all doing the same thing.'

Annie couldn't help thinking of Will. She was missing him desperately tonight. She fought back the tears. 'When are you going to Africa?' she asked, changing the subject.

'Very soon. In the New Year.'

'I'm going to miss you.'

'You could come with me.'

'What? My poor father would have a fit.'

Sister Harris laughed. 'I suppose he would. What time is he coming to collect you?'

'About now.'

Sister Harris smiled. 'You're very lucky to have such understanding parents. Rose told me what happened that night. She was worried they might not let you join us. Did you ever find out what became of the family you tried to help?'

'No. I know it was a long time back when it happened, but I'm always looking out for them. I ask people about them too, sometimes if I think they might know them.'

To Annie's surprise Sister Harris looked stern.

'Annie, you mustn't let them become an obsession,' she said, shaking her head. 'It is very rewarding to care for people, but you must not feel too disappointed if things don't always turn out the way you would like them to. You have to find an inner peace within yourself, then things will fall into place without you trying to push them all the time.' Sister Harris smiled and gently patted her hand.

Annie swallowed hard. 'Yes, I do understand that.' She turned back to the window. 'Here's Dad,' she said, almost relieved. 'I must go. Bye.'

Annie rushed out to the van and, clambering up into the passenger seat, gave her father's cheek a big kiss. 'Thanks for coming.'

'Your mother would have had my guts for garters if I hadn't.'

Annie laughed, her feelings under control at last. She knew Sister Harris was right. She had to work out where she belonged, and just now she knew it was with her family.

After Christmas dinner, Lil came round. It was like old times again as they laughed and giggled opening their presents. This time it was Annie who was in awe at the lovely silk dressing-gown Lil had given her.

'Look, I'm still wearing the earrings yer gave me last year,' Lil laughed. 'I always wear 'em on the stage, yer know. They're me lucky earrings.' She smiled and gently touched her ear. 'And I still got old Julian's necklace.'

'Do you miss him?' Annie asked, curious.

'Na, not really. I can be meself now, and sing what I like. And I gets all the money.'

'I must say you're looking very well, Lil,' said Mrs Rodgers. 'And you've put on a little weight. It suits you.'

Annie quickly glanced at Lil, wondering if she would say anything. She must be almost six months' gone and Annie could see she was blooming. She still didn't show though, but she was certainly more rounded. Over these past few months, every time Annie had broached the subject of how Lil would manage with the baby, she had told her not to worry.

Lil laughed and shrugged her shoulders. 'It must be all the beer I gits down me,' she said, answering Mrs Rodgers. She patted her stomach. 'It's a good job Annie 'ere don't try ter reform me.'

'We were all a bit worried about that,' smiled Mr Rodgers.

175

'Come on, let's not talk about that,' said Annie. 'It's time we laid the table for tea.'

'Did Annie tell you Georgie Bates came in the shop with his mother yesterday?' said Mr Rodgers.

'No she didn't,' said Lil. She gave Annie a look.

'Well, I've not had a lot of time, have I?' Annie protested. She suddenly felt as if she was being got at from all sides.

'Well, what did 'e look like?'

'Very well,' said Mr Rodgers. 'His old mum's so pleased to have him back home.'

'How long's 'e up 'ere?'

'For good,' said Mrs Rodgers. 'He's been discharged.'

'That's good. I'll 'ave ter go round and see 'im,' said Lil. 'I sent 'im a Christmas card, yer know – I wonder if 'e got it?'

'He told me he's got to start looking for work. Don't know how, poor lad,' said Mrs Rodgers. 'It's so sad to see him hobbling along on crutches.'

Annie stood up. 'At least he's still alive,' she sobbed as she hurried from the kitchen.

Chapter 18

Nineteen thirty-eight heralded a year of increased tension in Europe. It seemed that Mr Rodgers was forever studying his newspaper.

'Ben, you're getting on my nerves,' Mrs Rodgers scolded one afternoon. 'You've always got your nose buried in the paper. Either that or you're listening to the wireless.'

'Well, I'm worried. The news don't look so good, Mother.'

Mrs Rodgers was sceptical. 'Nothing will happen here. When we saw that nice Mr Chamberlain on the newsreel at the pictures the other day he said we've got nothing to worry about.'

Without comment, Mr Rodgers folded his newspaper and went down to join Annie in the shop.

Now winter was over spring had started blowy but dry, and today the watery sun had some warmth in it before it disappeared down behind the rooftops. Annie was pleased that the long cold winter seemed finally to be coming to a close. She didn't like standing on street corners singing when the cold wind tossed paper and leaves round her legs. Suddenly the bell rang and she looked up in surprise as she saw Lil come into the shop.

'Hello, Lil, been shopping?' Mr Rodgers nodded at Lil's paper carrier bag. 'What are you doing here today? Don't often see you on a Thursday. Got the sack?'

Lil smiled. 'No such luck.'

'Are you all right?' asked Annie, concerned. She could see Lil was pasty-faced, despite all her make-up.

'Course I am. Are yer busy?'

'No,' said Annie. 'Just thinking about closing for the night. Come on upstairs.'

'Would yer mind if Annie and me went out fer a walk, Mr Rodgers? We might go for a cup of tea later, if that's all right with you?'

Annie didn't query Lil's request. She knew just by looking at the dark circles under Lil's eyes that something was wrong.

'No, go on with you. I must say, Lil, you don't look all that well.' Mr Rodgers turned back to his shelves.

Annie walked round the counter. 'What is it?' she whispered to Lil. 'Are we going to be out long?'

Lil shook her head. 'I don't know – go and tell yer mum, we don't want 'er worrying.'

'Why, what's all this about?'

Lil shook her head again. 'Just git yer coat.' This time her tone was abrasive.

'I'll just go and tell Mum I'll be out for a while,' called Annie as she raced through the shop and up the stairs.

When she got back, Lil had wandered outside and was staring in the haberdashery window. 'Right, now what's all this about? And what have you got in there?' asked Annie, marching up to her.

Without turning, Lil said quietly, 'I'll tell yer later. Annie, I fink I've started.'

'What?'

'Shh, keep yer voice down.' Lil's steps were hesitant as they began walking down the Mews.

'Good night, Mr Day, Bessie,' said Annie as they passed the greengrocer's. Mr Day and plump Bessie who was helping Mr Day take in the last of the boxes of apples before they shut their shop turned and together said their goodnights. Annie moved closer to Lil. 'But you said it wasn't due for weeks yet.'

'I know. I worked it out. It should be about in April sometime.'

'What are you going to do?'

'I don't know.'

Suddenly they were interrupted by a commotion outside Day's. Annie and Lil stood at the end of the Mews looking at Bessie who was jumping up and down, screaming at a dog that had just cocked his leg up on the last of the apple boxes. Bessie grabbed a broom and began chasing it.

They both smiled and Annie went to move on.

''Ang on a minute.'

Annie looked in alarm at her friend. 'Lil, let me dad take you to the hospital.'

'No.' Lil hung on to the lamp-post as she bent over with pain.

'Oh Lil, you can't stay here.' Annie quickly looked back at Day's greengrocer's, but Mr Day and Bessie had gone in. Annie saw the lights were being doused. 'Please let me get you to the hospital.'

'No, Christ, I could 'ave gone there on me own. Annie, I want yer ter 'elp me.'

'Me? How? I can't. I don't know nothing about having babies.' Annie was beginning to panic.

'Yer don't have ter know much. They can manage it on their own.'

'Lil, you can't have it in the road.' Annie's voice rose as she looked wildly about her. 'Let me take you home, your mum will know what to do.'

'Annie, she don't know.'

'What?' exploded Annie. 'But I thought . . .'

'All the time I didn't show I didn't fink it was worth worrying 'er about it.' Lil stopped for breath. 'And I suppose in a way I fought it might go away. So yer see it'll come as a bit of a shock if she finds out this way that she's gonner be a gran, and I don't suppose me old man would be all that pleased.'

'Look, I'll run back and get me mum.'

'No.' Lil's tone was forceful. 'I've managed ter keep it quiet this long, so I don't want anybody else ter know about it now.'

Annie was almost hysterical. 'But, Lil, we must tell someone – we must get help. Let me take you to the mission. I'm sure Rose will help.'

'No, I ain't going nowhere like that. We can cope. Remember I 'elped me mum with 'er last one.'

'Yes, but that was in your house, not out here in the street, and it was born dead. Besides, what are you going to do with it when it's born?'

179

'I fought I'd wrap it up and leave it on the 'ospital's doorstep.'

'What?'

'Why not? They'll know how ter look after it.'

'Lil, you can't do that.'

'It's no use, Annie, I've made up me mind.'

'You can't leave it on a doorstep.'

'Talk sense. How can I look after it? If I leave it there someone will give it a good 'ome.'

'Well, I don't approve of that.'

Lil gritted her teeth. 'Well, I didn't fink yer would. All right then, if yer don't want ter 'elp me, then go on 'ome. I'll get by on me own.' Lil's tone was full of anger.

'Lil, you can't.' Annie knew it was useless to argue with her, and put her arm round her shoulder. 'OK. You win, but where are we going?'

'I fought we'd find a quiet place somewhere.'

'What do you want me to do?'

A faint smile lifted Lil's drawn face. 'Just stay with me, will yer?'

Annie nodded, almost on the point of tears.

'What about when the baby's born. What'll we put him in?' she asked.

'I got some clothes and other bits and pieces in this carrier bag, and a little blanket. Don't want 'im ter catch cold.' Lil stopped and leaned against a wall, her face a mask of pain.

'Oh my God,' wailed Annie. 'What am I going to do?'

'Keep calm fer one fing.'

Annie struggled to do as Lil told her.

'We'd better make our way nearer the hospital, just in case.'

'Yer, but remember, I ain't going in.'

'But what if something goes wrong?'

'Why should it? Women 'ave babies all the time, that's what they're made fer.'

'Yes I know, but it should be in the right conditions.'

'The poor cows in the jungle don't 'ave the right conditions.' Lil forced a feeble laugh. 'They just go behind a bush and 'ave it.'

Annie didn't have an answer to that.

Slowly they made their way towards the hospital, Lil stopping every few yards as the pain increased. Annie felt helpless. 'Would you like me to run into the hospital to fetch a cup of tea?' she asked nervously, at a loss as to what else she could say.

'No,' gasped Lil. 'Let's git round the back.'

The bright lights streaming through the entrance hall of the large impressive building looked warm and inviting. With a great deal of difficulty Lil walked upright through the gate. Annie wished she would faint or fall over, then at least she would have an excuse to call for help. They continued on past the door and round the side, and found a sheltered corner close to an outhouse. 'I can't believe I'm doing this,' said Annie as she helped Lil lower herself to the ground.

''Ere, I 'ope yer not gonner fall ter yer knees and start praying. I don't want none of yer allaluas.'

'Don't talk daft,' said Annie, trying feebly to make her friend comfortable.

Lil leant against the wall, holding on to her knees. 'I tell yer, Annie, it don't 'alf 'urt.' She groaned with pain.

Annie knelt beside her. 'Don't scream out, or else someone will hear you.'

'I'll try not ter. Give us yer hankie ter shove in me mouth, that might 'elp.'

For an hour Annie held Lil's hand, trying to comfort her as each contraction became stronger, biting her lip with anxiety. She knew she shouldn't be doing this. What if something went wrong? What if Lil died? What if the baby was dead? She wiped Lil's forehead: it was bathed in sweat. If only someone would come and find them, they would make Lil go into the hospital – they were so near. Annie looked up hopefully at the light that shone from a window high in the red-brick building, then looked down at Lil's face. Her friend gave her a weak smile. This was so wrong, Annie thought desperately, Lil lying outside on the hard ground bringing a new life into the world. She should be in a warm room and in a bed. Tears stung the back of her eyes.

'I fink it's coming,' gasped Lil, quickly pulling off her knickers. She pulled her knees up and opened her legs wide. 'I've got ter push. Can yer see its 'ead yet?'

181

Annie felt embarrassed as she peered at Lil's exposed private parts. 'No,' she croaked.

Lil panted and pushed and then lay back against the wall and closed her eyes with exhaustion.

'What's happening?' cried Annie. 'What's wrong?'

'It's all right. I just need a little rest.'

Annie shivered as she continued to mop Lil's damp brow with the towel Lil had brought. 'I fink this'll be it,' said Lil, straining with all the strength she could muster.

'I can see it, I can see it,' shouted Annie excitedly, and all thoughts of modesty vanished as she touched the baby's bloody, slimy head. 'It's coming,' she said enthusiastically, as, bit by bit, she helped the little mite into the world. 'It's a boy.' Annie was beaming. 'Lil, you've got a baby boy, a dear little baby boy.' Annie was laughing and crying together. 'He's ever so small. Look, I can hold him in one hand.'

The baby gave out a small rasping sound.

'Git the muck out of 'is eyes, and you'll 'ave ter cut the cord,' Lil said wearily.

'What? I can't – besides, what with?'

'You'll 'ave ter. There's some scissors in that bag, and a piece o' string.'

'What do you want the piece of string for?'

'Ter tie round the cord, and wrap 'em in that blanket.'

'It seems you've thought of everything,' said Annie, as with her free hand she feverishly felt in the bag. She brought out the scissors and string and gingerly cut the cord that had bonded Lil and her son together.

'Just bend it over and tie it. When 'e gits inside they'll take care of it.'

Annie did as she was told, and when the baby was free from Lil she wrapped him tightly in the blanket.

Lil was shivering, and she gave a long groan.

'Lil, what's wrong? What's the matter?'

'The afterbirth, it's just come out.'

Annie stared in amazement at the shining red blob. 'What we going to do with it?'

'Chuck it in the bushes.'

Annie handed the baby to Lil, picked up the soft, spongy mess in the newspaper Lil had brought too, and took it over to the bushes and tossed it in. Lil was sitting up looking at her baby.

'Shouldn't he be crying or something?'

'Na, look, he's breathing. Annie, fanks.'

'That's all right. I still can't believe it. Me helping to bring a baby into the world.' She touched his tiny hand. 'Lil, do you have to give him up?'

'Stop being all daft and sentimental – course I 'ave.' She paused. 'Annie, would yer mind going 'ome now and leaving me ter meself.'

'But, Lil . . .'

'Please. After all, this is the last time I'll see 'im.'

'I don't know,' Annie said doubtfully.

'I'll be all right.'

Annie hesitated. 'Well, if you think so. Where are you going tonight?'

'I'm going 'ome, just fer tonight. I've got the night off fer a change.'

'I don't like leaving you alone.'

'I'll be all right,' repeated Lil softly, looking down at her son.

'If you're sure.' Annie staggered to her feet. 'It's a bit cold, so don't hang about too long before you leave him.'

'No, I won't.'

'When will I see you again?'

'Dunno, Monday I expect. And, Annie, fanks again. And yer promise yer'll keep this ter yerself won't yer?'

Annie took a last peep at the baby and nodded. 'Bye,' she said thickly as the tears began to well again, and she quickly hurried away.

As Annie wandered home her thoughts were full. How could Lil bear to give away such a beautiful baby? And what should she tell her parents when they asked her where she'd been? She had to keep her promise to Lil so she had no choice but to lie to them. As she passed a fish-and-chip shop the mouthwatering smell made Annie suddenly feel very hungry. She'd go and get something to eat, she decided, then realized that in her hurry to get out she hadn't taken her handbag with her. She walked back in the direction of home and as she passed under a streetlamp she noticed blood on her coat. She panicked. It was up her sleeve so she couldn't hide it. What could she tell them about this? She walked on, her mind reeling but as she neared Albert Mews a story began to form in her mind. Bit by bit she forced herself to relax. She had to be convincing, for Lil's sake.

'We were beginning to worry about you, love. Where have you been? Have you had something to eat?' Her mother coughed painfully as she finished her sentence.

'Sorry about that, Mum, didn't mean to be so late. Me and Lil only had a cup of tea.' She took off her coat.

'Lil don't normally come round here on a Thursday. I was telling your mother I didn't think she looked all that well.'

'No, she said she didn't feel too good.'

'She could have caught this cold,' Mrs Rodgers said. 'It's beginning to get on my nerves.'

Annie looked away from her parents' gaze. She hated telling lies, but she had made a promise to Lil. 'When we were coming home we saw this boy,' she announced. 'He'd fallen down and hit his head and his face was all covered with blood. Look, I've got some on my coat.' She held up the coat sleeve that had Lil's blood on it.

Her mother jumped to her feet. 'The poor boy.'

'Where was this?' asked her father.

'Round Paradise Street.'

'They're a rough lot round there,' he muttered.

'Are you all right, love?' her mother asked, concerned.

'Yes thanks, Mum.'

'We'll get that blood off before it sets too hard.' Her mother took the coat to the sink and, under the running tap, began feverishly rubbing the sleeve. 'Is the boy all right now?' she asked over her shoulder.

'Yes, I think so.'

'Did you take him home?' Mr Rodgers was looking over his newspaper.

'No.' Annie was beginning to get flustered. She didn't like all these questions. 'He looked fine, so we left him.'

'So we won't be going to look for him to tuck under your wing.' Her father returned to his paper.

Annie gave a faint smile. 'No, not this time.'

Chapter 19

On Saturday morning Annie tried to busy herself in the shop. All yesterday she had worried over Lil and the baby, wondering if Lil was all right, and if the baby had been found. She scanned the newspapers, but nothing had been reported.

'What's up with you, Annie?' said her father, pulling at a half-empty sack of sugar to make room for the new stock. 'Every time I look at you you're miles away.'

'I'm all right.' If only she could tell her parents.

The shop bell rang and Mr Barrett walked in.

'Hello, sir,' said Mr Rodgers. 'Don't often see you these days.'

'Well, now the weather has improved a little, I thought I'd like to have a stroll round and see how my tenants are getting on. And how's little Annie these days?'

'I'm fine, thank you.'

'Your father was telling me you've joined the Salvation Army.' Mr Barrett smiled. 'I expect you look very pretty in your bonnet?'

Annie blushed. Although she'd glimpsed him around the Mews, the last time she'd seen Mr Barrett to talk to had been at his party and she felt uncomfortable in his presence. She hated it when elderly men commented on her looks. She remembered how she'd felt when Mr Hobbs had remarked that she was 'nicely proportioned' when she gave him her measurements for her uniform. She shuddered, thinking back to those men who had tried to attack her. What was wrong with them? Perhaps she was being silly, or was it because of all the dirty old men Lil was always telling her about – the way they leered and made rude remarks, and tried to touch her – that made Annie think that all older men would like

187

to act in this way? 'I'll go on up and see if Mum's got the list ready for the veg she wants from Day's.' Annie opened the door behind the counter.

'You knew of course that Peter was married?' called Mr Barrett after her.

Annie stopped in the doorway. 'Yes, Dad told me. He married Belinda I believe. Are they all right?'

'Yes, and you'll never guess, I'm going to be a grandfather.' Mr Barrett stuck out his chest, making the gold watch chain that he always wore tighten. He gave a loud laugh and slapped Mr Rodgers on the back. 'Well, what do you think of that?'

'Very many congratulations, sir,' said Mr Rodgers, warmly shaking his hand.

Annie glanced back ruefully at her father as she walked up the stairs. Would he have liked the baby's mother to have been her? She couldn't see Belinda with a baby, though. And, she thought sadly, if Will hadn't been killed her father might have been a grandfather anyway despite his disappointment over Peter. And what about Lil? If that baby had been Julian's, she might have been married by now and living in a nice house, not having it round the back of the hospital, and leaving it on the step for someone to adopt. Annie sighed. 'How could Lil leave him like that?' she said out loud and pushed open the kitchen door. Her mother who was still not well was in the bedroom. 'Mum, what did you want from Day's?' she shouted.

'The list's on the table,' called her mother huskily. 'I'll be getting up soon.'

Annie suddenly realized this was the first time she had known her mother to stay in bed with a cold.

'There's no need to get up; I'll see to this,' said Annie, picking up the scrap of paper.

'Hello, Annie,' said Mr Day. 'Don't often see you out shopping.' He nodded at the basket hanging on her arm.

'No, Mum's not well so she asked me to get these few bits.' She handed the list to Mr Day.

'Bessie,' he yelled. 'What yer doing out there?'

Bessie came bustling back into the shop straightening her overall. 'Cor blimey, gov, can't I even 'ave a pee in peace? 'Allo, Annie love, how's yer mum and dad?'

Annie smiled. 'Not too bad.'

'Look after Annie while I see ter those beets. I reckon they should be boiling be now.' He passed on the list.

Bessie began weighing out the greens. 'Yer know young Georgie Bates came in in the week,' she said over her shoulder. 'Did yer see 'im?'

'Yes, he always pops in when he's round this way. It's a long way for him to come on his crutches.'

'Yer, 'e was telling me 'e's trying ter git a job, but not many will take on a feller with only one leg.'

'Yes, it's a shame.'

'Still, 'e's still a bit of a laugh.' Bessie looked at the back door, and came closer to Annie. The smell of her cheap perfume almost took Annie's breath away. 'D'yer know what that saucy bugger done when 'e was in 'ere?' She grinned, and patted the back of her blonde hair.

Annie shook her head.

'Well, when I was bending over gitting the apples, you'll never guess what 'e done with one of 'is crutches?' Before Annie could answer she went on. 'Stuffed it up me skirt 'e did, saucy bugger.' She threw her head back and laughed. Then she clapped her podgy hand over her mouth. 'Sorry, Annie, I forgot you're in the Sally Army and don't like that sorta talk.'

'I haven't changed, Bessie, and I don't expect anybody else to when I'm around. Georgie's a nice boy, and he always enjoyed a joke.'

'Yer, well. It's nice ter know 'e ain't lost 'is sense of humour. It's a damn shame, 'im losing 'is leg like that.'

Annie didn't answer.

'Right love, that's the lot on the list. I've put how much yer owes. Don't bother paying now, I'll pop along for it later when I gits me fags.'

Annie left the shop deep in thought. Did her being in the Salvation Army put people on their guard? Lil still seemed the same, but then she'd known Lil a long while. What about the Murphys? They'd upped and moved when they found out she wanted the Salvation Army to help them. She'd joined the Salvation Army after Will's death because helping other people seemed to help her. But it didn't mean she was any different from what she'd been before. She hoped people realized that.

When she got back to the shop, Mr Barrett had left.

'Fancy that son of his going to be a father,' Mr Rodgers said as soon as she walked in. 'It's a pity you two didn't see eye to eye.'

Annie tightened her lips. 'That was over a long while ago; if Will hadn't been killed you might have been a grandad too.'

Mr Rodgers put the boxes he was carrying on the counter, and leaned forward. 'Annie, I do hope you meet someone one day. I don't like the idea of you going through life on your own and finishing up like those two old dears next door.'

She smiled. 'I'm not on my own, I've got you and Mum. Besides, I'm only nineteen, and at the moment nobody could take Will's place.'

'And I don't suppose anyone will, but I would like you to go out more, and meet different people.'

'I've got plenty of time to meet someone else,' she said firmly, 'but he'll have to be very special after Will.'

The shop bell rang again and Mrs Turner waddled in. She sat on the chair next to the counter and pulled her shawl round her shoulders. ''Allo there, Annie, Ben. Gis a couple o' rashers fer me old man's tea.'

'Where have you been? We haven't seen you for a while,' said Mr Rodgers. 'We wondered if you'd been ill.'

'Well, yer didn't bloody well come round ter find out, did yer?'

'I was going to, but you know how it is, what with one thing and another.' Annie's father was used to Mrs Turner's forthright ways.

Suddenly a yelling in the Mews sent them hurrying to the door. Outside Day's, Bessie was standing with her hands on her wide hips shouting at Mrs James.

'I ain't 'ad nuffink ter do wiv yer old man,' she bellowed.

Mrs James, a thin, mousy woman, with hunched shoulders, who always had her hair scragged back in a hairnet, was constantly worried about her husband going out with other women. 'I knows it was your lipstick,' she squawked. 'Yer dirty cow. Yer going ter finish up in the family way if yer don't watch out.'

Everybody except the two Miss Pages had come out of their shops.

'Yer must fink I'm 'ard up ter fancy your old man,' scoffed Bessie.

'Well, yer no bleeding oil painting under all that muck on yer face, and yer'll 'ave anyfink yer can grab as long as it's in trousers.'

'Don't be ser bloody cheeky. I'll 'ave that bleeding 'airnet orf if yer don't watch out.'

'Go on then, Bessie, we dare yer,' shouted the kids from the ironmonger's.

Bessie looked at her audience, loving it. 'I reckon 'er wig'll fall orf then,' she laughed. 'Go on, piss orf out o' it. Go 'ome ter yer old man, I've got work ter do!' She waved her fist at Mrs James and walked back in the shop.

'Don't you freaten me,' called Mrs James after her.

Mrs Turner began laughing.

Mrs James turned on her. 'What yer laughing at?'

'Bessie,' said Mrs Turner quickly. 'Ben, yer gonner finish gitting me order?' She hurried into the shop.

'You were in a hurry to get in here,' said Ben Rodgers.

'Yer, well, I 'ave ter be careful. 'Er kids are little buggers, and I could end up wiv a couple o' broken winders.'

Mr Rodgers continued slicing the bacon. 'Anyway, where have you been hiding?'

She sat on the chair and a big smile filled her round face. 'Been staying at me son's, ain't I? 'E's got a smashing place out in the country.'

'Whereabouts?'

'Dagenham.'

'Is that where Day's eldest daughter lives?'

'Dunno. Anyway, our Bill's got a lovely 'ouse, three bedrooms and a barfroom. Tell yer what, it's lovely ter sit on the bog and not 'ave the wind whistling round yer legs and spiders 'anging from the roof waiting ter drop on yer 'ead.' She laughed and put her shopping bag on the counter. 'And guess what? I'm gonner be a granny.'

'Well I'll be blowed, d'you know you're the second today. The landlord was telling us earlier that he's going to be a grandfather.'

'Well, they say everyfink comes in threes, so I wonder who'll be next. 'Ere I 'ope those rashers ain't too fatty, Ben.'

Annie picked up her basket of veg to take upstairs. Mrs Turner was right, everything did come in threes, and Annie knew who the third baby belonged to.

It was six-thirty on Monday when Lil walked into the shop. 'We still going ter the pictures ternight?'

Annie hurried round the counter and hugged her. 'Oh, Lil, I'm ever so pleased to see you. Are you all right?'

''Ere, give over, someone might walk in. Course I'm all right.' Lil sat on the chair.

'Well, you don't look any different.'

'I'm a bit thinner.'

'Have you been round to your mother's?'

'Yer, been round there all afternoon – why?'

'Did you go back there on Thursday – after – you know?'

'No.'

'Why not? Where did you go?'

Lil took a packet of Park Drive from her handbag, and before answering, very slowly lit a cigarette. 'I went fer a walk and finished up in a pub. I 'ad a few drinks with a couple of blokes then went back ter me own place. That's all.'

'You did what? Why was that?'

'I didn't fancy going 'ome to a lot of questions.'

Annie anxiously looked at the door. 'What about the . . . baby?' whispered Annie. 'Did you leave him on the doorstep?'

Lil nervously tapped the end of her cigarette into the ashtray, then stood up and walked across the shop. She looked up at the clock. 'Yer mum and dad don't get 'ere till seven do they?'

'They didn't go out tonight.'

'Why's that?'

'Mum's not too well. What's the matter, Lil? You did leave the baby, didn't you?'

'Yes, yes – course I did.'

'You didn't get caught?'

'No.'

'Did you wait till someone picked him up?'

Lil puffed hard on her cigarette. 'No.'

'But, Lil, why not?'

'Didn't see the point.'

'But what if . . .'

'Well, he ain't still there, if that's what yer worried about,' said Lil tersely.

'How do you know?'

'Cos after I'd 'ad a drink with these blokes I went back ter 'ave a look.' Without looking at Annie, Lil stubbed out her cigarette in the ashtray. 'Yer satisfied?'

Annie nodded very slowly. 'I'll start putting the lights out, you go on up, I expect Dad's made a cup of tea.'

Lil went up the stairs and left Annie with her thoughts. Who had that dear little baby now, she wondered.

Spring gave way to summer, and Annie, along with her fellow Salvation Army officers, was still going into pubs every Saturday night rattling their tins and selling the *War Cry*. At the meetings, and on Sunday mornings, she would be singing her heart out with them on one street corner, while the blackshirts were shouting Hitler's praises on the other, rattling about the pure race Hitler was going to have in Germany. Very often scuffles would break out between the blackshirts and their hecklers but Annie and the Salvation Army would carry on singing regardless. Annie and Lil continued going to the pictures every Monday evening. Lil had changed. To Annie she appeared more serious. Lil had told her her job and singing were the most important things in her life now. As for Lil's baby, if he ever crossed Annie's mind she quickly dismissed it, and neither Lil nor Annie mentioned him again. The newsreels were full of the problems in Europe, and everybody hoped and prayed there wouldn't be another war. But soon Annie's biggest worry was her mother. Mrs Rodgers had never completely recovered from the cold she had had way back in the spring; still unwell, she now seemed to be getting worse. For the second time in one week the doctor had had to be called out and today, as he emerged from Mrs Rodgers' bedroom, he looked grave.

'Annie, would you take this prescription to the chemist?' he asked politely.

'But what's wrong with her?' asked Annie pitifully. 'Is she going to get better?' Annie seemed to have fetched dozens of bottles of medicine for her mother yet she never appeared to improve.

'Your mother is very ill, and I want her to have an X-ray. I'm going to ask your father to take her to the hospital.'

Tears slowly crept down Annie's cheek. 'Why? What's the matter with her?'

The doctor shook his head. 'I'm not really sure. I'm very worried about her chest. She should be responding to treatment by now.'

The rasping cough had gradually got worse over the weeks, and it was making her mother very weak despite all the medicine and warm poultices. She had always been a thin woman but now her bones seemed to be almost sticking through her sallow skin, and her dull eyes had sunk deep into their sockets. It upset Annie to see her once active mother just lying there: she was desperately worried about her. No longer interested in going out, Annie didn't feel like going to her meetings, and sat at her mother's bedside most of the evening. All day she cooked and cleaned and attended to her mother's needs, as well as helping in the shop if her father had to make a delivery or collect goods.

Annie followed the doctor down the stairs and into the shop. 'I've got to go round and get this,' she said to her father, waving the prescription in the air. 'I won't be long.'

By the time she returned, the doctor had left.

'Annie.' Her father looked pale and worried. 'I've got to take your mother to get these X-ray things done. You'll be all right here on your own, won't you?'

''Course. When are you going?'

'The doctor said we could go right away. He's gone on ahead to make all the necessary arrangements.'

'I'll go up and get Mum ready.'

Earlier she had washed her mother, tidied her sparse hair, and changed her nightdress in readiness for the doctor's visit. It upset her to see her mother's energy fading away so fast. 'I'll get your slippers and a coat,' she said, trying hard to be cheerful. 'It's quite warm out.'

'I'm sorry to be so much trouble, love,' her mother said in a tired voice.

Annie fought back the tears. 'Don't be silly, you're no trouble. Now just 'cos you're allowed out I don't want you racing round the shops trying to buy up everything in the summer sales.'

Mrs Rodgers smiled. 'Chance would be a fine thing,' she croaked. 'You're a good girl, Annie.'

Mrs Rodgers never returned from the hospital. She was admitted right away, and a few weeks later died from tuberculosis. Annie was devastated.

On the day Mrs Rodgers was buried, the shops in Albert Mews closed as a mark of respect. Aunt Ivy, Uncle Fred and Roy came to the funeral, as well as most of those who lived and worked in the Mews, and many of their customers. It was a hot, sticky day, and in the well-filled church the smell from the mass of beautiful flowers was sickly and overpowering. Everybody hoped the threatening storm would hold off.

Throughout the service, and at the graveside, Lil held on to Annie. As they slowly walked back to the carriage Annie was still in shock. They wandered past the many graves, and her thoughts went to Will. He was in a different cemetery. I must visit him soon, tell him about Mum, she thought. Lil was speaking but Annie wasn't listening. Lil tapped the back of her hand, and in reply Annie gave her a weak smile. Over the years they had been through a lot together, and despite their very different lifestyles, they were still very close.

As they were being driven back home Annie, deep in thought, wondered how many more loved ones would be taken from her.

'Last year I lost Will, and now Mum,' she said sadly as, back at the house, she offered Aunt Ivy a ham sandwich.

Ivy put a comforting arm round Annie's shoulders. 'Why don't you come down for another holiday?' she said. 'You know you would be very welcome. Besides, Matthew and June are hoping to get married soon. They often talk about you and they *would* like you to come to their wedding.'

Annie wiped her eyes. 'That's nice of them. Give them my love when you get back. When exactly are they getting married?'

'The end of September, I think. Anyway, it's after the harvest. Think about it, love, it'll do you good.'

Annie studied her father's pale face anxiously. He was sitting with Ted the butcher who was busy talking to him, but Annie could see it wasn't registering. He looked lost and bewildered. She turned to Aunt Ivy. 'I don't think I could leave Dad just yet. He needs me.'

Aunt Ivy patted her hand. 'Our door's always open, so whenever you feel you'd like to come, love, just turn up. And, Annie, your mother wouldn't want you to grieve for ever – you've had more than enough sorrow in your young life already.'

Chapter 20

Annie couldn't believe her mother had gone: it brought home all too clearly how much she had meant to her. They had always been a close family, and now there was just her and her dad. Her father was looking old and drawn. Annie knew he wasn't sleeping well, and on many a night she heard him in the kitchen. At first she would get up with him and make them both a pot of tea, but after a while she'd realized he wanted to be alone with his thoughts. First he'd had John, his only son, taken away from him, and now his wife. Both he and Annie had lost people they loved and cared for, and he needed her. Sometimes Annie wondered how her father would have coped if she'd gone with Will to live in Carshalton. In a sad way, things had almost turned out for the best, it sometimes seemed.

At the beginning of September, as promised, Matthew sent Annie and her father an invitation to his wedding. Annie dearly wanted to go but her father said he couldn't face it, so she too declined.

At least, though, Annie was spending more time with Lil, now that her father no longer went to the pictures on Monday after-noons. One late September afternoon, the two of them were taking a leisurely walk round the park before they went to the pictures. Annie was commenting that the trees were now beginning to change colour, and another winter would soon be on them when Lil started waving to a couple of sailors sitting on the grass.

'Lil, stop it,' said Annie crossly. 'You make yourself look so common.'

'What d'yer mean? I know them, they come in the pub last night. They told me they've got a week's leave. That blond one's a bit of all right.' Lil nudged her arm. 'And they've always got a few bob to spend.'

Annie quickly glanced over her shoulder, and they waved back. She blushed at being caught. 'You wouldn't . . . You know, with them, would you?' Lil had been boasting earlier about how she was still earning plenty on the side.

'Don't be ser bloody nosy. 'Ere, d'yer wonner go over and talk to 'em?'

'No, I don't.'

'Please yerself. D'yer know, I reckon they'd take us ter the pictures if I asked.'

'I can afford to pay for myself, thank you,' Annie replied. 'Come on, let's get a move on.'

'Hello there, Lil,' a deep voice called from over their shoulder.

They both turned quickly to find the two sailors standing right behind them.

''Allo,' said Lil, her dark eyes shining.

'Will you be singing in the pub tonight?' asked the fair-haired one.

'Yer, yer coming over then?' Lil was grinning.

'I should say so, ain't that right, Sam?'

Sam had dark hair, and was taller than his friend. He was smiling at Annie. 'Will you be going to the Castle with Lil tonight?' he asked politely.

'I don't drink.' Trying hard to avoid his brown eyes, Annie began fidgeting with her handbag, and started slowly moving away.

'That's a pity,' said the blond sailor as they all fell in step with her. 'We could have made it a foursome. By the way, the name's Mike.'

'Come on, Lil,' said Annie, tugging at her friend's sleeve.

'Where're you two off to?' asked Mike.

'The pictures,' replied Lil.

'Who with?' It was Mike asking the questions, Sam just stood by quietly.

'No one, just us,' said Lil eagerly.

'We could take yer if yer like,' said Mike.

'No thanks,' said Annie as she continued to walk on.

Lil shrugged her shoulders.

'Well, please yerself.'

'See yer ternight, Mike,' said Lil as she reluctantly followed Annie.

'You're a right old spoilsport,' Lil whispered loudly when she'd caught her up. 'We could 'ave 'ad a good time with them two.'

'I'm not going to the pictures with any old sailor you care to pick up in the park,' said Annie indignantly, her pace quickening. 'The way you're carrying on I can see you ending up in the family way again.'

'Annie Rodgers, don't yer start preaching ter me – I ain't one of yer converts yer know.' There was an edge to Lil's voice.

'Sorry, Lil,' said Annie quickly, taking her friend's arm. The last thing she wanted was to lose Lil's friendship. 'If we hurry up we can have a cup of tea before we go into the film.'

The following Saturday, Annie decided she should go round to see the Hobbs. She felt guilty that she hadn't been in touch since her mother's death. It was time she took her Salvation Army work up again. Rose was busy in the kitchen when she called.

'It's nice to see you so willing and eager, Annie. I was afraid we might have lost you,' said Mr Hobbs putting his arm round her shoulder, and ushering her into the front room. 'How is your father these days?'

'He seems to be bearing up, thank you. I'm a bit worried about him though. He doesn't go out at all now.'

'Well, it's early days yet, give him time. I remember when I lost my wife – it does take time, though of course I had the good Lord to help me.' He gave her shoulders a gentle squeeze.

Rose came in the room, and Mr Hobbs quickly moved away. 'Annie, tonight we are going over Peckham way. Would you mind coming with us? We'll make sure you get home safely.'

'Will we be going into the Castle?'

'I should think so. Why? Do you know it?'

'That's where my friend Lil sings.' Annie smiled. 'She'll be surprised to see me walk through the door rattling my tin.'

*   *   *

199

When Annie pushed open the door to any pub, the heat and the smell of beer and tobacco always took her aback, and tonight the Castle was no exception. It was noisy with men laughing and shouting. A pianist was thumping away on a battered upright piano, while on the tiny stage Lil was singing her heart out. When she caught sight of Annie she waved, and most of the heads turned to see who she had waved to. Embarrassed, Annie bent down and put her tin under a couple's nose.

'Would you like a *War Cry*?' she asked, trying to make herself heard above the din.

'Yer, why not?' said the man.

"Ere, gis it 'ere,' said his lady friend snatching the paper from Annie. 'It always finishes up as bog paper.' The woman threw her head back and laughed, then picked up her drink and downed it. 'Our Lil's in good form ternight, ain't she, Fred?'

'Yer. 'Ere y'are, love, 'ere's a tanner fer yer orphans.'

'Thank you,' said Annie politely.

"Ere, Fred, you're gitting generous in yer old age, ain't yer?'

'Yer, well, yer wonner watch out, yer could end up in some 'ome wiv 'em, if I dump yer.'

'Bloody cheek. Git us another drink or I might end up dumping you.'

Annie left the woman to her loud laughter and off-key singing and moved on to the next table.

By now Lil was off the stage, and moving amongst the crowd, singing. Annie got closer, marvelling that such a strong voice could come from her friend's small body. She leant against the wall and watched and it brought back memories of when Lil first began to sing in pubs, and of Peter and Julian, and how all their lives had changed. Lil was moving around her audience now, and with the words of the song was making cheeky, titillating suggestions with her heavily made-up eyes. The people loved it, and they banged and hooted when she sat on the lap of the blond-haired sailor they had seen in the park last Monday afternoon. The other sailor who had been with him caught sight of Annie and gave her a friendly wave. She quickly turned away and moved to the other side of the room.

When Lil finished she pushed her way over to Annie. "'Allo, I didn't expect ter see you in 'ere. Did yer see me with that Mike. 'E's a nice bloke. 'Im and 'is mate 'ave been in 'ere every night this week yer know. They 'ave ter join their ship termorrer. It's sailing on the evening tide, so I gotter make the most of ternight.' She laughed excitedly.

'You can still hold an audience, Lil, I'd forgotten how good you are,' said Annie. She could see Mike's friend looking surreptitiously at her, and she felt embarrassed.

'Fanks.'

'Lil, 'urry up and git yer arse back 'ere,' shouted someone.

'That's Bill, me boss. I'd better go, see yer Monday.'

Annie watched her thrust her way through the crowd, duck under the counter, get behind the bar, and begin filling the empty glasses very efficiently.

As she went through the door Annie turned. Mike's friend caught her eye and, smiling shyly, waved.

That night when Annie was in bed, she gave a thought to Lil. Was she lying in Mike's arms? A small pang of jealousy touched her, and she wondered if she would ever be held close and kissed again.

Christmas was almost upon them, and Annie was on her way to see Rose, to tell her she wasn't going to leave her father to go to the mission this year. It was going to be hard enough for them both without her mother, and she knew she couldn't leave him alone.

'Come in, Annie,' said Mr Hobbs on opening the front door. 'Rose isn't here at the moment, she shouldn't be very long.'

'I've only come to tell you I won't be going out at all over Christmas, I'm staying in with Dad. I might even try and persuade him to go down to see my Aunt Ivy.'

'That is such a pity. Are you happy with us, Annie?'

'Yes.' Annie was always a little fearful of this man. He was tall and dark, and his bright button eyes always seemed to be darting about, devouring everything they landed on.

'I do hope you are not thinking of leaving us.'

'No, of course not. It's just that I think I should be with my father this Christmas.'

Mr Hobbs put his arm around Annie's shoulders, and she suddenly realized he'd been doing this more and more just lately. He continued in his sing-songy voice. 'Very charitable, my dear. But remember there are a lot of people out there who need you, and we need to spread the word of the good Lord.' Annie tried not to feel intimidated when he pulled her closer to him. 'It's a great pity your father won't come along to the mission with you. I'm sure he too would find a great happiness, and of course he'd discover many men who would be willing to talk to him, and perhaps help him find his way in the wilderness.'

'I don't think so, Mr Hobbs. Dad's not very religious,' said Annie, slipping away from him. 'I must go now.'

'Do you have to?'

'Yes, tell Rose I called.' She quickly left the house. Outside she began to smile to herself. Poor Mr Hobbs, he didn't know what a losing battle he was fighting trying to get Dad in uniform.

The following morning, Annie left her warm bed and ambled into the kitchen rubbing her eyes. 'Glad to see you've got the gas on, Dad. It warms this kitchen up a treat.'

'There's a Christmas card for you love, and it's got a foreign stamp on it.' Her father was turning over the envelope. 'Who do you know who lives in—' he studied the stamp – 'can't make out where it's from, it's all smudged.'

'I don't know anyone abroad, are you sure it's for me?'

'Miss A. Rodgers, look.'

Annie took the envelope and quickly opened it. She took out the card and a single page of a letter fluttered to the floor.

'Ah-ah, you have a secret admirer.'

Annie laughed. 'Not that I know of.' She peered at the Christmas card. 'It's from someone called Sam,' she said, mystified. She began reading the letter, and slowly it dawned on her who Sam was. It was the dark-haired sailor who'd waved at her in the Castle that night.

'Who is he then?' asked her father impatiently, his voice full of curiosity.

'Well,' she said, the word long and drawn-out. 'It's this sailor friend of Lil's I saw one time in the Castle when he was on leave a while back. I went in selling the *War Cry*. He knew Lil knew me as he'd seen us both in the park, but didn't like to talk to me then. Or so he says.' She turned over the page and began to read out loud.

'I asked Lil about you, and she told me you work in your father's shop. She gave me the address. I wanted to write before but didn't have the courage, so I can use this as an excuse. May I wish you and your father a very Merry Christmas and a Happy New Year. If you would like to answer this letter I would be very grateful.

Thank you,
Yours hopefully,
Sam Jarvis.'

Annie stood staring at the card and the letter.

'Well I'll be blowed,' said her father. 'What's he like?'

Annie blushed. 'I don't know,' she stammered.

'What d'you mean, you don't know?'

'I can't even remember what he looks like.' She looked down at the letter again. She did remember him, he had a nice smile, and his dark eyes had seemed to follow her all the time she was in the pub – but she couldn't tell her father that. 'I vaguely remember his friend, he was blond, and I seem to remember Lil said his name was Mike. I'll have to ask her all about this Sam.'

'Are you going to answer this sailor Sam, the one-eyed man, then?' He did a quick hornpipe round the room.

She giggled nervously, pleased to see her father happy and smiling again. 'I think so, there can't be any harm. What do you think I should do?'

Her father was suddenly serious. 'Well, if there is a war, I should think they'll want as much news from home as they can get. It won't hurt to drop him a line, Annie. Now, how about a nice cup of tea before I open the shop?'

'Yes, Dad,' she said dreamily. 'I'll make some toast.'

Christmas dinner was a very quiet affair, and Annie almost wished she was at the mission helping to hand out the meals. After they had done the washing up, they listened to the King's speech, then Annie went to her room to wait for Lil, while her dad read the newspaper. She hadn't seen Lil since she had received the Christmas card from Sam, and she was dying to know more about him.

It was nearly four when Lil came bursting in. Annie knew she would bring a bit of life into the house and eagerly kissed her painted rosy cheeks.

'Merry Christmas, both,' Lil said. 'Got yer a nice present, Mr Rodgers.'

'That's very kind of you, Lil, and I've got something for you.' He reached under his chair and brought out a small packet, neatly wrapped.

'Cor, thanks. Did you wrap it? It looks very nice.'

'You forget, I'm expert at wrapping parcels.'

Lil tore at the paper and was wreathed in smiles when she took a silver lighter from the velvet box. She rushed across the room and gave him a kiss. 'Aw, fanks, it's really smashing.'

'You'd better rub that lipstick off Dad,' said Annie. 'He might get talked about.'

Lil rubbed at his cheek. 'This is fer you.'

Mr Rodgers held up the beige cardigan.

'I hope it fits, Annie gave me yer measurements.'

He stood up and tried it on. 'It fits a treat. Thanks, Lil. You must have known I needed a new one. I'll miss Mother knitting for me now.'

'It ain't 'ome-made.'

'It's still very nice, thank you.'

A silence fell over them.

'Look what I got you, Lil,' said Annie quickly handing her parcel over to Lil.

Lil tore off the wrapping paper noisily. 'Thanks, Annie, I always like your taste in fings. Yer got a flair, and this 'andbag will go a treat with me new shoes.'

'Open it,' urged Annie.

'Aw look, look, Mr Rodgers, she's bought me a lovely gold compact as well. Fanks, Annie, yer a real pal. Now look at what I got you.'

'Your compact's not real gold,' insisted Annie as she opened her present from Lil. She smiled with pleasure at the large paisley scarf and, putting it round her shoulders, preened round the room. 'Lil, it's lovely, thank you.'

'Yer really like it? It's all the latest fashion, so the books say.'

'Well, you've something to write and tell that young man now,' said Mr Rodgers as he puffed on his pipe.

'What young man?' screamed Lil.

Annie handed Lil the Christmas card. 'I've got a letter from him as well.'

'Let's 'ave a look then.'

Annie reached up to the mantelpiece and took the letter from behind the clock.

''E's ever such a nice bloke, Annie,' said Lil as she read the letter. 'Bit too quiet fer me, though. I 'ope yer didn't mind me giving 'im yer address. Yer see, I didn't fink 'e'd write.'

'I can't really remember what he looked like.' Annie was trying to appear nonchalant.

''E's got dark 'air and brown eyes.'

'You had a good look then, Lil,' said Mr Rodgers. 'I couldn't even tell you what colour Annie's eyes are.'

'Oh, Mr Rodgers, I bet yer could. But yer see when yer singing yer 'as ter look at somefink, and it might as well be at people's eyes.'

'Where does he live?' asked Annie.

'Round Peckham way I fink. Yer gonner answer this?' Lil waved the letter.

'Well, it won't do any harm,' said Annie, taking it from her and putting it back behind the clock.

Christmas came and went. It was New Year's Eve and though Lil had tried hard to persuade Annie and her father to come to the Castle where she was working, they had both refused.

'I wish you would go out, Dad,' said Annie as she cleared the tea things away. 'After all, you don't have to get up in the morning. New Year's Day's a Sunday this year.'

'What about you? Why don't you go with the Hobbses?'

Annie shook her head. 'No, not tonight.'

Mr Rodgers got up from the table and sat in his chair. 'Have you lost interest in the Salvation Army then?'

'No, not really but, I don't know, so many things have happened.'

'I know what you mean, love. I'm pleased you stay in a bit more now; it's good to have you here.' He leaned forward and lit his pipe.

Annie sat and watched him. She often wondered about that night she had seen him with Bessie. 'Dad, why don't you go to the Eagle now?'

He sat back in his chair. 'I'd rather have a quiet drink indoors.'

Annie smiled, pleased the Eagle held no attractions for him. That Bessie thing before her mother died must have been a one-off, otherwise he wouldn't have needed any pushing to go out.

All evening they sat and listened to the wireless, laughing at the comedians' jokes and singing along with the bands till it was almost midnight.

Mr Rodgers stood up. 'I think we should have a drink to bring in nineteen thirty-nine, what do you say to that?'

'I think it's a good idea. I'll get the glasses.'

'A drop of port suit you?'

'Why not?'

Her father filled the glasses and, as Big Ben boomed out twelve o'clock on the wireless, they lifted their glasses.

'Happy New Year, love,' said her father, kissing her cheek. 'And for us, it can only get better.'

'Happy New Year, Dad.' Annie squeezed her eyes shut, hoping to stem the single tear that trickled down her cheek.

Chapter 21

Nineteen thirty-nine began with the talk of a war on everyone's lips. Annie wrote a short, cheerful letter to Sam, and thought that would be last she would hear from him – but to her surprise and delight, she received a reply a week later. In it, he told her all about himself and his family. Annie read it out loud to her father over breakfast. 'He lives in Peckham, his dad's a docker, and he's the eldest of seven children: he's got two brothers and four sisters.'

'No wonder the lad left home and joined the Navy. Should think it was a bit crowded with that lot.'

'He's a wireless operator, and at the moment his ship is back at Chatham,' she continued.

'So he's got a few brains then,' said her father approvingly.

That evening Annie replied to Sam's letter, telling him a little bit more about herself.

'You're keen,' said her father watching her.

'Well, I've nothing else to do.'

'You could go out a bit more.'

'It's a bit cold to stand around singing.'

Her father made no comment, just pushed his glasses further back up his nose, and returned to his newspaper.

Mr Rodgers wasn't the only one to notice Annie hadn't been out so much with the Hobbs just lately, and on Monday morning Rose came into the shop to ask her why.

'You haven't lost interest, have you?' she asked pointedly.

Annie was pleased her father was busy serving, and gently edged Rose to the other side of the shop. 'No, Rose, it's just that I don't like leaving Dad alone for too many nights. If I'm here we play cards and he listens to the wireless, but when I'm out I know he just sits and mopes.'

'But what about Sundays?'

'I like to get the dinner for him.'

'He should have some sort of outside interest. You have your own life to live, you know. Remember, I lost my mother too, and my brother. In lots of ways we're in the same boat.'

'I know,' said Annie, quickly glancing towards her father, hoping he hadn't heard Rose's remarks. She knew that she and Rose were very different. 'I'll come out with you on Saturday night,' she promised.

'Good. I'll see you about seven then. Goodbye, Mr Rodgers.'

'Bye, Rose.'

On Saturday afternoon, Annie was helping her father stack the shelves when the door opened and in hobbled Georgie Bates. Annie rushed over and closed the door behind him. She still had a soft spot for Georgie and couldn't help feeling protective towards him. She had been relieved when Lil had lost interst in him after she'd had her baby – much as she loved Lil, the last thing she'd wanted for Georgie was Lil using him as a convenient father for her child. But Georgie'd seemed rather crestfallen that Lil no longer paid him the attention she once had.

''Allo, Annie, Mr Rodgers. How are yer both?'

'We're fine, Georgie, how about your good self?' said Mr Rodgers.

'Not ser bad,' he said, sitting on the chair and resting his crutches against the counter. 'Wot's been going on in 'ere?' he asked, looking round the shop.

'It's Annie's idea,' said her father disdainfully. 'She thinks we ought to have a change round. Wants me to get in a lot of fancy things, but I keep telling her this is a poor neighbourhood, you can't expect me regulars to want posh stuff. And I'm not having 'em pay for it on tick.'

'Oh, Dad. I only said we should get in a few fancy biscuits, and different cheeses to start with. Then perhaps we could get some nice boxes of chocolates.'

'That's the trouble, if I start it I could end up bankrupt.'

'I must say I like the way yer done the shelves wiv that posh paper,' said Georgie.

'Mrs Turner swears I've put up me prices.'

'Don't listen to him,' said Annie. 'It's good to see you out and about again. How are you feeling.'

'It's great ter be able ter get out. I'm gitting quite clever on these.' He pointed to his crutches. 'But guess what me best news is?' His face was beaming. 'I've gotter a job.'

'Oh, Georgie, that is good news. I'm so pleased for you,' said Annie.

'It ain't much, but at least I'll be earning a few bob, and I'll be gitting out of the 'ouse. The old lady don't 'alf keep on about me gitting under 'er feet.'

'I know what you mean, son, you should hear Annie go on at me.'

'Dad,' Annie reproved him. 'Where're you going to be working, Georgie?'

'It's round at the old broom factory. I'll be sitting down all day at a bench so I 'spect it'll be boring. But there's plenty o' little darlings that work there, and who knows what greater fings it'll lead ter.'

'Yes, well, if there is a war, they'll be plenty of jobs then,' said Mr Rodgers.

'Don't be such a scaremonger,' said Annie.

Georgie shook his head. 'No, yer dad's right. Still, at least I knows I can't fight fer me King and country.' He held up the leg that finished just below the knee. 'They won't want them that can't run fast, so I'll stay 'ome and earn all the money, and take out all the pretty girls they'll be leaving behind.'

Annie laughed, glad to see him so perky. 'Trust you to think like that.'

'Anyway, Annie, that's what I've called round fer, ter ask yer if yer'd like ter come out with me ter kinda celebrate.'

'I'll go up and put the kettle on,' said Mr Rodgers. 'Fancy a cuppa, Georgie?'

'Yer, why not?' When her father left, Georgie asked, 'Well?'

211

'I'd love to. When?'

'What about ternight?'

'Oh, I can't make it tonight.'

'Why's that, gotter date?'

'Sort of.'

'Oh yer. Who's the lucky chap?'

'It's the Salvation Army.'

'Yer not still going about wiv that lot, are yer?'

'Well, yes.'

'I fought yer would 'ave chucked it be now. Annie, yer ain't doing yerself any favours standing on street corners singing.' He banged his crutch on the floor. 'Yer too pretty ter be wasting yer life. 'Sides, it won't bring Will back yer know, and yer've got yer own life ter lead.'

'I know that, and you're the second person to tell me this week – but I enjoy helping people, especially when I go to the hostel and give out the soup – some of the old men are real characters.'

'Yer wonner watch them, dirty old buggers some of 'em can be. When I was in 'ospital you should 'ave 'eard some of the fings they used ter say about the nurses.'

'I expect you were as bad.'

'Well, yer gotter 'ave a laugh.'

'Some of them are really well educated, and it makes you wonder why they fell on such hard times.'

'If the job folds, well . . . I expect they've seen a lot o' life though. I can see I ain't gonner change yer mind then?'

'No, sorry. But what about tomorrow?' she asked eagerly.

'Sorry, I told me mum I'd take 'er ter the pictures, and I don't wonner let 'er down.'

'No, no of course not.'

'Tea up,' said her father pushing open the door.

That evening, as she was getting ready to go out, she kept thinking of Georgie. She was torn: she wanted to go to the hostel, but she also felt Georgie should have some company. In the end she took off her uniform, put on her blue woollen dress and went downstairs.

'Dad, I'm going over to see if Georgie still wants to go out.'

'That's good. It'll do you good to go somewhere different for a change. Where're you going?'

'I don't know. I should tell Rose I'm not going first; they'll be waiting for me.'

'All right, love, I may even go out for a drink myself later on.'

Annie smiled approvingly. 'That'll do you good, Dad.'

'I'll wait up for you.'

'No, don't worry. I don't even know where we'll be going.'

Annie pulled her coat collar tighter at her neck, trying to shut out the cold wind. She felt guilty as she hurried along the road. A few months ago she'd been arguing with her father about joining the Salvationists, and nothing would have stopped her from going out with them, but now, since her mother's death, it seemed that any excuse could make her change her mind. *Was* she losing interest, like Rose said?

Mr Hobbs wasn't very pleased when Annie told him she wasn't going to the hostel that evening. 'I hope you are not going to play at this, Annie,' he said sternly. 'I must say I'm very surprised at you, I thought you were a true believer.'

'I've always told you, Mr Hobbs, the most important part of it for me is helping people.'

'Yes, we all know that, Annie,' said Rose kindly. 'Father, don't go on, or else you'll put Annie off for ever.'

'I'll be round in the week, Rose,' said Annie quickly. She didn't want them quarrelling over her.

She made her way to Georgie's house. He lived in a small terrace quite near to Fisher's. The factory was still puffing its smoke over all the local inhabitants and, according to the men that came into the shop for their cigarettes, the wall had been rebuilt and it was business as usual. It seemed that Will and Georgie had been the only two real victims that sad day. Everyone else who had been injured was now back at work.

As she turned into his road the memories came flooding back. The last time she'd been here had been to tell Mrs Bates that Georgie was in hospital. As she walked along the uneven pavement she wondered how Georgie managed so well on his crutches. She had never noticed if he wore gloves. His hands must be freezing.

I'll knit him some, she thought, as she hurried along.

As she neared Georgie's house, she heard a lot of noise streaming through an open window a few doors away from where he lived. Someone was banging away on a piano, and the singing was raucous and noisy. The loud music, the laughing and shouting, suggested that everybody was having a good time. As Annie walked past she could see people dancing. and she wondered if that was where he had planned to take her. She couldn't remember the last time she had been to a party; the last time she'd been to a dance was with her cousin Roy. She smiled when she recalled that week. Although it was just after Will had been killed, and she'd been feeling sad, she had enjoyed herself. The long walks over the fields with Nell trotting by her side had helped her to feel peaceful and serene. Perhaps she should go and see them again now that her father seemed a bit perkier.

She knocked on Mrs Bates's door. It was a while before the door was flung open. ''Allo, Annie, this is a surprise,' said Mrs Bates.

'Is Georgie in?' she asked.

'No 'e ain't, love. What can we do fer yer?'

'Oh, nothing.' Annie looked up the road.

'Come in fer a tick.'

Annie stepped inside the passage. It was gloomy as the light from the gas lamp was turned down very low. She followed Mrs Bates into the kitchen.

'Been doing a bit o' mending.' She quickly gathered up the sewing from the tapestry armchair. Annie noted the shirt had been neatly patched many times before. 'Gotter make 'im look smart fer 'is new job. Sit yerself down fer a minute or two. Did yer know 'e starts on Monday?'

'Yes.' Annie sat in the chair. 'He came into the shop and told me.'

''E's been in ter see yer then?'

'Yes,' said Annie.

''E's a good lad. Used ter be a bit of a tearaway, but all that's changed now.'

Annie knew Mrs Bates was a widow: her husband had died many years ago and she had brought up her two girls and Georgie on her own. The girls were now married and had moved. She was a good woman, and as Annie looked round she could see her place was clean and as comfortable as she could keep it on her small pension.

'How's yer dad keeping?'

'Not so bad. I wish he would go out though.'

'Give 'im time. That was a nasty shock, yer mother going like that.'

'Yes, it was. I bet you'll be glad to see Georgie back at work?'

'Not 'arf. 'E can't 'arf git under yer feet, and those bloody crutches of 'is always seem ter be in the way. I can't tell yer 'ow many times I've fallen over 'em. 'Sides, it'll be good fer 'im ter mix wiv people again.' She sat on a wooden chair next to Annie. 'Ter tell the truth, love, I've been a bit worried about 'im moping about all day, and I ain't got a lotter money ter give 'im ter go down the boozer. 'E gits a bit fed up wiv me, and about 'is leg, but I tells 'im 'e's gotter make the most of it, it ain't gonner grow back again. Cuppa tea?'

Annie looked at her watch. 'Do you think he could be at that party up the road?'

'Na, it's a wake. They're Irish, don't 'ave a lot ter do wiv 'em. They buried the old man this morning.'

Annie smiled. 'I wouldn't mind a cup of tea, if that's all right.'

'Just put the kettle on, I'll be back in a mo.' She left Annie and hurried into the scullery.

'Did Georgie tell yer ter come round 'ere then?' called Mrs Bates through the open door.

'No, he asked me to go out with him tonight and I said I couldn't, but I managed to get out of what I was doing, so I thought I'd come round and see if he still wanted to go out.'

Mrs Bates walked in with two cups of tea, but no saucers. ''E ain't been 'ome all day. I'll git the sugar.' She put the two cups on the table, which was covered with a thin, chequered tablecloth, went out, and returned almost immediately with a blue bag of sugar that had a spoon sticking up in it. 'Don't know where 'e gits ter 'arf the time.'

Annie put some of the lumpy, tea-stained sugar in her tea, and sipped the hot sweet liquid.

'How's yer friend Lil gitting on?'

'Fine, she works over Peckham way now.'

'Georgie used ter really look forward to you two going ter the 'ospital ter see 'im. I fink 'e 'ad a bit of a soft spot fer 'er. Does 'e know she works over there?'

'Oh yes, I think he's seen her round here once or twice. But she's very busy, what with her singing and her job.'

'Oh yer. More tea?'

'No thanks, I'll have to be going.' Annie stood up. 'You will tell Georgie I called, won't you?'

'Course, love. Mind 'ow yer go.'

When Annie passed the house with the party in full swing, she thought of her own mother's sad funeral, and asked herself, who was right?

As she walked along she wondered where she could go. It was too late for the pictures, and she didn't fancy going back home. A bus bound for Whitechapel was coming towards her, and on an impulse she clambered aboard it.

Seated inside, she let her thoughts drift. She knew she had to do something, her life was just slipping away. She got off and wandered into the mission.

'Hello, Annie, I thought you weren't coming tonight,' said one of her fellow officers. 'Sergeant Hobbs said you had to go out.'

'No, I mean yes. I was suppose to meet someone, but he wasn't home.'

'A nice young man, is he?'

'Yes, he was a friend of Will's.'

'Oh. Well, now you're here, perhaps you could give us a hand with cutting up some bread.'

'Are Sergeant Hobbs and Rose still here?'

'No, they've gone on.'

'I can't stay long. I mustn't miss my last tram.'

'You can go whenever you wish, don't worry about prayers.'

Annie went into the warm kitchen and stood at the table in front of the large window, and began slicing the loaves. She looked up. Outside, a rowdy crowd was hanging around on the corner. What if Daisy should walk past now? Would she want to talk to her after she had tried to help them? Perhaps she should just learn to mind her own business. After all, Daisy and her family were perfectly happy before she tried to put their house in order. Daisy's mother was to be admired, wanting to keep the family together. But it had been a cold winter, so where were they living now?

'I'll take this lot,' said the officer, bringing Annie out of her daydream.

'Do you want any more?'

'Please.'

Annie continued cutting the bread. Her mind wasn't really on what she was doing: she was miles away, trying to work out her future.

Annie was surprised to find her father was still out when she returned home. She made herself a cup of cocoa and sat at the table, thinking about the few changes she had been allowed to make in the shop. She wished they lived in an area where there was more scope for improvement. If only she could work in a big store and be in charge of a department – but she knew she would never leave her father.

It was after midnight when she heard his key in the lock.

'You still up?' He looked startled when Annie opened the kitchen door.

'Just made a cup of cocoa. D'you fancy one?'

'No, just had one in . . . Been in a mate's house.'

'That's nice. Anyone I know?'

'No. I'm off to bed now, love.' He disappeared upstairs.

Annie sat with her elbows on the table clutching her cup as tears filled her eyes. She was crying with a mixture of happiness and regret. This was the first time he'd been out since . . . Annie reflected on how well he looked when he walked in. He should go out more often, she told herself, and rinsed out her cup before going to bed.

The next day, just after dinner, Georgie came round to apologize for being out.

'Don't worry about it,' said Annie. 'It was really my fault for saying no in the first place.'

'D'yer fancy going out now?'

'We could go for a walk.' She paused. 'Sorry, Georgie, that was a bit thoughtless.'

'That's all right. Tell yer what, let's get the bus ter the park.'

'That'll be nice, I'll just pop up and get me coat.'

In the park they sat on a bench and talked, and watched the children playing with a ball.

'D'yer know, I fink that's what I miss most – me game o' football.'

'I didn't know you played.'

'Not the real fing, only mucked about.'

Annie told him about the letters she'd had from Sam. Since the accident she had found Georgie easy to talk to.

'Annie,' he said seriously. 'I fink there's sumfink yer ought ter know.'

She looked at him.

'It was 'cos of me Will got killed.'

'What?' She felt the colour drain quickly from her face. 'What d'you mean?'

'Well, when we saw that machine start to topple, we knew we couldn't git out in time, and we knew it would 'it the wall.' He stopped. 'When Will saw it, 'e flung 'imself on top o' me.'

Annie sat and stared at him.

'I'm sorry, Annie.'

She smiled weakly, and touched his hand. 'That sounds like Will. I'm glad you told me.'

George looked relieved. 'I've been wanting ter tell yer fer ages, but it never seemed ter be the right time. So yer see, I feel a bit responsible for yer, and I know it ain't none of my business, and Will was me best mate – but don't yer fink yer should go out with . . . Yer know? Yer very pretty, and well . . .'

'Go on with you,' Annie blushed. 'You always was an old flatterer.'

'No, honest. I don't fink Will would want yer ter just sit around and mope. 'Sides, I always fancied yer meself.'

'And I thought it was Lil you were after.' She laughed.

'Lil's a good mate, she'll always stick by yer. But she's got her own life to lead over in Peckham.'

'Yes,' said Annie. 'And she does like the high life.'

'Besides, I'm 'oping ter find meself a nice little darling in the factory.'

'Georgie Bates, you never change.'

'Why? D'yer want me to?'

'No.' She leant over and gently kissed his cheek. 'No, don't ever change.'

He touched his cheek. 'I won't wash this fer a week.'

Annie laughed. 'Come on, if you're taking your mum to the pictures, you don't want to miss the first film.'

'D'you wonner come with us?'

'No. You give your mum a nice treat – she thinks a lot of you, you know.'

Georgie smiled. 'Yer, I know.'

'Come on.' She handed him his crutches and pulled him up.

Holding her hand he said, 'Annie, I'm really sorry about Will, and I meant what I said. Don't mourn 'im for ever.'

Chapter 22

Over the next few months, several letters were exchanged between Annie and Sam, and she felt she knew so much about him. She knew he loved being in the navy, and it seemed he was very proud of the way he'd passed his exams to become a wireless operator. His ship mates were very important to him, and he told her of how, when they landed in strange countries he would have liked more time to explore further than the waterfront bars. She was surprised at how easy it was to tell him so many personal things, and always eagerly awaited his replies. In her fourth letter to him, Annie told Sam about Will, about how he had been killed and how she still thought about him. The letter she received in reply was full of sympathy and understanding. It also contained some exciting news.

'Dad,' she called, reading Sam's letter as she climbed the stairs after collecting Monday morning's post. 'Sam's coming home for the weekend.'

'That's nice,' said her father, looking up from spreading thick chunky marmalade on his toast. 'Does he say when?'

'Yes, this Friday. He wants to take me out on Saturday. Would that be all right?'

'I think I can manage one day without you. Where's he taking you?'

'He don't say,' Annie smiled.

'You'll have to bring him home. I'd like to meet this young man.'

She was annoyed with herself when her face flushed. 'You'll see him on Friday. He's coming over to tell me what time he's taking me out. And, Dad, I've told you before, we're only pen-friends.'

'Of course,' said her father, pushing his chair back. 'Come down when you're ready. What time will Lil be round?'

'About lunchtime as usual. That all right?'

Annie sat at the table and re-read Sam's letter. He did seem a very nice person. And she was really looking forward to spending a day with him.

Lil was also very enthusiastic about meeting Sam again when Annie told her he was coming home. 'Did 'e say if Mike's coming with 'im?' she asked eagerly, peering at Annie's reflection in her dressing-table mirror. Annie was sitting getting ready for their afternoon browse round the shops before going to the pictures.

'No. I expect you'll see Mike if he goes in the Castle.'

'Yer. 'Ere, what d'yer say we all meet up in the evenin', make up a foursome, and go up West after the pub closes?'

Annie frowned worriedly and turned to face Lil. 'I don't know. Sam didn't say we'd go to a pub.'

Lil sat on the bed. "E's a sailor, ain't 'e? And they like their booze.'

Annie still felt worried. 'I don't know about going into a pub.'

'Why not? They ain't the dens of iniquity your lot spout on about. 'Ere, 'ark at me!' She threw herself back on the bed and screamed with laughter. 'That's your fault, me using long words like that.'

Annie smiled. 'I don't know what I'll say if he asks me.'

Lil sat up and suddenly became serious. 'D'yer know, Annie, sometimes you can be a real pain. Surely you can go and enjoy yourself for one night. I bet some of the old men in the Sally Army likes a drink or two, and I can't stand secret drinkers. Bloody hypocrites most of 'em are.'

Annie turned to face the mirror again. 'I'll see what Sam wants to do first.'

'Anyway,' continued Lil, almost ignoring her. 'Yer ain't been going out with 'em quite as much as yer used ter. Why's that? Getting fed up with 'em?'

Annie stood up. 'No, it's just that I don't like leaving Dad too many times.' She picked up her handbag. She was already over-whelmed with guilt at not attending the meetings regularly now, and she didn't want to talk to Lil about it. 'I'm ready. Come on, let's go.'

On Friday, every time the shop door opened Annie eagerly looked up. She was really looking forward to meeting Sam, to seeing if he looked exactly as she'd remembered him, with his kind brown eyes and shy smile. But it wasn't until after they had closed for the night that there was a bang on the knocker and she raced down the stairs.

'Hello, Annie.' Sam stood on the doorstep with his hat in his hand. 'Sorry I couldn't get over before but I wanted to see me dad when he finished work.'

'That's all right,' Annie knew her voice was high and unnatural. 'Come on up.'

Mr Rodgers was already on his feet when Annie pushed open the kitchen door.

'Dad, I'd like you to meet Sam.'

They both shook hands with the same enthusiasm.

He stayed all evening. They laughed and talked; Annie had never thought someone could make them both so happy again. The way he fitted in, it was as though they had known him for years. When it was time for him to go, Annie slipped on her coat and said she would walk to the end of the Mews with him.

The crisp night air of April still had a bite to it and Annie pulled her coat collar tighter at her throat. 'Thank you for coming round tonight. Dad really enjoyed listening to some of your tales.'

'What about you, Annie?'

She was pleased it was dark, with only the dull yellow glow from the gas lamp lighting up the end of the Mews. She stopped to look in the haberdashery window, and he couldn't see her blush. 'I'm glad I've met you at last,' she said, and hurriedly added, 'have you thought where we're going tomorrow? We still haven't decided.'

Sam turned her round to face him. 'Annie, I'm so pleased you let me write to you. I really look forward to your letters.'

'Two old spinster ladies own this shop,' she gabbled on. 'They

are very sweet; both of them lost their fiancés in the war.' Annie
was trying hard to keep the conversation lighthearted.

Sam obviously realized this, as he asked, 'Is there anywhere in
particular you would like to go?'

'No, I don't think so. What about you?'

'I'll tell you what, you sleep on it. We don't need to decide now.
I'll pick you up about ten if that's all right?'

'Ten will be fine. Goodnight, Sam.'

'Goodnight, Annie.' Very lightly, he kissed her cheek.

When Annie walked into the kitchen her father was whistling.
She hadn't heard him whistle since her mother died. 'I like him,
he's a nice lad,' he said, moving away from the sink.

'Yes, Dad, he is. He's coming round at ten tomorrow. I don't
know where we're going so get yourself something to eat, don't
hang around waiting for me.'

'I've washed up the cups,' said her father, plumping up the
cushions. He picked up his newspaper and neatly folded it then
glanced at the headlines. 'I hope there's not going to be another
war – it'll be rough on young lads like that. I'm off up now. Turn
the gas out. I'll see you in the morning.' He too lightly kissed her
cheek.

Half an hour later, Annie lay in bed thinking about Sam. It
would be awful for everyone if there was another war. Without
realizing it, she began comparing him with Will. They were about
the same height, and both had dark eyes, but Sam's hair was darker
than Will's, and he was a lot broader. Sam had a handsome outdoor
face, and he seemed very nice. She quickly admonished herself for
thinking like that. Nobody could be as kind and caring as Will, and
nobody could possibly take his place. She turned over. Where could
they go tomorrow? It couldn't be up the Thames: Sam must have
had enough of boats. What about Kew? It would be nice to see the
gardens. With that thought in mind she finally fell asleep.

It was five to ten when Sam walked into the shop. 'Hello, Mr
Rodgers, Annie. It's a smashing day out.'

Annie smiled at Mrs Turner who was seated on the chair.

'Yer old man letting yer 'ave a morning orf then, love?'

'Hello, Sam.' Mr Rodgers continued weighing up the broken

biscuits, and said jokingly, 'She's always having time off. Didn't I let her have a whole week off, what, must be almost two years ago?'

'Slave-driving old sod. Off anywhere nice, girl?'

'Don't know yet. Bye, Dad, Mrs Turner.' They said their good-byes together as Sam and Annie left the shop, laughing.

'She means well,' said Annie, chuckling.

Sam smiled, his dark brown eyes twinkling, and she quickly looked away.

''Allo, Annie love, off out then, are we?' Bessie had been leaning over a box of apples. She straightened up and smoothed her overall down over her well-rounded hips, but it wasn't Annie she was looking at.

'Hello, Bessie,' said Annie politely.

'Everybody seems surprised you've got a day off. Is your dad a bit of a tyrant?' inquired Sam.

'No, it's just that, other than with Lil, I don't usually go out much.'

'Did you and Lil go anywhere exciting when you had your week off?'

'I didn't go with Lil. I went to my aunty's in Sussex. It was just after Will got killed.'

'I'm sorry, Annie, I should have guessed.'

'You weren't to know. Now, where are we off to?'

'You tell me.'

'Well, do you like flowers?'

'Yes, I suppose so. Don't see that many at sea. Why?'

Annie laughed. 'How about Kew Gardens?'

His face lit up. 'That's a really smashing idea. D'you know, I've never been there. We can have a spot of lunch, and see how the time goes from there. Did you have any other plans for this evening?'

Annie looked down and pushed on the fingers of her glove. 'No.' Sam knew she was in the Salvation Army, and that she often went to the mission on a Saturday night, so she was waiting for him to say something. But he only took her arm and said, 'Good. So the rest of the day's ours.'

For hours they wandered round Kew, admiring the banks of spring flowers. They sat on a bench and had a sandwich. Annie was still amazed at how easy it was to talk and laugh with him.

Sam leaned back. 'Annie,' he said quietly. 'I know no one will ever take Will's place, but now we've met, we do seem to hit it off. Will you come out with me when I'm home again?'

'I should think so,' Annie replied, gazing studiously in the direction of a sea of daffodils.

'You will still keep writing, won't you?'

'Of course. I really enjoy your letters.'

'Our ship's finished its trials, so we'll be sailing next week.'

Annie turned her gaze away from the daffodils and looked at him. 'Will you be away long?'

'Don't know yet. But I'll let you know.' He sat up. 'We could finish up on some wonderful South Sea Island, with lots of hula girls.'

Annie was relieved he had stopped being serious. 'I hope you don't get up to anything, you know . . . ?' she smiled.

He threw his hands up in the air, and with mock horror on his face, said, 'Heaven forbid.' He scrambled to his feet. 'Come on.' He held out his hands to pull her up. 'Let's go and have an ice-cream.' As she stood up he pulled her close, and for a second or two they looked into each other's eyes. Their hands were still firmly clasped when some children rushed past yelling and shouting. The spell was instantly broken.

They left Kew and went into a Lyon's Corner House. After ordering Sam asked, 'What shall we do this evening?'

'I don't mind.'

He sat back and, taking a packet of cigarettes from his pocket, offered Annie one. 'Sorry, I forgot you don't smoke,' he said when she shook her head.

'Would you like to go to the pictures?' she asked quickly.

'We could do.' He leant forward and tapped the end of the cigarette in the ashtray. 'I told Mike that we might see him in the Castle later. Would that be all right with you?'

The waitress had brought the tea and Annie began pouring. 'I don't know. You see it could be rather awkward. Some of the

Salvation Army officers go there collecting, and it wouldn't look quite right if I was sitting in there drinking.'

'No, I suppose not.' Sam puffed on his cigarette before stubbing it out in the ashtray. 'Not even if you only have a lemonade?'

'I'd rather not. Look, you can drop me off if you like, then you can go and see Mike.'

'He's not that important. I'll be sick of the sight of him soon enough. Be seeing him for months when we set sail.'

Annie was pleased he preferred her company to Mike's.

That night she lay in bed reflecting on the day's events. In the cinema he had held her hand and she hadn't pulled it away. On their way home, as they were strolling through the Mews, Sam had nudged her arm as they passed Sally the ironmonger's eldest daughter locked in a deep embrace with her boyfriend.

'Looks like you might be having a wedding here soon,' said Sam.

Annie giggled. 'She's still at school.'

When they reached her doorway, Sam again only gently kissed her cheek. She was pleased he hadn't made any more advances.

Now, in the dark, Annie touched her cheek. She was restless and couldn't sleep. She liked him, and couldn't believe what she was feeling. Was this grasping at straws? Was it because she was lonely, and Sam was the first person to come along since Will's death? But this wasn't like her. She told herself over and over again that he wasn't Will, and she mustn't be silly. He was a sailor, a pen-friend, and would always be off to some foreign place, perhaps for years. She was seeing him again tomorrow afternoon, and they were going for a walk in the park before he went back to his ship, but then he'd be gone. She must be sensible . . . with that thought she closed her eyes and tried to sleep.

She was drifting off when she heard the kitchen door shut. She recognized her father's footsteps. What was he doing wandering about at this time of night? Had he just come home? She'd assumed he was in bed when she came in. Should she get up and see? It would be such an effort; sleep was beginning to overtake her. He hadn't said was going out. He'd been going out a lot lately, and he wasn't telling Annie who with. She turned over and cuddled her pillow. Well, that's his business, she thought sleepily. I've been too fond of poking my nose in other people's affairs, and I usually finish up doing more harm than good. He'd tell her, if and when he wanted to.

On Monday Lil was full of her weekend with Mike. It seemed they'd had a good time together. 'What about Sam? We fought we might 'ave seen somefink of yer. Where did yer git to?'

'We went to Kew on Saturday.'

'Kew? What, Kew Gardens?'

Annie nodded.

'That must 'ave been really boring. Whose idea was that?'

'Mine, and we had a very nice day.'

Lil screwed her nose up. 'I bet Sam didn't fink so.'

'Why? What makes you say that?'

'Well, 'e's a sailor, ain't 'e? 'E ain't interested in flowers, and I bet 'e missed 'is pint.'

'He didn't seem that concerned. I did tell him he could go over to see you and Mike, but he said he could see Mike at any time.'

Lil gave Annie a playful push. ''Ere, looks like yer got yerself a fancy man.'

'Sam's very nice, but we're just friends.'

'Sounds like it,' said Lil knowingly.

'He is nice,' said Annie firmly.

'Bet yer didn't tell 'im about Will?'

'As matter of fact I already have, in my letters.'

'Oh yeah, and what did 'e 'ave ter say about it?'

'He was very sympathetic.'

'Oh yeah,' repeated Lil.

Chapter 23

It was a warm day, and Annie looked up from the order book as Bessie came sauntering through the open door. 'Is yer dad about?'

'He's doing a delivery at the moment – can I give him a message?'

'Na, it's all right, I'll catch 'im later.' Bessie caught her reflection in the glass case that Annie had placed on top of the counter to hold the new cheeses and fancy water biscuits. She pursed her bright red lips together and patted her blonde hair. 'I like the new stuff yer gitting in,' she said, continuing to wander round. 'Them posh boxes of chocolates are smashing.'

'You've had them before?' asked Annie in surprise.

'Yer, yer dad gave me a box.'

Annie was suddenly very interested. 'When?' she asked sharply.

'When we was out fer a drink the other night.'

The colour drained from Annie's face. 'You've been out with my dad?'

'Yer, quite a few times. Don't look ser shocked. 'E's good company, and it makes a change ter go out wiv someone who ain't trying ter git yer knickers orf all the time.' Bessie's white overall was undone and she smoothed her tight skirt over her rounded hips.

Annie came from behind the counter and, shutting the shop door, stood defiantly in front of it. Her face was full of anger. 'Now you listen to me, Bessie. You leave my dad alone. We all know what you're like.'

'Wot? Well, fanks a bunch. Yer gitting ter be a right stuck-up little madam. First yer takes over trying ter run the shop, now yer wants ter take over yer dad's life. Why can't yer leave yer poor old

229

feller alone – 'e can go out wiv who 'e likes.'

'Not with the likes of you.'

'If I wanner go out wiv 'im I will, and you ain't gonner stop me, so git out the way – I ain't standing 'ere ter git a lecture from you. Why can't yer leave yer dad ter do what 'e wants?'

Annie stood her ground. 'I don't want to see him made a laughing-stock by going out with the likes of you. Why can't you leave him alone?'

Bessie laughed, and Annie was reminded of that night years ago when her father had tried to climb the lamp-post. 'How long has this been going on?' she demanded.

'You're a silly cow. D'yer fink I'm interested in yer old man? Christ grant me wiv a bit o' savvy. I only said I'd go out wiv 'im fer a drink' cause 'e was lonely and fed up after yer mum died, and you was no 'elp, orf singing wiv the Sally Army.'

Annie suddenly felt flooded with guilt. She realized she was doing it again – getting involved in other people's business. She moved away from the door and walked round the back of the counter, the wind taken completely out of her sails. 'I'm sorry, Bessie. If my dad wants to take you out, well, then that's up to him.'

'I ain't that bleeding 'ard up fer a bloke,' sniffed Bessie. ''E's old enough ter be me dad.' She opened the door, her nose in the air.

'What did you want him for anyway?' asked Annie, quietly.

'Nuffink, just tell 'im I can't see 'im ternight – I've got a date.' She walked out of the shop.

Annie didn't want her father to know she had been trying to interfere with his life, so when he came in she told him casually that Bessie couldn't go out that night. She didn't make an issue of it, and when her father wasn't forthcoming, she let the matter pass.

As the summer progressed, so did the preparations for a war with Germany. The newspapers, wireless and newsreels were full of the problems, and traumas that were going on in Europe.

When Annie related her fears in her letters to Sam, he told her there was nothing to worry about. His letters had been very different since he returned to his ship, more loving. Annie tried hard to keep her letters to him on a friendly, interesting basis.

One day, at the beginning of July, Annie and Lil were on their way to the pictures. When they reached Silwood Street they stood for a moment or two watching the men unloading huge sections of tin air-raid shelters from off the back of lorries, and taking them into the houses.

'They keep saying there ain't gonner be a war,' said Lil. 'So what they giving 'em out for?'

'Got to be prepared, I suppose,' said Annie looking at the large lumps of silver corrugated metal stacked on the lorry.

'What 'appens if yer ain't got a yard? Where they gonner put 'em?'

'Don't know, we haven't got anywhere to put one,' said Annie.

'And they ain't got anywhere in Victoria Gardens. 'Ere, they'll 'ave ter move old Reeves' 'orse out. Phew, when they dig down there, that'll stink!' She laughed. ''Ere, I 'ope them shelters don't start ter grow up like rhubarb, with all that 'orse shit on the ground.'

'Lil,' said Annie in her disgusted voice, but she was smiling.

As they slowly walked along they laughed at some of the antics going on around them. Men, with sacking padding their shoulders to protect them, strained and struggled, their knees bending with the heavy weight of the long unyielding sheets of iron as they pushed and shoved them through the open front doors. The sound of swearing and cursing came floating through the air as the men fell over the prams and other paraphernalia that were piled up in most of the passages.

One large woman, with her hair in metal curlers and her hands locked under her floral pinny, was clearly agitated; she looked very angry as she followed the men out of her house. She stood in her doorway and began shouting. 'Yer jus' broke me winder!' she yelled. 'Now yer've gorn an' trod on me bleeding cat. It's run up me curtains, Gawd only knows 'ow I'm gonner git it down.'

The men, leaning against their lorry and having a smoke, began laughing. 'Sorry, missis.'

''It it wiv a broom,' one of them called out.

'You'll fank us when yer old man's busy putting that in the ground. It'll give 'im sumfink ter do, and it'll keep 'im off yer back,' shouted another.

'Ger off wiv yer, yer saucy bleeders.' She waved her fist in the air and the top of her arm wobbled. 'I bet yer didn't tread on Lizzy Procter's cat. Too busy upstairs. I saw yer. She ain't 'aving a shelter in 'er bedroom, is she? Yer dirty sods.'

Annie and Lil, along with the many other passers-by, laughed.

'Looks like that lot 'ave found themselves a nice cushy little number,' said Lil, nodding towards the men.

'They say we've all got to have gas masks. I don't fancy that,' said Annie as they walked on. 'And they want to evacuate all the children from London.'

'What, all of 'em?'

'Yes.'

'Christ, that'll take for ever. There's a lotta kids in London. 'Sides, where will they put 'em all?'

'Don't know. In the country I think.'

'Do they say who'll go?'

'All of those at school.'

'Well, that's all our kids.'

'And the mothers with little ones under five can go with them.'

'That'll really be somefink ter see. Annie? D'yer fink there'll be a war?'

'I don't know. Me dad says it all depends on Poland. It seems we've got some kind of agreement with them.'

'Oh,' said Lil thoughtfully. 'Mind you, I wouldn't mind going in the Army. It could be quite a laugh.'

'I suppose it could,' said Annie. 'Are you old enough?'

'I fink so.'

As they made their way to the tram they were both deep in thought. Annie's were about Sam. He would be very vulnerable on a ship, and she knew her feelings for him were growing more intense.

July slipped away and August was bringing further evidence that a war could be coming soon. There seemed to be a lot of activity all around them. Gas masks were delivered and fitted, air-raid shelters were erected where possible, and in the park a lot of men were busy filling sandbags, whilst all the valuable paintings had been removed from the art galleries. Avidly, Annie's father read the newspaper and listened to the wireless. She had almost stopped going to the mission, and Rose and her father no longer asked for her help. Her letters from Sam were the one thing that really made her happy, but he warned her that in the event of a war they would be censored. He had told her that his ship's name had been painted out, and the name had also been removed from his hat-band. He was upset at that, as he was very proud of his ship.

Every day brought news of something happening. On the Tuesday after the Bank Holiday Lil came into the shop crying. Annie rushed round the counter to comfort her friend.

'What's the matter?'

Lil blew her nose. 'It's me mum, she's ever so upset about the kids going.'

'When are they going?' asked Annie, even though she knew the big evacuation was beginning at the weekend.

'Saturday. I don't care what old Bill says, I'm 'aving that day off.' Lil was angry. 'I've gotter see 'em off, ain't I? Dunno when I'll see 'em again. Poor mum, she's in a bit of a state.'

'It must be very hard for some parents.' Annie was thinking of some of the men who came in from Fisher's telling her how much they'd miss their kids, while others said they'd be glad to see the back of them. 'They may all be back before you have time to miss them.'

'I 'ope so,' sniffed Lil. 'D'yer wonner come with us?'

'I'd like that, Lil. Would you mind?'

Lil shook her head. 'I fink I'll need a shoulder ter cry on.'

On Saturday Annie went with Lil to the station. She was amazed at the vast number of children haring around them. With brown labels tied to their coats, to tell the world who they were and where they used to live, they emerged from the buses and underground like ants. All had the newly issued gas masks in brown cardboard boxes bouncing on their behinds. Some of the poorer children, whose coats were too small, or who had buttons missing, carried brown paper parcels, while others who were smartly dressed in their school uniform, proudly marched along with their brown attaché cases.

Every time a train expelled its steam, some of the youngsters, who had never been on a train – or even in a station – before, clung crying to their parents; the fear in their eyes told it all. This upset Annie.

'I wonder who organized this?' she said, looking around in disbelief as they were swept along.

'Dunno,' said Lil, hanging on to young Elsie's hand.

'I didn't know there were so many children in London,' said Annie, trying to keep up a conversation as they were pushed and jostled.

'Now, just make sure you all keep together,' said Lil's mum as she gathered her flock around her. Mrs Grant's voice was panicky and edgy. 'And as soon as yer git settled, write and let me know where you are, and I'll try and git down ter see yer. You listening ter me, Ernie?'

Mr Grant, who hadn't said a lot, clipped Ernie round the head.

''Ow, that 'urt.' Ernie held his head.

'Well, yer should listen when yer mother's talking to yer.'

'I was.'

Lil put her arm round her brother's shoulders. 'You will write, won't yer?'

'Course. Lil, I don't wonner go. S'pose the old lady don't like us?'

'Course she will.'

'What if we all finish up in different 'ouses?'

'Mum's asked for yer not ter be separated.'

Sally Grant moved closer to Annie. 'Annie, there ain't a war yet, so why're we being sent away now?' she asked.

'It's just in case,' said Annie.

'I don't want ter go and live in some strange 'ouse.' Sally's tears were beginning to fall.

Annie took a hankie from her pocket and gave it to Lil's young sister. 'It might not be for long,' she said comfortingly.

They had been told where to queue when they got off the bus and, as they steadily shuffled along, the noise from the tannoy, the children and the trains was deafening.

'What district?' a woman in a WVS uniform asked Mrs Grant.

'A what?' shouted Mrs Grant, bending her head closer to the woman.

'Where do you live?'

'Rovverhive.'

The WVS woman looked down at her clipboard. 'Make your way over to Platform Number Six.' She quickly moved on.

At the far end of the platform, a fight had broken out between the high school boys and some of the others. Parents rushed forward to separate them.

'Looks like there's gonner be a bit o' trouble on that train,' said Mrs Grant.

'They want a few men ter look after that lot,' said Mr Grant.

'They've got the teachers,' his wife said.

'I said men, not that right marmy-pandy-looking lot o' ponces,' said Mr Grant, turning his nose up.

All too soon it was time for the children to board the train. After all the kisses, hugs and tears, the guard blew his whistle and, high above their heads, he moved his green flag backwards and forwards. Very slowly the train hissed, clanked, and jerkily moved away, carrying its precious load to only a few knew where.

As the train gathered momentum, the intoxicating high spirits of shouting and waving died down and most of the crowd on the platform stood silently watching as it finally snaked out of view. Many of the women were crying and Mr Grant had his arm round his wife's heaving shoulders.

'If there's a war we might never see 'em again,' she sobbed.

'Come on, old girl. Don't talk daft, they'll be back under yer feet next week and yer'll be wishing 'em further.'

Annie was surprised to see how the parting had affected Mr Grant as she watched him trying hard to put on an act full of bravado. 'Look, it's opening time,' he said as they turned to leave. 'How about a quick one ter cheer us all up?'

'I don't mind,' Annie said, 'but I mustn't be too long, Dad's got a delivery to make.'

Lil shot her a glance full of astonishment. 'We'll just 'ave the one – that all right with you, Lil?' asked Mr Grant.

'Yer, yer, Dad.' She pulled Annie back and whispered, 'What's up with you? Going inter a pub?'

'I think a lot of things have got to change now, Lil,' said Annie thoughtfully.

The following morning, Sunday 3 September, at eleven o'clock, Mr Rodgers, along with thousands of others, was intently listening to the wireless when Mr Chamberlain announced to the world that Britain was at war with Germany.

'Well, that's it, love,' her father said, banging out his pipe into the ashtray. 'God only knows what will happen now.'

'What d'you mean?' asked Annie.

'We'll just have to wait and see.'

'D'you think a war will last for very long?'

'Wouldn't like to say.'

Annie was thinking about all those children who had left their homes yesterday. Many of them had believed they would be home before long, but now . . . Suddenly a loud wailing sound filled the air. Annie screamed. 'What's that noise? What is it?'

'The bastards!'

'Dad!' Despite her fear Annie was still shocked. She had never heard her father say that word before. 'Dad? What is it?' She put her hands over her ears.

'Quick, love, let's get outside. It's the siren, it's the air-raid warning.'

'Are we going to be bombed?' Annie was panicking, frightened, not knowing what to do.

'Don't know. Come on, move yourself! Don't hang around up here.' His voice was harsh as he grabbed her hand and rushed down the stairs.

When he flung open the door, Annie was surprised to see everybody was outside already.

Mrs Day rushed up to them weeping. 'What we gonner do, Ben?' she sobbed.

Ted the butcher came racing over, his face red and full of anger. The vein on his neck stuck out as he shouted, 'They said on the wireless we're s'posed ter go to a shelter. I ask yer? Where's the nearest bleeding shelter to us?'

His wife was puffing close behind him. 'He won't finish up getting bombed. He'll end up 'aving an 'eart attack first if 'e ain't careful,' she said to Annie, and anyone else who was listening.

When the noise from the siren drifted away, the Mews fell eerily quiet.

The small and mild Miss Page from the haberdashery shop gently touched Annie's arm. Her voice was shaky. 'I'm very frightened,' she whispered.

'Stop being such a moaner, Dorothy,' ordered her sister.

'We are all frightened, Miss Page,' said Annie abruptly. She'd never spoken to Miss Page like that in her life before.

'Exactly, and we've got to keep a stiff upper lip.' Maud Page stood her ground, and in a loud voice went on, 'We're not going to let Mr Hitler get us down.' Her audience broke into a round of applause, and Annie half expected them to start singing 'There'll always be an England', or some other patriotic song.

A man on a bike, wearing a navy blue uniform and a tin hat with the word 'Warden' emblazoned across the front, carefully manoeuvred his way over the cobbles as he cycled along the Mews. He stopped and everybody pounced on him, erupting with questions.

'Where's our shelter?' shouted Ted.

'We could all soon be bloody dead if the bombers come over.' Bill Armstrong the ironmonger, who had been pacing up and down, stopped and looked up at the sky. 'Fank Gawd me kids are safe out of 'ere,' he muttered.

Everybody followed his gaze, but the bright blue sunlit sky was clear.

'You'll 'ave ter go along ter Fisher's shelter fer now, that's the nearest at the moment,' said the warden, taking advantage of the brief moment of calm.

'Fisher's!' the cry went up.

'I tell yer we could all be killed 'fore we git over there,' said Bill Armstrong.

'You're a right bloody Jonah,' said the baker's wife.

The warden cleared his throat. 'I've 'eard they're going ter start building yer one round the corner.'

'When?' was the response.

'I did hear talk of tomorrow,' he said and, jumping on his bike, quickly rode away.

'I reckon 'e only said that to fob us off,' said the baker. 'Mind you, I don't reckon the cellar in the pub would be a bad idea.'

Ted's face lit up. 'Now that's what I call the first sensible idea ter come forward terday.' His voice was drowned by a long pure note. 'That's the all-clear!' he shouted.

'Is it all over?' asked Annie.

'Sounds like it,' said her father. 'I reckon they were only trying it out. You know, making sure it worked properly.' He took her arm. 'Come on, love, let's get on upstairs. By the way, Bill, you getting in any of that mesh stuff we've been told to stick over the windows?'

'Should be 'ere in the morning. I ordered it last week. Come along about nine.'

'I'll 'ave some of that,' said Mr Day.

As Annie closed the door she could see all the others making the same arrangements.

She pushed open the door that led into the shop, and stood surveying it. Soon all the pretty windows in the Mews would be covered in mesh. She felt sad. What would this war mean to all their lives now?

Dinner was a quiet affair, and after they had washed up Annie sat and wrote to Sam. Today she felt she needed to include a little more of her real feelings towards him. Now the war had started, who knew if they would ever meet again?

Chapter 24

After that first siren, nothing much else seemed to happen, and people went about their business in the normal way.

Although Annie knew Sam wrote almost every week, some of his letters took over a month to arrive, and then she would get a batch all together. Every day she eagerly watched for the postman; gradually she began to realize how much Sam meant to her. His letters to her were beginning to get more loving, and he was pleased that she had told him that she was fond of him.

At the end of the year many of the children who had been sent away began drifting back into London. Lil's mother and father had decided to go up north and live with their children after they found out the kids had been separated and were all very unhappy. Mr Grant found a job, they rented a house, and settled down to a new life. Lil spent Christmas with them, and told Annie afterwards that they had had nothing to stay down here for; they were happy in their new place and Lil was pleased for them. Christmas for Annie and her father had been very quiet without Lil, and at times Annie wished she hadn't turned her back on the Salvation Army, although she knew it pleased her father to have her around.

It was only at the beginning of 1940 that the war started to become a reality for those living in the Mews. So far only the blackout, and the evacuation of the ironmonger's children had affected its occupants directly, but now the baker's two sons were being called up, and food was rationed.

'I'm glad I've only got Annie here,' said her father to Mrs Turner when she was telling him about her son having to go into the Army.

'Wot we gotter do about these 'ere ration books, Ben?' She

settled herself on the chair, and plonked the buff-coloured book on the counter.

'Don't ask. You should see the forms and paperwork I've got to do.'

'I ain't worried about your bloody troubles.' Her tone wasn't her normal lighthearted bantering one and there was no smile on her face as she spoke.

It wasn't like her to be aggressive, Annie thought. This war was beginning to change people.

The old lady pulled her scarf tighter at her throat. 'I only asked yer a question, I don't want yer bleeding life 'istory.'

'You have to register with us,' Annie said patiently. 'Dad has to put his name in your book, here, see?' She turned to the page. 'We have to cut out these coupons for some things, and cross out these for others.' She pointed to a page with numbers on.

'Oh, yeah. We ain't gonner git very much it says in the papers.'

'I think they'll have to see how it goes. It's a big thing getting it all organized,' said Annie.

'Yer, I s'pose it is.' Mrs Turner stood up. 'I'll take me bacon now, Ben, if that's all right? How much do we git?'

'Four ounces.'

'What?'

'Four ounces,' repeated Mr Rodgers.

'I did 'ear.'

'And that's got to last you all week.' Mr Rodgers began turning the handle on the bacon slicer. 'Got a nice bit of back here.'

'Yer, well, just make sure yer scales are right. Wouldn't want yer ter give me too much.' She looked over her shoulder. 'Might 'ave old 'Itler coming in 'ere fer 'is rations if 'e fought 'e'd git a bit extra.' She laughed. Annie was pleased things were back to normal.

The shop bell went again, and a couple of men from Fisher's hurried in. They quickly closed the door behind them, but the icy blast made Annie shiver.

'Christ, it's bloody cold out there,' said Mr Harrison, banging his arms across his chest. 'Wouldn't be surprised if they don't ration coal next. D'yer know? I 'eard that even a bit of the Thames froze over.'

'Could be 'cos there ain't ser many boats up and down there now,' said his mate, blowing on his hands. 'Read about that in the paper. I see we're losing a few of our ships though. Feel sorry fer the sailors, poor buggers. Fancy being chucked in the sea this weather.'

'That's if yer don't git blown ter bits first,' said Mrs Turner, getting back on the seat.

'Still, they sunk the *Graf Spee*,' said Mr Harrison.

'And a bloody good job too,' said Mrs Turner.

'How're the boys, Mr Harrison?' asked Annie quickly, anxious to get away from this conversation. She had been very worried about Sam ever since she had read about the German submarines sinking a lot of ships; he couldn't tell her where he was as his letters were now heavily censored. 'Did you have a nice Christmas, Mr Harrison?' she asked.

'Really great.' His face lit up. 'You should see 'em now. They've really shot up, even got a bit o' colour in their cheeks. All that country air's doing 'em the world of good. The youngest is still 'omesick though.'

'I think a lot of them are,' said Annie.

'Yer, and from what little David told me I fink some of 'em are being treated like skivvies.'

Mrs Turner put her ration book and bacon in her bag. 'Yer well, I don't suppose it's any different from being at 'ome fer some of 'em, from what I used ter 'ear what went on.' She sat up. ''Ere, did yer 'ere what old Mrs James's kids went and done?'

'No,' said Mr Rodgers. 'She don't come round this way very often since that bust-up with Bessie.'

'Well, 'er boys,' said Mrs Turner, clearly loving the attention she was getting, 'seems they was breaking their necks for a jimmy and the old dear they was staying wiv wouldn't let 'em in the 'ouse wiv their muddy boots, so they went and piddled down the old boy's well.'

'No?' said Mr Rodgers.

'What 'appened?' asked Mr Harrison and his friend as they doubled up laughing.

'They told 'im they fought it was the outside bog.' She threw her

241

head back laughing. 'The old boy went mad!' she screamed.

'What did he do?' asked Mr Rodgers.

Mrs Turner wiped her eyes and tried to compose herself. 'Made 'em take the kids away. Seems they finished up in a school teacher's 'ouse.'

'Bet they don't like that,' said Mr Harrison.

'No, they've gotter mind their Ps and Qs there. Right, I'm orf. Bye, Ben, Annie.'

Mr Harrison and his workmate left the shop too, still laughing and talking about Mrs James's boys.

'I'll go up and make us a cup of tea, Dad,' Annie said as the shop fell quiet.

'Good idea, love. Eh, I'm glad we ain't got a well!' He laughed and, picking up his glasses, continued to pore over the papers the Ministry of Food had sent him.

Annie was still smiling as she went up the stairs. In the kitchen she filled the kettle and stood staring at the blue flame as it licked the side of the kettle. Her thoughts were suddenly full of Sam again. She couldn't help worrying about him. She found she was thinking a lot about him these days, and at times felt guilty about it – did she like him more than Will? No, it wasn't a question of more or less: it was just different. But was it just because of the war that she was feeling like this? Could it really be she was in . . . Somehow she couldn't bring herself to say the word 'love', and the kettle's loud whistling quickly brought her back to reality.

Many weeks had gone by when one afternoon the shop door was flung open and Lil came in singing 'Wish me luck as you wave me goodbye'.

Annie started laughing. 'What are you doing here on a Thursday?'

'I've just been and signed on. I fought I'd pop in and tell yer. I'm joining the Army, and guess what? I'm 'oping to go in ENSA.'

'What's that?' asked Mr Rodgers. 'What does it stand for?'

Lil took a deep breath. 'Entertainments National Services Association.' She giggled. 'They entertain the troops.'

'It's a bit of a mouthful,' said Mr Rodgers.

'Yer, s'pose that's why they always call it ENSA.' Lil looked smug as she sat on the chair. 'I can't believe it. I could be on a stage singing ter thousands of soldiers and airmen.' Her face was wreathed in smiles.

'When do you go?' asked Annie despondently.

'I've got ter 'ave a medical, but it shouldn't be too long.'

'I'm going to miss you,' said Annie.

'I'll write. I ain't very good at it, but I will write. Then I can tell yer all about what's 'appening.'

The following Saturday, Georgie Bates came into the shop.

'Guess what?' he said cheerfully. 'I'm going to a factory in Surrey.'

'Whereabouts?' asked Annie. 'Me and Will went there once.'

'Don't rightly know. It seems they want workers, and me and Pam both said we'd go.'

Annie smiled. She hadn't seen Georgie for quite a while, but his mother had been in the shop and told her all about his girlfriend. Pam worked with him at the brush factory, and they were going steady. Mrs Bates liked her and Annie could tell Georgie was rather sweet on her. She sighed. 'All my friends are going away . . . Did you know Lil's going into the Army?'

'No,' he laughed. 'She'll bring a smile to a lot of blokes' faces when she gits going.'

'She's hoping to go into ENSA. It's the entertainment side, you know.'

'That would suit 'er. Must go, Annie, though. Meeting Pam. When I'm up this way again I'll pop in and see yer.'

Annie walked round the counter and held the door open for him. 'I hope so. Good luck, and take care.' She kissed his cheek.

He smiled. It was a broad smile that Annie could see reflected his feelings. She hadn't seen him this happy since the accident. 'I hope they'll be happy together,' she whispered under her breath as she closed the door.

Automatically she began tidying up the sacks of dried goods that stood on the floor. These days they weren't so full as they used to be. She knew her father was beginning to find it difficult to get stock, and she wondered what would happen if they ran out. Her thoughts went back to Lil and Georgie. Soon everybody would be gone. Should she start thinking of joining something? She wondered how long it would be before it was compulsory to go into a factory or the Forces? Things were all on the move once more.

In March, Aunt Ivy wrote and told them how upset she'd been when Roy went into the Army. Ted the butcher was unhappy too, upset about the new meat rationing. One day he came into Mr Rodgers' shop moaning about it.

'How the 'ell am I gonner cut a bloody great side o' beef into bits that cost one-and-tuppence?'

'The same way as I have to cut up the bacon. Very carefully.'

'Ha, ha. Very funny.'

'You'll get used to it,' said Mr Rodgers.

'Yer, but what about me profits?'

'You'll manage.'

'Fanks fer yer sympathy,' he sniffed.

'Remember, there's a war on,' said Mr Rodgers, smiling.

'Yer don't 'ave ter tell me.' He opened the door. 'Now look, it's bloody well raining.'

After he closed the door, Annie and her father looked at each other and burst out laughing.

'Poor old Ted,' said her father. 'He can't stand all these changes.'

So many changes were going on all around them.

When Lil went into the Army, she wrote, as promised, to Annie. Her letters were very short, but she gave an outline of her new life, and how much she was enjoying herself. In the last letter, Lil had said she was expecting a weekend pass as soon as her training was over.

Annie was overjoyed when on Friday the shop door opened and Lil walked in. She rushed round the counter and threw her arms round her, then she stood back to admire this very well-turned out girl in her neat uniform.

'I must say you look very smart, Lil,' said Mr Rodgers.

She did a quick twirl on the ball of her foot. 'Not bad, eh?'

'You look smashing,' said Annie.

Lil laughed. 'I tell yer, Annie, it's a great life. The square bashing's a bit 'ard, but it's really good apart from that.'

Mr Rodgers smiled. 'You two go on upstairs, I'll manage down here. You can bring me down a cup of tea later.'

They rushed out of the door giggling.

'I'm really pleased to see you,' said Annie, sitting at the kitchen table. 'I'm thinking of joining up or doing something soon. There's not a lot of life round here now you've gone.' She looked sad as she ran her fingers over the tablecloth.

Lil sat next to Annie. 'What's up with yer? After all, I only saw yer once a week when I was 'ome.'

'I know, but I miss going out with you,' Annie sighed. 'Sorry about that. Shouldn't be such a misery. Now what are we going to do while you're home?'

Lil looked at Annie. 'I'd like to go to the Castle, but don't worry if you don't want to come. I only 'ope me bed's still there.'

'Don't worry about that – you can stay here,' said Annie cheerfully. 'And I don't mind going to the Castle.'

'Yer don't?'

Annie shook her head. She leaned forward. 'What d'you say we ask me dad to come with us? We could go in the van then.'

A grin spread across Lil's face. 'Why not. 'Ere, d'yer fink 'e would?'

'I could ask. It'd do him good to have a night out.'

'And we wouldn't 'ave ter 'ang about in the cold waiting fer a bus. 'Urry up and make that tea, then go down and ask 'im.'

'You two don't want an old man like me going out with you,' he said when they asked him.

'We do, Dad, honest,' said Annie, passing him his cup of tea.

'Yer, come on, Mr Rodgers. It'll be good, and we won't 'ave ter worry about a bus.'

He laughed. 'You crafty pair. D'you know, I wouldn't mind taking you out. I reckon I'll be the envy of all the boys.'

'Just ser long as yer don't cramp me style,' said Lil, patting the back of her hair.

'Come on, let's go upstairs. Do you want anything of mine to wear?' asked Annie over her shoulder.

'Na, I'll keep me uniform on. It looks all right, don't it?'

'It looks lovely, and it really suits you,' said Annie closing the kitchen door.

'I feel ever so smart,' said Lil as they trotted up the stairs. 'Don't reckon much to the drawers though – look!' She lifted her skirt to reveal a pair of baggy khaki knickers.

Annie laughed. 'D'you have to wear them?'

'Not all the time. The shoes don't do a lot for yer, do they?' She lifted her foot.

'At least they've got soles. I remember when your shoes didn't.'

Lil smiled. 'Yer, that's right. I 'ad ter put bits o' cardboard in 'em ter keep me feet dry. Cor, that's going back a few years. It is good ter see yer again, Annie.' She gave her friend a quick hug. ''Ere, I nearly forgot. Guess who I saw at the station?'

'Who?'

'That kid we 'ad ter climb frew that winder for.'

'Daisy?'

'Yer, that's it, Daisy.'

'Daisy? What was she doing at the station?'

'She said sumfink about she'd been to 'er uncle's funeral.'

'Did she say if it was Chalky White's?'

'I didn't ask.'

'Was she all right? Did she remember me?'

'Yer. It was 'er who spotted me. It didn't click who she was at first. She looks a lot different now.'

Annie plonked herself down on the bed. 'Daisy – after all these years.' She leaned forward. 'Where are they living now? What about the family? Are they still together?' Lil's news was exciting.

''Ang on a mo. One question at a time. I didn't 'ave a lot o' time to talk to 'er. She said 'er train was due.'

'Where was she going?'

'Up north, I fink. But she did tell me ter tell yer you done 'em all a favour when you made 'em move on.'

Annie looked hurt. 'I didn't make them move on; they just upped and went.'

'Yer, well it was your fault really. Anyway, it seems that as they were moving about the mother got worse, and collapsed in the

246

street. She was taken ter 'ospital, then the kids was looked after by the welfare.'

'Is the mother all right?'

'She didn't say.'

'Were they split up?'

'I don't fink so, 'cause when the war started she said they was all evacuated ter the country. It seems the boy loves it wiv all the animals, and the two girls are gitting on fine.'

'I'd love to see her again. Did you get her address? Can I write to her?'

'No, I didn't.'

'That's a pity, but at least I know Daisy's all right.' Annie smiled. 'I can't believe it. Fancy seeing Daisy after all these years. I'm so pleased everything worked out fine for them. Did she look happy?'

'Yer, she did. 'Er 'air looked nice, and she's got a nice little figure now. Must be all the good food she's gitting.'

Annie pulled her knees up and hugged them. 'I still can't believe it. After all these years.' Slowly tears began to run down her face.

'Come on, yer soppy old fing.' Lil sat on the bed and put her arm round Annie's shoulders.

'I can't help it. I'm really so pleased for them.'

'That's cheered you up, ain't it?'

Annie nodded. 'Are you happy, Lil?'

Lil took a packet of cigarettes from her handbag, and lit one. She puffed the smoke high in the air and smiled. 'D'yer know, I didn't fink life could be this good.'

'I'm so glad. When Dad closes the shop, I'll get us a bit of tea – then it's off to the high life.' Annie was thrilled at the thought of going out somewhere. Even going to the pictures wasn't the same now she was on her own. And knowing the Murphys were safe and all right after all this time was indeed the cherry on the cake.

When they arrived at the Castle, Lil was treated like a long-lost soul, and all evening Annie and her father laughed and sang along with her as she went through tune after tune. Annie couldn't remember her father enjoying himself so much, and they had so many drinks bought for them they could hardly drink them all. Once or twice Annie looked guiltily around her, in case someone from the Salvation Army had come in; as it was Friday she knew she was fairly safe, though it didn't stop her conscience from bothering her.

At closing time, Annie was feeling a little squiffy as they staggered out of the pub. But she hadn't had as many as her father and Lil, who were giggling together as they tried to hold each other up. Finally they settled down in the van and made their way home.

'Good job there's not a lot of traffic about,' said Mr Rodgers, peering through the windscreen. The van bumped against a kerb, making Annie and Lil laugh even more as they fell against each other. 'Can't see a damn thing with these silly covers on the head lights,' he said, struggling with the wheel.

At home, they all had their cocoa and went to bed. Annie lay on her back listening to Lil's deep breathing. After a while she pulled herself up on her elbow and looked down at her friend sleeping on the floor beside her. A smile crept across Annie's face. Lil was so happy. She lay back down. What would happen to Lil when the war ended? And what about Sam? Would he still want to take her out when all this was all over? Her thoughts milled haphazardly around in her head. When would this war end? And what could she do to play her part?

The next morning, Mr Rodgers said Annie could have the day off, so she and Lil went shopping in the afternoon, and to the pictures in the evening. Then all too soon it was Sunday and time for Lil to go back. After they finished dinner, Mr Rodgers said he would run them to the station. As Annie stood on the platform, hugging Lil, she couldn't stop her tears from falling.

'I'm going to miss you,' she croaked.

'Me too,' said Lil hurriedly.

Mr Rodgers hugged Lil too, then quickly walked away. 'See you by the van,' he shouted to Annie as he pushed his way through the throng of people on the platform. Like Lil, they were mostly service personnel, and as Lil climbed on the train she was lost in a sea of uniforms of all colours.

Annie was very quiet all the way home, and for the next couple of weeks she carefully began to mull over what she should do. She was growing tired of feeling the world was moving on without her.

Annie looked up at the clock. Ten o'clock. She had filled her hot-water bottle and clutched it to her, gently humming a tune that had been on the wireless earlier.

Suddenly the peace was shattered by someone knocking on the door.

'Who the hell's that, banging at this time o' night?' Mr Rodgers, who had been dozing, jumped, startled, but he was quickly on his feet and out of the kitchen.

Annie stood at the door. She could hear voices. She pulled her dressing-gown tighter around her. Voices drifted up the stairs. Her father's was loud, but it wasn't angry. She didn't recognize the other.

'Look who's here, love,' said her father, pushing the door wide open.

Annie gasped. 'Sam!' She threw the hot-water bottle on to the chair and, unthinking, fell into his open arms.

He kissed her lips long and hard. Mr Rodgers coughed.

Instantly they broke away. Annie stepped back, embarrassed at her uncharacteristic behaviour and, blushing, looked at the floor.

'Sorry it's so late,' Sam said. 'I can see you're just off to bed. I'll come back tomorrow.'

'You'll do no such thing,' said Mr Rodgers. 'I'm just off, so that'll give you two time to have a little chat.' He kissed Annie's cheek. 'Goodnight, love. Sam.' He shook Sam's hand. 'It's good to see you home again. She needs a bit of cheering up.' He left the room.

'It's so nice to see you,' said Annie, trying to control her voice which was uncommonly high. She hastily began tidying up the room.

'I've been dreaming of this moment,' said Sam, still holding his hat and standing in the doorway.

Annie plumped up the cushions 'Would you like a cup of tea?'

'Yes, if that's all right and not too much trouble. I'm not keeping you up, am I?'

Annie fluffed up the back of her hair, wishing she wasn't wearing her scruffy old slippers and dressing-gown. If only she had just a hint of make-up on. 'No, no. How long are you home for?' she asked.

'Only the weekend. Got to go back on Sunday.'

'Lil was home two weeks ago, she only had a weekend . . .' Annie's voice faded away as Sam threw his hat on the chair and slowly moved towards her.

He took her into his arms. 'I haven't stopped thinking about this moment. I've been going over and over in my mind what I would say to you. I love you, Annie.' She went to speak but he put his finger on her lips. 'I know how you felt about Will, and I don't want to force my feelings on you. I know from your letters that you're fond of me, but could you . . . ?'

'Sam,' whispered Annie. 'Yes, I did love Will, and I don't know if it's possible to love two people.' She held her face up to his. 'But I can try.'

His mouth covered hers and she was suddenly filled with a longing she had never felt before. Sam held her close, whispering her name.

When they broke away he said, 'I think I'd better go. I'll be round in the morning.'

'Yes, yes, it's getting late.' Annie half laughed nervously. 'I expect Dad's still awake, wondering when I'll get to bed.'

Sam picked up his cap. 'Will your dad let you have tomorrow off?'

'I should think so.'

'Good. I'll be round about ten, will that be OK?'

'Yes, yes, that'll be fine.' She opened the kitchen door and they went downstairs.

Sam kissed her again. 'You don't know how happy I am,' he whispered.

Annie stood at the open door, and in the moonlight watched him leapfrog over the bollard at the end of the Mews. Annie laughed. He turned and threw his cap in the air then, blowing her a kiss, disappeared round the corner.

As Sam rounded the bend he felt he could have danced all the way home. He did a little skip, and whistling joyfully made his way to the bus stop. Annie closed the door and leant against it for a few moments, hugging herself with happiness. She too could have jumped over the bollard – even the moon. She suddenly felt cold and, taking the stairs two at a time, ran upstairs.

As she snuggled down in bed she closed her eyes and tried to analyse her feelings. She knew she had been in love with Will, but somehow her feelings were different with Sam. With him it was more . . . Will had been a very kind, gentle person, but with Sam – it was more exciting. The words of Aunt Ivy and Georgie Bates came back to her. 'You mustn't mourn Will for ever', and deep down she knew he wouldn't want her to. After that first brief meeting, and during all these months she had been writing to Sam, she had known she was falling in love with him. She suddenly opened her eyes. What if anything happened to him? What if he got . . . ? Tears began to run down her face and she hastily wiped them on the sheet. 'I can't lose two,' she whispered. 'Please, God, keep him safe. Watch over him for me – please.'

Chapter 25

It was before ten the following morning when Sam walked in the shop.

'Annie's getting ready. She'll be down in a tick.' Mr Rodgers moved round to the front of the counter. 'Seen much action out there, son?'

'A bit.' Sam twirled his hat round and round. He was surprised at how nervous he felt in Annie's father's presence. Perhaps it was because he loved Annie so much and wanted to make a good impression.

'You allowed to say where you've been?' asked Mr Rodgers.

Sam nodded. 'The Atlantic run. There're a lot of German subs out there.'

'I read they're playing havoc with the cargo boats.'

'It's a bit better now they go in convoy with us protecting them. That's the trouble with being an island. All our food has to come here by ship. He lowered his voice. 'Don't say anything to Annie, but we got hit.'

'No. Did your ship sink?

'No, fortunately. It was just holed by a plane.'

'Many hurt?'

'A few, we were lucky. That's why I'm home now – we've been in for repairs.'

The door behind the counter opened.

'Hello, Sam,' said Annie nervously. 'Been waiting long?'

'Just got here.' He opened the shop door politely for Annie. 'Bye, Mr Rodgers, I won't keep her out too long.'

Mr Rodgers smiled. 'Enjoy yourselves.'

Annie slipped her hand through Sam's arm as they walked through the Mews. She was so excited, like a child on its first outing, and her heart was beating fit to burst. Sam was head and shoulders taller than her, and she could feel many eyes on them as they walked along – she was half expecting Bessie to jump out with some ribald remark. 'Where are we going?' she asked, breathlessly.

'First of all I want to show you off to me dad.'

Annie stopped. 'Why does he want to see me?'

'Because I've been on and on about you. He gets a bit down now Mum and the kids have been evacuated. He asked if we'd like to go over for a bit of dinner, then I thought we'd go up West and see a show. Is that all right?'

'I can't let your dad cook my dinner. I can't take his rations.'

'Don't worry about that. I've brought my ration card home, and he does all right. He's a very good cook. 'Sides, he likes me being home, it makes a change for him to have a bit of company. He can't get used to the peace and quiet after a house full of noisy kids. It's strange.'

'I suppose it is. But are you sure it'll be all right?'

'Course. It might only be mutton stew. D'you fancy seeing a show this evening?'

'Sounds lovely. At the beginning of the war a lot of the theatres closed, you know, but I think some of them are open now.'

'Well, we can see what's on when we get there. Here's our bus.'

When they got to Peckham Mr Jarvis greeted Annie warmly. 'Sam mentioned yer the last time 'e was 'ome. It's nice ter see yer, love. Take yer coat orf, I'll put the kettle on.'

Sam followed his father into the scullery.

'Well, Dad?' he whispered.

'I think she's a little smasher,' beamed Mr Jarvis.

'So do I.' Smiling, Sam made his way back to the kitchen. And, he thought, I'm going to ask her to marry me.

Annie was looking round the small room. She found it hard to imagine seven children all sitting round the table. 'You must miss the family,' she said as Mr Jarvis returned to the kitchen from the scullery.

'Yer, at first I fought it was a good fing, glad ter see the back of 'em. But it gits a bit lonely, and the quiet gits on yer nerves. Sam, bring in the tea, I 'ave made it. And don't fergit the sugar. Sam tells me yer dad's got a shop?'

'Yes, it's a small grocer's.'

'Bet you don't go short then.'

She smiled. 'It does have its compensations.'

'Don't she talk nice,' he said as Sam put the tray on the table. 'Did Sam tell yer 'e passed a scholarship? Could 'ave gorn ter 'igh school.'

Annie nodded.

'But what did 'e go and do? Joined the Navy.'

'Well, you must admit, Dad, it wasn't easy to get a job.'

'Yer, well, I suppose so.'

'I didn't feel I could live off you for ever.'

Sam had told Annie that his father had made quite a few sacrifices for him, and she could see he was very proud of his eldest son.

Annie found that, like Sam, Mr Jarvis was easy to talk to. They finished dinner, washed up, and reluctantly left.

'That was a nice picture of your mum on the mantelpiece,' said Annie slipping her arm through Sam's.

'She was quite a smasher in her day, so me dad reckons. Even after having seven of us she's still full of energy, and she'll still give any of us a clip round the ear if we don't behave.'

'Don't you miss the family?'

'Can't say I do. Haven't seen a lot of the youngest, they were born after I'd left home.'

'It must be nice coming from a big family.'

'Not really. Not when money's tight. Dad's good to us all, but he can't work miracles.'

'My dad would get on like a house on fire with yours,' said Annie as they strolled along.

'Yes. It's a pity you don't live a little nearer, then they could go for a drink together. Come on, let's get the tube to Piccadilly Circus, then we can wander round Green Park for a while before finding a show we fancy.'

Although it was late March, the sun already had some warmth in it and there were many other couples wandering around the park, most of the men in uniform. When they found an empty bench they sat down, and Sam put his arm round Annie's shoulders.

'Annie, I do love you.'

'I'm very fond of you Sam,' she answered quietly. Although Annie knew she loved him, she still couldn't say it.

He kissed her. 'I knew I loved you from the first moment I saw you, and I couldn't stop thinking about you when I went back last time. I've never felt like this about anyone.'

'I thought sailors had a girl in every port.' She was trying to keep the conversation lighthearted.

'Some do.' He took hold of her hand, determined to say what was on his mind. 'I know this is a bit sudden, but . . . I would like to marry you.'

She quickly pulled her hand away. 'I can't.'

'Why? Why not? Give me one good reason.' He felt hurt.

'I don't know.' She turned away.

He turned her face to his and his hand lightly brushed away her tears. 'Why are these tears falling? You do love me, don't you?'

Annie nodded. 'Yes, I do.'

'Well then, what's stopping you?'

'I'm afraid.'

Sam took a deep breath. 'Of what?'

Annie ran the flat of her hand over her face. 'I'm afraid . . . After Will . . .' She fumbled in her handbag for a handkerchief. 'I might lose you, and I couldn't stand that.'

Sam took her in his arms and kissed her long and passionately. She felt she was flying. This was a wonderful, new sensation; she knew she loved him, truly loved him, and she couldn't bear him to go away.

He buried his head in her neck, and gently kissed it. 'Nothing's going to happen to me, and when this war is over,' he whispered, 'I promise I'll never leave you.'

Annie sobbed.

'You're crying again.'

She laughed as the tears ran down her face. 'I can't help it, I'm so happy.'

He hugged her close, thrilled. 'I feel like shouting to the world.

256

Annie Rodgers loves me, she's mine, all mine.'

'You are daft.'

'Yes, about you.'

The sun began to sink quickly behind the trees. Annie shivered.

'You're cold,' said Sam. 'Come on, let's go and have a cuppa, then it's off to the theatre.'

'Look,' said Annie as they walked along. '*Pygmalion*'s on there. Would you mind very much if we went to the pictures instead?'

'Course not. Let's have our tea first.'

Annie smiled up at him. She loved him, and wanted to spend the rest of her life with him. Of that she was absolutely certain.

All too soon the evening was nearly over. Sam was joining his ship the next day. He was leaving about lunchtime and Annie was upset that he didn't want her to go to the station with him.

But Sam had made up his mind. 'I don't want to remember you amongst a sea of faces,' he said. 'I want to keep in my thoughts a picture of you as you are now, waving goodbye at your door.' He kissed her. 'When I'm on leave again we'll get you an engagement ring.'

'You don't have to worry about that,' she said, snuggling up to him.

'I want everyone to see you belong to me.'

'Oh, Sam.' She held up her face, and once again he kissed her.

'I must let you go in,' he said, but in his heart he didn't want to let her go. 'Your father will be wondering where you are.'

'It's a pity it's so late, otherwise you could have come in.'

'No, I don't want to disturb him. Bye, my darling.'

'Bye,' she whispered. She watched him hurry away. He didn't jump the bollard this time, but he did turn and blow her a kiss.

'Didn't hear you come in last night,' said her father as she wandered into the kitchen. 'Was Sam with you?'

'No, it was late so he said he didn't want to disturb you.' She yawned and rubbed her eyes.

'Did you go to a show?'

'No, we went to the pictures, saw *Pygmalion*. It was very good. More toast?'

'No thanks. I'll have another cup of tea, though.'

Annie sat at the table and poured out the tea. Her elbows resting on the table, she clasped her cup with both hands. 'Dad. Do you like Sam?'

Her father slowly stirred his tea. 'Course I do. Why?'

'He's asked me to marry him.'

Mr Rodgers' spoon made a clatter as he dropped it in the saucer. 'Annie, oh, Annie. What did you say?'

She leapt out of her chair and flung her arms round his neck. 'I said I would. Do you mind?'

'Oh, Annie,' he said again. 'Mind? I'm so pleased for you. It's about time you had a bit of happiness.' He fumbled for his handkerchief and blew his nose. 'Any idea when?'

'No, we hope to get engaged when he's on leave again. We'll sort it out after that. Are you really happy about it, Dad?'

'I should say so. He seems a nice lad.'

'He is, and his dad's nice as well. You'd like him.'

'You've met his father?'

'Yes, we had dinner there – he's a good cook.'

'Where's his mother?'

'Evacuated with his brothers and sisters.'

'Just as long as you are sure this is what you really want?'

'I am, Dad. I really am.'

For the rest of the day, Annie did her chores singing. That evening she wrote to Lil telling her her good news.

The last thought on her mind was the war.

Chapter 26

It seemed to Annie that after Sam had gone back to his ship the war began to worsen. Newsreels were full of the terrible things happening in Europe, and of the Germans pushing British soldiers across France. Sam's letters were very irregular and Annie wouldn't get any for weeks, then in one week there would be a few every day.

Lil was still writing as well: her letters were full of the good times she was having, and of how her singing was taking her all round the country. She was bursting with happiness at Annie's news, and wanted her to wait till she was home before they got married so she could be a bridesmaid. Annie smiled at that particular letter.

In the shops, goods were beginning to run short, and so were people's tempers when they missed anything that was off-ration and now considered a luxury. If their customers knew they had a box of tinned fruit in, Mr Rodgers would find queues outside when he opened up, and tins of salmon almost brought a riot. But on the whole most of the customers would queue quietly.

A brick air-raid shelter had been built round the corner of the Mews, and it caused a lot of interest when it was finished.

'Don't think I'd fancy spending a night in there,' said Dorothy Page, screwing up her nose as she looked in for the first time.

'You will if he sends over his bombers,' said her sister.

'Don't say things like that, Maud. Now that nice Mr Churchill's in charge he's said he'll sort things out.'

Bessie came out of the shelter laughing. 'Reckon we could 'ave some right old fun and games in there,' she guffawed, moving closer to Annie. The smile faded as she added, 'If yer ask me I fink fings are going ter get worse. We ain't got hardly any fruit, and I can see old Day giving me the chop soon.'

'Where will you go?'

'Fought of joining the Land Army. 'Ere, can yer see me in those breeches milking a cow?' She laughed. 'How's your mate Lil getting on? She looks good in 'er uniform.'

'She loves it, she's part of ENSA now,' said Annie as they strolled back to the shops.

'She must be seeing a bit o' life.'

'I think so, by the sound of it.'

At the end of May, the great evacuation of Dunkirk began. Annie, along with her father, read every page of the newspapers, and at the cinema the newsreels had become almost as important as the film.

'I wonder if Sam's ship is helping?' asked Annie as they listened to the wireless.

'Wouldn't like to say. I know he was on the Atlantic run, but if he was over this side of the water they could well be involved,' said her father.

One June Monday afternoon, just after the evacuation had finished, Lil walked into the shop. As she put her suitcase on the floor, Annie ran towards her.

'Lil, Lil,' she shouted as she held her close, 'it's so good to see you.'

Mr Rodgers hurried round the counter and kissed her cheek. 'You look smashing, as usual.'

Lil sat on the chair, looking round the shop and up at the half-empty shelves. 'Where's all yer stock?'

'It's getting hard to get, and a lot of it has to go under the counter,' said Mr Rodgers quickly, glancing behind him in case someone had walked through the open door and was listening.

'How long are you home for?' asked Annie eagerly.

'Till Sunday night. I fought I'd go up and see me mum.' Lil took a cigarette from her handbag. She was quiet, and not her usual bubbly self.

'Is anything wrong, Lil?' asked Annie. 'You look tired.'

'No, it's just that we've been down doing some shows for a lot of the fellers that came over from Dunkirk. Only finished last night.' She drew long and hard on the cigarette. 'Some of 'em are in a terrible state.'

'Would you like a cup of tea, Lil?' asked Mr Rodgers.

'Please. Ain't 'ad one since breakfast.'

'Come on up,' said Annie. 'I'll bring you one down, Dad.'

Upstairs, Lil told Annie about some of the soldiers, and the wounds they had. 'Reminded me of Georgie Bates when I saw 'em hobbling around on crutches. Then there's them with only one arm. I was talking to some of the blokes and the things they told me what went on in France. I tell yer Annie, gawd 'elp us if 'Itler ever gits 'ere.'

Annie bit her lip anxiously. 'Don't say things like that. I'm very worried about Sam. I haven't heard from him for quite a while.'

For the first time that afternoon a smile lifted Lil's face. 'I was ever so pleased ter 'ear about you and 'im. When yer thinking of gitting married?'

'Don't know. It could be difficult to make plans with this war. When are you going up to see your mum?'

'Fought I'd go tomorrow. All right if I stay 'ere the night?'

'Course. Do you want to go out anywhere this evening?'

'Not really. Would yer mind if we stayed in?'

'I never thought I'd hear you say that.'

'Yer well, a lot's changed. But don't worry, I'll be back ter me old self before long.'

During that evening Lil brightened up and she soon had Annie and her father laughing when she did her impersonations of some of the other performers in their show. The following morning Mr Rodgers took Lil to the station.

'Did she get off all right, Dad?' asked Annie when he got back.

'Yes, I think so. But I don't like to see Lil so down.'

'Perhaps she'll feel better after seeing the family. She's coming back here for the weekend so I expect we'll go out then.'

'Did she say what day?'

'She hopes to get back here on Saturday. She said she'd like to go to the Castle in the evening. You could come with us, Dad.'

261

Her father smiled. 'Why not? It was good the last time we were there.'

The next day her father had to go to the wholesaler's. It had been hot and dusty all day and Annie left the shop door wide open whilst she leant on the counter reading the paper. She looked up as a shadow fell across the page she was reading and thought her heart would stop.

'Hello.'

'Sam, Sam,' she croaked. She rushed from behind the counter and fell into his arms. He smothered her face with kisses. 'I can't believe it, it's you. It's really you,' she said between kisses.

'I hope so. Or do you normally fall into every sailor's arms when they walk through the door?'

She laughed. 'Oh, Sam . . . I can't leave the shop, Dad's out. He shouldn't be too long.' She closed her eyes in disbelief. 'I still can't believe it,' she repeated.

He held her round the waist, unable to believe that this moment had arrived. 'Do you want me to pinch you?'

'No.' She stood back and gently touched his face. 'You look tired, when did you get home?'

He kissed the palm of her hand. 'Yesterday. I've been without sleep for days. Our ship's been helping with the evacuation. We've been back and forwards across the channel I don't know how many times. Must have picked up thousands of survivors.'

'You poor thing. How long are you home for?'

'Till Sunday. Got to go back about midday.'

She settled in his arms again. 'Good, that gives us almost five days. You'll never guess, Lil was here, she's been singing to those troops.'

Sam nodded. 'There's so much activity going on round those ports, I've never seen so many ships. Even little boats were helping.' He sat on the chair and pulled her close. His face was drawn and suddenly his mind filled with thoughts of their future. 'It's only the Channel that's stopping him now. Annie, you do love me, don't you?'

'Yes, Sam,' she said gravely.

'Annie, will you marry me?'

'I've already said I would.'

'Yes I know, but I mean now, this week.'

She gasped and stood back. 'But how . . . ? We . . . ?'

He laughed. 'All I want is a yes or no.'

'But how can we?'

'Special licence, we could be married on Friday.'

'Friday,' she repeated. She was in a state of shock. 'I don't know. Why so quick?'

'I think the way things are we should grab all the happiness we can, and I don't know when I'll be home again.'

'Friday,' she said again. 'I've got nothing to wear.'

'I'm sure your father would . . .'

'Dad, what about Dad?' she interrupted. 'I'm under-age. Do you think he'll sign the consent papers?'

'We can only ask.'

She began laughing, and tears began to roll down her face. 'I always dreamed of my fiancé going down on his knees and proposing in some romantic place. Not sitting on a chair in a grocer's shop!' She kissed him, and knew that this was what she wanted.

They were still laughing and making plans when her father returned.

'Sam,' he said, struggling in with a stack of boxes. 'Well I never, it's all happening this week. First we had Lil home, now you. How are you, son?'

'I'm fine thanks. Mr Rodgers, I have something to ask you.'

'Go on then, ask away.'

'I'd like to marry Annie.'

'Didn't Annie tell you? You know you have my approval about that.'

'Yes she did, but we'd like to get married on Friday.'

He dropped the large cardboard boxes he was carrying on to the counter. 'What? This Friday?'

'It would be by special licence, Dad,' said Annie softly.

'Well yes, I suppose it would be. But why? What's the hurry?'

'I'm worried about the future, and I feel we should take the opportunity while we can.'

Mr Rodgers blew his nose. 'Yes . . . Yes. Well, I can see your point. And I give you both my blessing.'

Annie threw her arms round his neck and hugged him. 'Thanks, Dad.'

Sam took his hand and shook it. 'Thanks, Mr Rodgers.'

'Now, we've got a lot to talk about. Can you stay to tea, Sam?'

'Yes, sir.'

'Have you told your dad?' asked Annie.

'No,' he grinned. 'I didn't want to count my chickens.'

'Right, now how about a cup of tea, Annie?'

'Yes, Dad. I'll go up and put the kettle on.'

'You'd better go with her, Sam.'

When they were in the kitchen, Sam took her in his arms and kissed her passionately. 'This time next week you'll be Mrs Jarvis.' He buried his head in her neck, kissing it gently.

'Mrs Jarvis,' she whispered. 'I can't believe it.' She let his hand travel over her breast, and the thrill sent shock waves through her body. 'I shall always love you.'

'I think I shall die having to wait till Friday before you're mine.'

She gently pushed him away. 'We've only got a few days before the wedding, and I'd rather wait. Lil!' she suddenly burst out. 'Lil, I promised her she would be bridesmaid.'

'Where is she? Can you contact her?'

'No, she's at her mother's, up north somewhere.'

'When's she coming back?'

'Saturday I think.'

'That's a shame, if she was still in camp we could have phoned her.'

'Poor Lil, she'll be so disappointed.' But there didn't seem to be much Annie could do.

All evening they laughed, talked, and made plans about the wedding. After Sam had gone, Annie was so excited she couldn't sleep, and was sitting at the kitchen table when her father walked in.

'Couldn't you sleep either?'

She shook her head.

'Happy, love?'

She looked up at him, her eyes shining. 'Yes, Dad.'

264

'He's a nice lad.'

'I think so. I'll try not to be out too long tomorrow.'

'Take as much time as you like. After all, it's not every day a girl goes shopping for her wedding dress.'

'I wish Mum was here.'

'So do I.' He swallowed hard. 'Annie, you do know all about the birds and bees, don't you?'

'Oh, Dad.' She giggled. 'Having Lil around all these years, I think I've learnt something.' What would he say if he knew she had helped deliver a baby?

'Yes, I expect you have. It's a pity Lil's not here to go shopping with you.'

'Yes.' Annie thought about the baby again, wondering where he was now. 'Yes, she'll be really sorry she's not going to be a bridesmaid.'

'Are you disappointed you won't be having a big white wedding?'

'Not really. I would have liked Aunt Ivy and Uncle Fred to have been here though.'

'Yes, that would have been nice. Now come on, love, let's go back to bed. We've got a very busy week in front of us.'

'Goodnight, Dad.' She cuddled him close, and he gently patted the top of her head. She knew that, like her, he was thinking of her mother, and wishing she could have been with them at this special time.

The following morning, Annie went shopping. After some difficulty, she bought a smart white suit with a navy trim, a white hat, gloves and shoes. She knew Sam was getting the licence, and making all the necessary arrangements. They were going to have a quiet meal afterwards, with just Mike, his best man, and their two fathers. Then they were going to spend their wedding night in a hotel.

'I'm exhausted,' she said, staggering wearily into the shop. Falling on to the chair, she kicked her shoes off.

'Did you get everything you wanted?' asked her father.

'Yes, in the end. I didn't realize how little stock the shops have got. One old Jew took me out the back and tried to sell me a tatty wedding dress – you should have seen it, I reckon it was his mother's.' She rubbed her foot. 'Had to pay a bit more than I wanted to, though.'

'I told you not to worry about the cost. I've got a surprise for you.' He was grinning. 'Ron from the baker's has been in, and guess what?' Her father was almost jumping up and down with excitement. 'You know you said you couldn't have a cake made in time. Well, he's started making you one now.'

'No? That's really kind of him. How did he get all the ingredients?'

'I haven't got a shop for nothing, you know.'

Annie gave him a hug. 'Thanks. Will it be iced?'

'Yes, and an ornament on the top as well. It's your wedding present from them.'

'Oh, that's very nice of them.'

'And that's not all.'

'What?'

'Everybody in the Mews wants to help. The two old dears next door are going to lend you a blue lace handkerchief, so that's your something old, borrowed and blue taken care of. And now you've got your something new.'

'Dad. I didn't know you were such an old softy.'

'And . . .' he said it long, and was smiling broadly. 'When Charlie Day goes to the market on Friday morning, he's bringing back some flowers, and his missis is going to make them into a posy or whatever you call it – she used to be a florist. What d'you think about all that?'

Annie laughed. 'I can't believe it. You certainly have been busy.'

'Everybody's so pleased for you, Annie. You're very well thought of you know.'

She blushed. 'Dad.'

'What time is Sam coming over?'

'Don't know, when he can. He's got to go round to Mike's. I'm still upset that Lil won't be here for the wedding, though. Still, perhaps we can all go out together on Saturday night. We can have a real celebration then.'

'That'll be nice.'

All Friday morning people were in and out of the shop, bringing their good wishes and the best present they could afford. The baker came up with the cake and Annie was amazed he had produced such a lovely creation in such a short time.

'We 'ad a few silver bells and fings ter decorate it with. It's a pity we couldn't get 'old of any marzipan. Still, I ain't forgotten how ter use the old piping bag.'

Annie kissed his cheek. 'Thank you. It really is lovely. It seems a shame to cut it.'

'Good job yer dad 'ad some icing sugar. I 'ear they're making cardboard covers for the cakes now. Trust someone ter fink of somefink.'

Annie laughed. 'But you can't eat cardboard.'

The baker shrugged his shoulders and they both burst out laughing once more.

Later in the morning, Mrs Day brought along the bouquet, and buttonholes for Sam and the few guests.

'I've bought yer another bunch for upstairs. I 'ad a few over and fought yer might like 'em for the 'ouse. It's a shame, these don't last that long once you've put wires frew 'em.'

'Mrs Day, it's really lovely. Thank you very much.' Annie stood admiring the beautiful spray of flowers and cascading fern. 'You're very talented, I'm surprised you didn't do these for the shop.'

'I fought about it, but after that trouble with Amy, well, I lost interest – now it's too late.'

'Do you ever hear from her?'

Mrs Day shook her head sadly. 'Na, more's the pity. Anyway, put these in a drop of water, just ter keep 'em fresh. It's a bit warm terday for 'em.'

'Yes I will, and thank you. I don't know what I would have done without everybody's help.'

'It's been a pleasure. What time's the wedding?'

'Three, I'm going in Dad's van.'

'We'll all be out ter give yer a wave, and ter wish yer luck.'

'Thanks.'

At two-thirty Annie and her father left the shop and walked down the Mews. She was surprised at how many people had turned out. Apart from all the shopkeepers there were a lot of their customers too, familiar faces she had known for years.

Mrs Turner was dabbing at her eyes. She put her basket on the floor and grabbed Annie's hand. 'Yer looks lovely, girl. Good luck.'

'Thanks.' Annie smiled; her mouth was a gentle pink, for she had been very careful with her make-up.

'Good luck, Annie,' shouted Bessie. 'And if yer can't be good, be careful. And don't do anyfink I wouldn't do.'

'Christ, that gives yer plenty of leeway,' said Ted the butcher.

Everybody was laughing, shouting their good wishes. Annie felt like a princess, she was so happy. She took her father's arm and, as they headed for the van that was parked at the end of the Mews, everybody was singing, 'All the nice girls love a sailor'. She turned and waved.

'I've never seen the old van look so posh,' said Annie.

The two Miss Pages had put white ribbons on the door handles.

'I even gave it a clean. Come on, climb up.'

Annie had one foot on the step when she heard her name being called. She almost fell out of the door. 'Lil, Lil. It's you!' She gasped when she saw who it was.

'What the bloody 'ell yer doing gitting married without me?' Lil was breathless through running.

Tears ran down Annie's face. 'What you . . . ? How did . . . ?'

'I just came frew the other end of the Mews, and there was all these people standing around laughing and singing. When I ask 'em what was up, they said yer was just off ter git married, and if I 'urried I'd catch yer. So I dropped me case, and 'ere I am.'

'What made you come down today?'

'Got fed up up there. Not a lot ter do. Anyway, we going to a wedding?'

'Yes. Lil, will you be my bridesmaid?'

'Yer, why not? Mind you, I always fought I'd 'ave a long frock, not be in army uniform. Anyway, where's me flowers?'

'Flowers?' repeated Annie. 'Dad, we've got those upstairs. Could you go and get them?'

'Just so long as we're not late. Don't want Sam to think you've got cold feet.'

'It's a bride's privilege ter be late,' said Lil.

'Be back in a tick,' said Mr Rodgers, running back up the Mews.

'Put some paper round them, Dad,' shouted Annie after her father. 'Lil, oh Lil.' Annie hugged her. 'You've really made my day.'

'Glad I made it. By the way, Annie, I like yer suit. You look really smashing.'

'Thanks,' she grinned, feeling like the happiest person in the world.

Chapter 27

After the simple ceremony, and all the hugging and kissing, they stood outside on the steps of the Registry Office, posing for a friend of Sam's Dad's who was going to take a few pictures.

The restaurant was only a few streets away, and when they'd finished their meal they all climbed into the van and headed back to Albert Mews.

'Fancy Lil turning up like that,' said Sam.

Annie hugged his arm as they walked through the Mews. 'I still can't believe that. I'm so happy, and everybody has been so kind. You wait till you see the cake.'

'We're not going to stay too long, are we?' whispered Sam, stopping and pulling her out of earshot.

'No. Just long enough for me to pick up my overnight case.'

'Good.'

Mike had been thrilled when he'd seen Lil walk in with Annie. 'Got someone to have a few drinks with tonight,' he said, his arm round her waist as they all squeezed into the shop.

'We all going to the Castle later?' asked Mr Jarvis.

'Don't see why not,' said Lil. 'You two coming?'

'I don't think so,' said Annie.

'You mustn't have too much to drink, me old mate. Well, not tonight anyway,' said Mike, giving Sam a playful punch.

'From what I can gather, he had more than enough last night,' said Annie smiling.

''Ere, 'ark at the missis,' said Mike, laughing. 'It *was* 'is stag night, and I didn't keep 'im out *too* late.'

271

'I know,' said Annie. 'Pity Lil wasn't there to keep an eye on you.'

'Yer gonner 'ave trouble with that one, I can see,' teased Mike.

Sam kissed Annie. 'I don't think so.'

'Yer can stay at my place ternight as well as tomorrow, Ben,' said Mr Jarvis to Annie's father. It had been arranged that Annie and Sam would have the flat to themselves on Saturday night.

'Thanks all the same, but I must open up this place in the morning, otherwise I'll have all the old dears knocking the door down for their rations. But I'm coming to have a couple with you lot tonight. Annie and Sam, are you sure you don't want me to take you both to the hotel?'

'No thanks, Dad. We're getting a taxi. Got to arrive in style. I'll just put these flowers in water. What about yours, Lil?'

'D'yer mind if I take 'em with me? Don't often git flowers.'

'Course not.'

After cutting the cake and drinking a toast it was time for them to go. At the door, Annie held her father close. 'See you tomorrow, Dad. And thanks for everything. It's been a really special day.'

'Bye, love,' he croaked. 'Sam.' He shook Sam's hand.

Annie slipped her hand through Sam's arm, and at the bottom of the Mews they turned and waved.

When Sam closed the door of their hotel room, he took Annie into his arms. 'I have loved you for so long. I never dared think you would marry me. Oh, Annie, my Annie.' His lips were on hers.

She was overcome with happiness, and her tears flowed as she responded to his passionate kisses. She was his; Mrs Jarvis. 'I'll just take my suit off,' she whispered breathlessly, breaking away.

He gazed at her as she stepped out of her skirt, unable to believe she was his. Annie was wearing white french knickers, and as she carefully placed her skirt on the chair he could contain himself no longer. He kissed her.

She shuddered.

'Are you all right?'

She nodded and turned her head.

'What is it? What's wrong?' He held her at arm's length.

'Sam, I've never . . . You know.'

He laughed and hugged her close. 'Don't worry,' he whispered, tenderly kissing her ear. 'I promise I'll be gentle.'

They were both lying on their backs, Sam blowing smoke rings in the air. She looked at her left hand and, smiling, twisted her plain gold wedding ring round and round. He took her hand and kissed it. He put his cigarette in the ashtray and, propping himself up on his elbow, kissed her cheek.

Annie sighed.

'Happy?'

She nodded.

'You really are Mrs Jarvis now.'

She giggled. 'D'you think that man at the desk knows what we've been doing?'

'I should think so, and he's probably very jealous of me.'

'I won't be able to look at him when we go down,' said Annie coyly.

'Don't worry about it – he's used to it. Now, how about us going out and having something to eat. All that exercise has made me very hungry.'

'Oh you . . . Is that all you've got to say?'

'Only that I love you very much.' He kissed her, and Annie knew at last she had found what she had been looking for.

That night, after making love, Annie lay awake listening to the comforting sound of Sam's steady breathing. She gently touched him to convince herself he was beside her, that she wasn't dreaming. It was a warm night so they had pulled back the black-out curtains before getting into bed and now the moonlight was lighting up the room. She slipped quietly out of bed and wandered over to the open window. Their room was near the river and she could hear the low sound of the ships' hooters as they made their way up the Thames. As she looked at that small part of London everything appeared so normal and peaceful and, so far, untouched by the war. She was still unable to grasp what had happened to her in such a short while. This time last week she could never have guessed

273

she'd be married. Sam moved, still fast asleep. She smiled as she looked at him. As her gaze returned to the window she was suddenly filled with fear. She remembered what Lil had said. What if Hitler did get there? A tear slowly trickled down her cheek. She never wanted this week to end.

Suddenly two warm arms folded round her. She snuggled into them, feeling safe and secure. 'You're awake?' she whispered.

'I panicked. I thought I'd been dreaming, and you'd got away.' Sam kissed the back of her neck.

'You're never going to lose me now,' she said, turning her face to his. They were both determined this war wasn't going to spoil their happiness.

The following evening the wedding party went to the Castle. Lil was in fine voice and had everybody singing. Annie, with Sam's arm round her, laughed and sang too. Suddenly she stopped and sat upright.

'What is it? What's the matter?' asked Sam.

She nodded towards the door. 'I'll go in the lav,' she said hastily.

'No, don't, Annie. There's no disgrace in having a drink. Do you know them?'

She shook her head. She couldn't recognize any of the faces in the familiar Sally Army uniforms.

'Well then, relax.' Sam pulled her close.

'Annie. How are you? This is a surprise.'

Annie turned, the colour draining from her face.

'Hello, Rose,' said Mr Rodgers, standing up from across the table. 'How are you?'

'I'm fine,' said Rose, still looking at Annie.

Sam stood up. 'Let me introduce myself. I'm Sam, Annie's husband.'

Rose quickly recovered, and took the outstretched hand. 'Is this why we haven't seen much of you lately, Annie?'

Lil's round of applause quashed any conversation for a few moments.

'Can I get you a drink, Rose?' asked Sam.

'No, no thank you, not while I'm on duty.'

'I've heard all about you, and your mission. You're doing a good job with those kids.'

'Haven't got any now, they've all been evacuated. I was going to go with them, but decided to stay here with Dad. Annie, when did this happen?'

'Yesterday.'

'Congratulations. I'm really pleased for you.'

'Thank you, Rose.'

'Well, while I'm here, I might as well sell you a *War Cry*.' Rose smiled.

Annie kissed her cheek. 'Thank you. I'll never forget you,' she whispered, holding her close.

Rose nodded and left.

'I thought you said you didn't know them?'

'I didn't, Rose must have come in after the others.' Annie heaved a happy sigh of relief. For her that had been the last hurdle, and now she knew that part of her life was over for good.

On Sunday morning, Annie cooked the breakfast with a heavy heart. She wasn't hungry as she sat and watched Sam. He was going at midday, and he had insisted she didn't accompany him to the station.

Sam looked up from his empty plate and grinned. 'Didn't know I'd married such a good cook, especially one whose Dad owns a grocer's shop.' He sat back in his chair. 'Did meself a bit of all right there.'

Sam was trying hard to remain cheerful but tears were beginning to fill Annie's eyes.

He stood up and put his arm round her shoulders. 'Come on now,' he whispered. 'We don't want any tears.'

She held him close. 'I love you, Sam.'

'And I love you.' He kissed her long and hard. When they broke away he held her tight. 'I'll write every day if I can.'

'I'll never stop loving you.'

He took her face in his hands. 'Promise.'

'I promise.'

When her father arrived from Mr Jarvis's later in the morning,

Annie was very quiet. In her bedroom Sam held her tight once more. 'Remember that, whatever happens, I'll always love you, Annie,' he whispered.

She waved from the end of the Mews till the van was out of sight. In the quiet of the kitchen she sat and looked at her bouquet. She couldn't believe so much had happened in just a few days. She loved Sam so much, and prayed that the war would soon be over and they could spend the rest of their lives together. She suddenly felt so alone. Even Lil would be on her way back to camp now. Then the photo of her mother caught her eye. 'If only you had been here,' she sobbed. Eventually she wiped her eyes and pulled herself together. She'd take her wedding flowers to her mother's grave, she decided. She wrote a note for her father and left.

At the cemetery she pulled up a few weeds and generally tidied up, filled the urn with water and arranged her flowers. After a while she began to walk slowly back for the bus. In the far corner, under the bushes by the cemetery gate, some bright flowers caught her eye. She stopped, curious that fresh flowers had been put in such an odd place. As she peered under the bush she realized they were the same as Lil had had for the wedding. They had been put in a glass jar. Getting up closer Annie could see a slight lump in the ground. She froze. These *were* Lil's flowers. Who had put them here? And what was under that small mound? She put her hand to her mouth. She couldn't have – not Lil. Annie sat on the ground and stared at the flowers. Should she tell the police? Tell them what, that she thought there could be a baby under the ground? And what if it *was* Lil's? What would happen to her? Time slipped by as Annie sat there, her mind full of the night the baby was born. Had he died? If so, why hadn't Lil told her? If she was right and the baby had died, why did Lil bury him here? Annie shivered: the sun had gone down. She looked at her watch; her father would be wandering where she had got to. She picked up her handbag and made her way home. I must write to Lil and find out what had happened that night, she said to herself. The sadness of Sam leaving had been overshadowed by a new problem.

Chapter 28

That evening Annie wrote two long letters, one to Sam and the other to Lil. She had to find out the truth behind what she had discovered.

The following week she had a very loving letter from Sam, but it was almost two weeks before she received a reply from Lil. As soon as she recognized the writing, Annie raced up the stairs, tearing at the envelope.

Dear Annie,

I tried to write this letter to you, over and over again and many times in the past I've wanted to tell you what happened that night but I didn't think it was fair to upset you as I know what you're like.

This is going to be very hard to write but in many ways I'll be pleased that after all this time I'll be able to share everything with you just as we've always done, you've been more than a good mate to me, so please don't think too bad of me.

After little Joe (that's what I called him) was born I sat for a long while holding him. He was such a dear little thing, I couldn't believe he was mine. I wanted to keep him and started wandering around the streets trying hard to work out what I should do. His little fingers were clutching mine, and I knew I couldn't part with him.

The pages had become blurred so Annie had to stop to blow her nose and wipe away her tears.

Then after a while I realized he was dead. He'd gone all cold and I'd been so carried away with worry I hadn't realized what had happened. Annie I was scared stiff. What could I do. At first I thought about going back to the hospital, but I knew they couldn't bring him back and I might even get chucked in clink. Then I thought I'd come and see you but be now it was gone midnight and I knew you was in bed. I was at me wits end. What if the police found me. I sat cuddling him and crying for hours. I know what I did was wrong but I did so want to keep him. I should have listened to you. It's my fault he's dead and I'll be carrying that with me to the day I die.

Anyway when it started to get light I made me way to the cemetry where your mum was buried. I knew he couldn't have a proper funeral as he ain't been christened. So I managed to scrape out a bit of a grave, said a few words over him and laid him under the hedge.

Annie's mouth had dropped open, and tears were streaming down her cheeks. She was relieved her father was in the shop and couldn't see her.

I've never put flowers on him before as I thought someone might see me. But now I don't care. After seeing some of the things what's happening to people through this war, I know my little Joe is at peace, and he was loved Annie, really loved. I hope you'll keep my secret. And please don't think to hard of me, and don't stop writing.

All my love,
Lil. XXX

P.S. I'm glad you married Sam, I think he's smashing.

Annie put her head on the table and wept.

After she had read the letter several times, Annie answered it. There was no reprimand. It was a loving, caring letter, and she knew Lil would be pleased about that.

For Annie, after the excitement of June, July was warm and

uninteresting. She received many letters from Sam, but she never told him about Lil, for she knew his letters were censored, and she didn't want any strangers reading about Lil's tragedy. The evening his dad's friend brought round the photos of the wedding she sat and cried at the happy memories, and for Sam's safety. She only knew he was on the Atlantic run, and the war was getting worse.

It was at the end of August that the doctor confirmed what Annie knew for sure, that her morning sickness wasn't due to an upset stomach, but to the fact she was pregnant. Her father was delighted, and couldn't wait to tell everybody.

'Dad . . .' Annie reproached him gently as he gushed on about it to Mrs Turner.

'Well, love, you can't keep it a secret these days, not if you're going to get a green book for your extra rations.'

'Just yer make sure yer get yer oranges when old Day gits some in,' said Mrs Turner.

'I don't think she's got any worries there,' said her father proudly.

'And take all those iron fings as well. Does yer old man know yet?'

'I've written and told him, I'm waiting for a reply. I should think he'll be pleased.'

'Lil. You know Lil?' Mr Rodgers was addressing Mrs Turner. 'Well she's going to be godmother.'

Annie smiled. This baby was going to get plenty of love and attention.

'It's all 'appening round 'er, ain't it?' Mrs Turner picked up her ration book. 'And fancy that Bessie going in the Land Army as well.'

'Are you coming to her do in the Eagle tomorrow night?' asked Mr Rodgers.

'Wouldn't miss it fer the world – don't git many nights out. Right then, I'm orf. See yer termorrer.' She gathered up her shopping and stuffed it in her bag.

When Bessie had first announced she was going into the Land Army, everybody in the Mews had decided to give her a party at the Eagle. So tonight the beer was flowing, the singing loud and the pub full, its regulars having been joined by some of Day's customers. When Mrs James came in, Bessie staggered over to her and put her arm round her shoulder. ''Allo, love, come ter say goodbye ter me then?'

'I ain't yer love, and I've only come ter make sure yer going,' said Mrs James, pulling away.

'Course I'm going,' she laughed. 'Come and 'ave a drink on me.'

Mrs James pulled her cardigan across her flat chest. 'I ain't drinking wiv the likes of you. Yer nuffink but a Jezebel.'

Bessie laughed even louder. 'What, me a Jezebel? Cor, fancy that. P'raps I should 'ave gorn on the stage. Would 'ave been more fun than milking cows.'

Annie was sitting quietly in the corner, talking to the butcher's wife.

'Looks like there could be a bit of a trouble if Mrs James don't stop keeping on at Bessie,' said Ted's wife, eyeing the two of them.

'We don't see so much of Mrs James since her boys went away,' said Annie.

'Did yer 'ear about 'em piddling down that well?' asked Mrs Turner who was sitting with them.

Annie laughed and nodded her head.

Mrs James had a shrill voice, and it was rising. 'I still ain't fergiven yer fer chasing after my Arfur and leading 'im astray.'

''E didn't need a lot o' chasing.' Bessie was trying to make herself heard above the din of the pub.

'Yer painted 'ussy.' Mrs James's quick beady eyes darted round the room. Her brown hair was held close to her head with a fine hairnet, and with her sharp nose and twittering, fidgety movements, she looked more like a bird to Annie than ever.

'I wouldn't touch your old man wiv a barge pole,' said Bessie, patting the back of her blonde hair.

'That's wot yer say now. I bet yer flashed more than yer stocking tops at him, yer big fat cow.'

'Who you calling a fat cow, yer skinny moo?' Bessie grinned at her audience, then turned back to Mrs James. 'And yer should 'ave seen wot 'e flashed at me,' she taunted. Although Bessie was laughing, the edges of her mouth had turned white, and her face was showing signs of anger. 'Now go on, git out of it. We don't need the likes of you round 'ere, yer dozy cow.'

'Don't you call me a dozy cow.' Mrs James went to raise her handbag but she was too late.

Bessie gave her a push. She lost her footing and fell against a table, screaming. As the glasses crashed to the floor the beer slopped over Bessie.

'Now look what yer gorn and done, yer silly cow! Look at me new frock!' She leapt at Mrs James like a tiger. Mrs James looked terrified as Bessie grabbed her hair, her fingers becoming entangled in her hairnet. For a second the net dangled limply like a spider's web before Bessie tossed it away and wrenched her head back. Suddenly all hell was let loose and the pub seemed to erupt, with everyone jostling to get a better view of the fight.

'Come on, Annie, let's scarper, it could get nasty. 'Yer gotter take care in your condition,' said Ted's wife.

Annie quickly moved round the table and out into the fresh warm air.

Later that evening, her father told her that the party had broken up shortly after that, and added that Bessie could be sporting a nice black eye when she went off on Monday. Mrs James hadn't proved quite so much a weakling as her scrawny frame made her look.

After the party, the dog fights over the south of England became a major talking point, with the inhabitants of Albert Mews keenly adding up how many enemy planes had been shot down.

One day, Ted wandered into the shop with his newspaper tucked under his arm. 'Seen this?' He opened the paper. 'If yer ask me I reckon we're in fer a right old bashing if 'is planes gits frew.'

Mr Rodgers looked worried. 'Those boys are doing a fine job though.'

''Eard from Sam lately, Annie?' Ted asked.

'Not lately.'

'Does 'e know 'e's got a kid on the way?'

'I have written, and I'm just waiting to see what he's got to say about it.'

'I reckon 'e'll be dead chuffed. I know I was with the first one, then after that the novelty wears off.'

'I only hope Sam will see it before it gets too old.'

'Yer, well, we all 'ope fer that. See yer later, ben.'

They watched him stroll across the Mews. Mr Rodgers put his arm round Annie. 'I've been thinking, love. Don't you think you ought to go away? You know, down to Ivy's. I'm sure she'll be pleased to see you.'

'What about you? I couldn't leave you on your own.'

'If things get bad I think you should.'

'Well, I'll think about it. Dad, do you think it's wrong having a baby now – with this war?'

'Course not. 'Sides, I'm looking forward to being a Grandad. And what about Ivy? She was thrilled to bits when you wrote and told her she was going to be a great-aunt.'

'It was a pity she couldn't come to the wedding.'

'She'll make a big fuss of Sam when she sees him.'

'I hope so. I was very upset when I heard about what happened to Matthew's June. She was such a smashing girl.'

'Yes, that was a shame. Still it's a good thing the baby survived the birth; at least it gives Matthew something. Annie, you're not worried about the same thing happening to you, are you?'

'No, course not.'

'Remember, dying in childbirth is very rare these days.'

'Yes, I know. Poor Matthew. And his daughter,' said Annie almost to herself.

On the following Saturday, 7 September, the day started off like any other, but at five o'clock everybody in the Mews knew that their lives were about to be changed.

As soon as the siren finished its wailing, the droning of bombers filled the air.

'Quick, Annie, in the shelter,' shouted her father.

She quickly grabbed her handbag and raced out of the shop. 'Miss Page, hurry,' she shouted, pushing open the haberdashery door.

Ted was looking up at the sky. 'Look, there's hundreds of 'em, quick, git in the shelter.'

'Miss Page,' cried Annie in alarm.

'Don't worry, we're just coming . . .' The rest of the conversation was drowned as a loud explosion stopped them dead in their tracks.

'Git on the floor!' yelled Ted. 'Fer Christ's sake git down.'

Those who were in the Mews instantly obeyed.

'Now run fer it!' shouted Ted again. And as one, they scrambled to their feet and ran to the shelter that had been built at the end of the Mews.

Inside, Mrs Day was weeping.

'It'll be all right,' said Annie, sitting beside her on the slatted seats that ran along both sides of the wall. 'We should be safe in here.'

'It's me cake, I've gorn and left it in the oven. It'll be burnt to a cinder,' Mrs Day sobbed.

'I told 'er ter move 'erself, but all she wanted ter do was take the bloody cake out the oven. I ask yer. We're all about ter be blown ter pieces, and all she worries about is that bloody cake.'

'I took me a long while ter save up me dried fruit,' whimpered Mrs Day, looking up at her husband.

He tossed his head and tutted, then with his hands thrust deep in his trouser pockets, he moved down nearer the door to where the men had gathered.

They had all sat in the shelter before, but most times it had been a false alarm, and had turned into a big joke. This time it was for real.

For what seemed a lifetime, bombs rained down on London. The shelter shook and heaved with every explosion, and everybody sat quiet with a grim expression on their faces. As the dust gently floated down, Annie guessed that, like her, they were all saying their own prayer.

'D'you think these things are safe?' asked Maud Page in a hushed tone as she looked round the shelter.

'The government reckon so,' said the butcher.

When they did talk, they spoke in whispers. There was no crying or screaming.

The air was becoming stifling, and when the all-clear finally went, the door was flung open and they all rushed out. Outside they stood open-mouthed. They turned this way and that, looking at the great palls of smoke rising from behind houses that miraculously were still standing. The acrid smell of smoke got down their throats and made them cough.

'Bloody 'ell.' Ted pushed back his straw trilby and scratched his head.

The rising thick black smoke was blotting out the sun.

'Look at all the damage,' said Miss Dorothy Page softly. 'All that broken glass.'

'All the shops are OK,' shouted Bill Armstrong from the iron-monger's. He had gone on ahead.

'Looks like the docks got it bad,' said Mr Rodgers. All the time they stood taking in the scene before them, more explosions were rending the air. 'Looks like we're in for a rough night.'

Annie shuddered. She wanted to cry, but knew that wouldn't help things.

'Right, now before we worry about clearing up all the glass, let's start to think about tonight.' It was clear Mr Rodgers was going to take charge of the situation.

'What d'yer suggest, Ben?' asked Ron Jones, the baker.

'I think we ought to get some kind of bedding in the shelter, some flasks of tea and sandwiches. Got any hurricane lamps, Bill?'

'Yer, and I got some candles as well. Anyfink else yer want?'

'Can't think of anything at the moment. Can anyone else? And don't forget to bring your torches.'

'What's the point?' said Miss Dorothy Page bleakly. 'We're all going to be killed anyway.'

'Dorothy,' said her sister sternly. 'Don't be such a silly defeatist.'

'Those fires are gonner light up London like a beacon ternight. I reckon yer can see 'em miles away,' said Mr Day.

Ron Jones looked up. 'Those bloody chimneys of Fisher's stick up like sore thumbs. That's gonner be a right target.'

'Yes, well, that's why we've got to sort ourselves out,' said Mr Rodgers, clearly getting angry.

'Wouldn't be surprised if 'e didn't come in fer the kill ternight,' said Ted.

'Don't be such a bloody Jonah,' said his wife.

'Sorry, love,' Ted muttered, biting his lip nervously.

Maud Page turned to Mr Rodgers. 'Perhaps one of you kind gentlemen would help me to bring a mattress down.'

'I'll give yer a 'and,' said Mr Day.

'I fink we ought ter 'ave a bucket down the end, Ben,' said Ted's wife. 'I 'ave a bit a trouble wiv me bladder in the night.'

'That's a good idea. We should put a sheet or something up, just to give us a bit of privacy.'

'It won't be very private piddling in a galvanized bucket,' said Bill Armstrong.

'Well, we'll all 'ave ter sing out loud when someone 'as a jimmy,' said the baker's wife.

A smile at her remark lifted most faces.

Mrs Day emerged from her shop carrying a burnt cake. 'Look, bloody burnt to a cinder.' She looked up at the sky. 'I'll never fergive yer fer this, 'Itler, and if yer ever shows yer face over 'ere, I'll chuck it at yer.'

That brought forth gales of laughter, and a cheer for Mrs Day.

For the next hour things moved very rapidly, everybody helping. Some of the women swept away the glass in Albert Mews, for every shop had been affected. What little stock they had on show was taken out of the windows, packed away, and tills emptied. The men took the bedding down to the shelter and allocated spaces for everyone. The sheet was put up with a bucket behind. A dartboard appeared, and a folding table complete with a pack of cards and a crib board. The hurricane lamps and candles were duly set out. They were ready.

'D'ye fancy egg and bacon for your tea, Dad?' asked Annie, as they went back inside.

'That'll be nice. Are you all right, love?'

'Yes,' her voice was shaking with emotion.

Her father held her close. 'Whatever happens tonight, remember I love you.'

'Oh, Dad.' She held on to him, and her tears flowed. 'I don't want to die. What about Sam? And the baby?'

'There's nothing we can do about it. We've just got to pray it's not our time to go.' He kissed her cheek. 'Now, how about this egg and bacon? If there's time we're all going to have a drink in the Eagle.'

'That's a good idea.'

'I bet there'll be a few bottles in the shelter tonight.'

They finished their tea almost in silence.

'I'll just do the washing up, then I'll be ready,' said Annie.

'Leave that.'

'But, Dad, it'll be stuck by the . . .' her voice drifted off. Would there be a morning?

'Just get your coat, and anything else you want to take with you.'

Annie went to her room and picked up Sam's letters, the photo of her wedding, and a snapshot she had of her mother. She put them in a bag her mother always kept the policies in, then stood for a few moments looking round her room. Annie swallowed hard and touched her stomach. 'Remember, my little one, you were really loved.' She turned and closed the door.

Chapter 29

''Ave a whisky, Annie, it's on the 'ouse,' said Ted.

Annie looked anxious. 'I don't know.'

'Go on, love, it won't do yer any 'arm,' said his wife. She fussily patted her handbag and, nodding towards her husband, added, ''E's chucking it down 'is throat like water.'

Ted's wife was sitting beside Annie once again, and she was reminded of Bessie's farewell party. 'Does anyone know where Bessie went to?' she asked.

'Na. D'yer know, I reckon she must 'ave known sumfink, getting out o' London when she did. 'Ere, yer don't reckon she's a spy?' She threw her head back and roared with laughter. Annie smiled; she could see by her neighbour's flushed face that she'd had quite a few drinks.

'All right, love?' asked her father. He too had bright eyes and rosy cheeks. 'Might as well all get drunk.'

'Well, at least that way we won't know what 'its us,' said Bill Armstrong.

Annie was sipping her second whisky. She didn't really like the taste, and the smell of it brought back memories of that dreadful night long ago. As she toyed with the glass her thoughts went to the Murphys. She supposed in the end all that had turned out for the best. She hoped they were safe now, away from London as Lil had said.

'Come on, Annie,' said Ted's wife, bringing her back to the present. 'Git this one down yer.' She plonked another glass on the table. 'It's medicinal, and it might 'elp yer sleep.'

Deep down, Annie knew that they were all hoping it would help deaden the pain, and blot out what was in front of them tonight.

'Listen!' shouted Bill Armstrong.

Everybody cocked their heads; the sound of a distant siren wailing brought a sudden chilling silence to the bar. Fear immediately filled every face.

'Drink up, Annie,' said her father sharply. 'Let's get in the shelter.'

Annie gulped her drink down, its raw taste at the back of her throat making her choke. She picked up her bag and quickly joined the others.

In the shelter, the two Miss Pages had already settled themselves. Miss Dorothy was clutching a bible, while Miss Maud was reading an Agatha Christie. There were a few books and papers inside the door as well as a box of biscuits Ben Rodgers had put in, and Annie noted a crate of beer partly hidden under the seat at the front.

The loud tone of the nearby air-raid warning sent shivers down Annie's back, and she began to pray.

Very quickly the first wave of planes came droning overhead. The whistling of the first bomb sent them falling to their knees, flattening themselves on the hard concrete floor, holding their heads. More and more bombs began dropping near them and the ground beneath the shelter shook and heaved with every thump – it was as if some giant hand was picking it up, shaking it, then dropping it down again. The whistles of the bombs screaming through the air were loud and long, the crack of the explosions horrifyingly close. The clatter of falling walls, masonry and glass was terrifying. Slowly the smell of dust and soot found its way into the shelter, filling their nostrils and mouths. In the brief moments of quiet between explosions no screams or shouts came from the shelter's inhabitants, just a gentle crying from Dorothy Page and Mrs Day.

Annie sat with her father. Her head was spinning, mostly from whisky, and she couldn't think straight. She wanted to speak, but the words wouldn't come. The deathly silence after the bombers had emptied their bomb-bays, done their job, and turned for home, lasted only a few moments: all too soon they could hear the low deep drone of the next wave of approaching planes. Wave after wave continued to come over. The atmosphere in the shelter was stifling and suffocating and, building up inside her, Annie could feel an urge to get out, to run away from all this horror. Suddenly a loud explosion blew the shelter door open. Bill Armstrong, who was standing just behind it, was thrown the full length of the shelter and the racket as he crashed into the galvanised bucket brought forth nervous, suppressed giggles.

'You all right, Bill?' shouted Mr Rodgers.

'Yer, I fink so.' He was squatting on the floor with the sheet draped over his head. In the half light from the hurricane lamps he looked like an Arab. 'It's a bloody good job the bucket ain't been used yet.' He laughed.

'Christ, yer might have been covered all over wiv . . .' Ted stopped abruptly.

Annie guessed his wife had poked him in the ribs.

'Violets,' continued Ted. 'That would 'ave been just my luck.'

'Yer can wash yer own clothes if that 'appens,' said his wife.

At least that incident brought a little light relief.

'Where d'yer reckon that one was?' asked Mrs Day, as another crash made the ground shake. 'Don't worry about that,' said her husband. 'We'll know soon enough when we gits out.'

'If we gits out,' Mrs Day said softly.

Annie was a few seats away from the two Miss Pages, but she could hear muted words being exchanged between them and knew that Miss Dorothy was weeping. Suddenly Miss Dorothy stood up. 'I'm going to ask Mr Rodgers.'

Maud tried to pull her down but she shrugged her off.

'Mr Rodgers,' began Dorothy Page, quickly glancing towards her sister. 'I wonder,' she turned to Mr Rodgers, 'when things get a little quieter . . . Do you think you could come back home with me?'

'Dorothy. Come back here and stop being a nuisance,' Maud Page's voice was loud and powerful.

To everybody's amazement her younger sister ignored her. 'You see,' she went on, 'I've left my engagement ring in the flat. That's all I have left of . . .' Her voice faltered, and Annie guessed she was trying hard not to cry out loud.

Annie was full of pity for the frail little old lady. How would she feel if the only thing she had of Sam's was in danger of being blown away for ever?

Her father was speaking. 'I'd be only too pleased to. Don't worry about it, but we'll have to wait till it eases up a bit.'

'Yes, yes of course. Thank you. I'm sorry to put you to any trouble. We must wait till it's safe.' She dabbed at her nose.

'It's no trouble.'

She settled down beside her sister, and Annie knew there would be words over what Miss Dorothy had just done.

Gradually the group began to quieten down. Heads began nodding, only jerking up at a loud, close explosion. Whether it was the whisky or sheer exhaustion, Annie finally drifted off, dozing fitfully. Once she had to move her leg through cramp. When she opened her eyes again she was disorientated. She strained her ears, then realized it was quiet outside. She sat up. Was it all over? She wanted to shout out for joy that they were still alive. Tears ran down her face and she fumbled in her pocket for her handkerchief.

'You all right, love?' whispered her father.

'Yes, Dad. Is it all over?'

'We haven't had any planes over for about half an hour.'

She cuddled against him. 'We're still here then?'

'Yes. We're still here.'

There were gentle murmurs disturbing the air as people began sitting up, undoing flasks, and generally taking stock.

''As the all-clear gone yet?' asked Mrs Day.

'No, not yet,' said her husband.

'Are you awake, Miss Page?'

'Yes, Mr Rodgers.'

'I think it's safe enough for us to see if we can get in the shop. Are you ready?'

'Yes.' She stood up. 'Won't be long,' she said to her sister.

'Bring your torch,' instructed Mr Rodgers as he made his way to the door.

'I wonder what they're going to find out there,' said Maud Page.

Bill Armstrong had the shelter door open. 'Can't see much. The sky's blood-red with all the fires.'

They sat quietly, listening to the sounds of fire-engine bells and a distant ambulance filtering through the open door.

'I'll be glad when it's light,' said Mrs Armstrong. 'Don't care much fer the dark.'

Annie realized Mrs Armstrong hadn't said a lot all night. She was always a very private person, so different from her husband.

'Ben's coming back,' shouted Ted, who had been outside.

Miss Page and Annie's father sat down.

'Well? What's 'appened?' asked Ron Jones.

Miss Page began crying. Her sister put her arm round her shoulder.

'Ben, fer Christ's sake, what's 'appened?' asked Ron Jones again, his manner agitated this time.

'The shops are still standing, but there's no slates on the roofs, and all the doors are off. Fisher's is still there, but those houses near there look like they've caught it, and that's as far as I could see.' He put his head in his hands and Annie moved closer to him.

Everybody was very quiet.

'I was walking on all the lathes and plaster from the ceiling,' Miss Page softly whispered. 'There's dirt and dust everywhere. Everything's ruined. The water pipe's burst and water's been running down the stairs.'

'Be careful when you get back. I think by the smell of it, the gas main's fractured,' said Ben Rodgers.

'That'll be just my bloody luck. Survive a night of being bombed, only ter be blown ter kingdom come by our own bloody gas.' Mr Armstrong laughed at his joke.

It was just after five when the uplifting sound of the all-clear filled the air, and they all hugged and kissed each other.

'Thank God we're all still alive,' sobbed Dorothy Page.

Carefully they made their way back to Albert Mews. Lumps of concrete, splintered wood, and glass seemed to be everywhere.

'Looks like we've got a lot of work to do,' said Mr Rodgers, standing looking at the row of shops.

'It's not ser bad fer me,' said the ironmonger. 'My stock don't perish like yours.'

'How we gonner manage without gas?' asked Mr Jones. 'We can't bake bread without gas.'

Annie was standing watching the early morning sun slowly rise. Despite the smoke that occasionally blotted it out, and the destruction all around her, to her it was a wonderful sight.

A warden came along, weaving his bike precariously round the obstacles. 'You ain't got no gas or water,' he shouted. 'They're trying ter git it sorted out as soon as they can.'

'Is there any way we could git a cuppa?' asked Mrs Day.

'I'll send a WVS van round.'

'Many injured round here?' asked Mr Rodgers.

'Not too bad, most of 'em were in their shelters. I fink Victoria Gardens got it pretty bad though.'

'D'yer need any 'elp?' asked Ted.

'Not at the moment. I don't fink old Reeves's 'orse will ever see the knacker's yard. Blown ter bits, so I 'eard.' He jumped on his bike and, wobbling over the rubble, disappeared out of sight.

'Poor old Reeves's 'orse,' said Mrs Day,.

'Good job most of 'em 'ave gorn from Victoria Gardens,' said Ted.

Annie stood in silence. Thank goodness Lil's family had moved up north, away from there.

'Come on, love, let's try and get a bit cleared up,' said Mr Rodgers, pushing what had been the shop door to one side. He studied it, then called out, 'Got any hinges, Bill?'

'Yer, I'll git some sorted out.'

'I reckon I'll be able to put both these doors back on,' he said, looking at the wooden surround. 'These have been ripped right off.'

Annie carefully stepped into the shop, and stopped. She couldn't believe her eyes as she tried to take in all the damage. The gas lamps were hanging from the ceiling at a dangerous, drunken angle and all the mantles were broken. The glass in the counter that held the sweets had gone. The few sacks of pulses that had been stacked neatly on the floor were split wide open, the contents spilled out and mixed with the plaster and glass. The window – the beautiful bay window she had always loved and admired – had gone, leaving a gaping hole: its frame was now a pile of matchwood joining the rest of the debris.

She carefully pushed open the door behind the counter. At least that was still on its hinges. Slowly she made her way up the stairs. They too were covered with rubble, and she had to run her shoe over them to get a firm foothold. It was light, she noticed. That wasn't right, there were no windows on the staircase. She looked high above her head and realized she could see the sky through the missing slates. When she arrived in the kitchen everything was covered with plaster and glass though all the cups and plates on the dresser were still intact. Annie looked at the table which had been laid for last night's tea; under the debris she knew were the dirty egg and bacon plates. 'I knew I should have washed them up,' she said out loud. 'It's going to take me for ever to get them clean.'

'Everything all right up there, Annie?' shouted her father.

'It's a bit of a mess.'

'Well, take care, I'll bring up a bucket for the rubbish. And mind your hands on that glass. And, Annie, don't go lifting anything heavy.'

She stood at the top of the stairs. 'No, Dad. What are we going to do for water? I've got to wash up.'

'Don't worry about that, just try and do the best you can.'

'Didn't Miss Page say that she had water running down her stairs?'

'Yes, that was from the waste pipe, it got disconnected. It's all right now, I've seen to it. We're all going to the warden's post to see if they know where we can get some tarpaulins to put over the roofs.'

'Dad, be careful.'

'I'll see if I can get hold of some tea first.'

'Please. I'm dying for a drink.'

Annie wandered into her bedroom and was greeted with more dirt and destruction. She tied a scarf turban-fashion round her hair, put on one of her overalls, and got down to work.

She had only just cleared the kitchen table when someone shouted up the stairs.

'Cooee, Annie. Are yer there?'

Annie came out of the kitchen and looked down.

'Got some tea fer yer.' It was Ted's wife.

'I'll find a clean cup and I'll be right down.' Annie quickly wiped the dust out of the largest cup she could find and hurried down the stairs.

Someone had brought a wooden chair out and a large brown enamel teapot stood on it. Annie's mouth suddenly felt parched and dry.

'It's got sugar and milk already in it,' said Mrs Day.

'Where did it come from?' asked Annie.

'That warden brought it.'

In the Mews the two Miss Pages were sitting on chairs they had brought out of their shop. 'What are we going to do after we've cleared up this mess?' asked Miss Dorothy. 'It all seems a bit pointless if you ask me. We could all be blown to kingdom-come tonight.'

'Dorothy, will you please stop carrying on.' Her sister was clearly getting very cross. 'Now drink your tea and let's get back to work.'

They quickly went back inside.

'She's right, yer know,' said the baker's wife. 'It does seem a bit daft working all day and fer what?'

'They may not come over tonight,' said Annie.

'Don't you believe it, love,' said Ted's wife. 'Now 'e's started I reckon 'e'll be like a dog wiv a bone, and 'e won't let it rest till London's finished orf.'

'You're a right bloody Jonah, ain't yer?' said Mrs Day. 'I'm gonner carry on till me old man gits back, then I'll see wot 'e says.' She picked up her cup and shuffled away.

Annie too went back to her chores. She coughed and spluttered as she brushed pieces of plaster off the furniture. Then she pulled down the rest of the curtains which were hanging in ribbons, and began to sweep out the two bedrooms. Dust was flying all around her. 'If only we had some water to lay the dust,' she said, rubbing her nose.

Up on the roof there was plenty of banging. Orders and curses were being shouted from all the men in the Mews as they worked together pulling the large tarpaulins over the holes. As she worked below them, Annie was afraid one of them would come through.

'Annie,' yelled Ted's wife. 'There's a cart down 'ere wiv water. Bring yer kettle and a couple of saucepans.'

Annie hurried down with as many vessels as she could carry.

All day they toiled. It was well into the afternoon before Annie realized they hadn't eaten properly, and had only been nibbling at biscuits. Someone had lit a couple of fires and now kettles and saucepans were being boiled for tea. 'I'm starving, Dad,' she said as he emerged from his labours in the shop.

'That warden said a coffee-stall was being set up outside their post. Let's have a wander round there and see what he's got left. Bring the flask.'

The hot tea and sausage sandwich went down a treat, and as they walked back home her father said, 'Annie, I'm taking you down to Ivy's tonight.'

'What about the shop? That warden said there were looters about. Will we take all our stuff?'

'No. We'll have to take a chance. I'll only stay the night.'

'Why can't you stay for good?'

He shook his head. 'I can't, people are rationed with me, and I've got to get stock.'

'Let them go somewhere else.'

'I can't, Annie, you know that. Besides, it's our home.'

She linked her arm through his. 'Sorry, yes I do know. But I'm not going away without you.'

'You must. What about the baby?'

'We'll take our chance with you. Besides, we may not get a raid tonight.'

But Annie was wrong. Night after night, for many weeks after that, the raids continued. Despite her father's protestations, however, Annie had made up her mind: she was going to stay in London with him. But every morning when they left the shelter, they were unable to believe Albert Mews was still there, and that they were all still alive.

Chapter 30

The two Miss Pages stayed only a week after the first raids. They decided that perhaps Bournemouth would suit them better. Annie was sorry to see them go. Even when Fisher's was razed to the ground, everyone else in the Mews was determined to stay. They were beginning to take the raids as part of their lives, and tried to get back to normal as quickly as possible. Sam's letters were still very spasmodic. Annie guessed it was getting difficult for him to write. She would sit and read them over and over again: they were always so very loving, and he was thrilled about the baby. Annie was pleased he said he favoured a girl but wasn't really that fussed just so long as they were both all right. She didn't see any point in worrying him about the air-raids, so she said nothing about what they had to go through night after night. Lil's letters came through a little better and of course Annie told her about what was happening to her old home territory: Lil was sorry to hear about Victoria Gardens, and old Reeves's horse.

The shelter was now very well equipped, with shelves for the hurricane lamps and candles. The slatted benches had been moved around and pushed together to make beds, some comfortable chairs had been brought in, and a door had been fitted in front of the galvanized bucket.

Outside in the Mews, Annie and her father had boarded up the shop windows and so far they hadn't lost a customer.

'I 'ear Mrs James is going ter stay wiv 'er boys,' said Mrs Turner one day.

'Yes, I'm surprised you haven't gone to your son's,' replied Annie.

Mrs Turner shrugged her heavy shoulders. ''E's in the army now, and I don't git on that well wiv 'is wife.'

'I thought you did.'

'Yer, I used ter, when she lived round 'ere, but when they moved away and got the 'ouse she got all toffee-nosed. I ain't good enough for 'er now.'

'It's a shame you don't see a lot of your grandson.'

'Yer, well – it can't be 'elped.'

That made Annie feel sad. How could Mrs Turner's daughter-in-law leave her here on her own in London? Her own father-in-law had been to see her after the docks had been bombed. He was being sent away to work and had wanted to see her before he left. She liked Sam's father very much.

'Bye, Annie,' said Mrs Turner, bringing her back from her daydreams.

'Bye, Mrs Turner.'

'I 'ope yer dad manages ter git a few extra bits in fer Christmas. Could do wiv a nice tin o' ham.'

'I'll ask him to put you one by.'

'Fanks.' She closed the door behind her. Annie missed the familiar tinkle of the shop bell – that had gone along with so much else.

It was the end of November, and as usual after tea they made their way to the shelter. Before the Miss Pages left they had given Annie some reels of ribbon and a lot of baby wool, so now Mrs Armstrong, Ted's wife, and Mrs Day were all busy knitting for the new baby. The baker's wife didn't knit but she was crocheting a lovely shawl. Despite all their problems, the neighbours had become very close. The men spent most evenings in the shelter playing cards and having a few bottles of beer and they were all pleased that so far the Eagle, despite having no windows, and some slates missing, was still standing.

''E's a bit late ternight,' said Mrs Day, casting her eyes up to the roof of the shelter. 'What time is it?'

'It's gorn twelve,' said her husband. 'I'm gonner git a bit o' shut eye while I can.'

'Good idea,' said Mr Rodgers.

'Be quiet, Ben,' said Ted's wife. 'Annie's trying ter git a bit o' sleep.'

Annie smiled to herself. Being pregnant and sleeping on these slatted benches wasn't an easy feat. What wouldn't she give to get in between nice clean sheets, and pull the soft cosy blankets up round her chin. She cuddled her hot-water bottle near to her, wishing Sam was holding her close. Her father had been very cross about her staying in London, but she knew she would never leave him. Perhaps, she thought to herself, after the baby was born she might go down to see Aunt Ivy. As she drifted off to sleep, her thoughts milling round her brain, she was aware that before long the planes would be over, and it would be another broken night.

Someone was moving about. Annie opened her eyes. There was no noise; all was quiet. She sat up.

'It's all right, love,' whispered her father. 'I'm just getting up.'

Annie's eyes gradually became accustomed to the half light. 'What time is it?'

'Seven.'

'What, seven in the morning?'

He laughed. 'Course. He didn't come over last night.'

She swung her legs to the floor. 'You mean there wasn't a raid?'

'That's right,' said Bill Armstrong. 'Reckon 'e's frightened of old Winny.'

The whole shelter was stirring, unable to believe they had had a night without bombs.

The morning papers told them why London had been spared; the Germans had changed their tactics and were now going for other cities. Over the following weeks, they continued to make their way to the shelter every night, but still there were no raids on London.

'Dad? D'you think we could risk one night in bed?' asked Annie one morning, rubbing the small of her back.

'Don't know, could be a bit dodgy. It's a bit of a way to run if we get caught.'

'Just over Christmas.'

'OK, but only if it's still safe.'

Annie gave him a hug. The thought of a nice comfortable bed seemed like heaven.

Sam slumped on his bunk. It was his turn to get some sleep. The engines were throbbing healthily deep in the bowels of the ship; they were on their way back to England and he hoped he might get some leave. As he lay looking up at the metal girders his thoughts were full of Annie. It would be Christmas soon, their first Christmas. He wanted so much to be with her, to buy her a nice present. He turned over and took the photo of their wedding from under his pillow. It was becoming dog-eared from so much handling. As he studied it he could almost hear her laughing. In March he was going to be a dad. He ached for Annie's warm lips on his, her soft hair nestling against his chest. He loved her so very much, and desperately wanted to be home with her, to hold her close, to make love to her, and to see their baby when she arrived. He had made up his mind, he wanted a daughter, but if he wasn't lucky this time, there could always be another. He reached up for her last letter.

The loud sound of the klaxon calling them to battle stations quickly brought him back to reality. As he jumped from his bunk, an almighty crash and a blinding flash of light threw him against the side of the ship. He didn't know what had happened. He was hurting, but didn't know where. He was floating. He was in the water. It was cold, bitterly cold. Annie was holding out her hands to him. He was floundering and thrashing about. He tried to grab them, but he kept slipping away. He was being dragged down. Water was filling his ears and eyes, and he was cold, so very cold. 'Annie,' he shouted, 'Annie, save me.' No matter how hard she tried, she couldn't reach him. He tried to call her name again. He was holding her hand, but she didn't answer. He couldn't see her, it was black, she had gone, and he didn't hurt any more.

Christmas was very quiet for Annie and her father. She had put up the few paper chains she had found undamaged, but without Lil and Sam they both knew it would be lonely. Her father had wanted to take her to Aunt Ivy's, but the van had been badly damaged, and he didn't think many trains were running as a lot of track had been blown up. But they were sleeping in their beds, and next year Annie prayed she would be with Sam and their baby.

The Friday after Christmas Ted came into the shop. ''Allo, Ben. All right then?'

'Not too bad.'

'We've all been 'aving a little chat, and we fink we ought ter 'ave a bit of a do in the Eagle next Tuesday, New Year's Eve. What d'yer say ter that?'

'I reckon that could be a good idea, Annie could do with a night out.'

'I'm gonner start a kitty, so if yer've got five bob, yer in.'

'Done.'

So far, everyone in Albert Mews had been spared the real horror of war. Only their property had been affected. The baker's two boys were in the catering corps, and as far as anyone knew they were fine. Ted's daughters lived out of London, as did the Days' girls. The ironmonger's children had all been evacuated, and the two Miss Pages were safely in Bournemouth. So when, on the Saturday afternoon, the telegram boy slowly cycled up the Mews, everyone left their shop to see where he would stop.

Annie's face drained when he walked into their shop.

'Mrs Jarvis 'ere?'

'I'm Mrs Jarvis,' Annie knew she was speaking, but it wasn't her voice that was going round and round inside her head. Her hand trembled as he handed her the small buff-coloured envelope that everyone was in dread of receiving.

Her father was at her side. 'Here, love, sit on the chair.'

Slowly she lowered herself down. 'I can't open . . .'

'Shall I do it?'

She nodded as her eyes filled with tears.

Mr Rodgers quickly tore at the envelope. He glanced over the words before speaking. 'Annie love,' he croaked. 'It's Sam. He's missing, believed killed in action.'

Annie tried to speak. Her mouth opened and closed, but no words came. She felt as if she was floating away and a hand grabbed her as a blackness settled over her.

* * *

301

'It's a bloody shame.' A voice was echoing in her head. 'She's coming round.'

'Git 'er a drink o' water,' said another voice.

A glass was put to her lips and she automatically swallowed.

'Annie, Annie love.' Someone was tapping the back of her hand.

She slowly opened her eyes. The light hurt them so she quickly blinked them shut again. She was trying to put everything together. 'Dad,' she whispered, looking round her and struggling to sit up, 'what happened?'

'You fainted. Are you feeling better now?'

She realized she was sitting on the floor; Ted's wife and Mrs Day were standing over her. Then it hit her why she had fainted. 'Sam!' she screamed. 'No, not my Sam.' Tears flowed from her eyes as she tried to get to her feet. Her father was helping her. 'Where's that telegram?' She snatched it from his hand. 'It can't be,' she sobbed. 'They've made a mistake.'

'I'll give yer a 'and ter git 'er upstairs, Ben,' said Ted's wife.

'I'll make 'er a nice strong cuppa,' said Mrs Day. 'I'll put plenty o' sugar in. Got a drop of whisky I can put in it?'

'Upstairs, in the bottom of the dresser.' Mr Rodgers was leading Annie up the stairs, and being followed by Ted's wife and Mrs Day.

Annie threw herself on the bed and cried. It was a heartfelt, pitiful cry. 'Sam, oh Sam!'

'Leave 'er be fer a while,' said Ted's wife. 'She needs ter be on 'er own. If I was you I'd go round and git Dr Black. 'E might give 'er sumfink ter calm 'er down.'

''Ere, Annie, I've made yer a cuppa tea,' said Mrs Day. 'I'll put it on this table. I'll sit 'ere an' keep an eye on 'er if yer like, Ben.'

'Thanks,' said her father quietly. 'I'll go round and get the doctor.'

Annie was aware of the doctor coming and giving her some medicine. She knew her father was sitting in the chair, but it was Sam who occupied her thoughts. She held out her hands and called his name. He smiled. She tried to hold on to him. She wanted to believe he wasn't dead. She had to keep thinking about him, willing him back. If there was one glimmer of hope, she would hold on to that.

Annie opened her eyes. It was morning, Sunday morning. Her father was still sitting in the chair. He needed a shave, and he looked old. Her head clearing, Annie knew she wanted to touch him, to tell him she loved him. How must he have felt when he'd lost Mum? Annie swallowed hard. For one small family we have had such a lot of grief, she thought miserably. First there was Will, then Mum – now . . . But she wasn't going to let herself believe Sam was dead.

Her father moved and opened his eyes.

'Hello, Dad,' she said, her voice thick through crying.

'All right, love?' He sat on her bed.

She nodded.

'Annie, I'm so sorry. I liked Sam.'

She threw her arms round his neck. 'Oh, Dad.' The tears began to fall again. 'What'll I do without him? I won't believe he's gone.'

'It doesn't hurt to live in hope.'

'I'm never going to believe he's dead.'

He patted her back. 'Come on, now. D'you fancy some breakfast?'

She bit her bottom lip and wiped away her tears. 'No, not really, but a cup of tea would go down well,' she sniffed.

'Stay there and I'll bring you one up.'

A few minutes later he walked into the room carrying a tray which he set down on the dressing-table. 'Annie, I've made up my mind, you're going down to Ivy's. I don't want any excuses. I don't want the baby to be in any danger.'

'But we haven't had any raids for weeks now.'

'That's not to say we won't be getting them again.'

'What about you, Dad? I don't want to leave you.' She looked up at him. 'You could be all I've got left now.'

Mr Rodgers turned his back on her and began stirring the tea in the pot. 'You've got your baby to think about.' His voice was filled with emotion. 'I'm not going to argue with you. Do you feel up to going today?'

Annie was watching him through the mirror. She didn't want to leave him. 'Not really . . . Let's leave it a week. I should feel more like fighting to get on a train by then.'

'Well, all right. We'll go next Wednesday.'

She nodded. 'That'll give me time to get everything ready.' She gave him a weak smile as he handed her her tea. 'Thanks, Dad.'

All day the neighbours were popping in to ask how she was. It was a comfort to know they had so many caring people round them, and that if she went away, her dad would get plenty of company. But still Annie moved around as if she was in a dream, her thoughts full of Sam.

That night, just as they were going up to bed, the siren began its mournful tone.

'Oh no, not again,' said Annie, her face red and puffy from crying. 'I don't think I could face going into the shelter. I think I'll stay up here. It could be a false alarm.'

'No, come on, we're not taking any chances.' Her father was firm.

Reluctantly Annie looked at her cosy bed, put on her slacks and a thick jumper and made her way downstairs.

'Have you got your bag with everything in?'

'Yes, Dad,' she said wearily.

Everyone from the Mews was in the shelter, and it seemed that as soon as the door was closed the ack-ack guns started firing and the bombs began to rain down once more.

During a lull Mr Armstrong looked out. 'Bloody 'ell. There's loads o' fires, and look, there's parachutes coming down.'

The men rushed to the door.

'Please God, don't let us be invaded,' cried Mrs Day.

There was a loud explosion..

'It ain't 'is army,' said Mr Armstrong closing the door quickly. 'It's bloody land-mines.'

The words had barely left his lips when a loud rushing noise filled their ears. A ball of fire seemed to explode all around them. Annie felt the breath forced out of her; the noise in her ears was deafening.

She fell to the floor and her father, who was coming towards her, was blown to the ground with her. Bricks, dust, rubble, and pieces of concrete were thrown high in the air and then crashed back to earth. It was dark, pitch black. Annie quickly blinked, trying to adjust to the dark. She began to panic. What had happened? She lay quite still, terrified. The air was thick with the dust that was settling on them; her mouth was filled with dirt and grit but she was surprised to find she could still bring her hand up to wipe it away. The baby, was the baby safe? There was a heavy weight on her legs. Someone was moaning. They were calling for help and she didn't recognize the voice.

All at once a babble of voices filled the air. Everyone was calling out.

'Annie. Annie, are you all right?' It was her father shouting.

She suddenly felt safe. 'Dad, Dad, where are you?' she called, her voice shaking with fear.

'I'm here. I'll try and touch you.'

Suddenly a warm sticky hand was feeling over her leg.

'That's my leg, Dad.'

He squeezed it. 'Hang on, love.'

'Ben, is that you?' A loud whisper close by came from out of the darkness.

'Yes, Mrs Jones.'

'I fink me leg's broken,' she stated.

'Don't move,' said her husband.

'I can't move, yer silly bleeder. I just told yer, I fink me leg's broken.'

'Someone will be here soon,' Ron Jones replied in a quavery voice.

'Ted, where are you, Ted?' shouted the butcher's wife.

'I'm all right, I think,' he shouted back.

'Charlie, Charlie.' Mrs Day was crying. 'I can't make Charlie answer me,' she shouted hysterically.

'He might just be unconscious,' said Mr Rodgers. 'Can anybody move?'

'No, don't fink so.' It was Ron Jones the baker's voice that came out of the darkness.

'Are we gonner die?' sobbed Mrs Day.

'Course not,' came her husband's deep throaty tone.

'Fank Gawd. Charlie, yer all right?'

'I 'ope so. Mind you, I ain't 'arf got a bloody great lump on me 'ead though.'

'I fink I can move me arm a bit.' It was Ted speaking. 'If only I could git this bloody great lump of wood orf it.' There was a crash of something falling.

'You all right, Ted?' shouted Mr Rodgers.

'Yer. I'm standing up now. Could do with a torch though.'

Suddenly a couple of lights were being shone. 'You OK in there?' They couldn't see a body, but the voice was comforting.

'Not really,' said Mr Jones.

'Well, 'ang on, 'elp's on its way,' said the voice.

'If yer give me a 'and I'll 'elp the others,' said Ted.

'Right. D'yer know 'ow many's in there?'

'There's eight of us.'

'Fred, try and git an ambulance.'

The sound of timber being thrown aside, and the clatter of falling concrete made Annie wince. She wasn't in pain though; in fact now she felt quite calm, pleased that her dad was still holding her leg.

Gradually one by one they were lifted from the rubble that had been their shelter. It seemed that only the corner by the door had collapsed, and the seats that had been blown along the shelter were what was holding them down.

Mrs Jones did have a broken leg, and Mr Day had a badly cut head. His wife was just frightened. Annie was bruised and shaken, but all right, but her father, who had fallen in front of her and stopped the chairs from hitting her, had ripped the sleeve of his jacket, revealing a deep and bloody gash down his left arm. Mr Jones and Ted were fine, and so was Ted's wife. Mr Armstrong had been right by the door, and he was now lying unconscious on a stretcher. Annie sat in the ambulance trying to comfort his wife; Mrs Jones, Annie's father, and Mr Day all sat in the back with them.

The ambulance bumped and lurched over hose-pipes and debris.

'Sorry it's such a rough ride,' said the driver, braking hard. 'It's

306

nasty tonight, mostly land-mines and incendiaries.'

Through the darkened windows they could see fires burning in all directions; many buildings were well alight.

'I'll try to get you there all in one piece.'

'Thanks,' said Mrs Jones, catching her breath and wincing with every bump. 'I hope the baby's all right,' she said to Annie, trying to put on a brave smile.

'I can feel it jumping around, so that's a good sign,' said Annie.

'Well, that's it, young lady, you're off to Ivy's as soon as possible,' said her father, grim-faced.

'But, Dad, what about the shop?'

He sat silent for a few moments, then said softly, 'It's gone, love. There's nothing there. That land-mine hit it.'

Annie sat back. Everything in the world that she possessed had gone. Tears began to fall. 'Then all we've got is what we stand up in?' she sobbed, gazing down at her dirty clothes.

''Fraid so, love,' said her father.

Annie wiped her tears with the back of her hand. 'D'you think they'll find my bag in the shelter?'

'Wouldn't like to say. Why?'

'The only pictures I had of Mum and Sam are in it.' She clutched her father's hand. 'This baby is more important than anything else in the world, and that picture was all I had left of Sam to show our baby.' Her last words were hardly audible, lost in her sorrow.

Her father put his good arm round her heaving shoulders. No one spoke. They all had their own memories of Albert Mews to cherish.

Chapter 31

As soon as Annie had been checked over and – despite the ordeal of the bombing and of losing Sam – found to be in good health, they were allowed to leave the hospital, her father with his arm stitched and dressed. They spent hours filling in forms and waiting about for clothes, temporary ration books, identity cards, travel warrants and money, then finally they were on their way to Downfold.

The train journey to Horsham was, as her father had predicted, a very slow affair with many stops and changes. It was late evening by the time they were knocking on Ivy's door.

'I don't believe it,' she said after the shock of seeing them on her doorstep. Even old Nell rose from her warm fireside to greet them with a wagging tail and a wet nose. The kisses and cuddles were interspersed with tears from both Ivy and Annie.

Ivy ushered them into the warmth of the kitchen. 'You both look done in. Fred, put the kettle on. What about a bit of supper?'

'No thanks, Ivy, we've eaten quite well today, but a cuppa would be very welcome.'

'Right, now sit yourselves down and tell me what's happened.'

Ivy's tears ran unheeded when she was told about Sam. Then Ben described the air-raid that had led to the day's events. Annie, sitting with Nell at her feet, in a comfortable armchair in front of a glowing fire, could hardly keep her eyes open.

'I think young Annie here could do with going to bed,' said Uncle Fred. 'Ivy's made up the bed for you in Roy's room.'

'Would you mind?'

'Course not, you go on up.' Aunt Ivy gave her a warm, loving smile, and held her close.

'Thanks. Goodnight, all.' As she passed the sideboard, Annie noticed with delight that the copy of her wedding photo which she had sent Aunt Ivy was proudly displayed there. Tears filled her eyes. Now at least she would have a picture of Sam to show to their baby. Sleep came quickly when her head touched the pillow.

It was light when Annie opened her eyes and looked at her watch. It was half-past nine. She strained her ears. There was no sound, where was everybody? She turned on her back and lay looking up at the ceiling. Then the full horror of yesterday and Saturday began filling her mind. Saturday she had had the terrible news about Sam, though she knew she would never accept that he was dead. And yesterday? That dreadful night. She couldn't believe so much had happened to them. They had been lucky, they could have been killed. Now they had simply walked away from it all. Tears trickled into her ears. Albert Mews had gone. All those people she had known all her life would be going off in different directions and she would probably never see them again. She suddenly thought about the Murphy family again, and how upset she had been when they walked out of her life. The baby moved, and she gently touched her stomach. 'You are part of me and Sam,' she whispered. 'And nobody is going to take you away from us.'

A light tapping on the door caused her to wipe her eyes quickly.

'Annie, are you awake?' came a loud whisper. It was Aunt Ivy.

'Yes, it's all right, you can come in.'

Ivy pushed open the door, and put the cup and saucer she was carrying on the table at the side of the bed. 'Brought you a nice cuppa. Your dad's already up.'

Annie sat up. 'It's lovely to stay in bed.'

'We're going to spoil you for a while.'

'You don't have to.'

Ivy sat on the bed. 'Course we do.' She patted her hand. 'We've got to look after you. After all, that baby's going to be the first of that generation in the family. Can't see our Roy ever getting married.'

'How is he?'

'Seems to be all right. He's up north somewhere, still a mechanic.'

'I was very sorry to hear about June.'

'Yes, that was very sad.'

'How's Matthew managing?'

'Quite well I think. He lives with his mum, and as they've got the farm, he's exempt.'

'That's a good thing then.'

'Yes,' she stood up. 'I'll be downstairs if you want anything.'

'I'm getting up now.'

'You don't have to.'

'I'd rather.'

'See you downstairs then.' Aunt Ivy left Annie to finish her tea.

It was a cold, crisp day, and Annie could see old Nell didn't want to go for a walk.

'Would you mind if I went out for a while, Dad?' she said quietly.

'No, but mind how you go, it's a bit cold.'

Outside she shivered, and was pleased she still had her winter coat. Aunt Ivy had given her some gloves and a headscarf, and she pulled that tighter round her ears. Her thoughts were full. She still couldn't believe Sam was really dead. She knew that she and her father had to start a new life now that the shop had gone. What was going to become of them, and how much more could they stand? The fresh, cold air brought tears to her eyes, and they mingled with her genuine tears of sadness. 'Please God, keep us safe,' she whispered. She thrust her hands deep in her pockets and turned for home. Tomorrow she would have to go shopping, and her father would have to register for work. Life would go on.

In the months that followed, Annie and her father were surprisingly happy, happier than Annie could have hoped. He was working in a factory that was only a bike ride away. The hours were long, and he was sleeping downstairs in the front room, on a bed Ivy had managed to get for him. Annie was also pleased to be getting plenty of sleep. She wrote to the War Office telling them her new address, always living in hope that they had been wrong about Sam. She had many letters from Lil, who promised that she would come down to see her as soon as she got some leave.

On one of her many walks she met Matthew again. At first they both felt very ill at ease, each aware of the other's pain, and it took many weeks before they could talk and laugh together freely.

Matthew's baby daughter June was a delight and, on fine days, if Matthew was busy and his mother had one of her women's meeting to attend, Annie was quite happy pushing her pram.

One Sunday morning, Annie and her father were going for a walk. Annie loved walking, and the changing season was bringing new delights every day.

'D'you want to come, Uncle Fred?' she asked cheerfully.

'No thanks, love, me old knee's playing me up a bit.'

'I think Nell's staying with you out of sympathy,' laughed Annie.

'Could be she's got more sense than you two. It's a bit sharp out there.'

'It's a shame about Fred's arthritis,' Ben Rodgers said when they were outside. 'He's in a lot of pain.'

Annie linked her arm contentedly through her father's. 'He's such a nice old man.' They continued their stroll down the lane. 'Look at all these lovely primroses.' With a great deal of difficulty, Annie bent down and picked a small bunch. 'D'you know, I like living in the country, do you, Dad?'

'Yes, I could get quite used to it.'

'I'm thinking of staying somewhere round here after the baby's born, and after the war.' She tried to sound casual and, without looking at him, she began to arrange the posy.

'What would you do?'

'Don't know. I get my pension.'

'I know, but that won't be enough to keep you both, and pay rent.'

Annie shrugged her shoulders. 'I've got to stand on my own two feet.'

'Yes I know, but . . .' Her father stopped. 'We should get some sort of compensation after the war. What if we bought a small grocer's shop and ran it together?'

Annie's face was wreathed in smiles. 'What, near here? In the country? Would you, Dad? I'd like that. That would be really smashing.'

'I've been thinking about us getting a place of our own very soon. Some of the blokes at the factory have managed to find places to rent.'

'We can't, Aunt Ivy would be most upset if we moved out.'

'I know. But after the baby's born, it's going to be a bit crowded. After all, they've only got the two bedrooms, and I feel it's wrong me sleeping in their front room. And Fred's none too nimble on his feet.'

'Aunt Ivy don't mind.'

'No, I know. Anyway, we'll see. Come on, let's get back, dinner should be ready by now. And, Annie. Don't say anything to Ivy, not just yet, anyway.'

She squeezed his arm. 'Course not.'

It was the end of March when Annie's little girl pushed her way into the world. All the time she was in labour and in a warm bed, she was reminded of Lil and that night behind the hospital.

Hazel, as Annie called her, had a mop of dark hair and big dark eyes. Her small rosebud mouth was the finishing touch to this perfect little face. Everybody was thrilled. Matthew had sent a beautiful bunch of flowers to the hospital and Aunt Ivy and her father came to visit her at the first opportunity. Her father couldn't leave his granddaughter alone.

'She's lovely, Annie.' He kissed Hazel's hand again.

'You'll kiss them away,' said Ivy, but she too was besotted with this six-pound-three-ounce bundle of joy.

When her visitors finally left, Annie lay looking at her daughter as she cradled her in her arms. Tears filled her eyes, and her thoughts turned once more to Sam. 'If only your father could see you,' she whispered, her lips gently caressing the soft downy cheek. 'He did so want a daughter. I'm going to tell you all about him, and show you his picture. We're never going to forget him, or stop loving him.'

The long hot summer months quickly sped by, and Annie was soon as happy as she had ever been. When Lil came to see her on a long weekend pass there were more kisses and hugs, and on

Saturday night Aunt Ivy looked after Hazel while Lil, Matthew and Annie went to the local dance.

As usual Lil was the belle of the ball, even though she was in uniform. She had bleached her hair and looked good, and when people saw the ENSA flashes at the top of her arm she was invited up on the stage. She was in her element. Annie danced, laughed and was happy, and it was almost as if, at that moment, the war didn't exist.

As they all walked home she was reminded of the last dance she'd been to with her cousin Roy, just after Will had been killed. Behind her, Lil and Matthew were busy talking. Annie shivered. Her mood of joy had changed. Suddenly she felt very unhappy as Sam came into her thoughts.

They reached the gate, and Matthew kissed Lil's cheek. She giggled.

'I'd already heard all about you from Annie,' he said, looking down and kicking a small stone.

'All good I hope,' interrupted Lil.

'But I didn't realize you'd be such a . . . smasher.'

Lil took his face in her hands. 'Thanks, Matt.' She quickly kissed his lips. 'I'll see you tomorrow, about six.'

'I won't be late. Bye, Annie.'

'That's nice of 'im ter take me ter the station,' said Lil as they walked up the path.

'I think he's got a soft spot for you.'

'Na, it's just that I'm a bit, well, you know, well travelled and all that.'

'Be quiet going up the stairs,' whispered Annie, closing the front door.

In the bedroom, Lil began to giggle.

'Shh, you'll wake the house up.'

'Sorry. It's this damn 'ome-made country wine. I'm a bit tipsy. Me, who can normally drink anyone under the table.'

Lil carefully placed her uniform over the chair. She sat on the bed wearing just her pale pink camiknickers.

'I see you're not wearing those khaki passion killers,' sniggered Annie. 'This must seem a bit tame after your usual life-style.'

314

'It makes a nice change not to 'ave every bloke trying ter git yer outside just ter git 'is leg over. D'yer know I've really enjoyed meself ternight. Did you?'

'Yes, it was a nice change to go out.'

'Don't you and Matt – you know?'

'No, we're just good friends.'

'Annie.' Lil pulled at a loose thread on the bedspread. 'I was ever so upset when I 'eard about Sam. Don't you ever fink about going out with someone else?'

Annie pulled her nightgown over her head, and sat next to Lil. 'No. I feel . . . I can't . . . I don't know. D'you know that was the worst weekend of my life. I can still go over it minute by minute.'

Lil threw her arms around Annie. 'Thank gawd yer still 'ere,' she sobbed. 'I couldn't bear it if anyfink should 'appen ter yer.'

Annie patted her back. 'Nothing's going to happen to us, not down here.'

Lil sat back and wiped her eyes; her mascara had streaked down her cheeks. 'I fink Hazel is the sweetest baby I've ever seen, and I'm glad I'm 'er godmother, even if I wasn't 'ere.'

'Lil,' Annie hesitated. 'Do you ever think . . .'

Lil stood up. 'No, that's in the past, and I don't wonner talk about it. Come on, let's git ter bed.'

Annie turned out the light. She was pleased they were still good friends. The two of them had been through a lot of ups and downs in their lives.

In the year that followed, Annie's father found a small cottage not far from Ivy's. They bought some odd pieces of furniture, and settled in very quickly. They were happy, and to them the war seemed a million miles away. London was still being bombed and, after Pearl Harbour, America joined the war. Annie and her father would often sit in front of the fire talking about Albert Mews, wondering what had happened to all the people who used to live there. In the summer of 1942, Annie began helping Matthew, working on the farm, or looking after both the girls when he and his mother were busy. She was teaching Hazel to say 'Dad', determined she would know all about Sam. Her father was delighted by his beautiful granddaughter, who was the apple of his eye.

As the years rolled by, the news of the war wasn't so good, and everybody was calling for a second front. Since Annie and her father had moved to Downfold, their lives had been unaffected. Annie continued to tell Hazel about her father, and now she was talking and taking an interest in his photo.

By September 1944 the Allied forces had landed in France, and everybody was hoping that victory was now in sight.

One warm sunny afternoon, Annie was in the fields helping Matthew stack some hay. Both the girls had chickenpox, so they were staying with Ivy. A lone plane came droning overhead and Annie and Matthew shielded their eyes as they looked up.

'He's a bit low,' said Matthew.

'I don't like it when . . .' Annie hadn't finished speaking when the rat-a-tat of a machine-gun filled the air. Suddenly bullets were flying all around them. She screamed and screamed, frantically looking round for a place to run. Matthew grabbed her and threw her to the ground. He quickly threw himself beside her and, with her hands over her head and Matthew's arm protecting her, she lay trembling and sobbing. 'Not again,' she whimpered. 'Please, not again.' She was shaking and crying uncontrollably.

'The bastard,' shouted Matthew. He hit the ground in anger.

Annie didn't answer.

Slowly he turned over and carefully raised himself up on his elbows. 'I think he's gone. He must have thought we were easy game.'

Annie didn't move.

'Annie. Annie, are you all right?' he yelled, his voice full of fear as he cradled her in his arms.

She opened her eyes, and tears ran down her pale face. He hugged her and whispered, 'Annie, are you all right?'

'I'm so frightened.'

He held her close, and, as they lay together, their lips met. It was a long, tender kiss.

'Oh, Annie.'

She quickly sat up. 'I'm sorry, Matt, I shouldn't . . .'

He took her hand. 'I won't pretend I don't have any feeling for you. And I understand that, like me with June, you'll never forget Sam.'

She put her finger to his lips. 'No, Matt, please don't. Don't spoil our friendship.'

He pushed her hand away. 'I must. Please, Annie, let me finish. Both our girls get on very well. So why can't we get married and all live together?'

'I can't marry you. I'm very fond of you, but I shall always wait for Sam to come back.'

'He's dead, Annie.' His voice took on a tone of anger. 'My God, even you must realize it by now. You've never heard from the War office, so . . .'

'I'm sorry Matt, but I'll never give up hope.' She turned her head. 'Please don't be angry, and don't let this come between us. I value your friendship too much.'

'I'm sorry, Annie.' He kissed her hand. 'Forgive me?'

She nodded and wiped her face with the flat of her hand.

'It's just that I don't want to see you throw your life away on a dream.'

'Deep down I know it's not a dream,' she whispered.

Chapter 32

All too quickly, winter was on them once again. On Friday nights Annie's father looked after Hazel while Annie and Aunt Ivy went into town to the cinema. The outing was a highlight of Annie's week: she'd always loved the pictures and all through the war the newsreels had become almost as important as the main film. Back in the summer, Annie had cringed when she saw the damage the so-called flying bombs had done to London, and the frightening memories had come flooding back. Now there was a new menace – the V2 rockets that were falling out of the sky without any warning. When would Hitler give up?

But tonight the news had been good, and it cheered them all when the newsreel showed the progress the Army was making across Europe. Throughout, Aunt Ivy had kept nudging Annie and whispering eagerly that she was sure every Army driver was her Roy. The entire audience was hoping that the end of the war was in sight at long last.

As Annie and Ivy stood waiting at the bus stop laughing and chatting about the Bob Hope and Bing Crosby film that had accompanied the newsreel, Aunt Ivy pulled her scarf tighter at her throat. 'This wind is getting raw. Wouldn't be surprised if we didn't have a white Christmas. I was talking to Matthew's mother the other day.'

'Oh yes,' said Annie, stamping her feet to bring back the life and warmth into them.

'She is saying she would like to see Matt married again.'

'Has she anyone in mind?'

'You, I think.'

Annie quickly brought her head up. 'What did you tell her?'

'What I always say when anyone asks me if you're going to get married again. You're waiting for your husband to come back.'

To the surprise of the other people waiting at the bus stop, Annie hugged Aunt Ivy. 'You don't think I'm wrong having hope, do you?'

Aunt Ivy shook her head firmly. 'No, love, I don't. Look, here's the bus.'

Christmas came and was full of excitement, and after Hazel had ripped open the few presents they had been able to buy or make, the rest of the day was spent with Aunt Ivy and Uncle Fred.

'That was lovely, Ivy,' said Ben Rodgers after they had finished their Christmas dinner. He sat back in his chair and patted his stomach. 'That's one good thing about living in the country, we never go short of food. I'm glad I haven't got the shop now. Can you imagine all of 'em queuing up and shouting for their dried fruit and tins of salmon?'

'Have you thought any more about opening a shop round these parts after the war, Ben?' asked Fred.

'Yes, but I'll have to wait and see what sort of compensation I get from the government first. I rather fancy another grocer's, don't you, love?' He looked at Annie who was busy wiping the dinner off Hazel's face with her bib.

'I think it would be nice, and I could do with something to do when Hazel starts school.'

'My God, how time flies. Young Hazel starting school!' said Uncle Fred.

Hazel looked at him and grinned. She wrinkled her nose and showed her lovely white, even, baby teeth.

'You've got a little while yet before that happens haven't you, my love?' said Aunt Ivy, gathering up the dinner plates. 'I'll get the pudding.'

'Me likes pudding,' said Hazel, throwing her head back and laughing. She loved being the centre of attraction as much as her Aunty Lil did, Annie thought fondly.

* * *

Nineteen forty-five came in with high hopes of the war ending soon. The Germans were being pushed back out of Europe, and in the spring everyone was talking about victory parties.

'I was pleased about the arrangements made at the mothers' meeting yesterday,' said Annie over the fence to Doreen, her next-door neighbour.

'I know there's not many children in this village,' said Doreen as she hung her washing on the line. 'But we're going to give them a party just the same.'

'I had a letter from Lil, you know Lil?' said Annie, coming closer to the fence.

'Is that the singer?'

'Yes, you've met her. She's been here a few times. Well, she's been all over the place, and she was telling me that when they liberate somewhere they all go mad. She's having a wonderful time.'

'Well, you can't blame them for celebrating. Thank God the Germans never got here.'

Annie put her elbows on the fence. 'When this is all over I'm going up to London for a few days to see if I can find out what really happened to Sam.'

'That's a good idea. Those Whitehall wallahs don't seem to bother about answering letters. Don't forget, I'll take care of Hazel for you.'

'Thanks,' Annie smiled.

'That's all right, she's no bother.'

On 5 May, a few tables and benches were placed outside the Women's Institute hall. There were only about twenty children in the village of Downfold, but that didn't stop everyone from making sure they would celebrate the end of the war. The tables were laden with neat sandwiches, cakes, jellies and lemonade. All the children were wearing paper hats and blowing on hooters: the noise was deafening.

'Are you coming to the dance tonight, Annie?' asked Matt, bending down to retrieve his daughter's paper hat for the third time.

Annie looked at her father.

'Course she is, I'm looking after young Miss here.' Ben Rodgers patted Hazel's head and grinned at Matt.

Annie ignored him. She and Matt had an understanding now – they were good friends.

Along with all the other grown-ups, Annie's father was busy fussing and helping with the proceedings, passing round cakes, dishing out jelly and ice-cream, mopping up lemonade when glasses were knocked over as young excited arms waved about wildly. His face was flushed which, Annie thought fondly, was probably due to his sampling the barrel the landlord of the Bird in Hand had provided. His paper hat had fallen over one eye, but he didn't care. Catching her gazing at him, he came up to Annie and put his arm round her shoulder. Pulling her close, he kissed her cheek. 'Well, love, we made it,' he said. He squeezed her tighter and then, looking down at the top of Hazel's red paper hat as she spooned jelly into her mouth, said proudly, 'The three of us have got a lot to look forward to now.'

Annie nodded and smiled. The war was over, and they were safe.

Chapter 33

Sam leant on the rail and, along with many hundreds of other service men, gazed in awe as the cliffs of Dover loomed in front of them. When they'd first come into sight the cheer that had gone up had been deafening, but now they all stood in silence, almost as if they were paying homage to some unknown benefactor. For hours the tannoy had been blasting out what Sam supposed were the latest records, and now it was Vera Lynn's 'White Cliffs of Dover' that crackled and faded away with every small, welcome breeze on this wonderful warm July day.

Since they had first set foot on the ship on the other side of the Channel, the nurses had been hovering amongst the wounded. Others, like Sam, wandered about helping those not so fortunate, but for all of them the war was finally over. They were on their way back home.

With his thumb and forefinger, Sam rubbed his eyes as the tears stung. Home, home to see his beloved Annie and the baby he'd never seen. He didn't even know if he had a son or daughter. He coughed, desperately trying to stem the tears that wanted to fall. He couldn't let anyone see him like this, it wasn't manly. He tried hard to picture Annie, but now after all these years the memory was blurred and fading. He had had photographs from her, but they had been lost at sea when his ship was torpedoed. That was four years ago. Did Annie know he was still alive? Although he had written to her when they were allowed to, he had never had a single letter from her in all the years he'd been in the POW camp. What had she been told? The Red Cross were marvellous at finding out what was happening to men taken prisoner, but the Germans were a wicked bunch: did they pass on all the information? Sam's thoughts were muddled. Since being released he realized his camp had been fairly relaxed. When he learned of the atrocities some of his fellow prisoners had suffered in other camps, he shuddered and gave up a silent prayer of thanks.

The ship's hooter brought him out of his daydreams, and he looked over the side at the hundreds of small boats flitting about. Those with sails were ducking and weaving dangerously around them like ants, the water cannons sending up huge sprays high into the air. Suddenly there was a carnival atmosphere as the men whooped, shouted and whistled. Some were even doing a jig. Sam caught sight of one or two youngsters standing alone, quietly crying.

After they docked, Sam, along with many others, was taken to a rehabilitation centre which doubled as a hospital. He was given a bath and clean clothes, and for the first time in years felt human. Then he was put in a ward and given a check-up by a doctor. Lying in bed quietly reflecting, Sam gently ran his hands across the clean white sheets. They were stiff, but to him they felt like pure silk.

The following day a WVS woman came round with paper and pens and, for those who couldn't write, help.

Sam stared at the blank white sheet of paper. Where could he start? Over the years he had written many letters to Annie, and it had never been a chore. Now he didn't know where to begin. Slowly a thought crept into his mind, the one thought he'd shut out all this time, that he had pushed right to the back of his consciousness. Now it had to be faced. What if they had been injured, or even . . . ? He had learnt that London had been badly bombed. What if they had stayed? That was the sort of thing Annie'd do. She wouldn't have worried about her own safety if she'd thought she could help others. He chewed the end of his pen. Her generosity was only one of the many wonderful things he loved about her. But she had the baby, and he knew how much she would love it. Surely the baby's safety would have come first? He put the pen to one side. He wasn't going to write. He had been given a clean bill of health, and he was leaving. He was going to find them.

As the bus took him through Dover he couldn't believe his eyes. The devastation was staggering. It was a miracle that anyone could have lived through this. He turned this way and that.

'Bit of an eye-opener, ain't it, mate?' The conductor held out his ticket. 'Just got 'ome then?'

'Yes. This must have been awful.'

'Yer, it was a bit sticky at times. Still, we've got the bastard now. Only got ter finish off the Japs then our kids will be safe. Where's home then, lad?'

'London.'

The conductor gave him a grave look. 'Been there since the bombing?'

Sam shook his head.

'Be prepared fer a bit of a shock. They got it real bad up there. Next stop's the station.'

As Sam left the bus, the conductor shouted, 'Good luck, mate.'

Sam hoisted his kitbag on his shoulder and gave him a wave. There was a sea of people, mostly service personnel, all waiting inside the station. He couldn't rest, so he paced up and down – everything seemed so slow.

As the crowded train entered London he saw for himself what the bus conductor had meant. He couldn't recognize any of the old familiar landmarks, and his heart sank. What if they'd . . . ? He couldn't bring himself to say the word. Annie had been his world, the one person who had been worth living for, her and his baby. When he'd lain rambling after being plucked almost dead from the sea, it had been the thought of seeing Annie again that had pulled him through. He had to make up to them both for the missing years. He closed his eyes. God couldn't take both of them away from him, not now.

As the train drew to a halt he jumped on to the platform and ran through the ticket barrier. Outside he hailed a taxi. He wasn't going to wait for a bus.

'Where to, mate?'

'Paradise Street.'

'Where's that?'

'Off Jamaica Road, I'll show you when we get there.'

'It'll cost yer.'

'Don't worry about that, and please hurry.'

'It'll take a bit o' time, a lot of the roads are still blocked off. Still dangerous, yer see, bomb craters, and a lot of the buildings are still falling.' The taxi driver glanced over his shoulder. 'Just got back then?'

Sam wasn't in a chatty mood. 'Yes,' was his short reply as he gazed out of the window.

Finally they reached what Sam thought had once been Paradise Street. The journey had taken far longer than he had expected, and the driver had been right, they had had to take many diversions. They seemed to be going round in circles. He couldn't believe this was London, his London, where he'd been brought up and lived all his life until he'd gone into the Navy when he was sixteen. He didn't know where he was. He paid the driver, picked up his kitbag and started to walk towards Albert Mews.

He passed what was once Victoria Gardens. Where Lil had lived was now a flat, open space. He wondered what she'd do now the war was over. The last he'd heard was that she was carving herself a great career with ENSA. He hurried on. The Eagle pub was still standing. The windows were all boarded up, but painted on the boards in bright red letters was 'business as usual'. The door was shut tight as it wasn't opening time yet. All around him the bright afternoon sun was shining on places which had hardly ever seen the light of day, and now the wild flowers that were growing out of the rubble had turned the stones and the dust into a mass of colour. As Sam walked on he knew in his heart that Albert Mews no longer existed.

Fisher's chimneys had gone, the great towers which had dominated the landscape all these years had vanished. Where the neat shops of Albert Mews had so proudly stood was now a large pile of debris sprouting with weeds. Why hadn't it been cleared away like some of the other bomb sites? Sam wondered bleakly. Perhaps because it was tucked out of the way. Lumps of concrete, some dangerously balanced, lay on the ground. As Sam got closer he could see the arm of the lamp-post sticking up. Annie had told him a long while ago that the bollards had been taken away for scrap metal. The front of the air-raid shelter had been blown in – it was now just a hollow shell with grass growing all round it. He shuddered. He knew they would have used that. What if they . . . ? He wouldn't let his mind think of that.

He scrambled over the wreckage, he didn't know why. What was he looking for? Was it hope? Was it some form of confirmation to tell him Annie hadn't been here when this dreadful thing had happened?

For hours he searched and dug with his bare hands. He found a reel of what had once been pale pink ribbon, which he knew must have come from the haberdashery. As he slowly and unconsciously unwound it, tears filled his eyes. What had happened to those two dear little old ladies? Then he unearthed some rotten cardboard; he could just make out the name, Park Drive. That must have been in Ben's shop. He tossed it aside, sank to the ground, and buried his head in his hands. Where was Annie? And who could tell him what had happened to her?

"Ere, mate. What d'yer think you're doing?"

Sam looked up. A policeman was walking towards him. Sam struggled to his feet and, stumbling and falling over the debris, rushed to meet him. Tears began running down his face and he wiped them away with his dirty hands.

"Ere, 'ang on, mate. You all right?"

To the policeman's surprise, Sam threw his arms round him, and all the years of pent-up grief, fear, horror, frustration, anxiety and war spilled out.

'Steady on, mate. You all right?'

Sam stood back. 'Sorry about that.'

'Just got back?'

Sam nodded as he wiped his face. 'My father-in-law, wife and baby used to live there.' He quickly glanced behind him.

'I'm sorry to hear that. Did they manage to get out?'

'I don't know. You see I've been a prisoner-of-war, and I've just got home. I haven't heard from my wife in all that time. You don't happen to know when this happened, do you? Or how many were . . . ?'

The policeman picked up his bike. 'I wasn't round this way then. Look, come back to the station with me and we'll see if we can find something out for you.'

'Thanks.'

'And I expect you could do with a cup of tea?'

Sam smiled, his hopes rising. 'I haven't had one since I left Dover first thing this morning.' And for the first time in years, Sam's step had a spring in it.

At the police station one or two of the old ones told him they remembered when the land-mine dropped on Albert Mews.

'That was a night that was. I tell yer, if Hitler had landed then I reckon he would be here be now. Almost flattened London that night he did. You should have seen one of the craters round at Fisher's. Could get two double-deckers in there easy.'

'How many in Albert Mews were killed?' asked Sam softly.

'Never rightly knew. I was busy over the other side of the water. I remember the night Victoria Gardens got it, blew old Reeve's 'orse ter bits. Bloody shame.'

Sam buried his head in his hands.

'Their shelter got 'it after that, but they may 'ave gorn away before that night. I knew all of them.' The policeman sat back in his chair. 'I remember that Bessie, she was always good for a laugh. She was one of the lucky ones, she went in the Land Army before it happened, so I heard. I bet she's chased a few farmers.'

'What about the Rodgers?' asked Sam.

'I knew Annie, and her father. Always got me fags there. She was a nice girl.'

'Did you ever see our baby?'

'No, can't say I did. I remember when 'is missis died. Wasn't young Annie in the Salvation Army then? Why don't you try them. They might be able to tell you who was found. Here comes yer tea, lad.'

'Thanks.'

The other policeman touched Sam's shoulder. 'I shouldn't hold out too much hope, son.'

Sam swallowed hard. 'Thanks, I think I'll go round to the Salvation Army.'

Sam finished his tea and left. It took him a while to get his bearings and, as he made his way through the bombed streets, he wondered all the while if the mission hall was still there. So many churches were gutted, leaving just skeletons, standing proud and defiant. He could never visualize what those days and nights of ceaseless bombing must have been like, or how women and children could have survived such hardships. In the years at the beginning of the war, his ship had seen plenty of action, and they'd seemed to thrive on it. When the end had come it had come very quickly. He couldn't imagine the night after night of suffering this part of London must have been through.

Sam quickened his pace as he came in sight of the little mission hall that Annie had once showed him. He knew Rose used to teach Sunday school there. It was standing alone; everything around it had gone. Annie had told him of the children who were forced to attend while their fathers had their afternoon nap. He knew all about that, as he too had had to attend Sunday school to get out of the way. He thought about his parents. He knew his mother had been evacuated with all the kids, but the address had been lost along with many other things. But what about his father? The docks had been badly bombed. Sam told himself that as soon as he found out about Annie he'd go and see if his old home in Peckham was still there. He suddenly caught sight of someone coming round the corner. She was walking away. 'Excuse me,' he yelled out. 'Just a mo.'

The woman, who was shabbily dressed and must have been in her forties, stopped.

Sam ran up to her. 'Could you help me?'

'What d'yer wanner know?'

'You don't happen to know if Rose Hobbs or her father are still alive?'

'Can't 'elp yer, lad. Yer see, I ain't from round these parts.'

Sam looked dejected. 'They were in the Salvation Army, Rose used to teach in there.' He raised his hand towards the mission.

'It ain't been open fer quite a while. Ain't been many kids left round 'ere. They're gonner be coming back now, but gawd only knows where they're gonner live.'

Sam looked at the wide open spaces. 'Thanks anyway.'

'Yer could try one of their hostels, I fink the one over White-chapel's still standing.'

Once more Sam had found hope. 'Thanks, missis, thanks a lot.' To her surprise he kissed her cheek.

She touched it tenderly. 'Go on wiv yer. You sailors are all the same.'

Sam made his way to Whitechapel. By now he was beginning to feel weary and tired. He hadn't eaten since his breakfast and now the sun which had been high in the sky all day was slowly sinking out of sight. His kitbag was heavy and digging into his shoulder, he felt alone and miserable, and wondered how all this would end. He knew there used to be a sailors' home near there, so perhaps, if he didn't have any luck, and if it was still standing, he could find a bed for the night.

At the mission he was told that Rose was in the Forces, and they thought Mr Hobbs was working away. Once again he had come up against a blank wall, and he made his way to the Seamen's Mission.

'Fancy a drink, mate?' asked one of his room-mates as Sam sat on the bed. 'We're going to the pub on the corner. Wonner come?'

'Why not?' Sam stowed his gear and followed the two sailors.

'What yer having?'

'What they got now?'

'The usual.'

'I'll have a pint of bitter. Thanks.'

When his new-found friend returned with the glass full of amber liquid, Sam suddenly realized it was years since he had had a drink. He picked up the glass. 'Here's to the future.'

His two mates lifted their glasses.

'Been home long?' asked the one with a beard.

'No, got back this morning . . . I'm looking for my wife,' said Sam, slowly supping the beer with relish. 'Blimey, I'd forgotten how good this tastes.'

'She gorn off with someone else then?'

'No.' Sam put the glass on the table and began telling them his troubles.

After a few more beers on an empty stomach, Sam got very drunk.

The following morning when he opened his eyes he was surprised to find himself in a bed. He raised his head. It began pounding.

'I see yer awake then,' said his bearded friend. 'Look, me and Dave 'ave got to join our ship. We only stopped off here for the night. I wish we could help yer, mate – I really do. Why don't yer go and see if yer dad knows something? Yer missis might have dropped him a line.'

'I'll go this morning. Thanks for bringing me back here.'

Under the full set of whiskers Sam could see the weatherbeaten face break into a grin, and bright blue eyes twinkling. The sailor gently slapped Sam's shoulder. 'That's all right, mate. I'm only sorry we can't stay and help.' He hoisted his kitbag on to his shoulder. The two of them turned in the doorway and gave him a wave.

Once more Sam was on his own and continuing his search for Annie's whereabouts. He discovered his old home had also gone, and as he wandered around looking for a familiar face, he turned the corner and to his joy saw the corner shop where as a kid, when he was lucky and earned a couple of pence doing errands, he'd got his sweets, and then, as he got older, his cigarettes. Although boarded up, it was still intact and the door was open. He ran and almost fell in the doorway. 'Mrs Moss, Mrs Moss.' Throwing his kitbag on the floor he flung his arms round the well-built, startled woman.

When she was finally released Mrs Moss stood back. 'Sam, Sam Jarvis! How are you, after all these years?' Tears began running down her cheeks, and she patted them with the bottom of her faded flowery pinafore. 'How are you, son?'

'Not too bad. And you don't look so bad.'

'We managed, just about, but we managed.'

'Mr Moss OK?'

'Yes, his heart's a bit dicky, but he got through that lot.' She pointed at the void outside.

'You don't happen to know if Mum and Dad are all right? Or where they finished up, do you?'

'Your dad had to go away after the docks got bombed. Scotland I think. You know your mum was evacuated with all the kids?'

'Yes, but I've lost her address. You don't know how I can find out about them?'

'I reckon the docks might be able to tell you where your dad is, and then he'll be able to tell you where you can find your mum. They can't come back here, can they? Mind you, they do say we're having a lot of prefabs round here.'

'What's that?'

'Houses that are made in sections, in a factory. Seen them on the pictures, they look very nice. I wouldn't mind having one. They've even got a bathroom and an inside lav.'

Sam laughed.

'Oh, it's so good to see you again, Sam.' She gave him another hug. 'Seen a lot of action then?'

'Not lately, I've been in a POW camp for the past four years.'

'No. Oh, you poor boy. I remember your dad telling me you got married? How is your wife?'

'I don't know. I'm a dad as well.'

'Fancy that, you a dad. Boy or girl?'

'I don't know.' Sam then told her how he was looking for Annie.

Mrs Moss sat down. 'Oh, my poor boy. I'm so sorry, so very sorry. There must be some way of finding out where they are.'

'Or if they're still alive.'

'Yes, yes of course. Look I'll just go up and tell Jack, he'll be really pleased to see you. He don't come down a lot these days, ain't much point really. We don't get a lot of customers now, don't know why I bother to keep it open half the time.'

Sam touched her hand. 'Well, I'm glad you did.'

Jack Moss was as pleased as his wife to see Sam, and after all the handshaking and hugging he suggested Sam go round the docks to see if someone there could help.

'Where're you staying?' asked Mrs Moss.

'I was at the Seamen's Mission last night.'

'You can bed down here tonight if you want to.'

'That'd be nice, as long as you're sure I won't be putting you to any trouble.'

'It'll be lovely to have you, son,' said Mr Moss.

'Look, I've got the dinner on, I'm sure we can find you a bite. That's if you fancy it?' said Mrs Moss.

332

Sam smiled. 'That'd be really great. I don't remember the last good meal I had.'

'Don't get excited – it ain't nothing fancy.'

'I'm sure it'll taste like manna. Then after, I'll go along to the docks.'

'Fancy a bit o' company, lad?' asked Jack Moss.

Sam smiled. 'I'd be glad of it.'

Mrs Moss's round rosy face beamed. 'It'll do you good to have a little stroll.' She turned to Sam. 'He don't go out a lot now. There ain't many of the old uns left for him to go out with.'

Sam came away from what had once been the thriving docks with a little hope.

Jack sat on a wall. 'I never thought it was as bad as this.' He was looking at the twisted metal and steel that had once formed the great barn-like buildings that used to house mountains of timber. What was left of them was burnt out, and they looked grim and hideous.

Sam sat next to him. 'It must have been horrible.'

'It was, son, it was.'

'I'm glad me mum and the kids were out of it. And now I know where Dad was sent I can send him a letter and find out where they're living.' He lowered his voice. 'They might know something about Annie.'

Jack Moss touched Sam's shoulder. It was a kindly gesture. There was no need for words.

After tea, Sam said he wouldn't mind going to the Castle for a drink. 'Is it still there?' he asked.

'As far as I know,' said Mrs Moss.

'D'you both fancy coming with me? Let me treat you.'

'Thanks all the same, son, but this afternoon fair done me in.'

'What about you, Mrs Moss?'

'Thanks, Sam, but I'll stay with Dad if you don't mind. You go on out and enjoy yourself. You've got a lot of lost time to make up.'

'As long as you don't mind. I won't be back too late.'

'I'll give you a key. I expect we'll be in bed by the time you get back.'

Sam's thought were mixed as he walked to the Castle. Did he want to go in there? The Castle was where he'd seen Annie when she was in the Salvation Army and really fallen in love with her. And it was where Lil used to sing. Lil: she would know where his beloved Annie was. Although they were so different, they were always such good friends, they were sure to have kept in touch if they could . . . But at least now he knew where his father was working. Perhaps it would be quicker to go to Scotland than write. He had a lot of leave, and a lot of time to think about his future. But what kind of future would he have without Annie?

He was relieved to see the Castle was still standing. He pushed open the door and the noisy, smoky atmosphere was still the same. To Sam it was almost like stepping back into the past. In the other bar they even had someone banging away on the old piano. Sam had a thought: perhaps Bill the landlord might know where Lil was. He quickly made his way to the bar, but all his hopes were dashed when he didn't recognize anyone serving there.

'What's it to be, mate?'

'Half of bitter.'

'Ain't seen you 'ere before – just got in?'

Sam nodded as he sorted through his change. 'How much?'

'Fivepence.'

'How much?'

'Fivepence,' he repeated.

'That's a bit steep. Gone up a bit since I was here last.'

'There's been a war, yer know.'

'I have noticed. Is Bill still the landlord?'

'Na, 'e bought it in the first raid. 'E was in the ARP. It was a shame, 'e wasn't a bad bloke.' The barman plonked the glass on the counter.

'Did you know Lil who used to sing in here?'

'Yer. 'Ere, yer ain't sweet on 'er as well, are yer?'

'No, she was a friend of my wife's.'

'Doing well in ENSA, so she said the last time she was in 'ere.'

Sam looked up. 'Lil comes in here?'

'Yer, when she's round this way.'

'Gi's a pint, Tony,' shouted someone along the bar.

Sam felt as if he was walking on air. Lil comes in here. He leant over the bar, impatiently watching Tony fill the man's glass. As soon as he put the money in the till, Sam called him over. 'You said Lil comes in here. You don't happen to know where she stays?'

'You know Lil, in anybody's bed. She ain't changed.' Sam remembered Lil with his friend Mike. 'She still keeps some of 'er stuff 'ere.'

'So she calls in here then?'

'Yer, but she ain't been round fer a while.'

'You don't happen to have a key to her room?'

'No I ain't. Why?'

'I wondered if I might find my wife's address in there.'

'Can't 'elp yer there, mate, but I'll tell yer what, if yer like ter leave a note I'll see she gits it. Don't know when, mind.'

'Thanks.' Tony gave him a pad and pencil. Sam took his glass and sat at a table. He had just finished his second beer and was thinking of leaving, when a great commotion came from the other bar.

''Ere, mate,' shouted Tony across the bar. 'It's your lucky night. Guess what? Lil's just walked in.'

Chapter 34

Sam raced round to the other bar. His hand was on the doorhandle when Lil's voice filled the air. He stopped. He had forgotten how good she was. The last time he'd heard her sing had been the Saturday night after his wedding. He was trembling. He wanted to go in, but . . . What would she tell him? He slumped against the door.

'Move over, chum, yer going in or not?'

Sam looked up at the soldier standing in front of him. 'Sorry, mate.' Sam stepped aside.

The soldier pushed the door open and Sam could see Lil. She was wearing a uniform, was still as trim, but now her hair was blonde. The door closed, and once more Sam was on the outside.

The last words of her song were completely drowned by the applause, shouting and catcalls. Sam opened the door and walked slowly across the room – Lil had her back to him, and was surrounded by men. She turned.

''Ere, what's up, Lil, yer've gorn as white as a sheet – yer just seen a ghost or sumfink?' asked one of her admirers.

For what seemed minutes they stood facing each other, then suddenly Lil sprang into life.

'Sam, Sam,' she yelled. 'It's you, it's really you.'

Sam smiled and went towards her. Lil darted forward with her arms outstretched. Tears ran down her face as she threw her arms round his neck. Much to the amusement of those in the bar, they hugged and kissed, Sam lifting her off her feet and whirling her round and round.

All the while, Lil was crying, 'Where have you been? We all

337

thought you were dead! Oh, Sam,' she sobbed as he put her back on the ground, 'it's so good to see you.'

'Is Annie still alive?' he asked, his eyes suddenly fixed on hers. Lil nodded.

'And the baby?'

'Where have you been?'

'Lil,' he was holding her shoulders. 'Lil, what about the baby?'

'They're all right. At least they were when I last heard from them.'

'When was that?'

'A couple of weeks ago. You've got a daughter.'

'A daughter,' repeated Sam. 'Where are they, Lil?'

'Come and sit down.' She brushed away her tears with the flat of her hand. Her mascara was smudged and her lipstick smeared. She took a packet of cigarettes from her handbag, and offered Sam one. He in turn took a lighter from his pocket and lit them. He drew long and hard on his.

'Where are they, Lil? I almost went mad when I saw Albert Mews, and I've been going round and round in circles trying to find out what's happened to them.'

'They're safe. They've got a place near Annie's Aunt Ivy's. They went down there after they 'ad a really bad raid and Albert Mews got bombed.'

'Is Annie all right?'

'Yer.'

Sam leant back in his chair. He could have cried he was so happy. 'I'd forgotten all about Aunt Ivy. I've never met her, do you have her address?'

'Course. Annie thinks you're dead.'

'What? What gave her that idea?'

'The War Office sent her a telegram saying you were missing believed killed.'

'I don't believe it.'

'Neither did she. Not deep down. So where're yer been all this time?'

'In a POW camp.'

338

'You poor darling.' Lil gently touched his cheek. 'So why didn't yer write?'

'I did, lots of times – but it must have been after the Mews got bombed, and she never got them.'

'And she couldn't write as she didn't know you were still alive. She told the War Office she'd moved.'

'I expect her letter got swallowed up in the system.'

'Wait till Annie sees you.'

'Lil. There's nobody else, is there?'

'Don't talk daft – you know Annie.'

'Yes. We've got a lot to talk about.'

'Yes, well, I'll get a drink. What'll it be, Sam?'

'A whisky. I need something to calm me nerves.'

Lil returned almost at once. 'These are on the house. Cheers.'

Sam looked at Lil. 'I can't really take this in. Me sitting in a pub talking to you.' He held her hand. 'And my Annie's alive. You've seen her, and the baby?'

Lil nodded.

'What does she look like? And what's her name?'

Lil smiled. 'Annie called her Hazel.'

'Hazel,' he whispered.

'She's lovely, Sam, really lovely. She's got dark hair and hazel eyes.' She put her head on one side and studied Sam. 'D'yer know, she looks a bit like you.' Lil laughed. ''Ang on. I've got a photo of them.'

Sam tried to hide his tears as he sat gazing down on a picture of his daughter and his beloved Annie. 'She is lovely,' he croaked.

'She's what, four. She'll be going to school soon.'

'Going to school,' repeated Sam. 'And I've never even seen her. Is this their garden?'

Lil nodded.

'I can't wait till tomorrow. Where do they live?'

'In Sussex. I've got her address here.' Lil dived in her bag once more, and this time brought out a little book. 'Got all me boyfriends' addresses in here. And a few Americans as well. When I'm demobbed I'm hoping ter go on tour with the lot I'm with now.'

'You can still give out a good song.'

With the cigarette dangling from her full red lips, Lil began writing.

Sam examined the piece of paper. 'Bay Tree Cottage, Downfold. Where's that?'

'You have to go to Horsham station and get a bus from there. You might 'ave ter wait a while, they don't run very often.'

Sam leant across the table and kissed Lil's cheek. 'Thank you, Lil. I'll be on the first train in the morning.' Sam played with his empty glass. 'When I saw the mess Albert Mews was in I never thought I'd ever see them again.' He looked up. 'I went past Victoria Gardens . . . Was your dad still there when . . . ?'

'No, thank God. You know me mum and the kids had already been evacuated, and then me dad went up north with 'em. It seems 'e was most upset when 'e found out what happened. I fink some of 'is drinking cronies bought it.'

'Did you lose everything?'

'Didn't 'ave a lot ter worry about. They're doing all right. Dad works in a munitions factory, and they rent a house.'

'That's good. Now, let me get another drink.'

'OK, and then you can tell me all what's happened to you,' said Lil.

Sam returned with the drinks, his face fixed in a permanent grin. 'And what about you? You look smashing, and I bet you've got a few tales to tell.'

She too smiled. 'Thanks. D'yer like me hair?'

Sam nodded. 'It suits you.'

Lil took a cigarette from the packet on the table. 'It looks like we've got a long evening together.'

For hours they sat and talked about all the missing years.

'What happened to Mike, Sam?'

'Never saw the going of him.' He toyed with his glass.

'That's a shame, he was a nice bloke. Where are you staying tonight?' asked Lil.

'At Mrs Moss's: she's the lady who owns the sweet shop near where I used to live.'

'You know you don't have to go back there tonight. You could stay with me upstairs.'

Sam laughed. 'Are you making an improper suggestion, Miss Grant?'

'I'd better not, Annie'll 'ave me guts for garters. But no, honestly, Sam, you could stay.'

'Thanks all the same, Lil, but me gear's at Mrs Moss's. When are you likely to see Annie again?'

'Don't know. Now the war's over I've got to see if I can get into show business. I've got a lot of contacts now, and I've met quite a few stars.' She sat back and puffed hard on her cigarette. 'I know I shouldn't say it, but this war has been a Godsend to me. D'yer know, Sam, I've seen places I didn't even know existed. Been to France, Holland, and even North Africa. God it was hot out there.' She laughed. 'And I've been in a few sticky situations, but I wouldn't have swopped any of it.'

Sam smiled weakly. He too had seen places he didn't know existed, and experienced a lot of things he would rather forget.

Lil continued. 'D'yer notice I try ter talk a bit proper now?'

Sam nodded. 'I don't care how you talk, you'll still be our Lil. So what are you going to do now?'

'Don't know yet. Perhaps I could find meself a Yank, then I'd get to America.'

'Time, if you please,' shouted Tony. As he cleared the glasses from their table he asked quietly, 'You staying the night, Lil?'

'Yes.'

'Well, wait till I've locked the door, then you two can carry on drinking – don't want the law on me back.'

'I'd better be going anyway,' said Sam. 'I expect Mrs Moss will wait up.'

They walked to the door. 'Give my love to Annie, and tell her as soon as I'm settled I'll let her know where I am.'

Sam kissed Lil. 'Thanks, Lil. I still can't believe my good luck bumping into you like this.' Sam held her tight as he fought back the tears.

'Come on, you old softy,' whispered Lil. 'Now remember. Don't do anything I wouldn't do. So that gives you plenty of leeway.' She smiled and the tears glistened on her cheeks. 'Bye, Sam.'

He turned and walked away. He could have flown, he was so happy.

Mr and Mrs Moss were still up when he returned.

'You look cheerful, son,' said Jack.

'Fancy a cup of cocoa?' asked Mrs Moss.

Sam was grinning like a Cheshire cat. 'They're alive, and I've got a daughter.' Sam went over and kissed Mrs Moss's cheek and, taking the paper from his pocket, waved it in the air. 'I've got Annie's address, and they're both safe.'

'That is good news. What's the baby's name?'

'Hazel.'

'Hazel. That's pretty.'

Jack shook his hand. 'That's really good news.' He patted Sam on his back. 'Where are they?'

'Near her aunt's place in Sussex.

Tears trickled down Mrs Moss's face. 'I'm so pleased for you, Sam, really pleased.' She wiped her tears. 'Look at me, silly old fool. Still, they say there's no fool like an old one. How did you manage to get it?'

Sam told them how he'd met Lil. 'I'll try and catch the first train in the morning.'

'I'll get you up, don't worry, and I'll get you a nice breakfast before you go,' said Mrs Moss.

'Thanks, but you don't have to bother.'

'It'll be a pleasure.'

Sam was bedding down on the sofa, but sleep wouldn't come. His mind was turning over and over. He tried to visualize their meeting – he went over and over the conversation they might have, and he shuddered with pleasure at the thought of holding Annie in his arms and making love to her. But what if after all these years she had changed and didn't want him? What if she had met someone else? And what if his daughter didn't like him? Little girls could be very funny.

Finally the first light seeped through the parlour window, the only downstairs window still intact. He was washed and dressed long before Mrs Moss came down. And after breakfast he left them to begin his new life.

He had taken a taxi from Horsham station and, as it bumped along the uneven lane, his heart was pounding.

'Right, lad, this is it,' said the driver.

Slowly Sam stepped out of the taxi, and it drove away. As he stood looking at the nameplate set in the ground, doubts began to fill his mind. He was alone. What if this was the wrong place? What if . . . ? He walked up the path and banged on the door. There was no answer. So he banged again, and once more doubts and fears began filling his mind.

A young woman wearing a brightly coloured turban looked over the fence. She took the pegs from out of her mouth. 'Annie's not in, she's up at her aunt's.'

'Where's that?'

'If you go up this lane, turn left at the crossroads, and it's the first cottage you come to.'

'Thank you. Can I leave my kitbag here?'

'Yes sure, that'll be . . .' She suddenly stopped. 'Here, you're not . . . ?'

He nodded, smiled and touched his cap. 'See you later.'

He dashed off leaving Annie's neighbour open-mouthed.

Again he was walking up an unfamiliar path. But this time he felt more confident. Everything looked so peaceful. Suddenly the door was flung open and a well-built woman filled the doorway. She walked towards him. As she got closer a quizzical look spread across her face. 'It can't be?' Her face turned ashen, and she ran towards him. 'It can't be!' she shouted. 'Fred, Fred,' she screamed out over her shoulder. 'Look. Look who's here!' She clasped Sam to her ample bosom. 'It is you! It really is you, Sam. You're alive?'

'Aunt Ivy,' was all he could whisper.

Fred too hugged him. 'It's good to see you, son.'

'Where's Annie?' asked Sam, looking towards the door.

'They're down the bottom field. Hazel's with her.' Ivy was crying. 'How did you know it was me?'

'I'd know you anywhere, I have your photo stuffed under me nose every five minutes.' She sniffed.

'Annie always said you'd come back. I'll show you where they are,' said Fred, trying to compose himself.

'I'll have a cup of tea ready for when you get back,' said Aunt Ivy, wiping her nose on the bottom of her pinny.

Despite his arthritis, Fred hurried along beside Sam. They went down the lane, into a field, and climbed over a stile. Fred stopped. 'That's them.' He pointed to a slim young woman, a tall man, and two small children playing in the far corner of the field. 'That's Matthew and his little 'un with them.'

Annie and Matthew were deep in conversation.

'Annie,' called Fred.

She turned and waved. She shaded the sun from her eyes with her hand. Sam was running and stumbling towards her. He could see her mouthing his name, but the sound didn't reach him. Matthew was staring. The children looked up. Sam swept her into his arms.

Annie cried, 'Sam! I knew you weren't dead. I knew it. I knew it.' Her tears fell as he smothered her face with kisses.

The only words Sam could whisper was her name. 'Annie, my Annie.'

There was a tug at his trousers. He looked down into a big pair of hazel eyes that were set in a tanned face and framed with straight, dark, shiny hair.

'Are you my daddy?'

Sam fell to his knees. 'Yes, and you must be Hazel. Do I get a kiss?'

'Yes.' She threw her arms round his neck.

Sam held her tight.

'Mummy said you'd come home one day. I've got ever such a lot to show you – will you stay with us for a long while?'

'For ever, my darling,' he whispered. 'For ever.'